I0586491

REDEMPTION

Redemption Duet
#2

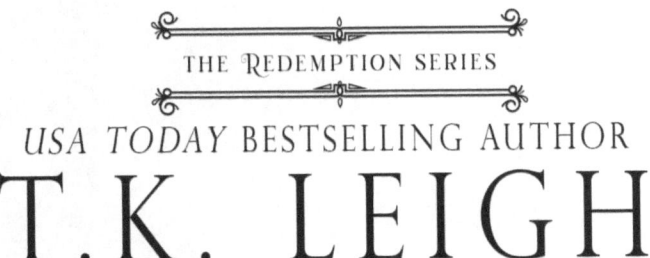

THE REDEMPTION SERIES

USA TODAY BESTSELLING AUTHOR

T.K. LEIGH

REDEMPTION

Published by Carpe Per Diem, Inc. / Tracy Kellam, 25852 McBean Parkway # 806, Santa Clarita, CA 91355

Edited by: Kim Young, Kim's Editing Services

Cover Image Viorel Sima

Used under license from Adobe Stock

BOOKS BY T.K. LEIGH

CONTEMPORARY ROMANCE
The Redemption Series
Promise: A Redemption Series Prologue
Commitment
Redemption
Possession
Atonement

The Dating Games Series
Dating Games
Wicked Games
Mind Games
Dangerous Games
Royal Games
Tangled Games

ROMANTIC COMEDY
The Book Boyfriend Chronicles
The Other Side of Someday
Writing Mr. Right

ROMANTIC SUSPENSE

The INFERNO Saga

The Beautiful Mess Series
A Beautiful Mess
A Tragic Wreck
Gorgeous Chaos

For more information on any of these titles and upcoming releases, please visit T.K.'s website:
www.tkleighauthor.com

CHAPTER ONE

BROOKLYN

ROBERT FROST IS FAMOUS for writing about the road not taken, about a traveler who comes to a fork in the road and is faced with a decision regarding which path to choose. Both hold uncertainty for the future. Both have advantages and disadvantages. Both can bring happiness or sorrow. With no knowledge as to what awaits him, the traveler goes with his gut, contemplating that he can always come back and choose the other path later.

But can he?

One road will lead to another, which will lead to another, then another. You're soon miles from where you started, unable to remember how to get back. Worse, you can't recall where you started in the first place. All because of what you believed to be an innocent decision to go down one road instead of another.

As I sit at the stoplight, the road ahead taking me one way, the interstate to the left another, Dave Matthews' voice brings me back to my high school years. In all actuality, I'm at an advantage, unlike Mr. Frost's memorable traveler. I've been down one of these roads before. Over. And over. And over. I've given that road chance after chance after chance. What has it given me in return? Heartache. Pain. Agony. But also love, as cruel and beautiful as it's always been between us. Can I put myself through that again? Is security and safety more valuable than passion? The answer becomes abundantly clear.

The light turns green and I take a deep breath to slow my racing heart. My foot eases off the brake, stepping on the gas as I take the road I believe will lead to happiness, to peace, to love. The entire drive, I'm certain this is the correct path for me. I need those things. Why should I settle for anything less?

When I finally pull up in front of the house and step out

of my car, making my way up the familiar walkway, everything seems different. This isn't like every other time I've been here. Something's changed. I've changed. Have I changed for the better? For his better?

Or does everything seem different because I've chosen wrong? Should I have taken the other path? There's only one way to find out.

I stare at the door, torn, wishing the correct answer were scrawled in the grains of the wood. When it opens, I inhale a sharp breath, staring into a pair of compassionate, soothing eyes. Ones that have always looked at me with nothing short of devotion, of pure admiration, of absolute love.

"Brooklyn..." His voice is husky but concerned, perhaps even relieved.

My lips part as I struggle to summon a single word. There's a reason I've chosen this path. So I don't have to look back anymore, so I don't have to face a daily reminder of my mistakes, of not being enough, of never being enough. This man staring at me with so much concern loves me. Unequivocally. Unmistakably. Unquestionably. His love is pure, untainted, with no hidden agenda. And he wants to spend the rest of his life with me. That should count for something.

No. That should count for everything.

The events of the past few days overwhelming me, my hands go to Wes' cheeks. Pulling him toward me, I crush my lips to his, kissing him fully, completely, holding nothing back, giving him everything I've denied him since the beginning of our relationship. He stills at first, his body becoming rigid. I bring myself closer, erasing the last bit of distance between us. My hands tugging at his hair, fingernails digging into his scalp, my body pleads with him to want me, love me, help me forget about Drew.

With a groan, he relents, melting into me, dragging me into his house and kicking the door closed. This exchange is completely different from our usual kisses. It's not tender, soft, sweet. That's not how I want it. Not right now. I need it deep, powerful, soul-crushing. I need to never have another reason

2

to think of anyone but Weston James Bradford. I'm his world. It's time he becomes mine.

I claw at him, tongues tangling and teeth clashing as our kiss becomes ravenous, primal...hot. He pushes me against the wall and I grind my body against his, his erection springing to life. No longer the same Brooklyn I was mere hours ago, I reach down, palming it. A low rumble falls from his throat and he tears out of the kiss, his heavy breaths hot against my skin.

"Damn, baby. What's gotten into you?"

"I want to turn over a new leaf. I want to be everything you want. In public..." Tilting my head up, I drag my tongue along his smooth chin and neck, suppressing the desire to have an unshaven jaw bruise and scratch my skin. When I pull back, I give him a coquettish grin. "And in private."

Growling, he dives in for another impassioned kiss, taking control as he presses against me, pulsing and thrusting. Hands are everywhere, tugging, yanking, scratching. His lips move to my neck, teeth clamping onto my skin. I whimper, craving the physical pain to help me forget about everything relating to Andrew Brinks. About the longing in his eyes when he learned the truth. About the despair covering his face when I drove away. About the way my heart still yearns for him, regardless that he's never brought me anything but torment, that he's done nothing but crush my dreams and break my heart.

"Harder," I beg, willing my body to react to Wes' touch, his kisses, his words. But I feel nothing, empty, broken. I squeeze my eyelids shut. Instantly, brown eyes flash before me, impassioned and hungry, bringing me back to that night seven years ago, the night I'd kept a secret from everyone for years. The hands on me transform from smooth and soft to rough and calloused as I succumb to the memory.

"Why aren't you dating anyone, Brooklyn?" Drew asked in a lazy voice as we both lay in my bed. Considering our history, it was irresponsible of me. But when he'd begged me to stay after I'd dropped off a water and a few aspirin to nurse the headache I was

certain would find him the instant he woke from his alcohol-induced slumber, I couldn't resist. I never could resist Andrew Brinks.

"No reason."

"Come now," he slurred. "Are you trying to tell me there's no one who's caught your eye, who's stolen your heart?"

I opened my mouth, my words stuck in my throat like tires in heavy mud. What could I say? That I'd been pining for the same person all my life? The same person who possessed my heart since the day he threatened a boy in my second grade class after he picked on me because my father came to Mommy and Me tea. The same person who gave Damian Murphy a broken nose for touching me inappropriately the summer before my junior year of high school. The same person I never stopped thinking about, even after he stood me up on the morning I thought I would lose my virginity. I was naïve and gave him my heart. Despite the passing of years, this man still had it, although I wished he didn't. Wished with everything I could pry it out of his cold, cruel hands.

He ran his thumb along my bottom lip, my breath hitching as a shiver rolled through me. I plumped it out, my insatiable hunger to feel his hands on me overtaking all sense of rationale, making me forget our past. All I cared about was now, about feeling this man's body so close to mine, to feel his heart beat in time with mine. I should have left, should have walked away, but I couldn't. The power this man had over me defied all reason, all sense of what was right.

"Brooklyn?"

"There's someone," I murmured in a barely audible voice.

"Who?"

As if able to read my thoughts, he inched even closer, his body flush with mine. My breaths came in pants as his erection pressed against my stomach. There was no hiding his need for me. But was it for me? Or did he just want to feel something after learning his wife was leaving him? Was I simply his last resort? Just someone he'd use for a night, then toss aside, like my father warned me he would?

4

"Do I know him?"

"You might." I lowered my eyes, staring at his muscular frame. His t-shirt had lifted slightly, a sliver of skin visible above his jeans. Just that small bit of exposed flesh made my entire body heat even more.

"What's he like?"

I couldn't help but smile as I considered my answer. *"Sweet. Charming. Although he'd never admit it. He likes to put on this front, make everyone think he's some macho bad ass, especially when he's around his co-workers."* I lifted my eyes to his. *"But I knew him before. And I can't help but think I'm one of the few people he can be himself around. That he doesn't have to put on a show to make me believe the public perception of him."*

His hand roamed the contours of my frame, stopping on my hip. My teeth chattered, my body having trouble reconciling the myriad of sensations coursing through it. When he pushed me onto my back, I gasped at the unexpected shift, my surprise silenced when he buried his head in my neck. I held my breath, briefly squeezing my eyes shut. Was I asleep? Was this just another dream I'd awaken from…alone?

"Do you love him?" he whispered, his lips ghosting against my skin sending a ripple through me.

My pulse increased, my mind hazy as lust for this man blinded me to everything. I'd been with a few guys before, but I'd never felt anything remotely close to this, to this incredible euphoria and need driving me mad.

"I shouldn't."

"Why?" He pulled back, his whiskey eyes searing mine.

"Because he'll only break my heart. Because as much as I want to be with him, it won't end well."

"How do you know?" He climbed on top of me, supporting his weight on his elbows. My legs fell on either side of him and I ran my hand up and down his back, as if this were a normal, everyday occurrence for us. The feel of his ripped muscles beneath his t-shirt made my mouth dry.

"Because he's always held all the power," I stated, more unguarded than I'd ever been. I didn't understand what possessed me to be so honest, why I admitted something I'd refused to acknowledge for the past decade. *"Because he has the power to destroy me in a way I'll never recover from."*

* * *

My words all those years ago hit me hard, practically knocking the breath out of me. When I muttered them that night, I had no idea how true they were. I only had to wait a matter of a few hours to learn I was right, that the promises he made in his alcohol-induced euphoria, then forgot about, would destroy me. Just like the promises he made the night before he left for college irrevocably changed me.

The hurt of everything plagues me and my chin quivers, tears spilling over my eyelids.

"What's wrong?" Wes asks, noticing the change in my demeanor. Pulling back, he searches my face. His concern makes me feel even more guilty for fantasizing about Drew. "Did I hurt you? Was I being too rough? I never want to do anything to—"

I grab the back of his neck, forcing his lips to mine so he can't see the indecision in my expression. He's hesitant at first and I can sense his internal struggle. It's classic Wes. He wants me but doesn't want to do anything to hurt me. He's never wanted to do anything to hurt me, always doing everything in his power to put a smile on my face.

"Please, Wes," I murmur, my tone bordering on desperation. "I need you." My mouth still against his, I nibble on his bottom lip. Any reluctance on his part vanishes, his kiss voracious and consuming as his tongue plunges inside my mouth. He fists my hair, his free hand gripping my hip somewhat painfully, but I make no move to get him to loosen his grasp or to stop.

I run my hands through his hair, tugging, attempting to take control of the kiss. My movements become slow, deep, reverent, reminding me of the kisses I'd been the lucky recipient of from Drew. Sweet, yet intense. Restrained, yet erotic. Memorable, yet too easily forgotten in the cloud of alcohol he consumed. It doesn't matter that years have passed. The pain I endured because of Drew's inability to follow through on his promise is still as prominent as if it had just happened. That pain is why I need to do this, why I need to marry Wes.

Tearing away, my chest heaves as I stare into Wes' midnight blue eyes, the pupils dilated. I reach for his chest, running my hands up and down, then ripping his t-shirt over his head. "Bedroom. Now," I demand in a breathy voice.

"You don't have to ask me twice." With haste, he grabs my hand, pulling me through the living room, up the stairs, and into the master bedroom. The instant we cross the threshold, I reach for his jeans, my fingers fumbling with his belt.

"Damn, baby." He palms my back, jerking me hard and fast against him. "What's gotten into you?"

"Nothing," I lie.

I can't tell him that my tear-filled confession to Drew pushed me over the edge. That while Wes had me pinned against the wall, it was Drew's hands I imagined on my skin. That when he kissed me, it was Drew's lips I craved.

"I just need to feel you." Another lie. I don't need to feel Wes. I just need to feel something other than the crippling reality that this is a mistake. I don't want it to be a mistake. I want it to be real, to give my heart to a man who'll never break it.

Yanking the belt from around his waist, I crush my lips back to his, my kiss filled with anguish. Wes is only too happy to match my eagerness, confusing my desperation for desire. He lowers the zipper of his pants, his mouth never leaving mine as he steps out of his jeans. Steering me toward his bed, he helps me out of my pants, both of us frantic to lose ourselves in each other, but for two completely different reasons. He needs me. I need him to help me forget.

With a hungered growl, he runs his hands up and down

my frame, peppering kisses along my neck, my collarbone, cupping my breasts. "Do you feel how hard I am?" He thrusts against me, pinching my nipple. I yelp, the pain remarkably pleasurable.

"I do." I close my eyes, letting the moment consume me.

"Do you want more?"

"Yes," I moan.

"You got it, baby." He grips my hips, spinning me around. A rough hand fists my hair and he forces my stomach against the mattress. He tears my panties from me and parts my legs.

Unsure how to react to this new, somewhat callous side of Wes, my body stiffens. The familiar sound of a packet opening echoes in the space. Before I can tell him this is a bad idea, that I shouldn't be doing this when I'm consumed by thoughts of another man, he pushes into me. I play along, pretending this is what I need. I want to need him like this, to enjoy it.

I still feel absolutely nothing.

"God, you feel so good like this," he hisses through his teeth, his motions increasing.

I moan once more, because that's probably what he wants. My hands clench around the comforter, balling it, and I shut my eyes, imagining a different man behind me, filling me, his hands on my skin. A tingle spreads through me at the thought. Instead of being in Wes' bedroom, I'm back in mine, back in that moment when I wish time could stand still.

* * *

My confession hung between us, my heart racing at what I'd just admitted.

"Because he has the power to destroy me in a way I'll never recover from."

How could I say that? How could I admit my feelings for Drew so freely? Sure, I didn't come right out and admit I was talking about him, but he had to know. Would he use this information to hurt me all over again? Was this all just part of whatever sadistic game he liked to play with my heart?

Before I could say anything to dampen the impact, Drew's strong hands cupped my cheeks, his eyes filled with sincerity. He pressed his lips to mine, causing my entire body to momentarily stiffen. I'd dreamt about his kiss since that summer ten years ago. I never thought I'd have the opportunity again, not after watching him date woman after woman, then come home and announce he'd married a hockey groupie he barely knew. Now, I finally had another taste, but for how long? Was this going to be just like last time? Would he avoid me for months, years, then pretend it never happened?

"Kiss me, Brooklyn," he whispered against my lips when I remained unmoving. "I'm so sorry about everything. How I..." He trailed off. His fingers grazed over my face, a stomach-clenching shiver rolling through me. "Please. Help me feel again." The raw emotion and vulnerability in those words cut me in two. It was so different from the cocky, self-assured man he'd turned into these past few years.

"Oh, Drew...," I exhaled, pressing my lips against his, our kiss warm, tender. I thought he was a good kisser all those years ago, but he was even better now, the way his tongue tangled with mine making it so I never wanted to be apart from him again.

I no longer obsessed about the possibility that this would be a repeat of ten years ago. That I'd give him my heart, only for him to shatter it. All I cared about was this moment, of enjoying everything Drew was willing to give me, regardless of how fleeting it may be.

Deepening the kiss, I ran my fingers through his hair. It was the off-season, so he kept it relatively short, the usual facial hair he sported during the hockey season replaced with a bit of two-day stubble. It was rough against my skin, but in a way that made me burn for him even more.

I hooked my legs around his waist, moving my hips with the rhythm he set as he kissed me so reverently, like he needed my lips on his to breathe, like he'd hungered for me for years, like his heart was made just to love me. In that moment, lost in the sensation of his mouth on mine, his body on mine, his fingers interlocking with mine, keeping my arms secured above my head, I felt it was.

"Brooklyn…," he moaned, moving from my mouth, down my jawline, nipping on my neck.

"Yes," I breathed, lightheaded, dizzy, the room seeming to spin around me, despite only having consumed one beer the entire evening. I was drunk on the man on top of me, thirsty for more of his intoxicating kisses.

"Do you have any idea how long I've thought about this moment? About how you would feel, how you would taste, how your body would respond to mine?"

I quivered, my core tightening, my soul singing.

"It's been so long," he continued, his tongue drawing a lazy line along my collarbone. "I've tried to stay away, do the right thing, fulfill the promise I made."

His fingers found the hem of my t-shirt and raised it slightly, exposing my stomach. I wanted to ask what he meant by that, but as he slithered down my body, a hunger I hadn't experienced in years swallowed my words. I tried to keep my breathing and heart rate under control. It was damn near impossible, especially when he reached my belly button and glanced up, meeting my eyes.

"I'm so sorry, Brooklyn."

He brought his mouth to my stomach, his kiss tender against my skin. Wanting to imprint everything about this to memory, I closed my eyes, focusing on his lips exploring my body. They were smooth, supple, unyielding.

"For too many years, I've imagined how your skin would feel, would taste. How your cheeks would blush with a desire you couldn't hide. Because I know you, Brooklyn…"

My eyes opened, meeting his that were dark with a wanton desire. He carefully lifted my shirt even more, exposing the bottom of my breasts. Every inch of me tightened in anticipation as his tongue unhurriedly made its way north.

"As much as you've tried to hide it, as much as you've tried to deny it, you can't. Not anymore. You want me. You never got over me. Just like I never got over you."

He raised my t-shirt the final few inches, exposing my alert nipples. Pausing, he leaned back, staring at me, not saying a word. My breaths filled the room, the only other sound that of an occasional barking dog in the neighborhood where we grew up. The pounding of my heart seemed to echo against my eardrums, the intensity of Drew's gaze unhinging me.

I sucked my bottom lip between my teeth, never feeling so vulnerable and exposed as I did at that moment. I wasn't fooling myself. I'd seen the women Drew had dated. While I had an ample chest, it was nothing compared to what he was used to.

"You are so fucking beautiful," he crooned lazily, the effects of the alcohol obvious. He brought his forefinger and thumb to one of my nipples and tugged.

Sparks shot through me, a carnal need for his teeth to do the same thing filling me. I arched my back off the bed, having trouble making sense of these unique sensations overwhelming me. I'd been intimate in the past, but they were all boys. Drew was a man. The only man I wanted.

"I'm a fool for hurting you, for not saying fuck it and giving you my heart." He lowered his mouth to my breast, his motions warm, reverent, loving, at complete odds with the fiery desire in his eyes. "I'm a fool for not making you mine a long time ago."

I moaned, needing more. More of his words, more of his touch, desperate to experience every inch of him. It was the only way I'd know I wasn't dreaming, because this was all so surreal.

"God, you taste better than I imagined. And I've certainly imagined." He lightly pulled on my nipple with his teeth. I wasn't sure how much more I could take. The fire that had been burning for him the past few years…hell, decades…was growing out of control, washing over me, desire turning into uncontrollable desperation.

"Drew, please," I begged, my hips thrusting against him. My brain no longer catalogued all the reasons this was a bad idea. The only thing I cared about was feeling Drew on top of me, his lips scorching my skin, our bodies joining so I couldn't tell where he

ended and I began.

"Say you need me." He lifted his eyes to mine, a vulnerability in his gaze.

"I need you, Drew," I breathed. "I've always needed you."

"I've always needed you, Brooklyn." He returned to me, his mouth poised on mine. His warmth tickled my lips, my nerves standing on end as I braced for his kiss.

He ran a light finger down my face, a chill trickling through me. The anticipation was killing me. If I didn't feel his lips on mine, didn't lose myself in him soon, I feared I'd perish.

Finally, he pressed his mouth back to mine, his tongue exploring me once more, as if discovering something new with each kiss. One hand digging into my hair, his other journeyed a torturous trail down my body before landing on my hip. I wrapped my legs around his waist, my core clenching at the heat of him between my thighs. Then he slid his hand along my hip bone and between our two bodies. With incredible expertise, it disappeared into the leg of my sleep shorts. I loosened my grip around him. He leisurely lifted the line of my panties, a moan escaping my throat when his fingers neared that spot I wanted them, that spot I'd only dreamed he'd touch ever since I'd developed hormones.

"Drew," I begged again, my heart racing, my chest heaving, my brain fuzzy. "Please. I need you."

"I can't tell you how long I've waited to hear those words come out of your mouth," he murmured against my lips, kissing me at the same time his finger landed on my center, both of us moaning. "Damn." He pulled back slightly, his fingers spreading my slickness all over me. I'd never been this turned on, this ready to fall apart in a matter of seconds. "You're so wet."

I bit my bottom lip, gripping the sheets in my fists as my body climbed higher and higher. My breathing grew labored as I did everything to think of something other than how perfect, how right, how fucking wonderful it was to have Drew's hand between my legs.

"More," I murmured in a throaty voice, then flung my eyes open. I reached for his neck, urging his lips back to mine. "I need *more of you. I need you inside me."*

He groaned, slipping a finger inside me, massaging me. "And I'd love nothing more than to be inside you, Brooklyn. You have no idea how much I've fantasized about this, imagined the look on your face as I make you come over and over again until you beg me to stop because you can't take anymore."

I moaned louder, every muscle in my body clenching as I loomed closer to the peak.

"But I want to be sober the first time I'm inside you..." He licked his lips. "You deserve to have all of me the first time I make love to you. Because this isn't just sex. It would never just be sex with you. So tonight, I'll make sure you're taken care of. Tomorrow, when I wake up with you in my arms, I plan on making love to you, Brooklyn. Because I love you. I always have."

* * *

"God, baby. You are incredible." Wes' voice snaps me back to the present, reminding me Drew isn't here, that I made a conscious decision not to be with him.

"Harder," I beg, praying the deeper Wes thrusts into me, the more I'll want him. But it only reminds me of Drew. Of the way his arms enveloped me as we slept together that night. Of the way his eyes looked upon me as if I were the only person he saw. Of the way his breath mixed with mine in the most tantalizing of ways. Of the way he made me drop my guard and love him all over again.

True, deep, passionate love.

Consuming, hypnotic, unparalleled love.

Painful, tragic, unrequited love.

Ignorant of my fantasies about another man, Wes' breathing grows more uneven, his hold on me tightening, and I know he's close to unraveling. So I moan louder, making him think I'm about to lose all control.

"That's right." He drives harder and harder, frantic and unbalanced. "I'm the only one who can make you feel this."

"I'm close," I lie, wanting this to be over. Wanting to

crawl into a corner and never come out again. Wanting to run away and start over where nobody knows who I am, nobody knows what I've done, nobody knows how ugly and black my soul is.

He reaches around, finding my center, his motions harsh and relentless, a complete one-eighty from the soulful and fulfilling experience when Drew gave me several of the most earth-shattering orgasms of my life. But I make Wes think I like it, my moans and pants coming quicker, faster, more intense, crying out as I pretend to come undone around him so he'll stop touching me. That's all it takes. He grunts, pumping a few more times as he finds his release.

I remain still, turning my head to stare out the windows, ashamed, like I just cheated on Wes by thinking of someone else during sex. Am I a horrible person because of that? Don't people fantasize about other things during sex all the time? Isn't that all sex is? Just one big fantasy?

"You drive me fucking crazy." Wes leans down, placing a soft kiss on my shoulder blade as he slides out of me.

I go to push myself up and he helps me, my muscles sore and shaky. I avoid his eyes, not wanting him to see the truth within.

"Hey." His voice is sweet. He lifts my chin, forcing my gaze to his. A small smile pulls on his lips. "Thank you."

I furrow my brow. "For what? Letting you fuck me?"

His expression lightens briefly. "Well, as incredible as it was, that's not what I mean. I wanted to thank you for agreeing to marry me."

"Why wouldn't I want to marry you?" I reply, but my words seem more like an argument I'm making to myself. "You're caring, compassionate, loving. And you love me." I place my hand on his cheek. "Out of all the women you could be with, you chose me. I'm the one who should thank you."

"I don't want a single day to go by that I don't tell you how much I appreciate you. I know things have been crazy lately and we've both been busy. I promise I'll never take you for granted. I love you, Brooklyn." He presses his lips to mine, his kiss gentle, a stark contrast to the way he just screwed me.

If I felt ashamed for fantasizing about another man while having sex with Wes before, that's nothing compared to the guilt I feel as his heartfelt words wrap around me. He'll never treat me with anything but the utmost respect and adoration, never take me for granted.

Why am I so willing to throw it all away for a man who will?

CHAPTER TWO

DREW

THIS CAN'T BE REAL. This has to be a nightmare. I'll soon wake up to the sound of two small voices giggling as I pretend to sleep, just as we do every morning. But we already did that today. Then I walked them to school, just like every other weekday, and was about to leave for work when my entire world crumbled beneath me.

My stomach churns, my chest tightens, my lungs constrict, a fear unlike any I've faced in my life coursing through me, leaving me anxious, panicked, on edge. I didn't know what else to do, so I hopped on the vintage Triumph motorcycle my dad left me and took off to see the one person I need, the one person who can hold me together when I'm minutes away from unraveling. I promised to give her space, but I can't. Not now. Not after opening the envelope the process server handed me less than an hour ago.

"Can I help you?" a short blonde asks as I continue past the reception area of the cramped office building.

When I don't acknowledge her, she jumps up and chases after me. I'd like to see someone try to stop me today. I've never been so filled with rage, so ready to break down and scream.

"Sir, please! You can't come in here unless you have an appointment!"

I storm down the narrow corridor past rows of cubicles and tiny offices, then round the corner, halting in the doorway of Brooklyn's office. I could have found my way here blindfolded, her familiar aroma of lavender flowing from the room.

She shoots to her feet when she sees me, blinking repeatedly, her eyes darting from me to the receptionist and back again, confusion wrinkling her brow. "Drew?"

"I'm sorry. I tried to stop him," the receptionist apologizes. "I can call security."

"Please...," I manage to say through the lump in my throat, my anger turning back to despair, to desperation.

Brooklyn's gaze narrows on me as she surveys my disheveled appearance. My eyes are red and full of worry, distress covering every inch of me. My expression is slack as I plead with her to help. This woman has seen me at my highest of highs and lowest of lows. But I doubt she's ever seen me so distraught, so out of sorts. She can't refuse me. It's not in her nature to turn away someone in need, regardless of how much I've hurt her.

When she remains silent, seemingly still uncertain about the reason for my presence, I throw the papers in my hand onto the desk in front of her. "I need you," I beg, my tone shaky.

She studies me with curiosity, then looks down at the papers, instantly flinging her shocked gaze back to mine once she reads the caption. The same questions I had when I received this earlier are written in the lines of her face.

Her jaw grows slack as she shakes her head, struggling to say something. I know exactly what she's going through. I was there an hour ago. Hell, I'm still there.

In an instant, she flips the switch and becomes the social worker I know her to be, spine straight, composing herself. "Natalie..." She returns her attention to the blonde. "There's no need to call security." She looks back at me, a peaceful air about her. Right now, I need to feel her soothing presence. It's the only thing giving me hope. "Drew's a friend who needs my help."

"Of course." With a smile, Natalie starts to close the door when Brooklyn calls out to her once more.

"And please rearrange my schedule for today. I won't be able to make any of my appointments. Do what you can to reschedule them for later in the week, even if it means after hours."

Natalie shifts her eyes to me, then back to Brooklyn, curious. "I'll update your calendar." She closes the door behind her.

"A complaint for custody?" Brooklyn presses once we're alone. Her expression is long, a slight tremble in her chin as she swallows hard.

I pull my bottom lip between my teeth, the ache in my throat becoming more painful. Hearing those words validates it, reminds me I'm not dreaming, that this is my reality. My crazy ex is trying to take my girls from me. And that's not even the worst of it.

"What am I going to do?" I tug at my hair, pacing, unable to hide my emotions any longer. It's a miracle I made it all the way here in one piece when everything around me seems to be spinning out of control. How am I going to pick up Alyssa and Charlotte from school today and pretend everything is okay? How am I going to smile, laugh, and play with them without my heart breaking over the idea I might lose them?

"It'll be okay, Drew." Brooklyn's voice is strong, assertive, a complete one-eighty from the sorrow filling me. "We'll fight this. You took care of those girls after she abandoned all of you. There's no way you'll lose custody. If worse comes to worse, you may have to share custody."

I fall into a chair, burying my head in my hands. "What about Charlotte?" I slowly lift my glassy eyes to hers, my stare distant and empty, a vice squeezing my heart.

"What about her?" Her tone is cautious, as if she doesn't want to hear the answer.

With a defeated sigh, I sit forward and shakily point to the second paragraph of the pleading. Brooklyn's hesitant but eventually lowers herself to her chair, scanning the paper. After a few seconds, she sucks in a quick breath. Her gaze shoots back to me, her chin quivering, tears forming in the corners of her eyes. Words seeming to escape her as she processes what she just learned, what I just learned, she silently pleads with me for an explanation. I wish I had one.

"She claims I'm not the biological father. That Chase..." I trail off. Parker had warned me when we met for drinks on Saturday. I didn't want to believe him, didn't want to think it could be true. I guess I was wrong.

18

She covers her mouth with her hand, but it does nothing to hide her sadness, her pain. It matches my own. It's in this moment I realize I'm not the only one affected by this. We all are. Those girls are as much Brooklyn's kids as they are my own. She helped raise them — changed diapers, put them to bed, bathed them, sang to them, played with them. This isn't just my struggle. It's hers, too.

Brooklyn's lips form a tight line as she continues flipping through the pleading. Then she stands from her desk, heading toward the door. "Come on. Let's go."

"Go?" I peer at her through forlorn eyes. "Go where?"

"To see a friend of mine. A lawyer. She'll know what to do, how to fight this."

Without giving me a minute to protest, she grabs my hand, yanking me from the chair and pulling me down the hallway. I should be thinking only of my daughters, but damn if her skin on mine doesn't cause a subtle jolt of electricity to course through me. She's by my side again. Even if the circumstances that brought us together are tearing me apart, I find comfort in the small victories.

When we emerge outside, she spies my motorcycle parked in the lot and scowls. "Didn't the doctor advise you against riding that thing? It could cause irreversible brain damage if you got in an accident!"

"I needed to see you, and the bike is easier to navigate through traffic."

"That was stupid, Drew. You're worried about losing your girls to Carla. What if something happened to you? They'd lose you. We all would."

"You've never liked that bike," I comment.

She stops walking as we approach her car. "No, I haven't. I don't like the idea of you speeding down the highway with little to no protection."

She unlocks the car and I head around to the passenger side. "Duly noted," I say before lowering myself into her car. It's a small sedan, so my long legs and large physique seem to take up the entire compartment.

As she sits behind the wheel, she glances at me, her eyes

19

hard. "If you'd followed doctor's orders and refrained from riding that deathtrap on two wheels, we could have taken your car and you wouldn't be squished. So don't even think about complaining." Her tone is clipped.

"Okay. Okay. I get it. You don't like me riding the bike."

"I can tolerate it when you're in your neighborhood." She inserts the key into the ignition and starts the car, carefully navigating through the parking lot and merging onto the street. "You're a good driver, but I don't trust any other drivers on the road." When we come to a stoplight, her eyes briefly lock with mine. "You're special to me, Drew." A strange expression washes over her features, almost as if having a realization of sorts. "I can't lose you."

I swallow hard, the way she peers at me hitting me deep in my soul. I'm still not sure where we stand, but I don't care about that right now. I just need to feel something real again, something that grounds me. Brooklyn's always been my anchor.

Reaching across the console, I squeeze her hand in mine. "You won't. As long as that's what you want."

Her gaze darts to our joined hands and she quickly withdraws, freeing herself from my touch. As the light turns green, she returns her turmoil-filled eyes to the road and grips the wheel with both hands, something she never does.

"I don't even know what I want anymore." Her words are soft, contemplative, spoken in a way that makes me think she's saying them for herself, not me.

I could press her, make a case for why she should choose me. Why she should take a risk. Why she should give me one more chance to prove I'm not the person she assumed I was when I disappeared from her life without saying goodbye. Instead, I remain silent throughout the drive toward the Back Bay in Boston. I'm unsure how she would react to the truth of why I stood her up. Her father's the only family she has left. I can't be responsible for destroying that, too.

CHAPTER THREE

DREW

A WOMAN I ESTIMATE to be in her early forties looks our way the instant we cross the threshold into a small office in a revamped brownstone. "Brooklyn, so good to see you." Her smile is heartfelt and kind. "I'm finishing up with another client." She gestures to the gentleman standing beside her. "Go ahead. I'll be with you two shortly."

"Thanks, Alice." Brooklyn leads me from the reception area, which was probably a living room before they refurbished this space into offices. "This way." She gestures down a narrow hallway. I follow her into a room at the end. The ensuite bathroom to the left gives the impression this was once the master bedroom.

We sit across from a vast desk piled high with briefs and files. Diplomas and awards hang on the walls, and a large bookcase displays what appear to be dozens of legal books. It's not as stuffy as some of the law firms I've been to, though. There's a touch of familiarity, personality...warmth. In addition to all her achievements, this woman proudly showcases family photos. I hope the love she has for her own family will translate into helping me keep mine.

I catch Brooklyn studying me, her eyes analytical and penetrating, revealing nothing. I offer her a tight smile, hoping to crack the armor she wears when around me now. "Thank you. When I received that request for custody modification, I didn't know what to do, who else to turn to."

She straightens her posture, sitting rather formally, hands folded in her lap, back stiff, eyes forward, legs crossed at the ankles. "You came to the right place. I've dealt with custody issues for years now. Granted, mine usually deal with the termination of parental rights, but—"

"No. That's not what I mean." Drawing in a breath, I

moisten my dry lips. "I didn't come to you because you have contacts in this area. I could have called the attorney who handled my divorce. I came to you because there's no other person I want by my side through this." I lower my voice. "Through everything."

"Drew...," she cautions.

"I know." I throw up my hands in frustration. "I'm an idiot."

She tilts her head to the side, her eyes narrowing into slits. Then she laughs, the soft sound like music to my ears after the morning I've had. "That may be the understatement of the year. Hell, the century."

"And I don't blame you for avoiding me. But things aren't like they seem."

"I'm not avoiding you. I just—"

"Do you know what I've always admired about you?"

She shakes her head.

"You don't trust easily, but when you do, you do so unequivocally. I ruined it by betraying your trust in the worst way possible, of taking advantage of your compassionate nature."

She looks down, avoiding my gaze as she fidgets with her hands. I notice her fingernails. They're usually manicured with a light shade of pink. Not today. She's been biting them, something she does when she's stressed.

"It doesn't matter. You didn't know. Anyway, it was years ago. I've moved on." She seems to shrink into herself, then chews on one of her nails.

"Have you?" I press. Everything about the way she's acting gives me the impression she's only saying that to convince herself of the validity of the words. She hasn't moved on any more than I have.

"I—"

"Brooklyn, sweetie," a voice cuts through and Brooklyn stands, breaking the moment.

"Alice. Thank you for agreeing to see us on such short notice." They briefly shake hands before Brooklyn turns to me. "This is my friend, Drew. I mean, Andrew Brinks."

22

I stand, my frame dwarfing Alice as I hold my hand toward her. She has a pleasant disposition, her eyes bright, expression kind. Her blonde hair is cut to right above her shoulders. She's not dressed in a suit, as most attorneys I've worked with have been. Instead, she wears a belted dress and boots that come up to just below her knees. It's unusual, but I don't care, as long as she can help me. If Brooklyn insists this is where I need to be, I have to believe I'm in good hands.

"Not the same Andrew Brinks who—"

"One and the same," Brooklyn replies, cutting her off.

"Well, shit." She beams, shaking my hand even more enthusiastically, all the professionalism she tried to exude waning when she realizes who I am. "Alice DeMico. I barely recognized you without the beard and hair."

"I usually stay somewhat clean-shaven these days." I run my hand along my jaw, a bit of scruff covering my skin. "My daughters like it better. They call me Grizzly Adams when I don't shave for a week." My expression immediately falls.

"Which is why we're here," Brooklyn states, taking charge of the conversation when she notices the sudden change in my demeanor.

"So, tell me..." Alice steps behind her desk, sitting down. We mirror her movement. "How can I help?" She fishes a notepad and pen from underneath a file and scribbles down the date along with my name.

"Drew received this earlier today." Brooklyn hands her the request for custody modification.

An unnerving silence falls over the room as Alice flips through the pages, making a few notes every so often. My leg bounces as I constantly clench and unclench my fists, my eyes darting around. The wait is killing me. I just want to know my chances at keeping both girls.

Suddenly, a hand grabs onto mine, my head snapping toward Brooklyn, who offers me a reassuring smile. The sympathy I see relaxes me. Without uttering a single word, she pacifies me, convinces me everything will be okay. I expect her to pull her hand away once my anxiety has diminished, but she doesn't. I run my thumb along her knuckles, relishing in her soft skin against my fingertips. It's known and familiar, exactly what I need right now. She's always exactly what I need.

"Okay." Alice looks up, addressing me. I rip my eyes from Brooklyn, devoting my full attention to Alice, although I keep Brooklyn's hand in mine. "First, do you consent to Brooklyn being here?"

"I'll leave if you'd rather," she says to me, pulling away her hand. "I don't mind. You need to speak with her openly and honestly."

"No. I want her here. She knows everything about me. She always has." I say that more for Brooklyn's sake than Alice's, a desperate attempt at reminding her what's at stake.

"Very well. We won't be getting into the nitty-gritty right now anyway. What I'm going to do is order a paternity test immediately."

I lower my head, nodding. I knew this would be the first step, but the idea of confirming the truth weighs heavily on my heart.

"For both girls."

I whip my head up. "Both girls?"

"I understand it's not what you'd like to hear, but I find it's best in these situations. It's imperative we confirm the assertions she's made in her request for custody, which include verifying that Alyssa is your biological daughter. You don't want any more surprises."

I swallow hard. It never even crossed my mind that Alyssa also may not be mine. The mere thought of Charlotte not being my biological daughter wrecks me. Losing Alyssa, too? I won't survive.

"How will that work? You'll need my DNA and..."

"Your daughters'. It's just a quick swab of the mouth. They're used to routine pediatrician visits, correct?" She lifts a brow and I nod. "Most of my clients who have had to do paternity tests told their kids it was the doctor making sure they were healthy. I'm assuming you don't want to inform them about any of this until you're certain one way or another, right?"

I stare ahead, blinking. "I haven't even thought about how or what to tell them."

Alice gives me a reassuring smile. "One step at a time. We'll get the paternity test taken care of. Your ex-wife may just be playing hardball. It's a common tactic. Go big to convince the other party to settle in the middle."

I look away, not saying a word. In my heart, I know this isn't a ploy. Maybe if Parker hadn't implied that Carla had been sleeping with Chase all along, I wouldn't be thinking this way, but I know the truth. It's too much of a coincidence.

"Now, Ms. Gale alleged she came to you requesting occasional visitation with the kids, correct?" Alice jots a few notes on the pad.

"Yes. About two weeks ago."

Brooklyn shoots her eyes to me, surprised by this news. I hadn't told anyone about it. I didn't think anything would come of it. I underestimated Carla.

"And you separated when?" Squinting, she flips through the pleading, turning to the appendix, which contains copies of birth certificates, as well as our divorce agreement, detailing custody and spousal support.

"Almost six years ago." I do my best to answer all her questions without involving any of my emotions regarding the past. "Charlotte was only six months old. I was forced into retirement because of an injury, and Carla decided she didn't want to be with me if I was no longer the hockey celebrity she thought she married. So she left without a word. A month later, I received her request for divorce."

"And the agreement signed by the court attached to this pleading is the one that's still in effect?"

I nod. "Yes. We went through the standard mediation required before a divorce. She gave me full physical custody of the two girls and requested no spousal support. My lawyer encouraged me to take her offer and run, considering I'd been playing professional hockey when we met and had quite extensive assets."

Alice looks over the rim of her dark glasses. "I would have advised the same. Now, after your divorce, how often were you in contact with Ms. Gale?"

"Never. I tried reaching out to her, but her phone had been disconnected. A few months later, I learned she was no longer with the guy she'd left me for. In all these years, she never sent either of the girls so much as a card on their birthday or for Christmas." I glance at Brooklyn and reach for her hand, my fingers intertwining with hers. "Then last month, Brooklyn and I took the girls to the science museum. We ran into her there. My girls had no idea who she was."

"And you are of the opinion that got her thinking about them again?"

"It must have."

"Okay." She blows out a long breath, absorbing this truncated version of my past with Carla. "I'll reach out to the lawyer who represented you on your divorce and request the files he has, just so I have everything." She flips to the back of the pleadings, analyzing photocopies of a birth certificate. "She never listed you on Charlotte's birth certificate." Deep lines appear on her brow as she lifts her eyes to mine. "Were you present at her birth?"

I slowly shake my head. "I was in the hospital, but I was two floors below the maternity ward."

"And why's that?" she asks, jotting down more notes on her pad.

"My helmet flew off during a fight on the ice. I was knocked unconscious when some asshole on the other team slammed my head against the wall."

Realization washes over her. "I remember that."

"I was in ICU for a week. I had no idea Carla even went into labor or that Charlotte was born until the doctors were able to bring me out of the drug-induced coma they initiated in order to control the swelling in my brain."

"I'm sorry." She holds my gaze for another moment before analyzing the papers in front of her. "Were you aware of her extra-marital affairs at any point during your relationship?"

I pinch my lips together, contemplating, then sigh, digging my fingers through my hair. "No, but I probably should have been. We'd almost divorced a year before."

A sour taste fills my mouth as I mentally rewind to that night once more. I can't remember much, despite trying to force the memories back to the surface. Everything about it is still fuzzy...everything until I woke up in Brooklyn's bed the following morning to my phone ringing. It wasn't until Carla learned where I was that she shared the news of her pregnancy. Now I wonder if she would have told me had I not been at Brooklyn's. Carla always insisted Brooklyn had a thing for me, but I brushed it off. I didn't see how she could after what I did to her. How could she still love me when I broke her heart?

"But you didn't?"

"The following day, she learned she was pregnant, said she wanted to work things out for our daughter and the baby on the way." I blow out a long breath. "I grew up without a mother. I hated the idea of my kids growing up in a divided household. Yes, Carla and I fought a lot, but we also had some good times together. I thought we'd be able to reconcile any differences we had for the sake of our kids, thought we'd both be mature enough to put their needs and well-being above everything else."

"Not to sound insensitive, but at any point did you question whether the baby was yours? If she filed for divorce, things must have been rocky between you two."

Pausing, I press my lips together. "I don't know. Carla was always passionate, I suppose. She definitely had a temper. We only dated for a month before we got married...if you can call what we did dating. I knew she cheated on me later in our relationship, after my injury. I didn't know she cheated on me before then. Maybe I just wanted to believe she'd remain devoted to me, that the party girl she was when we met left the instant she became a mother."

The pain in my throat is back and I swallow, trying to push my emotions down. How could Carla sleep at night the past six years knowing a man other than her daughter's biological father was raising her? How could she be so selfish as to not tell me the truth? How could she watch me rock

Charlotte to sleep those final days before she disappeared and not think it important to come clean? Maybe that's why she left. Maybe she worried the truth would eventually be set free and didn't want to be around for the fireworks.

Returning my attention to Alice, I clear my throat. I can't think about that right now. It won't change anything. I need to focus on doing everything I can to keep my daughters with me, to protect them from the pain this woman caused me all those years ago, the pain she's causing me all over again.

"So with all this, with me not being on the birth certificate, what does that mean?"

She sets down her pen, leaning back in her chair. "I don't want to worry you with a thousand what-ifs, not until we know for sure."

"But I need to know," I insist louder than I intend, but I can't control it. Those girls are my life. I can't lose either of them. Even the thought of walking by an empty bedroom guts me. "I need to know what I'm up against here." My voice shakes as I struggle to blink back my tears, a hand gripping my heart and ripping it from my body.

Alice studies me for a moment, then relents with a sigh. In her line of work, I'm sure she deals with emotional parents daily. "Regardless of the outcome of the paternity test, I'll file a motion contesting physical custody...of both girls. We start at the extreme and hope to settle somewhere in the middle. You have the law on your side here. You've been the sole caregiver for six years. You're financially stable and have built a solid support system. Carla abandoned them with no communication for six years. Not a stellar track record."

"And if the paternity test comes back negative?" My voice catches. When Brooklyn's hand rests on my thigh, I'm surrounded by comfort once more. In my life, I've done many things I'm not proud of, but I'm grateful she's able to look past it all for now, to be my rock when I feel like I'm ready to crumble.

"We'll ask for an order of non-parental custody. It's not easy—"

"What's required?"

Her brows pull in as she assesses me, debating what to say. Then she tents her fingers in front of her. "First, you have to show a long-standing relationship with the child and that you're able to care for her. Obviously, that won't be difficult to prove. You also must show it's not only in the child's best interests, but it would be to her detriment if she's taken from you. That one may be a little more difficult, but still not impossible. DCF will need to be involved, of course." Her eyes briefly float to Brooklyn, then back to me as she leans forward. "If I get this in front of the right judge, we have a good chance of prevailing, especially since granting full physical custody to Carla would rip Charlotte away from not only you, but the only life she's ever known, which could be extremely detrimental to her emotional development at such a young age." She reaches for the motion, scrutinizing it once more. "Now, this man she claims is the biological father of Charlotte... Chase Gardner." She perks up, looking at me from over the papers.

"Yes. It's that Chase Gardner."

"Do you know if he's still in the picture?"

I shake my head. "She was with a different man when I ran into her last month. I assumed it was her husband. She was wearing a ring and they had a little boy with them. Probably around three or so."

"Good. If the child's biological parents are married at the time we petition for non-parental custody, that usually works against you. All of this may become a non-issue anyway if the paternity test establishes you as the biological father. No matter what that test reveals, I promise I will protect your rights as those little girls' father, regardless of whether your blood runs through one, both, or neither of them. In my eyes, it doesn't matter. You raised them. You're their father. And I will work tirelessly to make the court see it that way, too."

"Thank you, Ms. DeMico. I can't even tell you how much I appreciate this."

"No need to thank me. And please, call me Alice." She jots down an address on the back of a business card and hands it to me, standing from her desk. "This is where you need to go for the paternity test. I'll call over there right now and tell them to expect you. This isn't something I'd put off. The sooner you all provide a sample, the better."

"How long does it take to get the results?" I raise myself from the chair, helping Brooklyn from hers. I place my hand on her lower back. I should be more conscious to keep my distance around her, but this feels right. Her warmth, her affection, her…love?

"It can take upwards of a month unless you request them to rush the results. In that case, it should only take about a week, depending on how busy the lab is."

"We'll rush them. I don't want to drag this out any longer than necessary."

"Of course. Once we get the results and know exactly what we're up against, we'll talk strategy. At this point, it's all conjecture. But no matter the outcome, we're going to fight this."

Briefly closing my eyes, I exhale. The weight that had been crushing me all morning seems to have lightened dramatically. I'm not out of the woods, but no matter what, I'm grateful to have someone promising to do everything to help me.

"Thank you, Alice."

"Of course."

After we say our goodbyes and Alice promises to be in touch very soon with her opposition motion, Brooklyn and I leave the office. As we walk along the sidewalk, I drape my arm around her shoulders, surprised when she doesn't shrug me off. I take that as a good sign and lean down, softly kissing her temple.

"Thank you, Brooklyn."

We stop walking and she peers into my eyes. Her expression is unreadable, so I brace myself for her rejection. Then a soft smile lights up her face. "Thank you, Drew."

I don't ask why she's thanking me. It doesn't matter. After everything, I feel like she's slowly coming back to me, just like she always does. This time, I have no intention of letting her go.

CHAPTER FOUR

BROOKLYN

"WHERE ARE WE GOING?" Drew asks as I order him back into my car after stopping by Kelly's, the aroma of the comfort food of our younger years surrounding us. "Aren't we going to sit on the beach and eat like we used to?"

I shrug, turning the key in the ignition. "I thought about it, but I figured I'd combine our two favorite pastimes into one. Grab Kelly's and sit on the roof of the café while we eat it." I lower my voice. "Like we used to with your dad. Figured you could use a little familiarity today."

"Don't you need to get back to work? You've already wasted so much of your time taking me to see Alice, then to get the DNA swab. I don't want to take up the rest of your day."

"There's no such thing as wasted time when it comes to you." I keep my eyes glued to the road as I steer toward downtown. The truth is, I have no desire to leave Drew's side. Not right now. Not after this. "I wouldn't be able to concentrate if I went back to work. All I'd be thinking about is..." A tightness in my throat prevents me from continuing.

When I saw him standing in the doorway to my office this morning, I assumed he was there to confront me about the bomb I dropped on him this past Sunday. Never would I have imagined it was to ask for my help so he could maintain custody of his girls. In an instant, nothing else mattered. All my other concerns and fears became insignificant and inconsequential. I wonder if it's the universe's way of leading me down the road I should have taken...toward Drew instead of away from him.

"What a vile bitch Carla is?" he finishes with a slight laugh, one that still makes my heart skip a beat.

31

A tiny part of me wishes I no longer reacted this way to his endearing voice, husky laugh, woodsy scent, but the truth remains, I do react this way. I always have. He's the only person who's made me feel things I didn't think were real, that I thought only existed in books or movies. This man has brought me to the highest of highs and lowest of lows, but at least it was something. And isn't something better than nothing? Do I really want to sacrifice that passion for security?

I shift my eyes to his, staring into dark pools of admiration and respect. It's so deep and poignant, it sends a shiver through me. Goosebumps pimple my skin, his gaze saying more than Wes ever has with words. Isn't that what I've always wanted? To physically feel someone's love, instead of just taking their word for it? If it weren't for our disjointed history, the decision would be easy. I thought Drew's inability to ever notice me was the nail in the coffin of our future. Now I'm not so sure.

"No," I say, concentrating on the road once more. "I need to be here for you." I grip the steering wheel a little tighter. I'm worried my words may give him too much hope. Then again, maybe that's not a bad thing. Maybe hope is exactly what he needs right now. "Just like I know you'd be here for me if I were going through something similar."

"You know I would, Brooklyn, despite what my past behavior may lead you to believe." He reaches for my hand and I willingly remove it from the wheel. The instant his fingers wrap around mine, a shiver rolls down my spine. It's subtle, but there's no denying how my body reacts to him. It's just as strong as it was when we were teenagers.

I keep my hand joined with his as I drive into downtown, a blush blooming on my cheeks whenever he steals a glimpse at me. I like to believe I don't pull away so he'll feel the comfort he needs, but that's not entirely true. Ever since I first linked hands with him earlier today, I've craved the warmth of his skin on mine, regardless of how innocent the touch is. As much as reason tells me to keep my distance, my heart seems to be the one calling the shots today.

"And we're all going through this," he adds after a long

silence.

"But they're your girls."

"You helped raise them, too. You changed diapers, gave them bottles, sang them to sleep, dealt with meltdowns, wiped their tears. They're your kids, too, Auntie Brook."

I inhale a shaky breath when he calls me that. How much longer will I hear sweet, innocent Charlotte say those two words? I've tried to remain positive all morning for Drew's sake, but my hope of this being smoke and mirrors is nonexistent. I remember the woman Carla was during their marriage. Drew may have been happy to ignore it, since he'd landed a trophy wife, but I saw it. We all did. There's a strong likelihood Charlotte, and possibly even Alyssa, isn't Drew's.

"You've always been a permanent fixture in their lives. They don't remember a time you weren't there to play with them, or sneak them a chocolate chip muffin, or read them a story before bed. This affects all of us." He pauses. Our gazes lock briefly before I refocus on the road. "How are you doing?"

I pinch my lips into a tight line, fighting against the emotions that have been coursing through me since I read the pleading earlier. I've done everything to remain strong and levelheaded for Drew's sake. Those girls are his weakness...and his strength, just like Drew's always been my weakness and my strength.

"I'm trying not to think about it too much, but it's hard." Tears form in the corners of my eyes and I blink them away. "Since the moment you walked into my office—"

"I'm not sure walk is the right word for what I did," he jokes, trying to lighten the mood.

"No." I smile, playfully rolling my eyes. "That's certainly true. You pretty much barged right in. But as I read those papers, all I could think was what if she wins? Did I waste the little time I could have spent with Charlotte by keeping my distance from you over the past month? Am I really that selfish?"

"Don't say that. You're the most selfless person I know. You've made a career out of putting others' needs before yours. There's no way of knowing exactly what's going to happen, but you'll always be part of Charlotte's life. We all will be. I don't care if I'm forced to mortgage my damn house to pay for the legal fees. I'll do it just to fight for her. At least she'll know I did everything I could to keep her mine."

"You're a good man, Drew." I pause, then add, "I'm sorry."

"I'm sorry, too," he replies. "More than you know."

I float my eyes to his, holding his gaze. The tone of his voice makes it apparent he's no longer talking about his current predicament but the past we share. For the first time since he learned the truth about that night, a part of me believes he truly does regret how things transpired between us. Shouldn't that count for something?

We sit in comfortable silence the remainder of our short drive to the North End. Once we reach the café, I pull my car behind the building. Our grease-laden bags in hand, Drew jumps out and rushes toward the driver's side to help me out. We walk toward the rickety fire escape, about to climb up the scaffolding, when he stops, his eyes zeroing in on my heels.

"Are you sure you'll be okay in those?"

I shrug. "They're not optimal, but I'll be fine."

"Says the girl who threw a fit when I tried to get you into a pair of skates several weeks ago. Yet you're happy to climb a fire escape in a pair of fuck-me heels?"

I inhale a sharp breath, my face heating and insides tingling. His fervent voice saying those words brings back memories of that one night together, the things he whispered as his hands roamed all over my body. My mouth waters at the thought of experiencing that again.

"I mean..." He averts his gaze.

Emboldened, I step toward him, ensuring my shoes are in his line of sight. I have to admit, they are hot. As much as I loathed the dress my future mother-in-law chose for me to wear at my bridal shower this past weekend, the beige Christian Louboutin pumps were a rather pleasant surprise, and a very nice addition to my shoe collection.

"You think these are fuck-me shoes?" I ask in a sultry

voice.

This isn't fair to either one of us, but we need something to take our minds off our problems. For a few minutes, I want to pretend I'm not engaged to another man. I want to pretend Drew may not lose his daughters. I want to pretend he did show up at my house the morning he left for college and this is part of the happily ever after I've fantasized about for so long.

When he returns his eyes to mine, they're dark, full of need. It sets those butterflies in my stomach into overdrive. He licks his lips, bringing his body within a whisper of mine. "Will you be upset if I say no?"

"I should be." I bite my lower lip, my core clenching. My skin flushes, my fingers aching to reach out, grab the back of his neck, and force his lips to mine.

"But you're not."

"I..." I trail off, struggling to form the words I should say. I'm so tired of lying, of pretending just to protect my heart.

"You?" He arches a brow, inching even closer but still ensuring our bodies don't touch, remaining just out of reach.

"I think..." I peer into his mesmerizing eyes, torn. How would I feel if Wes were in my position? If he still harbored feelings for an ex and was currently a breath away from kissing her? It doesn't matter that I may not love him. I still care about him. I can't hurt him like that.

Snapping out of my fantasy world, I step back, the connection breaking. "I think we should go eat before our food gets cold."

Drew's shoulders fall as he briefly closes his eyes. "Of course." Doing his best to pretend my rejection doesn't hurt, he starts up the steps. I kick off my heels, carrying them as I follow him up. He glances back every few seconds, making sure I don't slip, just as he did whenever we came up here during our younger days. When he crests the ledge, he hoists himself over, placing the bags of food on the ground before turning around to help me.

Once I have my footing, I pause to take stock of the roof. We used to come up here practically every day during our childhood. It's like no time has passed, like we've been transported back to our formative years. Stealing a glance toward the far end, I spy the remnants of the hockey net Drew's father set up so he could practice. It's the hockey net where I shot my first goal, thanks to Drew's insistence.

Being here with him reminds me how strong our bond is, how much we've been through and survived. Yes, we've had our fair share of difficult moments, some instances when I thought my entire world was falling apart because of him. But we've had some amazing memories, too. Shouldn't those outshine the darkness? Shouldn't those be the moments my mind focuses on instead of all the times I felt marginalized, forgotten, tossed aside?

A hand lands on my lower back and I shift my eyes to Drew's. He gestures toward a picnic table, and I allow him to lead me to it. We sit down to feast on lobster rolls, whole belly clams, and Kelly's famous roast beef. Neither one of us says a word as we listen to the buzz of the city below us, the aroma of tomatoes and garlic wafting up from all the restaurants lining the street.

When I can no longer eat another bite, I push my plate away, noticing Drew didn't eat as much as he usually would. I watch his profile out of the corner of my eyes. He's reflective, pensive, his brows creased as he stares into the distance. I wonder what's going through his mind, if he's wracking his brain for any piece of evidence Alice can use in his upcoming battle with Carla.

It takes no time for him to realize I'm staring and he meets my gaze, his lips curving up in the corners. He looks different than he did when I first saw him this morning. Yes, he has an uphill battle on his hands, but at least I was able to give him a little peace of mind that we'll do everything to fight this. I return his smile as a breeze blows my dark hair in front of my face, but I make no move to try to smooth it back. I simply revel in the solitude and serenity being up here with Drew brings me, pretending things between us never changed.

"Penny for your thoughts?" I ask when his eyes never shift from mine.

He smirks. "Care to up that to a quarter? Those legal fees won't pay for themselves."

I cringe. "Sorry. I can talk to Alice, see if she can work something out."

He reaches across the table, clutching my hand. "Don't worry. I can afford it." He pauses for a beat, then withdraws, the lack of contact leaving me longing for more. He assesses me for a moment, then leans forward, placing his elbows on the table and folding his hands. "Actually, I was just thinking of the night Carla asked for a divorce."

"Oh." I shift nervously on the wooden bench.

"The first time," he adds, although it's unnecessary. The timbre of his voice makes it apparent which time he's referring to.

"I'm not sure now's the right time to discuss this." I jump up, collecting our trash, avoiding his eyes as I busy myself. "I shouldn't have said anything. You were better off not knowing."

"Why do you think that?" He gets to his feet, helping me clear the area.

"I told you." I keep my head lowered, hoping he'll drop the conversation.

"Yeah, yeah. I know. I couldn't remember and you wanted to forget. I'm sure you've rehearsed that one for years." He brings his hand to my chin. I stop, losing myself in his familiar, soulful eyes. He leans into me, his mouth less than an inch from mine. "What's the real reason?"

"That is the real reason," I insist weakly, swallowing hard, my gaze focused on his lips. My heart pounds in my chest, the electricity running through me strong enough to light New York City.

"Talk to me, Brooklyn." His voice placid, he scrunches his eyebrows together as he pleads with me like a desperate man begging for clemency.

I shake my head, chewing on my lip. "You'll never understand."

"I think I will. More than you realize. Please… Just help me wrap my head around it. Then we never have to talk about it again. I promise."

I draw in a deep breath, trying to calm my overwrought emotions. I'm so tired of hiding the truth, of pretending we can be friends when that ship sailed long ago.

"Because if I had told you the truth, you'd be faced with a decision." Our eyes lock. "I couldn't stand the thought of you choosing her over me, which I knew would happen. So I decided for you."

"But it wasn't your decision to make." His neck is strained, the veins in his forehead throbbing.

"Maybe not. But after everything we've been through, everything you put me through, I figured it was my best shot at protecting my heart." Stepping back, I cross my arms in front of my chest, warming myself against a sudden chill, despite the pleasant temperatures. "Or at least I thought it was."

"But it wasn't?"

The hope in his voice is overpowering, enthralling, consuming. God, I want to tell him I moved on, that I no longer think about our past. About the way his lips taste. About the way his kisses breathe life into me. About the way his touch jumpstarts my heart. But I do. Constantly.

"We both know I'm powerless to control how my heart feels about you."

His lips part, his eyes wide as my confession hangs in the air. A confession I never should have made.

Embarrassed, I whirl around, grab my shoes, and hurry toward the fire escape. "I should get going. Wes is probably wondering why I haven't returned any of his calls."

"Of course," Drew scoffs as I'm about to climb down. "Just keep running away, Brooklyn!"

The tone of his voice gives me pause and I stop in my tracks, slowly facing him. "What the hell's that supposed to mean?"

"No. Please, go." He gestures to the fire escape, frazzled. "You've made an art form out of running from the truth. Don't stop now. Go. See the man you're marrying."

"Don't be jealous, Drew," I sneer, masking my truth with

anger. "It doesn't look good on you." I turn to climb down, but he storms toward me, grabbing my arm and forcing me to stare into his fiery gaze.

"Jealous?" he bellows through the wind. "You think I'm jealous?"

The intensity in his tone renders me speechless. The seconds seem to stretch into minutes, into hours, into an eternity as I wait to see what he's going to say next.

"Okay! You got me!" He releases his hold on me, digging his hands into his hair. "I'm jealous!"

I exhale a small breath at his admission, both excited and scared at the same time.

"I'm jealous of the rain that hits your skin because I wish I could be the one to know what that feels like."

"Drew…," I caution, but it does nothing to stop him. He's obsessed, a man desperate to finally put it all out there.

"I'm jealous of the sheets on your bed that get to keep you warm at night because I wish it were my arms doing that." His eyes glued to mine, he closes the distance between us. I'm frozen, unable to move, unable to breathe, unable to walk away. "I'm jealous of the wind that gets to blow through your hair because I wish it were my fingers."

He pauses, studying me, a subtle quiver in his chin as he struggles to say the next words. "Most of all, I'm jealous of how happy Wes makes you."

I push out a laugh, my reaction involuntary. "You really think Wes makes me happy?"

He opens his mouth, my words catching him off-guard. The silence stretches, my heart pounding like a caged beast begging to be set free.

"If he doesn't, why are you marrying him?"

"You're so stupid, Drew." I briefly lower my eyes as I swipe at my tears. "There's only one person who's ever made me happy." I return my gaze to his.

"Who?" His Adam's apple bobs up and down as he waits intently for my response.

I shake my head, wanting to lie, but I can't. I don't understand what I'm doing, why I'm admitting this. A force more powerful than any I've experienced is at play, turning me into a puppet.

My lips lift into a smile. "You."

Every muscle in Drew's body relaxes the instant that word falls from my mouth. He goes to close the distance, but I hold up my hand, stepping back.

"That summer before my junior year was the happiest I could remember. Then you broke your promise and, in doing so, my heart." My throat is tight as I struggle to say the words I've wanted to utter for too long now, tears spilling over my eyelids, cascading down my cheeks. "For years, I wondered if I imagined it all, imagined the feel of your lips, the warmth of your arms, the way my body fit into yours so perfectly. How could it have been real when you did everything to pretend I didn't exist?"

With each word I speak, my tears become more numerous, but I can't stop. I've kept this in for years, not wanting Drew to see the power he's held over me. No more. He needs to understand why I'm doing what I am, why I need to move on.

"No one ever made me feel more invisible than you did. I swore to myself I would afford you the same compassion you did me...none." I swipe at my tears, summoning the strength to continue with this exercise in torture. "Then you had a baby of your own and I saw a glimpse of the old Drew...my Drew." I point to myself, my voice strained. "Little by little, you came back to me, so much so that when I saw you that night Carla asked for a divorce... I don't know. I thought things would be different. But they weren't. You were still the same Drew you always were, the one who tossed me aside the instant something better came along. You never noticed me, never paid any attention to me...until I told you I was engaged to another man. So whatever this is, whatever you think you feel for me, I know it's not real. You're just scared of being alone and are out of options."

I turn around again, my hands shaking as I reach for the ledge.

"You think I never noticed you?" his voice thunders from

behind. It's so cutting and deep, I almost feel the ground tremble below me.

I glance over my shoulder, the passion in his expression reaching my soul. "I—"

"I've always noticed you, Brooklyn," he interrupts, stalking toward me. "Always. Even when you didn't think I was looking. I noticed you used to put half-and-half in your Americanos every morning, but recently switched to whole milk instead."

I part my lips, about to tell him that kind of thing is insignificant, but no words come. It doesn't matter how small the detail. This is something even Wes has never noticed, as evidenced by the fact he still stocks half-and-half in his refrigerator.

"I noticed you get this adorable look on your face when you're real excited about something. Your eyes have this gleam, and I wish I could be the reason for that excitement." His tone softening, he closes the distance between us, a slight smile building on his lips. "And I noticed you were always the one my heart wanted. Always. For the longest time, I refused to believe it because I knew I'd never recover if you didn't feel the same way about me. The truth is, Brooklyn Rose Tanner, you've had my heart since the first time I pushed you on the swing on the oak tree in your front yard and you asked me to make you go higher so you could fly."

My lower lip quivers as I listen to his heartfelt plea. Wes has never spoken to me with so much emotion, so much longing, even when he proposed. His words were sweet, but not full of meaning. Not like Drew's.

"Just being near you has always made me feel like I'm flying. Because of you, I'm the man I am. I'm the father I am. Because of you, I want to be a better person." He stares at me, swallowing hard, his chest heaving, his breathing labored. "So you're wrong, Brooklyn. I've always noticed you."

His confession rings out in the air, leaving me stunned mute, frozen in place. When I make no move to retreat, as I've been prone to do, he steps closer. The tension between us is no longer strained. It's something else entirely...something much more electrifying.

"Brooklyn, tell me something." There's heat in his eyes as he stares at me, licking his lips. "What exactly did we do that night?" His voice is husky, wanton. It makes the hairs on the back of my neck stand on end, a delicious shiver rolling down my spine.

"Just what I said to Molly." I swallow hard. "We stopped just short—"

"Yeah, yeah. I heard all that." He inches even closer still, only a whisper between us.

I want nothing more than to erase that last breath separating us, but I want this more. This heat. This need. This anticipation. I haven't felt this alive in years. Almost seven years to be exact.

Lowering his mouth, his breath intermingles with mine. "What. Did. We. Do?"

My eyes zero in on those lips I remember being pressed against mine so fully, so firmly, so perfectly. "We kissed."

"Did you enjoy it?"

"Yes," I breathe in a throaty voice. "It was the best kiss of my life." He doesn't need to know that, but I can't stop myself, a slave to this man and the way he makes me feel.

He smirks flirtatiously, a whisper between our mouths. I brace myself for his kiss, my lips tingling in anticipation. As much as I should, I won't stop him. I've been fighting this for years. It's time I wave the white flag and surrender to what my heart craves.

I wait, and wait, and wait, but his kiss never comes.

"Did I kiss you on any other parts of your body?"

I dart my tongue out, nearly skimming against his lips as I moisten my own. "My neck."

He brings his mouth close to my throat. Instinctively, I crane my head toward one side, giving him better access. But he still doesn't touch me. He remains just out of reach, not a single part of his body on mine. I grow even more unhinged as his breath caresses my skin. I have no idea what he's trying to do, but whatever it is has turned me into a ball of putty in his very capable hands. This is better than any foreplay I've ever experienced. I don't want the moment to end.

He inhales. "Mmm. Lavender." He shivers, as if overwhelmed with sensation, before returning his fiery eyes to mine. This is a new look for him, his gaze harsh, punishing, saturated with need. "Where else?" His words come out like a growl.

"My stomach."

He lifts his hands toward me, stopping just shy of clutching my hips. "Did I circle your belly button, dragging my tongue along your hip bone?"

I gasp. "You remember?"

He slowly shakes his head. "No. I always imagined doing that. Did I kiss you anywhere else, Brooklyn?"

My heart pounds as I contemplate my next answer. This entire scenario seems incredibly surreal. I've never spoken so boldly about these kinds of things before, not even to Wes. I certainly shouldn't be talking this way to Drew, but I'm glued to the spot, glued to him, reliving the past.

"My breasts," I answer finally, my voice barely audible.

"Fuck." He bites his lower lip with such force, I expect to see blood. Nostrils flaring, he clenches and unclenches his fists before slowly bringing his hands toward me. My breathing increases, my chest rising and falling with each shaky inhale and exhale. The nearness of his hands unhinges me, turning me into a tightly wound ball of need as I succumb to the moment...succumb to Drew

His mouth hovers over mine and I close my eyes, mentally returning to that night, to the incredible sensations I experienced, ones I've gone back to time and again just to feel something.

"Did I touch you anywhere else?"

I subtly nod.

"Where?"

His gruff voice causes goosebumps to prickle my skin. "You know where."

He readjusts his stance, brushing his waist against me. If I weren't overly sensitive and hyperaware of everything, I probably never would have noticed it. But his erection skimming me flames my lust, an insatiable desire sparking to life. I whimper, my body trembling from the nearness of him.

"Tell me, Brooklyn." The heat of his words skates across me. "Did I make you come?"

"You know the answer," I pant. "You overheard what I told Molly."

"That's true. But I want to hear you tell me." He licks his lips. "Did I make you come?"

I no longer hear the busy sounds of the Boston streets below us, no longer feel the wind on my face, no longer smell the city air. I'm in another world, in the erotic dream I've fantasized about for years now. For a moment, it's just us. No Carla. No Wes. No past. Like I always imagined it would be.

"Yes."

His jaw clenches, every muscle in his body tightening as my response lingers between us. He inches closer, leaving absolutely no room for the Holy Ghost, as Aunt Gigi would say. His mouth scrapes mine and I plump out my lower lip. I feel like an addict whose next fix is right in front of her, but she can't have it yet.

"With what?"

"Your fingers..."

He moans, harsh and volatile.

"And your tongue."

"Fuck," he hisses. I can tell he's barely keeping it together. And I don't want him to. I want him to lose control. And I want to lose control with him. "Did you enjoy it?"

"It was the best orgasm of my life. I'd never experienced anything like it before. And I haven't since."

A groan falls from Drew's throat as we remain locked in place, our bodies almost touching, his lips hovering over mine. Abruptly, he steps back, running a shaky hand through his hair and turning from me. It leaves me bewildered, confused, uncertain.

"You should go," he says firmly. He glances over his shoulder. "As much as I want you, you're not mine to have."

His words are like ice water thrown over me, the heat coursing through me just minutes ago sizzling out. The reality of what I almost did hits me hard. What if Drew weren't so concerned? Would I have been careless and allowed him to kiss me? Would I have kissed him back? I know the answers to those questions. I hang my head in shame.

"How will you get home? Your bike is—"

"I'll borrow Gigi's car," he snaps. "I just... I can't do this with you."

I nod, my heart heavy. It's not just Wes I'm hurting. I'm hurting Drew, too. I can't string them both along. I love Wes. We're a good match. But it's nothing compared to the way my heart pounds an erratic rhythm when I'm with Drew. Is that enough to sustain a relationship, though? How can I reconcile this Drew with the one who broke his promise to me, then pretended like it never happened?

"I'm sorry." I'm about to head down the fire escape when he speaks again.

"This wedding's a mistake, Brooklyn."

I lift my eyes to his. There's so much emotion. More than I've ever seen from Wes.

"I see it. Everyone around you sees it. What's it going to take for you to finally see it, too?"

I part my lips, then give him the only answer I can, the only answer that would make this decision easy. "Forgetting the past."

CHAPTER FIVE

DREW

"WELL, THIS IS A pleasant surprise," Gigi says when I step through the doors of the café after watching Brooklyn drive off. Part of me hoped she'd come back, tell me she was willing to forget all the past hurt I caused her and leave Wes. But she didn't.

It took every ounce of restraint I possessed not to kiss her, not to crush her body against me and lather her with promises to make her mine in every way possible. But I won't do that to Wes. I won't be the other man. If I'm the one she chooses, she needs to give me every part of her. Until she's willing to do that, I won't touch her, not the way I know she wants me to. And the way I want to.

"Hey, Gigi." I go to the bar and kiss her cheek, then pour myself a cup of coffee. The place isn't crowded, not like it is in the morning. The tables are only half-filled with people having lunch or a few drinks.

"Aren't you supposed to be working?" a familiar voice chimes in. I sweep my gaze to a table in the corner where Molly's furiously typing on her laptop, journals filled with notes sprawled on the surface beside her.

"I took a personal day."

"Why?" Molly stops what she's doing and studies me. With one glance, she can sense something's wrong. I suppose that's what happens when you've spent over thirty years together. She shuts her laptop, her brows furrowing in concern. "What's going on? Did something happen with Brooklyn?"

"No. Not Brooklyn." I sit across the table from her. "But something did happen."

I swallow hard, worrying my bottom lip as I stare at the dark liquid in my mug. I hate having to inform everyone about what Carla's doing. It forces me to relive the moment I first read her motion this morning, the moment I learned Charlotte may not be my daughter. That's the worst part of this. Repeating the story over and over, each re-telling making me kick myself a little harder at how blind I was to the truth.

When I lift my gaze back to Molly's, unease fills the lines of her face. Regardless of the outcome of the paternity test, Carla's still trying to take my girls from me. This affects my sister and aunt as much as it does me. "There's something I need to tell you." I look at Gigi. "Both of you."

My aunt's face falls. By my tone alone, she knows it's serious. She gestures to one of our employees to take over the register, then heads toward the table, sitting down. "What is it, Andrew dear?"

I rub my palms along my jeans, exhaling. "This morning, after I dropped the girls at school, there was a knock on my door. It was a process server."

Molly squints, shaking her head. "Process server? For what?"

I bounce my legs as I tap on the wooden table. How can I sit here and tell Molly and Gigi our family is about to be torn apart? It wasn't this difficult when I told Brooklyn. She's analytical and rational. Molly and Gigi tend to be very emotional. I've finally gotten mine under control. I need them to stay calm so my girls won't think anything's wrong when I see them today.

"Remember how I told you we ran into Carla at the science museum last month?"

Molly nods, her eyes remaining intent on mine.

"Well, a few weeks ago, she stopped by my office and asked to be a part of the girls' lives."

"And you told her to fuck off, right?" she retorts, her voice harsh. She crosses her arms over her stomach, pure distaste on her face.

"Essentially, yes." My tone is calm, a complete one-eighty from my sister's. "I told her I wouldn't let her hurt them again. Before she left, she basically threatened me, saying I couldn't keep them from her forever."

Gigi gasps, covering her mouth with her hand. "She didn't..."

I briefly squeeze my eyes shut. "She's asking for shared physical custody of Alyssa."

"And Charlotte, too?" Molly presses.

"She's asking for full custody of Charlotte."

"What?" she shrieks, her eyes glistening with tears. "She can't do that!"

I glance between Molly and Gigi, who wears a long expression. "She might be able to."

"How? You're her father!" She opens her mouth, struggling to come up with a compelling argument. "She can't do that!" she repeats.

"She can if I'm not her father."

Molly inhales sharply, her lips parting as she processes this information. "She... No..."

"What are you saying, Andrew?" Gigi asks in an uncharacteristic shaky voice. She's always been one of the strongest women I know. Her one weakness, all our weakness, is family. The idea of anyone trying to come between us is too much for any of us to bear, especially Aunt Gigi.

"In her complaint for custody, Carla alleged that Chase is the father."

"Your teammate?" Gigi lifts a brow. "The man she cheated on you with after your injury?"

"She claims the affair had been going on for much longer, without my knowledge. That Chase is Charlotte's biological father, not me."

"But you don't know for sure, right?" Molly grasps at straws, just like I did earlier today. I've had several hours to come to terms with the fact that my entire life is about to change, and not for the better.

"Not yet. I talked with an attorney earlier, then went to a lab. They took a DNA swab. I have to take Charlotte to get one. And the attorney also wants to have Alyssa's DNA checked against mine so there aren't any surprises. Once we do that, we can find out the truth, one way or another."

Molly pinches her lips together, her chin quivering. She

48

looks away, swiping at her cheeks.

"You're going to fight this, right?" Gigi presses.

"Without a doubt." My response comes quick, fevered. "Brooklyn took me to see an attorney she knows, someone she trusts to go to the mattresses."

"Only you would resort to using a Godfather reference when talking about fighting for custody of your daughters." Molly's voice lacks the teasing quality it normally has. Regardless, I'm grateful for the short moment of levity.

"Brooklyn took you?" Gigi gives me a questioning look, a sly smile gradually building on her lips.

"I didn't know where else to go, so I went to her office. Luckily, she was there. The attorney she introduced me to is infinitely better than that guy who represented me in my divorce. She actually has kids of her own. She promised to do everything to fight this and help me keep custody of Charlotte, even if it's proven she's not mine."

Silence settles at the table as they process this drastic turn of events. What can you possibly say to news like this? That it'll be okay? That it'll work itself out? I'm not naïve enough to believe that's the case. No matter what happens, this will change all our lives. Despite that, I don't feel as helpless as I thought I would. Spending the day with Brooklyn, being with her, seeing how her body still reacts to mine, gave me a small slice of comfort, regardless of the difficult position we find ourselves in these days.

"What are you going to tell the girls?" Molly asks after a while.

"I have no idea." I peek at my watch, seeing it's almost 1:30. "I have to go pick them up from school. I don't know how I'm going to peer into their eyes and pretend everything's okay. I'm not going to tell them anything yet, not until I have definitive answers. But at some point, I have to tell them something. How am I supposed to explain to a six- and eight-year-old why their mother abandoned them and wanted nothing to do with them for six years, but is now trying to take them from me?" I shake my head, my throat tightening.

Gigi places a reassuring hand on my shoulder. "You will,

and we'll be there when you do...if that's what you need."

I force a smile. "Thanks, Gigi." I place one hand over hers, then reach across the table, grabbing Molly's, as well. "Both of you. I can't tell you how much your support means. Not just with this, but with everything over the years. I'd be lost without you two."

"And Brooklyn," Gigi reminds me, constantly looking for an opportunity to bring her up. "She helped raise those girls. She's always been there for you. Even when you didn't realize it."

I nod, pulling away from them. "I know." On a long sigh, I stand, my attention focused on my aunt. "Can I borrow your car?"

"Where's yours?"

I shrug. "Home."

"Then how did you get here?"

"Brooklyn."

"Oh really?" She waggles her eyebrows.

"Like I told you. I went to see her and she took me to talk to an attorney."

"That's true," Molly interjects, standing. "But you left out how you got here if you don't have your car."

"Brooklyn drove."

"And she left without taking you back to get your car? I find that hard to believe."

"I told her it was okay. Normally, she'd force me into her car, but considering I took the Triumph to her office, I think she was more than happy when I said I'd get Gigi to lend me her car."

My aunt's eyes harden, her lips pinching in a tight line. The vein in her forehead throbs, evidence of her displeasure at this news. She hates that bike more than Brooklyn does.

"We grabbed Kelly's, then brought it back here and ate up on the roof," I finish before Gigi can berate me for riding my motorcycle.

"Her idea or yours?" Gigi asks.

"Hers," I answer, not seeing why that should matter.

"I thought you were giving her space to figure things out?"

Molly teases.

"That was before I received the motion for custody modification."

"Mmm-hmm."

"She's still engaged to Wes," I remind them.

"Are you really going to let that stop you?" Gigi crosses her arms in front of her chest, passing me a skeptical look.

I do my best to reel in my grin as I slowly shake my head. "Do you know what Dad said to me when I first started playing hockey?"

"What's that?"

"The word 'quit' isn't in our family's vocabulary. So give up on Brooklyn just because she thinks marrying Wes is the right decision? Not a chance in hell."

* * *

My eyes remain glued to the phone in my hand as I stand in the distance, waiting for that final bell of the day to ring, followed by the sound of the front doors of the school opening, swarms of kids barreling out. The women Molly refers to as the "cougar den" lurk close by, ready to pounce, but I'm in no mood today...especially today.

As I search Google for cases in this state where a non-parent retained physical custody of a child, which I probably shouldn't be doing since it doesn't seem to be a normal occurrence, a familiar squeal meets my ears. It's both heartwarming and heartbreaking, the mere thought that this loving, considerate human may not be mine. The instant I see Charlotte, it takes everything I have not to break down in front of her. My lungs constrict and my heart feels like it's shattering in my chest.

A breaking heart isn't simply an analogy used for dramatic emphasis. I now know it does happen. The agony coursing through me is more than I can stomach. Still, I can't let her know. Her life's about to drastically change. I need to give her a few more good days before that happens.

So I plaster on a smile, acting like everything's exactly as it should be and this is just like every other day I've waited outside their school to walk them home.

I click off my phone and shove it into my pocket before squatting, holding my arms wide. When Charlotte runs into them, I pretend the strength of her hug nearly knocks me over.

"I missed you, Daddy!"

Her words hit me hard and I squeeze her tighter, savoring her warm body, inhaling her powdery scent. How much longer will I be able to hug her like this?

I pull back, doing everything to swallow down the tears threatening to fall. As I stare into her dark eyes, able to make out flecks of gold identical to those in Chase's, my stomach sinks. How did I not see it all before?

"I made you something in art class!" she exclaims.

"You did?" I clear my throat, masking the slight tremble in my voice. "What's that?"

She places her backpack on the ground and unzips it, pulling out a piece of folded construction paper. "A Mother's Day card."

She hands it to me, a brilliant smile on her face. With every second that passes, every word she says, it becomes increasingly difficult to fight back my tears. I'm a man. I'm supposed to be strong, not let things like this get to me. Kids have that effect on you. If they hurt, you feel that pain tenfold, wishing you could do something to take it away. Right now, I wish I could do something to dampen the pain of what Charlotte's about to go through...what both girls are about to go through.

"I made one for Auntie Molly, Aunt Gigi, and Auntie Brook, too!" Excitement oozes from her as she shows me all the cards, oblivious to my internal struggle. "I couldn't get as detailed as some of the other kids in class since I had four to make and they only had one, but I still think they're good. Do you like yours, Daddy?"

Opening the card, I smile when I see her attempt at drawing a hockey player and a trophy cup with "#1" scrawled on it. "I love it, Char." I pull her against me again, kissing the top of her head. "But you didn't have to make me a card. I'm your daddy."

"I know. But you're my mommy, too."

I hold her at arm's length, studying her. It seems like just yesterday I cradled her against my chest for the first time. When Carla walked in carrying Charlotte after the doctors finally brought me out of the coma, I panicked, thinking over a month had passed. Charlotte wasn't due until March, but it was only February. That should have been a giant red flag. The last thing on my mind was whether Charlotte could be mine. Instead, my focus was on whether I'd ever play hockey again, my world feeling like it was crashing around me when my doctor insisted I retire from professional hockey due to the extent of my latest injury, which only exacerbated the prior brain trauma. Maybe if I had focused on my family, not the fact I'd never play hockey again, I would have put the pieces together. Or maybe it was a blessing in disguise. Maybe it was the universe's way of telling me I needed this tiny human in my life, just like she needed me.

"And I always will be," I say, kissing her one more time, my lips lingering on her cheek longer than normal, savoring the feel of her soft skin against mine.

"Hey, Dad..." Alyssa's voice cuts through. I turn to see her walking up to us, her backpack slung over her shoulders. The instant our eyes lock, she slows, her expression falling. She's inherited her aunt Gigi's observational skills. Normally, I consider it a good thing. Now I wish she weren't so intuitive. "Is everything okay?"

"Of course." I stand, tousling her hair and giving her a hug, although she tries to push away.

I hate lying to her, to both of them. I'm struggling to cope with the unknown myself. I can't put that on them, too. I want to enjoy my last few days where these girls think I'm their hero. I fear they soon won't.

"Let's go home and get you girls out of these uniforms." I look up at the sky, the May sun warming my face. "It's a perfect day to go rollerblading, don't you think?"

"Yes!" Charlotte says, her voice oozing enthusiasm.

Alyssa's not as convinced, eyeing me with skepticism.

"Are you sure everything's okay? You always make us finish our homework before we can play."

I lift a brow. "Do you have a lot of homework?"

"No. Just a few math problems. It'll be easy."

"Then let's do something since it's so nice out." Most other parents would probably be concerned about homework, but Alyssa's intelligent. Math comes easily to her. I used to try to help her, although she insisted she didn't need it. She was right. Numbers just click for her. In the time it took me to work through one of her problems, she'd successfully completed her entire assignment.

"You'd tell us if something was wrong, wouldn't you?"

"What's wrong?" Charlotte presses.

"Nothing is wrong. I didn't get to see you girls much during hockey season. I want to make up for that now. Unless you'd rather do homework this afternoon…"

"No!" they both reply simultaneously.

"Good. Then let's have some fun."

I hold my hands out for the girls to grab. Charlotte takes one immediately. Alyssa scrutinizes me for a moment. Then, instead of insisting she's too old to hold my hand, she takes it. I don't know if I should be happy or worried about this.

CHAPTER SIX

BROOKLYN

A SLIVER OF LIGHT from the streetlamp shines across the hardwood floor in Wes' master bedroom as I lay awake, sleep evading me, like it has every other night this week. Occasionally, a car drives by or a dog barks before silence resumes. Most people like the peacefulness of living in the suburbs. Not me. I prefer the sounds of the city. It reminds me that there are other people around, that I'm not alone in my troubles, that there are others with bigger problems than mine. I've never lived in a quiet neighborhood where the only sounds are chirping birds or the occasional breeze. I'm not sure I want to leave the city and live in a house in the middle of nowhere with Wes. Won't he miss the city, too? Or is he willing to make that sacrifice because he thinks I want the perfect house, an enormous yard, and beautiful landscape?

As I stare at the ceiling, there's a subtle jingle of keys, followed by the door opening. Footsteps sound on the floorboards of the first level before they shuffle up the stairs. I hear the exhaustion in them as they grow closer. When the bedroom door opens, I shut my eyes, steadying my breathing, pretending to be asleep.

Wes is quiet as he walks past the bed and ducks into the ensuite bathroom. Soon, the shower turns on. I blow out a breath, then glance at the clock. 1:45 a.m. Is this what I have to look forward to? Dinner alone while he works late? Him sneaking in after midnight? Only seeing him for a few minutes in the morning before the cycle repeats for another day? I'm not sure I want that life, a marriage in name only, to be at his beck and call when it's convenient for him to show up.

After ten minutes of trying to convince myself I'm just overthinking this, that these feelings are the result of seeing Drew again today, a warm body slides into bed, an arm

55

snaking around my midsection. Wes pulls me against him, my back to his front. I sigh as he plants a soft kiss on my neck. The aroma of his body wash finds its way to my senses and I melt into him, my muscles relaxing as I try to quiet my mind. His kisses become warmer, more seductive, hands roaming my stomach, my hip, my ass. He brings me even closer, his erection hardening behind me.

"Wes," I whine, my voice raspy. "Not tonight."

He exhales a long breath, his frustration evident. I hate turning him down, hate I've turned him down the past three nights. I should want to be intimate with him. But since Sunday, since fantasizing about Drew while Wes was inside me, I'm fighting a tumultuous tug-of-war. I feel guilty for thinking about another man when I'm with Wes. And I feel like I'm betraying Drew by sleeping with Wes. It's a reminder that no matter which path I choose, I'm hurting someone I care about.

"Did I do something wrong?" He lowers his voice. "Was I too rough the other night?"

"No."

Quickly, I turn over to face him, although I fear he'll see the truth I'm finding it increasingly difficult to hide, especially when I stare at Wes' lips and can only think about Drew and how I was a breath away from kissing him. Had he not put a stop to it, I would have. Lust controls me when I'm near him. When he's gone, I want to confess my weakness to Wes and beg forgiveness. I'm riding a constant seesaw. How much longer can I do this before I hit the bottom hard enough to shatter my world?

"I like it when you're not gentle with me." I stare at his chest, playing with a few tendrils of hair. "I don't want you to treat me like this delicate thing you put on a pedestal and worship."

He pulls me closer, rubbing his arousal against me. "But I like worshiping you. It's what you deserve." He lowers his mouth to my neck, dragging his tongue across my skin. I close my eyes, wanting to tell him I'm not in the mood, but how much longer will that work? Eventually, he'll want to know why I went from being happy to have sex every night to being cold and uninterested. How long will he buy the same excuse before he begins to suspect something? Do I want him to suspect something?

With a moan, I crane my head back, allowing him better access, telling him with my body I changed my mind. His skin is soft on mine, no hint of stubble. Before, I preferred clean-shaven men. Now, it's not what I want. I want the jarring, scraping ache of a man's unshaven jaw rubbing against my most sensitive parts, bruising, punishing, electrifying.

His fingers are quick and awkward as they lift my shirt over my head. In an instant, his mouth clamps onto a nipple. I sigh, pretending I like it. It used to do the job, but now it seems lacking. He moves to the other breast, giving it the same treatment before traveling down my stomach. He pauses as he reaches the waistband of my pants, floating his eyes to mine. Biting my lower lip, I nod. It's not eager, but not resigned, either.

Once my panties are gone, he kneels between my thighs, positioning himself. There's no attempt to make me feel good, and I wonder if it's always been this way between us. If it's always been about him but I was too blind to care. I could tell him what I want, what I need, and he'll give me whatever I ask for. I don't. After the past few days, I don't deserve that. I prop my legs up, bracing for his invasion, our gazes locked on each other. There's so much love, respect, and need for me in those eyes.

"Wait," I say, my voice sharp.

He immediately stops, looking at me with concern. "Are you okay?"

I open my mouth, burdened with a sudden urge to come clean, tell him the truth. Tell him I've been in love with Drew since the first time he kissed me seventeen years ago. Tell him it's Drew I want, crave, need. Tell him when he makes love to me, it's Drew I'm fantasizing about. Instead, I flip onto my stomach and prop myself onto my knees and elbows, glancing over my shoulder.

"Like this."

Wes' gaze darkens even more as he repositions himself. When he pushes inside, his motions filled with love and lust at the same time, I face forward, squeezing my eyes shut, fighting against the tears welling. This feels so wrong, so dirty, so unforgivable. The fact I'm letting him fuck me like this so I'm not reminded of his affection guts me. Wes always says I'm such a kind person, my heart so full of compassion. If he only knew the darkness that lies within, he wouldn't think so.

I'm on autopilot as I drown in my guilt. Finally, Wes' hold on my hips tightens, his motions increasing. He groans, his thrusts jerky as he finds his release. We remain still for a few moments. He reaches around, toying with me in an effort to bring me to orgasm, grinding against me as his erection slips out.

"It's okay," I say, scooting away from him. "I'm okay." I fling my legs over the side of the bed, collecting my clothes.

"Are you sure? I don't—"

"I'm okay," I repeat, avoiding his eyes. "I need to clean up. It's after two and I need to be up in three hours." I head toward the bathroom.

As I'm about to disappear behind the door, he murmurs, "I love you, Brooklyn."

I pause, lifting my gaze to his. I'm barely keeping it together, all the events leading to this moment like a weight crushing my chest, making it impossible to breathe.

An ache in my throat, I swallow hard, giving him the response he needs. "I love you, too." Then I close the door.

Drawing in a deep breath, I lean my forehead against the wood. In my solitude, I allow all the emotions I've kept under lock and key to fall forward. I'm being tugged in a thousand different directions. Part of me wants to go back to that fork in the road and choose a different path. Another part wants to stay on the current course to see what's waiting around the bend. Still another part of me wants to walk away from everything, to disappear and start over somewhere new where nobody knows who I am, what I've done.

I turn on the shower and step under the water, not caring it's not yet warm. Placing an arm along the marble tile to support myself, I close my eyes, choking out a sob. To an outsider, this decision would be an easy one. Choose love, they'd say. Follow your heart, they'd encourage. But they haven't lived through the heartbreaking knowledge of always being tossed aside when something better came along, of getting your hopes up, of dreaming, pining, planning for a future, only to have those dreams dashed in an instant with no explanation.

I wish life were easier, wish I didn't feel like I had to choose between two men I care deeply for, but in entirely different ways. I wish I didn't feel like the longer I wait to choose, the more I'll hurt them. That I'm struggling with this should tell me everything I need to know about which path is correct, and it does. It doesn't make the decision any easier.

I lose track of time as I stand under the water, allowing myself to cry. But who am I crying for? Me? Wes? Drew?

It's not until my skin prunes I realize I've been in here longer than I originally intended. I quickly finish up, then towel myself off. After pulling my yoga pants and t-shirt back over my body, I tiptoe into the bedroom. The light from the streetlamp now illuminates a small portion of Wes' slumbering face, his expression peaceful, serene, temperate. It's at complete odds with the turmoil filling my subconscious.

Slipping into bed, I try not to disturb him. When a small snore fills the quiet space, I know nothing will wake him. I close my eyes, but just like every other night I've lain beside Wes in this bed of lies, my troubled thoughts prevent sleep from finding me. I stare at the walls, exhausted, but wide awake. I pick up my phone, aware it won't help matters any. As I'm about to check my email, I click on my text icon instead, pull up my most recent exchange with Drew, and type out a message.

Me: Just wanted to make sure you're doing okay.

I hesitate before hitting send. It's nearly three in the morning. I doubt he's awake. What will he think when he sees the message? Will he wonder why I'm awake, why I'm texting him instead of slumbering in the arms of the man I'm supposed to marry in a month? I should let it go, but I can't.

I remain still, barely breathing as I watch the text pop up in our exchange, then the little note it had been delivered appear below it. When I'm about to close out of the chat, I notice a text bubble below my message, indicating he's typing out a response. My heart rate picks up and I stare at the screen. It seems like it's taking a ridiculously long time when it's probably only a matter of seconds. Finally, his reply comes through.

> **Drew:** *I'm doing as good as can be expected, I suppose. Can't sleep, though. What are you doing up?*

I carefully get out of bed and pad on light feet out of the room, heading down the steps. The last thing I need is for Wes to roll over and notice me texting Drew in the middle of the night.

> **Me:** I can't sleep, either.

As I lower myself onto the couch and snuggle up with one of Wes' comfortable throw blankets, my phone buzzes with what I expect to be an incoming text. Instead, a picture of Drew on the ice during his hockey days appears on the screen, indicating he's calling me. It's not unusual. He calls me all the time. At least he used to. But now I'm nervous, like a teenager whose crush is calling her. It's not that far from the truth.

"Hey," I answer, my voice breathy.

"Hey," he whispers back. He sounds tired, the lack of sleep clear.

"How are you?"

"I'm not sure," he sighs, the honesty refreshing. "After meeting with Alice, I felt better. But when I picked up the girls from school and saw Charlotte..."

My heart breaks from his pain. I want to go to him, promise him it'll be okay. The lines are already blurred. Driving to his house in the middle of the night would only make them even more indistinguishable.

"What happened?"

"She had art class," he replies, his voice wavering. "She made Mother's Day cards. And she made one for me. I just... I hated standing there, hugging her, knowing I may not be her dad."

"You don't know for sure," I remind him.

There's a long pause, then another sigh. "Yes, I do."

"Nothing's a certainty until—"

"When Carla told me she was pregnant, I didn't question her," he interrupts. "The only thing I focused on was that she wanted me back, that she wanted to work things out. I remember waking up to my phone ringing. When I saw her name on the screen, I didn't answer it at first, figuring nothing she had to say was worth my time. It wasn't until I lay there for a minute I realized I was in an unfamiliar bed."

"Drew..." I swallow hard, unsure if I'm ready to hear his side of that night...and the following morning.

"Please, Brooklyn." There's a vulnerability about the way those words leave his mouth. "I just... Let me get this out."

Swallowing hard, I nod, even though he can't see.

"I should have known Carla would never be faithful to me. That wasn't her style. She had a reputation for tracking down where every hockey team was staying, going to the hotel bar, then striking up a conversation with anyone who seemed interested. But there was this part of me that wanted to believe she'd honor the vows we made to each other, regardless of the fact they were made in a Vegas wedding chapel. Although I didn't love her like I should have, I took those vows seriously. To her, they were just words. Nothing more. Before Alyssa was born, we used to go at it all the time."

I try to remain attentive, but hearing about Drew's sex life with another woman is difficult. I'm not fooling myself to think he hasn't been intimate with his fair share of women. It still stings.

"No time or place was off limits. After she gave birth to Alyssa, things...changed. I figured she was just stressed with getting used to being a mom. We hired a nanny, but it didn't help. She wasn't happy. After that, we rarely had sex. I tried to initiate it, but she was never interested, always gave me some excuse how she was tired from having to take care of a colicky baby. Sometimes she even pretended to be asleep."

Hearing his story forces a pang in my heart, what Carla did ringing a little too close to home regarding my current situation with Wes. I always disliked her for how she hurt Drew, but aren't I doing the same thing to Wes? Carla led Drew on until she didn't think he had anything more to offer her. When you look at it, I'm no different than Carla.

"In the month leading up to her first request for a divorce, I can count on one hand the number of times we were intimate. I tossed my doubts aside, ignoring the giant red flag I constantly tripped over. Hell, I didn't even question her when Charlotte was born a month before the due date and was over eight pounds and twenty-one inches. I didn't question her when she seemed to schedule all her doctor appointments for when I was on the road with the team. And I didn't question her when I held Charlotte the first time and saw those flecks of gold in her eyes...which Chase has."

"That still doesn't mean anything."

"Yes, it does." He sounds more resigned than anything else. The sadness and anger he fluctuated between earlier today is gone. He's admitted defeat. "It means everything. There's no denying that when Charlotte was born, she was full term. Carla and I would have had to be intimate around the beginning of May the year before for Charlotte to be mine. We weren't. I remember that specifically because it was around Mother's Day. I flew home on a day off during a bunch of away games to surprise her, but she wasn't even there. Our nanny said she hadn't been home in over a week, leaving her to care for Alyssa.

"So I can sit here and say I don't know for certain until I get those test results back. A part of me hopes I'm wrong, but deep down, I know she's not mine. And I've known it all along."

"That may be so, but would that change anything? Does it matter whether you share the same DNA?"

"Of course not. She'll always be my daughter."

"Then don't waste your time thinking about all the other things you could have done differently back then. You're a good man, Drew," I say, hoping my tone relays the sincerity of my words. "And you're one of the most devoted fathers I know. Those girls are incredibly lucky to call you dad. Both of them. No matter what happens, no matter what those tests show, they'll always call you dad."

Silence settles between us as my words hang in the air. No father who puts the amount of effort Drew does into his daughters' lives should have to learn he was lied to, that the child he's raised and loved from the day they were born isn't his. The thought of walking into that house and only seeing one art project hanging on the wall, one pair of shoes thrown haphazardly around, one backpack sitting in the mudroom guts me. But I need to keep it together and be strong for Drew. If I lose hope, how much longer will he hold onto it?

"Well…" I clear my throat, sitting straighter on the couch as I glance around the darkened living room. "I should let you go."

"I suppose you should probably get some rest, even if I can't sleep. No sense keeping you up, too."

"I might just get ready and go into the office early."

"You're not going to sleep?"

"It's not worth it. I'll probably wake up more tired than I would if I just powered through."

Drew doesn't immediately respond. When I open my mouth to say goodbye, he interrupts. "Want to stop by for a cup of coffee first?"

"What?" My voice evidences my surprise.

"You don't have to," he adds. "I figured you might want some coffee. And I'd like to see you."

"Drew…"

"I know. I know. I shouldn't say things like that to you, but I'm not going to lie, Brooklyn. I do want to see you. I'm kicking myself for taking this long to pull my head out of my ass, but I need you in my life."

"I need you in my life, too." The words slip out before I

can stop them.

"Then come over. It'll be just like we're at the café except in the comfort of my home. I have a bag of grounds from the café, if that entices you." His deep voice is borderline teasing.

I bite my lip, my pulse increasing, a lightness in my chest as I consider his invitation. Can I do this? Can I really run out on Wes so I can spend time with Drew?

I stand from the couch, clutching my phone to my ear as I look around Wes' house. It doesn't feel like home. It's comfortable enough, in a refurbished historic home kind of way. Being the architect he is, his main goal when he bought this place was to incorporate modern technology while keeping with the historic charm of the Victorian house built in the 1880s. While he's done an impressive job, there are moments I feel like his house is a museum, like one of the Newport mansions I visited during a high school field trip. Will our new house be the same, like he's trying to get it into some architectural digest instead of focusing on building a home?

"Brook?" Drew asks when I remain silent.

I swallow hard. I know what answer I should give him, considering I'm standing in the living room of the house belonging to the man I'm engaged to. But what I should do and what I want to do are two different things. They always have been.

"I'll be there in about twenty minutes," I say with a smile, rushing to grab my bag, not caring that I'm only in a pair of yoga pants and t-shirt.

"Twenty minutes? It usually takes me at least thirty to get to your place."

I cringe. "I'm not at my place."

"Oh." I hear the disappointment in his voice. "Do you think it's a good idea then? You leaving before the crack of dawn to meet me?"

"I think it's a horrible idea," I respond in a firm voice before I soften it. "But I want to do this. I don't want to be here, not when you need me."

"I'll always need you, Brooklyn."

I close my eyes, basking in his words. Why couldn't he have said something like this to me years ago? Not when I'm just weeks away from walking down the aisle to another man.

"I know," I say, and I believe him. A week ago, I may not have. I would have allowed all the times I fell for his lies to overshadow everything. But now, after spending the day with him, after experiencing the overwhelming electricity coming off his body as he remained just a breath away, so close to touching me but not quite, I believe his words have merit. Maybe if I stopped blaming him for the mistakes he made years ago, some of which he didn't even know about, we wouldn't be in this situation, in this battle of who hurt whom more.

"Will you be okay to drive?"

"I don't sleep much these days. I'll be fine."

I find my flip-flops and step into them, doing my best to stay light on my feet and avoid the floorboards that creak. There's an adrenaline rush as I head toward the front door, remaining as quiet as possible so Wes doesn't wake up. I shouldn't have to sneak out like this, and it shouldn't matter that I'm going to have coffee with a friend. Drew isn't just a friend, though. I'm not even sure what he is anymore, not sure what I want him to be.

"So, see you in twenty?" I ask, confirming he still thinks this crazy idea has merit.

"Looking forward to it," he responds. I can hear the smile in his tone. "See you soon."

"Goodbye, Drew." Hanging up, I stick my phone into my bag. I bring my hand up to the doorknob, pausing. There's no turning back once I leave. A few days ago, I took the path I thought was the most sensible. Maybe I need to see what awaits me down the other road.

CHAPTER SEVEN

DREW

THE HOUSE IS STILL as I wipe down the counters, doing my best to clean up the kitchen and living room. Thankfully, Gigi came by last night for dinner, so the place isn't the normal disaster it would be. Most nights, by the time I get the girls to bed, the last thing I want to do is straighten up their mess. I usually save it until the following day or for my housekeeper to take care of on Friday.

As I clean, I'm riddled with nerves. I haven't been this on edge since high school, since that sleepless night before I was supposed to see Brooklyn and be her first everything, before my hope was crushed. It was impulsive of me to call her when I received her text, and even more so to invite her over. I never thought she'd agree. Why did she? Maybe our story isn't over yet. Maybe this is the start of a new chapter for us, one we both deserve. And maybe I can have that without coming clean about what really happened all those years ago.

I check the clock an obsessive number of times, but the seconds seem to drag. It's almost four in the morning and my mind goes in thousands of different directions, contemplating every reason under the sun Brooklyn's not here yet. What if she fell asleep at the wheel? Worse, what if she encountered a drunk driver while driving through the streets of Cambridge? It's not entirely impossible.

Anxious at the thought, I grab my phone out of the pocket of my shorts and press her contact. The line rings. And rings. And rings. Just as I'm about to hang up and try again, her voice comes on the line, light and beautiful.

"You're not calling to tell me you're heading to bed, are you?" she jokes.

I close my eyes, blowing out a long breath. "No," I laugh, more out of relief than anything else.

"Is something wrong?" The concern in her voice is unmistakable. Or maybe it seems that way because I can sense how she's feeling from something as simple as a slight tremble in her tone. As simple as a furrowed brow as she sucks on her lower lip. As simple as the tapping of her fingernails against the closest surface. It doesn't matter I can't see her. I imagine her doing all those things right now.

"No," I repeat, my smile growing. "It was careless of me to ask you to drive over when you haven't slept. I was worried something might happen."

"I'll be fine, Drew. I'm only five minutes away. I'll see you soon."

"I'm sure you will be fine," I reply before she has a chance to hang up. "I'd prefer if you stay on the line."

"Why?" she teases. "Worried about me?"

"Always," I answer with more sincerity than she's probably ever heard from me. I wish that weren't the case, wish I'd been more compassionate toward her over the years instead of doing everything to forget about her. "I'll always worry about you."

There's a pause on the line as our conversation takes a turn, the playfulness and frivolity gone. I don't care how difficult it is for her to hear these things. I've kept it from her and everyone else for years. I can't go back to hiding my true feelings. And I want her to stop doing the same.

"So..." Her voice cuts through the strained silence. For once, she doesn't caution or berate me for my words. "What shall we talk about?"

"I don't know." I shrug. "I don't normally sit and talk on the phone. I don't think I've done that since middle school. Even then, I didn't get much phone time since Molly was always tying up the line."

"She always was on the phone, wasn't she?"

"Most of the time, it was with you, even though you only lived a few streets over. She could have just gone pool jumping and been in your yard in no time at all."

"Oh, my god! Pool jumping! I forgot about that summer! We almost got arrested, thanks to your crazy idea to go to some of the rich neighborhoods and jump the fence into their pools. I should have known they'd all have security systems or something!"

I chuckle, my chest expanding at the memory. "Where else were we going to find an in-ground pool with a diving board and killer slide?"

"It's a good thing the officer was a friend of your dad's," she reminds me. "Otherwise, we would have all ended up in juvie. If you thought my dad hated you just because you were a guy, imagine what he would have thought if he learned you were the reason I was shoved into the back of a police car in handcuffs."

"Nah," I brush her off, ignoring her comment about her father. If she only knew how much that man really did despise me. "We were only trespassing."

"And what was the argument you made to the police officer?" Her voice is contemplative. I picture her squinting her eyes, trying to force a memory back to the surface.

"I studied socialism in my history class the previous year." My expression lights up, my eyes shining as I recall the precise thing I told the police officer when Molly, Brooklyn, and I got caught cooling off in someone else's pool on a hot August day. "I argued I was practicing that by commandeering the state-of-the-art pool for the good of the community."

"That's right." She laughs louder. "You're lucky he didn't take it the wrong way. I'm not so sure how well that kind of comment would go over these days. Some may call you a traitor to the country."

"Because most people don't truly understand socialism, but I did. I think the officer was happy I paid attention in school instead of dozing off, so he let us go."

"After which you tried to convince us to go pool jumping at another house you heard about."

"Can you blame me?" I joke as a pair of headlights flash through the windows. I head toward the front door and step onto the porch, my eyes glued to her car. "Figured we already got caught once. What were the chances we'd get caught twice in the same day? In my defense, the other pool was in a different neighborhood. Molly was on my side, but someone talked us out of it."

"One of us had to be the voice of reason," she chides. "And it certainly wasn't going to be the two of you."

The car comes to a stop, and she turns off the ignition. The lights stay on for a while longer before they're extinguished. When I meet her eyes through the windshield, I can't help but smile. It's not forced, my lips curving in the corners as out of my control as the racing of my heart. Electricity courses through my veins at the knowledge that she's a few feet away, just seconds from being near me.

"That's always been your role in our trio."

"True." She keeps the phone up to her ear as she steps out of the car and walks toward me. I make my way down the steps to meet her. "I've always been the voice of reason. Molly's always been the wild one."

"And what about me?" I ask, my voice becoming low, husky.

She slows her steps as she approaches, the atmosphere between us intensifying with a powerful current, a magnetism drawing us to one another. Still holding her phone to her ear, she licks her lips. A slight breeze blows in the air, her addictive aroma of lavender circling me, comforting me.

"You've always been the one I can't let go." Her voice is thoughtful, filled with meaning. I study her, my eyes drawn to everything about her, but the smile building on her plump lips stands out. It's a smile I've seen for years, one I thought demonstrated how happy she was without me in her life. Now that I know the truth, it's remarkable how much a smile can hide.

"I don't want you to, no matter what happens," I murmur, keeping my phone against my ear.

Neither one of us speaks for a protracted moment, our eyes locked, our chests seeming to rise and fall in time with each other. I click the end call button and drop my phone into my pocket. She does the same, but we don't make any move to go inside. I can't stop staring at her, at how beautiful she looks, the moon shining through the trees highlighting her stunning features — vibrant emerald eyes, adorable freckles I've always been drawn to, lips I'd give anything to taste again. But until she's no longer wearing that ring, it's not an option, regardless of my past attempts to kiss her.

I step back, breaking my gaze from her before I do something that will make our situation even more painful. "Coffee?"

She nods, snapping herself out of her trance. "Of course."

"Come on then." I gesture up the steps, allowing her to walk in front of me.

I open the front door for her, then follow her inside. The house is quiet, as it should be in the pre-dawn hours. When Carla first left and I struggled to care for a toddler and six-month-old, I often woke before dawn to get a jump on the day. There was something peaceful about being awake when the world was still sleeping. That same peace fills me now.

"Thanks for coming over," I say as we enter the dim kitchen, the only light coming from over the sink. Heading to the counter, I grab the canister of grounds and scoop some into the French press.

"Thanks for inviting me. Better than heading into work early, even though I'm behind on my caseload."

"I'm sorry." I offer her an apologetic look before returning my attention to the tea kettle, filling it with water and lighting the stove. "I didn't mean to interfere with your work."

"You're not." She saunters up to the refrigerator, taking stock of the girls' most recent art projects. She usually admires them when she's here for Sunday night dinner, but she hasn't been around much lately. Glancing over her shoulder, she meets my eyes. "I'd rather be with you."

"I'm glad you're here. With me."

She smiles, holding my gaze for a moment before looking back at the refrigerator, focusing on a drawing of a plane Charlotte did in art class.

"That's us on our trip to Disney World," I explain as she takes in the stick figures sitting in the seats. "She's very excited about going on a plane."

"And who are all these people?"

I approach, standing behind her. Like an addict, I inhale a deep breath, basking in the memories her scent brings back. Reaching over her, I point to the drawing. "That's me."

Brooklyn laughs. "The hockey stick is a dead giveaway. I'm not sure they'll allow that in the cabin. They'd probably consider it to be a weapon."

"I'll be sure to put it in our checked luggage." I smirk, then look back at the drawing. "And here's Alyssa and Charlotte." My finger glides over the two girls on either side of me, both holding my hand.

"And who else?"

I adjust myself behind her, bringing my body even closer to hers. It would be so easy to place my hand on her stomach and drag her to me, tilt her head to the side, and kiss her neck. My jaw tightens, the need I have for her overpowering all sense of rationale. I can almost taste her skin, feel her core trembling, hear her moans of pleasure. But as much as I want that, as much as it's killing me not to have her, I don't touch her.

"That's Gigi." I point to a woman holding a tray of muffins, then gesture to the figure beside her. "And of course Leo. And Molly and Noah." My finger floats over the drawing of my sister with a round belly. Charlotte made sure we could see the baby inside her stomach.

"And this?" Brooklyn points to the woman on the other side of Charlotte.

"That's you. You're a part of this family, too, Brooklyn. No matter what path you take. Just like Charlotte always will be."

"She's a sweet girl, Drew." She turns around and meets my eyes, smiling. "You should be proud of what an amazing person you raised. You're an incredible father and an even better human." Shaking her head, her expression falls. "I'm so sorry I avoided all of you the past month."

My lips form a tight line. "I get it now."

"You do?" Her gaze searches mine.

"I haven't made things easy on you. I get why it's so

71

difficult for you to be around me."

"I didn't think you and Wes could co-exist in my heart," she murmurs, licking her lips.

"And now?" I place a hand on the refrigerator and lean on it, inching toward her. She doesn't bat an eye, doesn't attempt to step away. My mouth is so close to hers I can taste her sweet breath.

"I still don't think you can." Her chest becomes more noticeable as it heaves with her increasingly deep breaths. Her cheeks flush, that charge building between us again.

"But?" I ask, sensing there's more.

"My heart isn't ready to let go of you. I doubt it ever will be."

I exhale a relieved breath. It's difficult not to sweep her into my arms and kiss her. That won't help anything. I've hurt her. We've hurt each other. Repairing the damage we've caused won't happen overnight, but I'm convinced it can happen.

"I should check on the kettle." My voice trembles, demonstrating how on edge I am by her mere presence. I'm like a hormonally imbalanced teenager who's about to have sex for the first time. In reality, I'm a thirty-five-year-old man who has one month to convince the woman I've always loved not to marry another man. It's a daunting task.

I walk to the stove, turn off the burner, and bring the kettle to the counter, adding the boiling water to the press. Once the coffee is ready, I pour it into two mugs, stealing a glance at Brooklyn. If she's upset I refuse to touch her, she doesn't let it show. Then again, she's always been an expert at masking her emotions. She never lets anyone see what's hidden underneath.

After preparing her coffee the way she prefers, I hand her the mug. She raises it to her mouth, closing her eyes as she takes that first sip. I don't know what it is, but the sight of her savoring that first drink in the morning is one of my absolute favorite things. For a moment, she seems relaxed, a look of genuine happiness crossing her face. I wish I could be the one to make her feel that way. Wish someone could make her feel that way.

We stand in silence for a moment, staring at each other, unsure what to say. I don't want to say anything. I just want to be with her. Gesturing out the French doors, I notice the moon shining through the heavy trees surrounding my property. It won't be much longer until the sun replaces it.

"Want to go watch the sunrise?"

A smile lights up her face. "I'd love to."

I place my hand on the small of her back and head toward the door, opening it for her. She's careful as she steps down from the deck, descending the path toward the fire pit. She sits on one of the stone benches and I join her, our bodies touching. There's a slight chill in the air, but it's refreshing. I look at Brooklyn when I feel her body tremble, a shiver rolling through her.

"Want me to light a fire?"

"You don't have to," she insists. "I don't mind the cold. It reminds me I'm alive."

Switching my coffee into my left hand, I drape my right arm around her shoulders, pulling her close. She does nothing to fight me. Instead, she readjusts so she's leaning against me, her head nuzzled against my chest.

"I like this," she reflects. "Having coffee with you and watching the sunrise. It feels…"

"Right," I finish when she struggles to complete her thought. I glance down at her, our eyes meeting.

She blinks, contemplating. "Yeah."

I hold her gaze a moment longer, then slowly look back at the horizon. Neither one of us says a thing as the world gradually awakens, the morning glow painting the sky a beautiful pink and orange hue. I simply bask in her body enclosed in my embrace.

It doesn't make any sense to someone who doesn't understand our dynamic. Most men in my position would write Brooklyn off since she's engaged. I can't do that. I know her better than to think she's just stringing me along. I can feel the turmoil coursing through her as she stares into the distance. I can't blame her for struggling with this decision.

Her heart yearns to find out if this connection we both feel is as strong as it was all those years ago. But her brain reminds her of every instance I chose someone else over her, of every instance I made a promise and broke it. Looking back, I realize I all but carried her up the aisle and placed her in front of Wes. All I can do is try to show her I am the man she thought me to be before I let fame and notoriety get to my head. I can be that person again.

"I should get going," Brooklyn says once the dawn has chased the night away, propping herself back up. "I'm sure the girls will be awake soon, and it's probably best they don't know I'm here." There's a slight ache in my arm from where she had been resting her head, but the pain is well worth it.

"Of course." I stand, taking the mug from her as I help her to her feet. We silently walk back into the kitchen, our voices hushed and steps light.

"Thanks for the coffee. And the company." She meets my eyes, a thoughtful expression on her face. "It's exactly what I needed."

"Me, too."

She stands on her tiptoes and places a gentle kiss on my cheek, her lips soft. It doesn't matter how innocent the gesture is. It lights me up in a way no other woman ever has.

"Have a good day, Drew." Her mouth hovers on my skin for a moment longer, then she pulls back, turning toward the front door. Placing our empty mugs on the island, I follow, watching the sway of her hips as she makes her way down the porch.

When she's almost at her car, I call out softly. "Hey, Brooklyn?"

She glances back, our eyes locking. There's something about her as she awaits my response, the early morning glow illuminating her. I don't think she's ever looked so beautiful.

I lick my lips, my heart pounding. I may come to regret what I'm about to do, but like I've said repeatedly, I'm almost out of options. Almost. I still have a little time, and I plan to use that time to my advantage.

"Want to come over for coffee tomorrow?"

I expect hesitation or indecision, for her to wage her typical battle between her head and her heart. Instead, she beams a breathtaking smile that makes me feel like a teenager who just asked out his crush. "I'd love to."

"Great." I return her wide smile. "I look forward to it."

"Me, too."

I turn, heading back into the house. As I'm about to close the door, I hear her soft voice.

"More than you know."

Four words. That's all it takes to know it's not over yet.

CHAPTER EIGHT

BROOKLYN

I SHOULD BE EXHAUSTED, should need toothpicks to keep my eyes open, but I'm wide awake, my brain on overdrive. Electricity courses through me as I reminisce about how perfect it was to watch the sunrise while enclosed in Drew's familiar, soothing arms. It was romantic, spontaneous, and exactly what I needed.

I've known Drew most of my life, but the Drew I spent the morning with was different. It almost reminded me of the Drew I fell for during my high school days...before he became Andrew Brinks — hockey superstar and one of the most sought-after bachelors in professional sports. Maybe my Drew has finally come back.

As I sit at the desk in my office, my only thoughts that of having coffee with him again tomorrow morning, my phone buzzes. I glance at the screen, my happy demeanor diminishing when Wes' face pops up. I vacillate between answering and ignoring his call. But as I stare into the image of his vibrant blue eyes, a pang of remorse finds me. I try to rationalize my early morning disappearance by saying Drew's a friend, that it's completely normal to meet a friend for coffee, but I know that's not the case. Drew knows that's not the case. I have a feeling Wes knows that's not the case, too.

On a deep exhale, I press the answer button and bring the phone up to my ear. "Hey."

"Hey," he responds. There's a brief pause before he continues. "Is everything okay?"

"Why wouldn't it be?" My tone is defensive, or maybe it seems that way because of the Catholic guilt plaguing me. The guilt isn't severe enough for me to cancel my plan to see Drew tomorrow, though.

"You weren't in bed when I got up. I missed waking up

with you in my arms." There's a seductive quality to his voice.

I squeeze my eyes shut. I should put an end to this right now. The fact I'm considering that Wes may not be the right man for me should be the only clue I need that I'm on the wrong path. But can I be sure Drew is the right man for me after just one morning of him being the person I once thought him to be? If Drew weren't in the picture, would I even be thinking this way? Most likely not. Drew's only recently showed an interest. Who's to say that will last? Can I throw away everything I've built with Wes because of one man's promise when that man has a track record of breaking promise after promise?

This is one of the times I wish my mother were still alive. Based on the love she shared with my father, I know what she'd tell me to do.

Follow your heart, Brooklyn.

If only it were that easy.

"I'm sorry. It's been a crazy week," I say before he can read too much into my absence from his bed in the pre-dawn hours. "I had to take some time off from work yesterday, so I'm behind on my caseload. And I have a hearing this afternoon for a TPR in one of my cases."

"TPR?" he asks. "What's that?"

"Termination of parental rights," I respond dismissively. I don't like talking about my work that much, especially with someone who will only pretend to sympathize with these kids. Wes doesn't understand what they're going through. He's never gone to bed hungry, never had to go to school wearing clothes that didn't fit because his parents neglected him. Never had to worry about his parents selling him into forced servitude, as happened in this case.

"Oh. Does that happen often?"

"More than I wish it did. I wish it didn't happen at all, but there are certain circumstances that require it. And this case is one of those."

"I'm sorry to hear that."

"Me, too." I bite my lower lip, an awkward pause on the line as I wait to find out the reason for his call. It's rare for him to call me. It's not simply to hear my voice. Wes is sweet, but he wouldn't do something like that. "Is there anything else? Because I need—"

"Why did you take some personal time yesterday?" he interrupts.

My spine instantly straightens, my breath catching. "What?"

"You said you had to miss work. Why? Did my mother send you on another wedding errand?"

"Thankfully, no," I answer, my tone lightening. "If I have to look at one more cake topper I'm going to lose my mind."

Wes laughs, deep and throaty. "I can only imagine. You should have seen her when we went to pick out vests for the tuxedos. I'm pretty certain the poor guy working there submitted his resignation after we left."

I smile, relaxing into my chair at how effortless our conversation is. Shouldn't I be uneasy discussing the preparations for our fast-approaching nuptials? I'm not. It doesn't bother me, which only confuses me more. When I'm with Drew, he's all I want. When I'm with Wes, I find solace in his commitment. Is that enough?

"So, yesterday?" he asks after a moment.

"Right..." I swallow hard. "Well, Drew paid me a visit."

There's a pause. I can only imagine what Wes is thinking, considering everything we've been through lately. "You took personal time to spend the day with Drew?"

"It's not like that," I insist, the hurt in his voice clear.

"Oh really?" His tone changes. It's one he's never used before, at least not with me. "Then tell me how it is, Brooklyn. Is that why you finally slept with me last night after denying me all week? Was it just a pity fuck to try to cleanse your conscience?"

My heart drops to the pit of my stomach. His words hold some merit, but in a different way than he thinks. "You don't know what you're talking about, Wes." I try to keep my voice low, the walls in this old building paper thin.

"Because you don't talk to me. I feel like I'm constantly prying a stubborn jar open to get any information. Don't you want to share your life with me?"

"Of course I do."

"Well, that entails sharing your day with me, not going behind my back to see a man I know you have feelings for."

"I don't have feelings for Drew," I respond, although my words aren't as confident as I wish.

"Then why were you with him yesterday?"

"Because he needed me, Wes."

"There are times I need you, too, but that doesn't seem to have the same effect."

I close my eyes, trying to draw strength to get through this without saying something I shouldn't. "You've never needed me like this."

"Like what?" he presses. "I understand he's your friend, according to you, but it seems you're always choosing him. Is that how it will always be?"

My mouth opens but refuses to form the words assuring him it won't, that this was a special circumstance.

"It's his ex." I blow out a breath, avoiding Wes' question. "She's asking for a custody modification."

"His ex?" His voice softens. "I didn't think she was still in the picture."

"She's not. That's why this is difficult. She left six years ago and granted him full custody. He hasn't heard from her since...until a month ago when he saw her again."

On a deep inhale, I do my best to recount everything that led up to the events of yesterday — running into Carla when he was with the girls, how she went to his office and asked to be a part of their lives, his reaction to her demand. Drew's always been stubborn. Yes, he can be caring and compassionate, but if someone he loves is threatened, he won't hesitate to fight for them. I witnessed that first-hand all those years ago when he treated Damian Murphy to a broken nose for touching me inappropriately.

Maybe if Drew handled Carla's request with more empathy, she wouldn't have felt the need to involve the court. That didn't happen. Now we have to figure out which way is up, hopefully coming to a resolution.

"When Drew received her petition for custody modification, he didn't know what else to do, so he came to me for help."

"Why? You're not a lawyer."

"No, but I work in child services. I know which lawyers will fight for what's in the best interest of the child and which are just going through the motions to get in their billable hours."

"He's fighting it? Doesn't she have a right to shared custody if they're her kids? I don't mean to sound insensitive, but can he expect to keep them from her?"

"That's not the problem."

"It's not?"

I pause, a lump forming in my throat as I'm taken back to yesterday when I first read the pleading, Drew frantically begging for my help to figure this out. "Carla claims Charlotte isn't his daughter and is seeking full custody."

Stunned silence falls over the line. When Wes finally speaks again, his voice is no longer firm or angry. It exudes all the sympathy and compassion I've come to expect from him.

"Brooklyn, I... I don't even know what to say. I know how much you love those girls."

My chin quivers as I fight a new wave of tears. I've successfully kept them at bay all morning as I allowed myself a moment of happiness. But the worry about Charlotte being taken from Drew, from all of us, is back.

"That's why I spent the day with Drew. Because he's a friend," I bite out harshly. "And as a friend, he needed me. I have a feeling once we get the paternity results, he'll need me even more. I'm not going to abandon him. Not now, not when he may lose his little girl. He can't lose me, too," I add softly, my words surprising me.

"I'm such an ass," Wes breathes. It doesn't matter I can't see him. I know him well enough to know his shoulders are slumped, his head hanging low as remorse fills him. "Is that why you were crying last night?"

"What?"

"Last night. When you went to take a shower, I heard you

crying in the bathroom."

"You did?"

"Yeah." His voice is quiet, thoughtful. "I wanted to ask if you were all right, but you've been distant lately. I figured you might just need your space. Now I feel like an absolute prick. You needed to be comforted, yet here I am, accusing you of being unfaithful when I know that's not who you are."

I look at the ceiling, his words like the slash of a blade against my skin, each one cutting a little deeper, exposing me for who I truly am. If he only knew what's been going through my mind, he'd be singing a different song. True, I haven't been unfaithful, but I've been walking a dangerous tightrope these days. I like to think I won't stray from the innocent touches I've shared with Drew. But are they innocent? Maybe to an outsider. Deep down, I know the truth. That as I sat enclosed in his arms this morning, I yearned for more.

"It's okay. We're both under a bit of stress." I glance to the time on my computer screen and stand, using my shoulder to hold my phone up to my ear as I collect my things. "Listen, I need to get downtown."

"Of course. I won't keep you any longer. Will I see you tonight?"

I pull my bottom lip between my teeth. "I'm really tired, Wes."

"Then let me take care of you. We'll order sushi and I'll rub your feet."

"I promised Molly I'd get together with her," I lie, although now that I've said it, a girls' night sounds like a fantastic idea. I haven't seen her since Sunday when I told her I'd been in love with her brother for as long as I can remember.

"Oh." I hate hearing the disappointment in his voice.

"I'm sorry..."

"Don't be. I guess I've gotten used to seeing you every night. I like coming home from work knowing you'd be there."

"And you'll have years of doing that," I remind him, hoping he doesn't pick up on my uncertainty. For the first time, I begin to doubt whether there will be a wedding next month. "I just need some time with my best friend. It'll be good for both of us. You can work as late as you want while I spend some time with Molly."

"Okay," he sighs. "I don't like the idea of falling asleep without you, but I get it. I'll miss you."

"I'll miss you, too," I say through the thickness in my throat, his sincerity making me feel inadequate. "I really do need to go."

"Sure. I'll text you later. I love you."

Swallowing hard, I struggle to repeat those words back to him. It's never been a problem before, even if I didn't feel as though I loved him. Everything's shifted, but it's still too early to tell if it's for the better.

"I love you, too."

CHAPTER NINE

BROOKLYN

MOLLY'S HOUSE IS QUIET when I let myself in later that evening. The lack of sleep over the past few days is starting to catch up to me, but I need a night with my friend to figure things out.

The instant I step into the kitchen, Molly rounds the corner from the den, her eyes filled with a myriad of emotions. I expect her to hound me for information about what's going on between Drew and me, assuming he told her we spent yesterday together, but she doesn't. Instead, she heads toward me and wraps her arms around me tightly.

"I'm so happy you're here." Her voice catches. "I was worried we wouldn't be friends anymore."

"Oh, Molly." I return her hug, rubbing her back. "We'll always be friends. Nothing will come between that." I pull back and meet her eyes.

I've been so wrapped up in my indecision regarding Drew and Wes, I never stopped to consider Molly. She reached out to me several times this week, yet I didn't respond to any of her calls or texts. I assumed she'd want to talk about Drew. Never did I think she was worried about our friendship.

"Promise," I add.

"Pinky swear?" She lifts her pinky, just like we used to during our adolescence when we'd agree not to go after the same boy. It was never a difficult thing to ask of me. Her brother was the only boy who interested me.

"Pinky swear." I hook my pinky with hers, giving her a reassuring smile.

Our fingers remain linked for several moments before she releases her hold on me. "Come on. There are drinks and food in the den. Your text came at the perfect time. Noah's on call, so he's sleeping at the facility tonight."

She heads into the den and I follow, sitting on the couch beside her, pouring a glass of wine from the bottle of cabernet she'd opened. I sip on the liquid as I try to figure out what to say. Earlier, I would have loved to have a mother to discuss what was going on. All throughout my life, Molly was the only person I could talk to about everything... Well, almost everything. I never talked to her about Drew. During our younger years, it was because I didn't want her to tease me. Now that we're adults, I'm worried I won't get the neutral opinion I crave when faced with a life-altering decision.

"I really am sorry, Brook." Molly's voice cuts through my thoughts.

I snap my eyes to hers. Just over her shoulder, I spy a framed photo on the side table. The same photo of Drew, Molly, and me as kids that sits on my coffee table. I wonder if this is another instance of the universe reminding me of how deep and profound my history with Andrew Brinks is, that I shouldn't throw it away because of a mistake he made when he was eighteen. I've made my fair share of mistakes, too. Would I want someone to hold a grudge against me for years because of those?

"What are you sorry about?"

"Everything." She shakes her head, taking a moment to compose her thoughts. "I always knew there was a connection between you and Drew, but never in a million years..." She trails off, her lip quivering as her emotions overtake her once more. "If I had known, I never would have teased you about dating him all these years."

"It's okay. You didn't know. But now..." I pause, considering the situation. For so long, I'd made it my mission to keep the past a secret. I refused to let all the heartache Drew caused define me. Maybe that's not such a bad thing. "I'm glad you do." Our eyes lock so she can see the truth in my words, then I take a long sip of my wine.

"He's an idiot, if you ask me," Molly states. "The doctors warned him about potential memory complications from the number of concussions he's suffered. He knew alcohol would only impair his memory even more. They told him not to drink like that. I'm sorry you're the one who had to suffer because of his stupidity."

I swallow hard. I've had a lot of time to think lately. As angry as I want to be at Drew, I can't blame him, not when I hold some of the blame, too. "I could have told him the truth."

Molly regards me thoughtfully, her eyes pensive as she considers my words. "No, you couldn't," she says finally.

"Wha—"

"I know you, Brooklyn. One of the many things I love about you is that you are my polar opposite. That's why we've always gotten along so well, why we've stayed friends our entire lives when other people have grown apart. Not us. And because we've been inseparable the past three decades of our lives, I know things about you most people never would...even Drew. If I were in your shoes, you know damn well I would have told the prick exactly what happened. In explicit detail. Hell, I probably would have embellished a little and added sound effects for good measure." She waggles her eyebrows, smiling mischievously. My laughter fills the space and I'm thankful for the break in tension.

"But that's not who you are." Her voice turns sincere as my smile fades. "Your entire life, you've put other people's needs ahead of your own. So when you overheard Drew talking to Carla, you figured you had only one option. It didn't matter what you wanted. As much as it pained you, you did what you thought was best for Alyssa and the baby on the way. It's what you've been trained to do in your line of work."

I hang my head, biting my lip, nodding.

"When are you going to start doing what's best for you, Brooklyn?"

Her question hits me hard, almost knocking the breath out of me. I shoot my eyes to her, blinking repeatedly. "What do you mean?"

"I understand why you feel your relationship with Wes is the right thing. I get it. He's dependable, committed, devoted to you. Even better, he's never hurt you."

I raise my wine glass to my lips to hide my quivering chin. It takes everything I have to keep from breaking down, from sobbing into her chest and telling her how much I want Drew but the past is holding me back.

"I don't know..." She's contemplative as she stares at the ceiling, shaking her head. "If I'd secretly been in love with someone as long as you've loved Drew and he constantly took advantage of me, I'd probably write him off, just like you tried to do. But that's the difference between us. I would have written him off, regardless if he was my best friend's brother. Not you. And now..." She squints as she observes me, seemingly trying to read the thoughts circling my mind.

"I'm scared to death I'll never find anyone else like him," I say when I can no longer take her scrutiny, the truthfulness of my words surprising me. "Worse, I'm scared I don't want to."

Blowing out a breath, Molly wraps her arms around me, pulling me against her. All it takes is one show of compassion and the floodgates open, my tears spilling down my cheeks. It feels good to let it all out, to not have to keep it in and pretend everything is okay.

"I don't know what I'm going to do," I confess. Now that I've finally given voice to these concerns instead of allowing them to fester, a weight's been lifted. "My heart burns for Drew, but my head..." I trail off.

"Remembers all the times he made you feel invisible," Molly finishes.

"You have no idea what it was like. Every time I was at your house after he left for college, I could still smell him there. And when he came home on breaks..." I shake my head, transported back to those days. I'd never felt more invisible in my life than when I was at Molly's house and he walked right past me, not saying a word, not even acknowledging my presence. A part of me wants to tell Molly about that summer, as well, but it's too hard, too raw.

"You're right. I don't know what it was like." Sympathy covers her expression as she rests her hand on my bicep, squeezing. "And I can't tell you what to do now. I can't even attempt to empathize with what you're going through." A thoughtful look lights up her face. "But I can tell you what a wise person once told me when I was unsure of the path I should take."

"Oh yeah?" I swipe at my tears, knowing all too well this will entail yet another one of Aunt Gigi's pearls of wisdom. "And what's that?"

"If this doesn't scare you, it's not love."

I lift my gaze to hers, my chin trembling. "And if it does?"

She shrugs, giving me a knowing look. "Then maybe you have your answer."

I lean back into the couch. Molly places her arm around my shoulders, kissing the top of my head, her gesture soothing. "No matter what I do, someone ends up hurt."

"Or two people."

My eyes meet hers. "How so?"

"You're thinking about everyone else again. You're not even taking yourself into consideration. You think you'll hurt either Wes or Drew, but you never even stopped to consider your decision may hurt you, as well."

I stare straight ahead, pondering her words. They're alarmingly accurate. "So I should choose the safe bet."

"That's not what I'm saying."

"Then what are you saying?" I sit up, looking at her.

With a sigh, she smiles. "What I'm saying is people shouldn't be forced to pay for their mistakes for the rest of their lives. People change. You see that on a daily basis. How many cases have you had where the mother or father completely turned their lives around to give their kids a better chance?"

I shrug, averting my gaze. "A lot."

"It sucks it took state involvement to make them finally open their eyes, but at least they had the opportunity to make things right. What is it you always say when people ask why you spend the time you do developing action plans for families?"

"Everyone deserves a second chance," I answer as a voice in the back of my head reminds me of all the chances I've given Drew over the years. Can I find it in my heart to give him one more?

"I know this isn't an easy situation," Molly says as I sip my wine. "And I know you don't think Drew ever noticed you, but he has. He put everything on the line for you."

"I wish I could believe that was true, but he's never sacrificed anything for me. Not like I'd have to in order to be with him."

Molly opens her mouth, then snaps it shut, worrying her lower lip.

"What is it?" I can't help but think she's keeping something from me.

"It's not my story to tell. But trust me when I say things aren't as they appear." Her expression turns severe. "Some things were out of his control."

"What are you talking about?"

"You know how you didn't tell Drew about that night?"

I nod, guilt bubbling in my stomach.

"Why?"

"There were a lot of reasons."

"But one of them was to protect him, right?"

I nod again, the motion almost imperceptible.

"Well, he's done the same. I'm not so sure I agree with it, but I can see where he's coming from. Just like you, he was faced with a choice, and no matter which he chose, he would lose something he cared about."

"What did he lose?" I ask, unsure I want to know.

She contemplates an answer, then shrugs. "Everything."

CHAPTER TEN

BROOKLYN

E VERYTHING.
That word hangs in the air for the rest of the evening as I wrack my memory for what Molly can be referring to. What secret did Drew keep from me? And what did he lose?

I always assumed he had all he ever dreamed of. As a freshman in college, he was starting center and helped his team win the Division I championship trophy. The following year, he was in Salt Lake City and won a silver medal in the Games. From there, scouts knocked down his door to sign with a professional team upon graduation, which was what he did when the ink wasn't yet dry on his diploma. If anything, Drew has gained everything over the years. His success was nothing short of rapid and awe-inspiring. He became a household name, which made it even more difficult for me to forget about him. Or perhaps there's a different reason, a deeper reason, I never could.

I'm so lost in my thoughts as I drive home, I don't even notice Wes' car parked in front of my house until I walk up to my door.

"Hey."

I practically jump out of my skin as I spin around to face him. "Shit, Wes. You scared me."

He grimaces, running a nervous hand through his hair. "Sorry. I didn't mean to."

A ball of dread forms in my stomach as I consider why he's here when he knew I was spending time with Molly. Is he checking up on me? Making sure I'm telling him the truth? Or did he come over in the hopes I'd ask him to stay the night?

"What are you doing here?"

"You weren't answering your phone."

"The battery died."

"I figured there was a reason other than you avoiding me. That's not usually your style."

I remain silent, my expression flat.

"But I'm glad you're here. I didn't want to leave without seeing you first."

My heart drops to the pit of my stomach, my mouth growing dry. "Leave?"

"Yeah. Last-minute trip. I need to go to Dubai tonight."

I briefly close my eyes, releasing a relieved breath. "You're going to Dubai." Wes hears it as more of a question.

"Mother's assured me all the wedding preparations are handled. I don't want to go, but my father's right. This contract to build a hotel over there is everything I've ever hoped for. I can take that profit and reinvest it in the charity house-building program. Low-income homes lost due to the recent hurricanes can be rebuilt, and then some. This is a huge deal for the company, and I need to be there to make sure the project kicks off correctly. I should only be gone ten days…two weeks max." He pauses, assessing me before he continues. "You can come with me. Get away from all this for a minute." His eyes plead with me to consider his invitation.

"Wes…" I don't have the ability to jump on a plane at a moment's notice. I have a job, people who depend on me. "I need to work."

"I figured you'd say that." His voice is melancholy. I'm not sure how to feel about the fact that he's grown accustomed to me constantly turning him down. Not only in the bedroom, but in life. Yet he still wants to marry me. It doesn't make sense.

"Why do you want to marry me?" I blurt out before I can stop the words.

"What?" he asks, shaking his head in obvious disbelief. "How could you even ask that?" His face reddens and he tugs at his hair. "We're less than a month away from our wedding. I'm about to get on a plane for the Middle East and will be gone for two weeks. Should I be worried about returning to an empty house?" His voice catches.

"Wes…" I run my hands down his arms, trying to placate

him. "I didn't mean it like that." Even though I kind of did. "I guess... I don't know." I blow out a long breath, collecting my scrambled thoughts. "You're risking a lot by being with me. Your relationship with your mother. Your role in the company. I'm trying to wrap my head around why you'd do that just to be with me."

His expression softens and he loops his arms around my waist, dragging me to him. "Because I love you, Brooklyn." When our eyes lock, confusion clouds his blue orbs. "Don't you love me?"

My lips part as I struggle to say the words he needs to hear, my eyes darting to my surroundings. Before Sunday, my response would have come easily. But the events of the past week have forced me to take a step back. I've faulted Drew for never making me a priority, for never noticing me until I had another man's ring on my finger. While Wes has noticed me, I'm not sure he's made me a priority like I once believed he did. Yes, he purchased us a beautiful piece of land and is building me the house of my dreams. He's bought me stunning pieces of jewelry, even though I've told him to save his money, considering I can't wear any to work. But these things are simply possessions, things I can't feel in my heart. I want to feel loved, like I'm a priority, like I'm the only woman he's ever seen.

As I think about it, I can say with all the conviction I possess I've never actually felt that from Wes. He claims he loves me. Has he ever shown me that love in a way other than buying me something extravagant?

"Brooklyn?"

His pained voice forces me back from my thoughts. I stare deep into his eyes, confirming what I told Molly earlier, what I've feared all week as my heart was pulled in two different directions. No matter which path I choose, someone will end up hurt. Wes has always been attentive and caring, in his own way. But Drew... The pain of our tainted history still rips me open.

But has he caused that pain? Or was it self-inflicted? There were many times he had ignored me, made me feel invisible. But there were other times he made me feel like I was the only person who mattered. Like when he'd go with me to visit my mother's grave on the anniversary of her death every year. Like the way he put his scholarship at risk and broke Damian Murphy's nose for touching me. Like the way he bought me the wedding dress of my dreams because it was what I wanted, regardless of how much my engagement didn't sit right with him. He buried his own feelings to give me the happiness he thought I deserved.

I've been so focused on the bad, I've forgotten about all the times Drew made me a priority. The truth hits me hard, knocking the breath out of me. He's done something no other man's ever done. He made me feel loved.

"Brooklyn?" Wes' pleading voice catches my attention. "Don't you love me?" he repeats.

I press my lips together, frowning. I do love him, but is it the type of love that will endure all our lives?

"I...I don't know," I answer honestly.

The instant those words leave my mouth, his body deflates. The pain I saw in his expression before is no match for the heartache filling him now. The lines on his face that were once filled with hope turn down, his lips parting, his chin trembling slightly.

"I'm sorry, Wes." I wish there were something more I could say, something more meaningful to relay how much admitting the truth I've fought to ignore wrecks me. "I never wanted to hurt you."

"Are you..." He swallows hard. "Are you walking away?"

"I don't know what I'm doing."

And that's the truth. I have no idea what my plan is. Whether I'm walking away from Wes, whether I'm ready to run toward Drew. I can come up with a dozen reasons why I should stay with Wes. But I can also come up with a dozen reasons why I should be with Drew.

"Are we moving too fast?" He grasps my hands in his, as if I'm his lifeline, his only source of oxygen and sustenance. "We can take a step back. Put the wedding on hold. I knew you were uneasy about getting married this June. We can have a long engagement, like you wanted. We can elope and not tell anyone. Anything you want, just..." He lets go of my hands and cups my cheeks, leaning his forehead on mine as he draws in a deep breath. "Don't leave me." A tear falls from his eye, landing on my cheek.

"I just..." I moisten my lips that have grown dry. "I need time to figure out what I want." I pull back, staring deep into his pale eyes filled with anguish. I bring my hands to his face, swiping away his few tears with the pads of my thumbs. "Maybe this time apart is what we need to be sure we're on the right path."

"But I don't want to lose you. If leaving right now seals our fate, I won't do it. I don't want you to think my job's more important than you."

I remain silent. He's done a horrible job of making me think otherwise lately.

"I'll do anything for you," he adds.

"I know you will." I lift myself onto my toes and place a soft kiss on his lips. "That's why I need you to get on that plane and go to Dubai." I release my hold on him, stepping back. "Maybe I'll take this time and go somewhere, too. Clear my mind."

"You deserve a break. You're burning yourself out with the number of hours you've been working lately."

"Says the man who's been working eighteen-hour days," I quip back.

"It's all for you." His hands land on my hips and he pulls me toward him. I don't resist when he brings his lips toward my neck and inhales. "Everything I do is for you."

When his mouth brushes my skin, I moan. It's not his lips that cause that reaction. It's the fact he hasn't shaven since this morning, his scruff rubbing against me. It sends a spark through me, reminding me of the roughness of Drew's kiss from all those years ago.

"I love you, Brooklyn." He palms my lower back, forcing me against him. "So fucking much."

"And I love you, Wes." I open my eyes, meeting his, surprised how easily those words flow when I couldn't say them a few minutes ago. "I'm worried it won't be enough."

A small smile builds on his lips, everything about him sincere. "It is enough. You're more than enough, Brooklyn. You always have been. And you always will be. I'll give you the space you need to figure things out. When I come home, we'll start over again. I'll propose all over again, and we can plan a new wedding years down the road we won't tell anyone about, if that's what you want. I'll always give you exactly what you want."

He brings his mouth to mine, treating me to a sweet kiss. It reminds me of the first time we kissed after our first date. He walked me up to this same door. We stood in almost the same spot. Nervous energy filled us, the anxious laughs and avoiding of eyes. Then he leaned in, brushing his lips so tenderly against mine. It wasn't deep or full, a complete juxtaposition to the first time Drew kissed me. At the time, I thought that was a good thing.

"You're the reason I smile," he murmurs, then steps back. "I want to be the reason you smile, too."

I pull my lip between my teeth, wishing I could tell him he was. When I don't say anything, he sighs, retreating down the porch, his steps sluggish. I can't help but feel like this is goodbye but neither one of us will admit it just yet.

His hand on his car door, he pauses, glancing over his shoulder. "I'll be yours until the end." The candor in his tone burrows deep into my soul. "I hope you'll choose me." Then he disappears into his Mercedes and drives off into the night.

CHAPTER ELEVEN

BROOKLYN

M Y ALARM JOLTS ME awake at four. Most would curse and stumble groggily from their bed. Not me. Despite the way I left things with Wes last night, I excitedly fling my covers off, darting into the bathroom. I throw water on my face, brush my teeth, smooth my hair back, and check my reflection.

Pulling out the top drawer of the vanity, I grab my compact, applying a bit of powder and blush before adding eyeliner. Content with my appearance, I head down the stairs of my townhouse, grin as I pass a photo of Drew and the girls on my entryway table, then grab my keys and continue to my car. My smile builds as I make the journey to Drew's house. The closer I get, the faster my heart races.

After a drive that seems to last much longer than thirty minutes, I pull up in front of his house, unable to stop the butterflies from flapping their feverish wings in my stomach when I see him sitting on his porch. His hair is messy from sleep and he hasn't shaven in a few days. He's wearing a plain white t-shirt and a pair of gym shorts with the Bruins logo on one leg. His tattoos peek out from the sleeves of his shirt and I bite my lower lip, my mind going to places it shouldn't. I love this look on him. He looks comfortable, and it warms my heart to know he can be himself around me. Just like I can be myself around him. I don't think I've ever felt like I can be the real me around Wes. That must count for something.

When I shut off the engine and step out of the car, Drew's eyes light up, zeroing in on me. With each step I take, my heart pounds a little harder, my lungs expand a little quicker, my skin tingles a little more. This man has always had this effect on me, even when he was just a boy, but it's different now, more intense, more pronounced, more... Just more.

After the morning I watched him walk out of my father's kitchen without a single look back, I promised I would stop torturing myself, that I would finally let go of my adolescent obsession with Andrew Brinks. Since then, I did everything in my power to convince myself I'd done just that. I dated. I watched his wife's belly get bigger and bigger. I dated more. I offered him my congratulations when he flew into the café with a bag full of pink onesies after learning it was another girl. I dated even more.

Then Drew's life began falling apart. Molly and I were in the stands when he was knocked unconscious and wheeled off the ice on a stretcher. I held his hand as he lay in ICU, begging him to wake up. My jaw dropped when Carla walked in carrying a baby, considering Charlotte wasn't supposed to be born for another month. We were so focused on Drew's recovery and rehabilitation, nobody ever questioned it.

Still, throughout his entire downward spiral, I remained strong, refusing to get tangled in his web again. Every time I felt myself growing weak, I rewound the clocks to the day he left for college, the day I was supposed to lose my virginity to him. To when we saw each other that following Thanksgiving and he acted as if I weren't even there. To all the times he paraded girl after girl in front of me, blind to the tears forming in my eyes. To the morning after he finally told me he loved me, having no memory of doing so. I've held onto the pain he's caused throughout my adolescent and adult life, using it as a reminder to keep my distance, to focus my efforts on finding someone who would do the one thing he never did...make me a priority.

Now, as I look into his eyes and see a yearning unmatched by any man who's claimed his love for me, I realize I bear a lot of the blame here, too. Like during my undergrad days when I purposely took a guy to a Bruins home game, then proceeded to make out with him so Drew would see. Like when one of his teammates showed an interest in me and I feigned interest right back, just to piss off Drew. Like when a charming man with a sweet southern accent asked me to dinner and I said yes, just to help me forget about Drew. To forget about the way something as simple as his easy smile lights up my world. To forget about how much I've imagined hearing his husky voice murmur those three beautiful words. To forget about how much I've yearned to say those three words back to him, even to this very day.

"Hey," he says, his voice low.

"Hey." My heart is heavy, but full. I can't help but feel this is the turning point we've both been searching for over the past few months...hell, years. I've been so caught up with wearing my pain like a badge of honor, I never stopped to consider I may have hurt him just as much.

My lips part as we remain frozen in place, unable to look away. I want to tell him everything, yet nothing. I want to spill my heart out, yet also lock up all my secrets and guard them with my life. I want to lose myself in him, yet keep him at arm's length. I know I'm walking a dangerous tightrope. One misstep and I fear, this time, I'll fall too far to ever come back.

Tears well in my eyes, wondering where we'd be if we hadn't played these games for so long, wondering if we would have found happiness with each other years ago.

"Brooklyn?" His concerned vision rakes over me, searching for any hint of what's causing me distress. Just like he did all those years ago when he pushed me on the swing and I tumbled down the hill. Just like he did a few weeks ago when I fell on the ice. His words from that day come rushing back.

"I won't let you fall. And if you do, I'll help you put the pieces together again. Like I always have."

"Like you always have," I murmur to myself.

"Brook?" he says, urging me to talk to him.

I'm overwhelmed with a thousand emotions I can't name, both satisfying and terrifying. "I'm sorry," I choke out.

In an instant, I'm in his arms, resting my head against his broad chest. It's warm and inviting. In a word, it's home. I inhale a long breath, relishing in everything this man is, everything he's always been, everything he always will be. As much as I want both of us to forget all the past hurt we've caused each other, it's not that easy. There's a lot we have to forgive first.

"What are you sorry for?"

"Being so blind." I pull away and meet his heartfelt gaze. He's not hiding anything from me, not pretending to be unaffected by this connection, this power that keeps forcing us together.

"I'm the one who was blind, stupid, and probably scared. I have to live with that for the rest of my life." He cups my cheeks in his hands, his mouth just a whisper from mine. The way he holds me, the way he speaks, the way his eyes bore into my soul make me never want to leave this place, this time, this moment.

"No matter what you want to think, no matter what path you choose, you deserve to know that I've always loved you, Brooklyn. Always. I was just trying to do the right thing. That night at Brody Carmichael's party..." He loosens his grip on me, a finger traveling down my jawline, ghosting over my bottom lip. It causes a shiver to roll through me, my nerve endings firing. "I was young, but I'd never felt anything remotely close to what I did when I kissed you. When you kissed me back..." His body grows taut, his mouth inching closer to mine. "I never wanted to stop feeling your lips on mine."

"Then why didn't you come see me the next day? Why did you leave without saying goodbye? Without..." I trail off.

"Do you think I wanted to leave you?" His voice thunders around me, the vibration making my heart speed up. "God, Brooklyn. I hated having to do that. For months, you were all I thought about, all I dreamt about."

"So why did you act like I didn't exist?"

He pulls his lip between his teeth as he stares down at me, assessing his next move. "I know I've never given you a reason to believe me. And as much as I want to tell you why I never appeared at your door at 7:01 on August 26th, 2001, I'm not sure I'm ready to do that yet, not when I know the truth will hurt you far more than my failure to show up did."

His words remind me of what Molly said last night, how

Drew was forced to make a choice. Was this what she was talking about? That night before he left for college? How would she know about that?

"But—"

"Please, Brooklyn." He releases his hold on me, increasing the distance between us. Lowering his head, he runs a hand through his hair. "I've spent years trying to convince myself that one night didn't matter, that it didn't affect me like it did. I did everything to forget about it, hoping it would dampen the pain. That's why I couldn't look at you, couldn't bring myself to talk to you. It hurt so fucking much. I brought home girls who couldn't hold a candle to you, hoping I'd feel something for them. I didn't want to believe it, didn't want to admit the truth."

"And what truth was that?"

He lifts his gaze back to me, the tension mounting. My heart hammers in my chest, the intensity in his gaze consuming me, making me want to bare my soul to him. "Without you, I was dead inside."

I crane my head back, his words resonating with me, pushing me forward when the old me would have run away. "When I saw you across the way at a bar, I made out with a guy just to see if you'd notice me."

He brings his hands back to my face, swiping away my tears, a slight smile building on his lips. "I avoided going home to visit because it hurt too much to see you with another guy."

"I once dated a Canadiens fan in the hopes it would help free me from the hold you still had on my heart."

He lowers his voice as he inches toward me, barely a breath between our two bodies. "I asked Carla to marry me because I thought it was the only way I'd ever forget about you."

I nod, swallowing hard at what I'm about to admit to him. But we're putting it all out there. No more lies. No more secrets. No more pain. Everyone deserves a second chance. Maybe this is ours. We'll never know unless we wipe the slate clean.

"I agreed to marry Wes so I could forget about you."

Resting his forehead on mine, all the tension that's been plaguing him since I announced my engagement seems to roll off him in waves. He places his palm on my lower back and pulls me against him.

"Have you forgotten about me?"

"Never."

"And Wes?" His question is filled with hope.

"He's in Dubai for two weeks. I told him I needed time to figure some things out. In his eyes, we're still together, albeit on shaky ground." I don't want to do anything to hurt him while he's away. But I think even he knows this is coming.

His Adam's apple bobs up and down as his mouth hovers over mine. "And in your eyes?" He arches a brow.

"There's never been a choice when it came to you."

He briefly closes his eyes, allowing my words to soothe his soul. When he returns them to me, they're bright, lustrous, radiant. "Come on." He gestures toward the house. "Time for some coffee."

I blow out a relieved laugh, grateful we've turned this corner, that he didn't turn me away as I so often have these past few months. The weight that's been crushing my chest for years, inhibiting my ability to breathe, has been lifted, allowing my heart to beat the way it's always wanted to. For Drew.

"God, I love it when you talk dirty."

CHAPTER TWELVE

DREW

THIS PAST WEEK HAS been absolute torture, but in the best way possible. I want nothing more than to scream about Brooklyn from the rooftops, take her out, show her off, treat her like the princess I've always believed her to be, but I can't. Not yet. Not until she wipes the slate clean with Wes. As much as I want to kiss her, wrap her in my arms, lose myself in her, I remind myself she's not mine yet. Until that happens, we've agreed to keep things the same between us…in theory.

In reality, things aren't the same, not when she's been at my house for coffee every morning. Watching the sunrise together has given me something to look forward to. There's an electricity between us as we sit in my back yard, drink our coffee, and watch the world come to life. This time with her has brought me back to life, too.

Brooklyn's become my ray of hope when I thought my world was falling apart. Her compassion, her devotion, her love has gotten me through the nights I've been plagued with thoughts of what will happen to Alyssa and Charlotte, whether I'll be able to keep our family together. My initial concern and fear when I received the request for custody modification is now a distant memory. With Brooklyn by my side, I can get through anything.

I've been so content with how things have been going, I've all but forgotten about the paternity test results…until I received a phone call from the lab last night saying they were ready. It took hours to work up the courage to open the envelope containing the results, unsure I wanted to come down from the clouds where I've been living.

Now, as I stare at the two pieces of paper containing various numbers in several columns, I wish I hadn't, wish I'd given myself one more night of happiness, wish the words on

Charlotte's test I've been reading over and over weren't real. But they are. This paper is real. The ramifications are real. My hatred for my ex is real.

I knew this would be the outcome. It still doesn't make seeing the truth in black and white any easier.

> The alleged father is excluded as the biological father of the tested child. This conclusion is based on the non-matching alleles observed at the loci listed above with a PI equal to 0. The alleged father lacks the genetic markers that must be contributed to the child by the biological father. The probability of paternity is 0%.

I want to believe I'm having a strange nightmare I'll soon wake up from. At least Alyssa's results were positive. Still, I want to find Carla and demand to know how she could have lied. How she could have pretended to love me when she didn't. How she could do something like this and show no remorse. Those girls are my life. What am I supposed to do now? Will I soon only be able to walk one of them to school in the morning? Will there be an empty seat at Sunday dinner? Will there be one less stocking hanging on the mantle this Christmas?

How am I going to peer into Charlotte's eyes and tell her I'm not her real father? How am I going to explain to Alyssa it may be just the two of us from now on? How am I going to walk past Charlotte's empty bedroom and not break down? How am I going to fill the hole her absence will leave in my heart, in all our hearts?

Lost in my sorrow, I don't even hear the front door open or realize there's someone in my house until a familiar voice pacifies the rage bubbling inside me.

"Oh, Drew…"

Instantly, a pair of warm arms wraps around me. Lavender assaults my senses, giving me the comfort I crave. Brooklyn's exactly what I've always hungered for, but now, I can't go another day without her. I won't go another day without her, regardless of the gray area we've been living in lately.

"It'll be okay," she continues. "It doesn't matter if she has your blood. She's still your daughter."

"How do I break the news to Charlotte that everything she thought was just a lie?" I choke out, feeling like my heart has been yanked from my chest, as if I'm about to lose part of myself. "That I'm not her father?" I lift my gaze to hers.

There's so much concern within her striking green eyes. After everything I've put her through, I'm unsure whether I deserve it. I vow to never do anything to lose the devotion she has for me. I could very well lose Charlotte. I can't lose Brooklyn, too.

She reaches for me, cupping my cheeks in her hands. "You tell her the truth. That this changes nothing." Her voice is strong, despite the pain etched on her expression. Pain for what sweet, innocent Charlotte is about to face. Pain for how much this is tearing her apart. Pain for what I'm going through. It's all there, exposed for me to see.

"You tell her that being a father is so much more than sharing the same blood or DNA. That your love and respect are what make you family. That no matter what happens, you will always be her daddy. That you'll still be the one who threatens any guy who comes to pick her up for a date, reminding him that she's your little girl and if he even thinks about disrespecting her, he'll have you to deal with." She swallows hard, blinking back her own tears, her voice softening. "That you'll put your own life on the line for hers without so much as a hint of hesitation. That you'll be the one walking her down the aisle to the man of her dreams on her wedding day. Absolutely no one will take that away from you, Drew. No one. You share a history, a bond. A stupid piece of paper can't erase it."

She pauses, licking her lips, her fevered eyes remaining locked on mine. She loosens her grip on my face, but her hands remained glued to my skin, her thumbs caressing the scruff on my chin.

"Those little girls are so blessed to call you Daddy. They already know that. We all know that. What Carla's trying to do, how she's trying to come between you and your girls, well… She forgot how fiercely loyal you are. And maybe she didn't know. Maybe she never saw that side of you. But I have. I saw it the day I met you. How protective you were of your sister. How protective you became of me, too. But that's nothing compared to how protective you are of those two little girls. That won't change. And I will be right by your side every step of the way. I won't give up on you."

Closing her eyes, she leans her forehead on mine. Wetness falls down my cheeks, but it's not from my tears. It's from Brooklyn's. I bring my hands to her face, wiping away her tears with my thumbs, both of us holding onto each other, hoping this connection, this bond, will be strong enough to help us navigate through the stormy and unknown waters we face.

"Will you be there when I tell them?" I ask softly.

She inhales a long breath and nods. "Of course, Drew. I'm here for you." She places a soft kiss on my cheek, the anguish that's plagued me since I picked up this envelope starting to evaporate.

"I always want you to be here for me." My words linger in the air for what seems like an eternity before she releases her hold on me, the moment breaking.

"Drew, we've talked about this," she reminds me, as she's been prone to do over the past week whenever I attempt to bring up what the future holds for me, for her, for Wes. She steps away, heading toward the kitchen to pour the fresh coffee I prepared. "Not yet."

I don't know what it is about this moment, about feeling like my life's falling apart, about knowing everything's about to change, but I'm done waiting. This entire situation with Charlotte reminds me there's no time like the present, that you may not get another chance to do something. I can't risk that anymore.

Jumping up from my barstool, I swiftly close the distance between us. Brooklyn spins around, gasping at what she sees in my eyes. I've tried to be strong, to give her space, but she's the only thing that can stop the despair right now.

I grip her hip and tug her to me. She sucks in a surprised breath, her eyes floating over my chest before coming back to my face.

"Drew…," she whimpers, making no move to free herself, to retreat, to walk away. Our gazes locked, I lower my lips toward hers, my breathing quickening as the space between us disappears.

"Please, Brooklyn. Don't tell me to stop." Desperation overtakes all sense of what's right and fair. This woman is my weakness, but also my strength. I need that strength more than anything right now. "I know you didn't want to do anything until you cleared things up with Wes, but we both know which path you've chosen. You haven't worn that ring in over a week now."

She glances at her hand, but still appears torn. A ball of guilt settles deep in my stomach over the idea of putting her in this situation, of forcing her to make her decision. Wes will be home in a week, but these past several days have been torture enough. I can't wait that long. Not any more.

"I need to feel something other than this pain." My hand goes to her head and I fist her hair. "You're the only person who's ever made me feel." I bring my lips even closer to hers, her pink flesh skimming against mine. "Help me feel again."

Her brows crease as she places her hand on my chest, pushing softly. "Please, don't put me in this position. It's not fair to any of us." Her expression begs me to understand where she's coming from. The rational side of me does, but that's not the side that's in control right now. The heartache is driving me.

"Don't you want this? Don't you want me?" I ask, my voice catching. I'm not sure how much more hurt I can deal with.

She searches my eyes, licking her lips. "I can't give you the answer you need. Not yet."

My shoulders falling, I lower my head. I spin away from her so she doesn't bear witness to my breakdown, placing my hands on the island to support myself. I feel her eyes studying me, but I don't look at her, keeping my gaze focused on the pattern in the marble slab of the island.

"You should go," I manage to say after several awkward moments. It's an asshole move to kick her out simply because she won't betray Wes and kiss me. I'll probably come to regret my behavior later. Now, though, she's the key to my freedom that's hanging just out of reach.

"If that's what you want."

I shake my head. "You know what I want. I wish I knew what you wanted." I lift my eyes to hers, barely able to even say the words through the lump in my throat. I hate that Brooklyn's seeing me like this. Then again, she's seen me at the lowest of my lows. If anyone would understand what I'm going through, it's this woman.

She opens her mouth, then hesitates. The seconds stretch into an eternity as I wonder what she's doing, what she's thinking. She chews on her lower lip, her gaze swinging between me and the door. Her brows pull in as she puffs out her cheeks then releases the breath. Her eyes close briefly before returning to mine, heated, passionate, unwavering.

"Oh, fuck it." She rushes toward me, grabs my face in her hands, and crushes her lips to mine.

I freeze, not moving, not breathing, not thinking, momentarily stunned by her unexpected assault, every synapse in my body firing. I've imagined this moment for too long now, using the memory of her kisses the night of Brody Carmichael's party to get me through the most difficult times in my life. I loved the taste of her back then, but that's no match to how amazing she tastes now, her lips no longer those of a young, timid girl. This is a woman who knows exactly what she wants out of life. And she chose me. Finally.

With a moan, my hands go to her hips and I lift her onto the island, forcing her legs around me as I deepen the kiss. I never want to stop kissing her, feeling her, being with her. I tug her even harder against me, but it's still not enough. Her tongue dances with mine, greedy but reverent at the same time. Her kiss lights me up, sets me on fire, the way her body fits into mine pure perfection.

Panting, I tear away from her, needing to make sure she's

okay with this, that she doesn't regret it. Her own chest rising and falling from her labored breathing, neither one of us says anything for several long moments. I don't know what to say. We've crossed the line both of us have fought against. I should feel guilty, should feel horrible for what I'm doing to Wes. This is Brooklyn. Not just some woman I'm hooking up with and never intend to see again. This is a woman I've loved my entire life, a woman I'll always love, no matter what happens.

When I don't say anything, she quickly lowers her head. "I'm sorry." She attempts to scoot off the island. "I shouldn't have done that. I shouldn't have—"

"Don't." I capture her protest with a kiss, preventing her from escaping. My hold on her tightens. "Don't apologize. I just need…" I trail off.

"Yes?" She meets my gaze.

I moisten my lips. "I need more."

With a growl, I bring my lips back to hers, kissing her as if my heart will stop without it, as if her mouth moving against mine is the only thing that makes sense, as if her breath filling my lungs is the only thing keeping me alive.

"I've been such an idiot." My voice is soft as I cup her cheeks, at complete odds with the ravenous way I just kissed her. My hand traces the edges of her face. It's one I've seen nearly my entire life. It's one I thought I lost years ago. I won't lose her again, no matter what it takes.

She drapes her arms over my shoulders, her fingers running through my hair. It's such an innocent touch, but it sparks a yearning deep inside. "We don't have to live in the past anymore. We don't have to live with our regrets. We can start over. Today. Right now. We can forget everything and start fresh." A thoughtful expression crosses her face. "We can go back to the start."

I can't help but chuckle at the memory her words conjures up. Almost twenty years have passed since I said the very same thing to her. "The start?" I arch a brow.

She nods. "Yes. The start. Where we don't have to let the past define us because there is no past. There's just right now."

"I like the sound of right now." I cover her lips with mine

as she hooks her legs around my waist. The subtle circling motion of her hips drives me crazy, making me forget about everything for a moment. No other woman has ever brought me peace like this.

I trail my mouth down her jawline, burying my head in the crook of her neck. She tightens her hold on me, her fingers clawing into my back, my thin white t-shirt not much of a barrier between our two bodies. The way she touches me is enthralling and hypnotizing, an insatiable thirst filling me. It doesn't matter how many times I kiss this woman, how many times I inhale her scent, how many times I taste her delicious skin. I doubt I'll ever get my fill.

With a moan, she throws back her head, giving me better access. My hands roam her body. She's warm, needy, and absolute perfection. She pulls me tighter, her breathing becoming even more uneven. My chest heaves as my lips travel down her neck, along her collarbone, and up her jawline. I have no memory of the last time I kissed her, made her moan, made her hum. I plan on relishing every nip, every tug, every whimper, never forgetting what it feels like to love Brooklyn.

"Drew," she begs, pulsing against me. I pull away, stealing a glance at her face. There's no mistaking the ecstasy filling her, her eyes closed, her cheeks flushed, her lips parted.

"Yes?" I say in a coy voice.

She meets my fiery gaze. This moment is more intense, more powerful, more gratifying than I thought it would be. Her hands grip my face and she forces my mouth back to hers. "Don't stop," she whimpers against my lips. "Don't ever stop."

I kiss her again, this time harder, deeper, more frantic, more greedy, more everything. She reaches for my t-shirt and fumbles with it, ripping it over my head, our mouths parting just for an instant. When she returns her hands to me, the feel of flesh against flesh makes me crave her even more. Delirious, I yank off her shirt, leaving her in just her bra and yoga pants. With a shaky breath, I step back, making her loosen the grip her legs have around my waist. As I run my hands through my hair, I take a moment to admire her.

Brooklyn's never been one to show off her physique, often covering it with t-shirts and jeans. She rarely wore tight-fitting shirts or dresses. I remember the attention she got in high school when she started filling out. I put the fear of God into anyone who so much as looked at her in a way I thought was inappropriate. Now, as she chews on her bottom lip, I can't help but think she's never grown comfortable with her body, which is ridiculous. She's one of the most stunning and alluring women I've ever seen.

"Drew…" Her voice is timid, a hint of fear filling her eyes as I study her.

She starts to cover herself with her arms, but I'm in front of her in an instant, preventing her from doing so. "You are so fucking beautiful," I murmur, bringing my lips back to the skin of her neck. "But I'm not quite sure that word does you justice, my bewitching, captivating Brooklyn."

In one swift move, I wrap an arm around her back and the other under her legs, scooping her off the island, cradling her.

"Drew! Put me down!" she whisper-shouts, swatting at me as I carry her toward the living room.

"Not a chance in hell. I'm never putting you down again."

As I lay her on the couch, she gives me a coquettish look, biting her lower lip. I go to her, slithering up her body. Her legs fall on either side of me, her hair sprawled out behind her making her look like the goddess I've always thought her to be.

Propping myself onto my forearms, our lips meet again. I leisurely run my hand along the exposed flesh of her stomach, then tear my mouth from hers, traveling down her body. I want to take my time, but a primal need to taste every inch of her fills me, pushing me forward. When I get to the line of her bra, I float my eyes back to hers. We're about to cross a very firm line. There's no turning back after this. There's no being just friends if it doesn't work out between us. Then again, we're fooling ourselves to think we've ever truly just been friends.

She eyes me seductively as she lifts herself up and unclasps her bra, tossing it onto the floor.

"Brooklyn," I groan as I lower my mouth to her, my tongue tracing circles around her nipple.

"Oh god…" Her words are like a prayer. She runs her fingers through my hair, her hips moving in a tantric circle below me. "I didn't think I'd ever feel this again." Her nails dig into my scalp, her breaths coming closer together. I take her nipple in my mouth, the taste of her better than I could have imagined. When I nibble, she moans, her legs tightening around my waist, her fingers gripping my hair.

"You like that?"

"Don't stop," she begs, almost as if she's in another world, another place, another time.

"Never. I'll never stop giving you everything you deserve, making you feel how much I crave you, letting you know how much I need you in my life." Fevered eyes meet mine. "But not just as a friend. Never as a friend again."

"Never," she murmurs as my lips find hers, two interlocking pieces of the same puzzle. I've made a lot of mistakes, more than most men my age. For the longest time, I thought the only thing I did right was being a father. But I must have done something else to deserve this woman, this moment, this second chance. I'll forever be grateful to whatever power brought Brooklyn back to me, despite our tortured past.

My mouth begins its journey back to her chest, wrapping around her other nipple. Her body warms beneath me, her hips circling. I float my hand down her side, her stomach clenching the farther south I get. When my hand disappears between our two bodies, every muscle in my body tightens. I rub between her legs, her pants a rather unwelcome barrier.

"I feel how hot you are for me," I groan, caressing and craving. Her eyes roll into the back of her head, her eyelids fluttering closed as she succumbs to me. "Say you want me."

"I want you," she repeats, a slave to my demand.

"Say you need me."

"I need you," she moans, her body writhing beneath

mine. "God, Drew, I need you right now." Her fists clench and unclench, her chest rising and falling with her frenzied breathing.

I move my hand to the waistline of her pants, dipping a finger beneath, licking my lips at what we're about to do. When I go to push her pants down, her entire body stiffens, her eyes flinging open, as if someone's flipped the switch, forcing her out of her desire-induced trance.

"Wait." She shakes her head, biting her lip. "We can't do this."

I blink repeatedly, swallowing hard, a giant bucket of ice water thrown over me. "I thought…"

Her expression lightens as she reaches for my face, cupping my cheek. "Right now. We can't do this right now." She runs the pads of her thumbs along my lower lip. "That night all those years ago, you stopped me right before I pushed your pants off. You told me you wanted to be sober the first time we made love."

My heart squeezes when I hear her speak of that night. I hate that I can't remember it, hate that I got so drunk and have no recollection of the first time I was with Brooklyn, regardless that we didn't have sex.

"You deserve the same from me," she says.

I furrow my brow. "But you are sober."

A breathtaking smile crosses her face and she brings her mouth to mine, her kiss leaving me desperate for more. "You wanted to be sober so I'd have all of you that first time."

I close my eyes, releasing a long sigh, knowing what she's referring to.

"You need to have all of me, and right now, you won't. You deserve a Brooklyn who's free from her past. I have loose ends I need to tie up. As much as I want you right now, and I can't even put into words how badly I want you right now, it's not fair to any of us."

My head hangs low as I draw in a long breath. We probably already did more today than she's comfortable with, given her current status with Wes. She needs to put that relationship to bed before beginning something with me. She wants to go back to the start. She can't do that with Wes still in the picture.

"It sucks, but you're right," I sigh. "We need a clean slate."

"We owe that to ourselves…and each other." She lifts her lips to meet mine. "Back to the start."

"The start," I repeat, then kiss her sweetly. Just the feel of that soft flesh sends me into overdrive again. "When does Wes come home?"

"Next Friday. His flight gets in around five in the afternoon."

"What do you plan on doing?" I shift my position so I'm no longer on top of her.

"I can't lead him on any longer than I already have." She throws her legs over the side of the couch and sits up. I grab a blanket off the back and wrap it around both our bodies, covering her up. "I'd hate to be all 'Welcome home. By the way, I don't want to marry you anymore.' I just don't see any other option. I told him I'd go over to his place and stay the night." She shifts her eyes to mine, smiling coyly. "But I believe my plans have changed."

"They have?"

She nods, chewing her lower lip. "Yes, they have." Her mouth brushes against mine. "I still need to go over there, but I'll no longer be spending the night."

Pulling her tightly against me. I leave a kiss on that sweet spot where her ear meets her neck and a shiver visibly rolls through her. "And what will you be doing instead?"

Her gaze darkens as she shifts her body, crawling onto my lap, straddling me. "I never kiss and tell," she murmurs in a seductive voice. "But if I were you, I'd see if Molly or Gigi can take the girls Friday night." When she grinds her hips against me, the erection that had started to die instantly comes back to life. She could ask me to kill someone and I'd agree, as long as she kept doing was she was currently doing. "Once I close this chapter with Wes, I'll come over and start the next one with you."

"And how do you intend to do that?" I give her a sly smile.

She tilts her head at me in playful annoyance. "Use your imagination," she breathes, arching into me, her chest nearly in front of my face. God, I want to bury my mouth in her ample cleavage.

"You should know, I have a very active imagination." I bring my lips to her neck, peppering soft kisses along her skin. "I've often fantasized of the day you'd be mine, when I can have you anytime and anywhere I want."

"Is that right?" She moves against me with more urgency. It takes every ounce of resolve to not rip off her pants and drive into her. Waiting until next Friday will make that first time even more perfect. I'm ready to fall apart right now. I can only imagine how thick the sexual tension between us will be after another week.

"That's right."

"Where would you have me first?"

"The bed." I inhale her scent. "Where I plan on worshiping every inch of you. Where I'll make up for all the years, days, minutes we were apart."

She moans as I tighten my hold on her, bringing her body harder against mine. The feel of her skin is everything I thought it would be. "Where else?"

"Then we'll move into the shower to clean up, but I won't be able to keep my hands off you." My mouth travels down the line of her neck to her chest and I take a nipple into my mouth again, sucking and savoring. "Just like I can't now. I'll make love to you on the bed, but once I get you in that shower…"

"Yes," she exhales, her eyes closed, relishing in every word.

"I'm going to fuck you like you've never been fucked."

"Oh god…" Her motions increase, her breaths coming quicker. She wraps her arms tighter around my neck, her body language giving off every indication that she's just as desperate for me as I am for her.

"Then I'm going to carry your beautiful naked body outside." My voice becomes softer, more sincere. The mood shifting, she slows the intensity of her movement, opening her eyes and peering down at me.

"I'll lay a blanket on the grass and we'll make love as the sun rises, the new day bringing in the start of our lives together. Because that's what this is, Brooklyn." I cup her face in my hands. There's a tranquility in her eyes as her gaze remains focused on mine. "The start of our lives together. I had to let you go years ago. I won't do it again. Never again. I love you, Brooklyn Rose Tanner." My words are a promise, one I intend to keep this time.

Tears well in her eyes as she presses her lips to mine, our kiss simple, yet full of meaning. "You have no idea how long I've waited to hear those words come out of your mouth."

I chuckle, enveloping her in my arms, savoring the feel of her. "Actually, I probably do."

CHAPTER THIRTEEN

BROOKLYN

I CAN'T STOP SMILING as I drive back to my house after leaving Drew. For the first time since Wes took of for Dubai, I want him to come home, just so I can do what I should have done before he left. What I should have done months ago. This next week will be torture, especially now that I've been treated to a taste of Drew's lips after too long, relished in the feel of his unshaven jaw scraping against my skin, lost myself in the sensation of his flesh against mine. It's going to take every ounce of willpower I possess not to cross that final line.

Then again, this time will allow us to focus on other things. It will allow him the opportunity to focus on other things. Now that he has indisputable proof that Charlotte isn't his daughter, he'll need to devote his energy to ensuring this doesn't adversely affect those girls. They're both at an age where something like this can have long-term effects. He needs to make sure they get through this, never doubting the love he has for them.

The neighborhood is just coming to life as I step out of my car and make my way up to my front door. A few people are out walking their dogs, the occasional early morning jogger dashing along the streets, but the frenzy to beat rush hour traffic hasn't hit yet.

"Is there a reason you're just getting home after the sun's already up?"

I jump, whirling around. "Mrs. Bradford," I exhale, surprised to see Wes' mother heading up the walkway toward me. She's wearing a light blue dress, her hair impeccably groomed, makeup expertly applied, despite the early hour. I had no idea she was even in town. "What are you doing here?"

"Everything I can to ensure this wedding actually happens." She narrows her eyes on me, her mouth a tight line.

"What do you mean?" I grit out a fabricated smile, pretending her presence doesn't unsettle me. Running a hand through my dark hair, I bring it over one shoulder, hoping she won't notice the redness on my neck from where Drew's beard bruised me during our make-out session.

I had no intention of being unfaithful to Wes like that. I suppose no one really does. I truly didn't want to kiss Drew until I'd broken things off with Wes. But he's on the other side of the world right now. I can't break off our engagement over the phone or via email. He deserves better than that. He deserves better than me kissing another man, too, but Drew was so pained, so lost. I couldn't bear to see him hurting. I wanted him to feel something. Truth is, I wanted to feel something, too.

"Judy from the dress boutique has been trying to get in touch with you for a week now."

I blink repeatedly, feigning ignorance at the reminder of the voice messages my dress consultant left on my cell. "She has?"

"Yes. Your dress has come in and she needs to arrange your first fitting. As I'm sure you're aware, the wedding is three weeks from tomorrow."

I do my best to keep my expression flat, not wanting to give anything away, like the fact that there will no longer be a wedding. Until I can talk to Wes in person, everyone needs to carry on as if there is, myself included.

"I'm aware of that."

"Are you? You haven't been acting like it. When I was engaged to James, I couldn't wait. The instant my dress came in, I booked the first fitting appointment possible so I could see myself in the dress of my dreams. But you…" She's contemplative as she scrutinizes me, her gaze hardened. If I were in her shoes and saw the woman marrying my son not get home until after six in the morning, I'd have my own misgivings, too. "You don't seem excited about the prospect at all. In fact, the way you've been behaving makes it seem like this is more of a prison sentence than anything."

"I'm excited about it," I insist. "I've been busy. Just like

Wes. He has a job he loves. As do I. Which I need to get to, so if you'll excuse me——"

She's in front of me before I can say another word, preventing me from continuing into my house. "I'm sorry to be the one to inform you, but your plans have changed. When Judy couldn't reach you, she had no choice but to call me. I hopped on the first flight and assured her you'd be there for a fitting this morning."

"But I have to work," I protest.

"And I have a million and one things on my to-do list today…" She places her hands on her hips, her eyes cold. "All of which I had to drop to ensure you made it to your fitting." One side of her mouth turns up in a sneer as she leers at me with a sanctimonious look. "We're all making sacrifices here, dear. It's time you do the same."

I bite my lower lip to stop myself from asking what sacrifice she's ever made in her life. She wouldn't know the meaning of the word if it was glaring at her in black and white. I wish I could end this charade right now. The thought of going to my dress fitting for a wedding that's no longer happening seems wrong, but what choice do I have? Until Wes returns, I don't have one.

"Fine," I say with a huff. "I'll take some personal time. When's my appointment?"

"Nine."

"Okay. I'll be there. You didn't need to fly all the way up here just to let me know about this. A simple phone call would have sufficed." I push past Mrs. Bradford, turn the lock, and step into my house, about to close the door when she forces herself inside.

"Apparently not, or I wouldn't have had to make the trip. I'll wait here while you to get ready. We can stop for breakfast on the way."

I raise my brows. "You're coming with me?"

"I certainly am. I need to make sure you show up this time."

"When have I ever not shown up?" The instant the words leave my mouth, I snap my jaw shut, wishing I could take them back.

"I seem to remember one such instance you failed to show up, worrying my Weston, only to find out you spent the day with another man."

She continues farther into my house, her nose wrinkling in disgust at her surroundings. It's not that I'm messy and disorganized. My townhouse is spotless and decorated in a style I like. She doesn't like it because it's small. Her garage is probably double the size of my house.

"I told Wes he should have left you after that, but no." She whirls around and faces me, the disdain she has for me clear in the way she regards me. Her posture is stiff, her stance wide, making her appear much more formidable than her five-foot, three-inch frame would normally allow. "He defended you, said it was his fault, a misunderstanding." She shakes her head, fire in her eyes as she continues to belittle me. "I thought it the second he brought you home. And I still think it now. Weston is far too good for you."

I inhale a deep breath, summoning all my strength not to break down into tears. Yesterday, I may have done just that. The feel of Drew's love surrounding me, although he's not physically here, gives me the strength and courage I've been missing for years.

I saunter up to Mrs. Bradford, holding my head high. She blinks, not used to this sort of confidence from me. "You know… You're probably right. Nevertheless, he still wants to marry me. It must be eating you up that you haven't been able to talk him out of it, out of marrying a girl from a blue-collar family. You can have all the etiquette classes and right upbringing possible. Those things can't change the cold, heartless shrew you are."

My response leaves her stunned as I head up the narrow stairs. When I step into my bedroom and close the door behind me, I blow out a breath. I take a minute, leaning against the door. As I attempt to collect myself, I laugh hysterically, never feeling so alive. I'm done doing what everyone expects of me, of putting everyone else's needs before mine. It's time for what Brooklyn wants.

And Brooklyn really wants Drew.

* * * * *

"Ms. Tanner," Judy says as I walk into the boutique, Mrs. Bradford clutching onto my arm in a way that makes me think she's worried I'll run. I doubt she cares whether I even want to marry her son. All she wants is to plan the social event of the year. This has never been about the joining of two people in love. It's about making her the center of attention in her ridiculous little social circles. "So wonderful to see you."

"You, too." I grit a smile.

Judy glances nervously at Mrs. Bradford, then back at me, her expression momentarily falling before she plasters that fake smile back on her face. "Your dress is waiting in one of the changing rooms. If you'll come with me..."

She turns on her heels and heads through the showroom. I follow her toward the same dressing room as last time. The instant we cross the threshold, memories of being here with Drew flood back. These comforting recollections help me through this ordeal when all I want to do is run away and never look back. Despite my strong distaste for Mrs. Bradford and the way she treats anyone she views as inferior, which is most of the human race, she raised a son with such a beautiful, caring soul. I owe it to him to get through today, to not let on that anything's changed, not until he comes home and I can tell him the truth.

"Right in here." Judy heads toward the private dressing room off to the side of the sitting area, gesturing for me to follow her. I leave Mrs. Bradford, thankful to be out of her judgmental eyes for a moment. "I'll give you some privacy while I grab the seamstress."

"Thank you."

She studies me with analytical eyes. I wonder if she can see the truth, that this is just something I'm doing but have no plan to follow through with. Then her tight lips turn into a smile and she blows out a breath, almost like she's relieved. I'm about to ask her about it when she spins, leaving me alone. I collect myself, brushing off Judy's strange behavior. It's probably nothing, just my over-analytical mind seeing things that aren't real.

When I turn my attention to the dress, a smile tugs at my mouth. It truly is stunning, the dress I always dreamed I'd wear on my wedding day. When I saw it hanging on the rack all those weeks ago, I knew it wasn't one of Mrs. Bradford's approved dresses, knew Drew probably put the fear of God into poor Judy to find a dress I'd like. I was reticent to accept it at first, but deep down, I think I knew I'd never walk down the aisle to Wes wearing this dress. I've just been in denial for months.

I'm about to undress to get this over with so I can get to some of my appointments when my phone pings with an incoming text. Worried it might be work, I retrieve my cell from my bag, a smile lighting up my face when I see it's from Drew.

> **Drew:** *I can't stop thinking of your mouth.*

Reeling in my grin, I type out a reply, my fingers flying over the screen.

> **Me:** I can't stop thinking of your mouth, either. In addition to lots of other parts of your body, especially considering where I am right now.

> **Drew:** *And where's that?*

I hesitate, unsure how he'll react. Then I remind myself he's a reasonable person. He'll know this changes nothing between us, that this is something I must do.

> **Me:** Getting fit for the wedding dress I'll never wear. Mrs. Bradford was at my house when I got home this morning. My dress came in last week. Judy's been trying to call me, but I never returned her calls. So she called Lydia.

I hit send, then shrug out of my top and pull my jeans down my legs so Mrs. Bradford doesn't accuse me of being slow, as well. Removing the sleek dress from the hanger, I adjust my strapless bra, about to step into the dress when my phone pings. I reach for it, my heart falling when I see Drew's response.

> **Drew:** *Oh.*

I know him well enough to know he's not too happy about this news. I could have lied to him, but we've both lied to each other so much, kept so many secrets from each other. We spoke of wiping the slate clean. We can't do that by continuing on the same path.

> **Me:** I didn't have a choice. Wes needs to be the first person who finds out. I can't tell his mother the wedding's off. You know how she can be.

> **Drew:** *Can you call me?*

I shake my head, even though he can't see me.

> **Me:** I'd love nothing more than to hear your voice, but Lydia's out in the sitting area, waiting for me to walk out in my dress, which I'm sure she'll have some rather choice words about. Just like she told me her son was much too good for me earlier this morning as she made herself at home at my place.

I put my phone on the chair, reaching behind and zipping up the dress the rest of the way. Judy was right. Now that it's ordered in my size, it's even more stunning than it was when she pinned and clipped it to my body. I hate to waste this gorgeous dress. Then again, I may not have to.

As I consider the thought, my phone chimes once more.

> **Drew:** *I'm going to call you. You don't have to say a word. I want you to hear my voice.*

I quickly click the sound off right before it buzzes. I hit answer, bringing it up to my ear, remaining silent.

"You are the most beautiful woman I've ever seen." Drew's voice comes on the line, and I clutch the phone tighter, smiling. "And the way you look in that dress..." His tone becomes throaty. "I remember the first time I saw you in it. I've watched you date other men, watched you kiss other men, but I never felt the jealousy I did at that moment, when I thought how fucking lucky Wes was to stand at the end of the aisle and watch you walk up to him. Now, I hope that lucky bastard will be me someday. So no matter what that awful woman says, no matter how small she makes you feel, I want you to know something."

"What's that?" I whisper, my voice barely audible. I wanted to remain silent, but it's impossible not to respond to Drew's heartfelt words.

"That I love you. That I've loved you my entire life. That I'll love you the rest of my life. I don't care what you need to do in order to do right by Wes. I'll still support you."

I close my eyes, my chest expanding, my body too small to contain my full heart.

I love you, too, I mouth.

"I'll see you tomorrow morning."

I nod, not saying a word, holding my phone to my ear as if it's the only thing that brings me comfort. In that moment it does. His words give me the strength to face Mrs. Bradford when the old me would have done everything to shrink into herself, would have allowed her to make me feel small, like I wasn't good enough for her son.

When I emerge from the dressing room and walk to the 180-degree mirror where Judy's standing with the seamstress, Lydia sneers. "I knew I should have insisted on going dress shopping with you."

My expression momentarily falls, my usual personality briefly shining through. I take a moment, closing my eyes as I repeat Drew's beautiful words in my mind. Straightening my spine, I create a cocoon of comfort around me, one strong enough that even Lydia's hate-filled words can't penetrate. Judy meets my gaze as I step onto the pedestal, silently asking if I'm okay. I smile at her. I can honestly say I am. Knowing I only need to put up with Wes' mom for a few more days makes me no longer care about her opinion.

"What were you thinking?" she continues.

"That all the dresses you chose were hideous," I quip.

She inhales a sharp breath, taken aback by my bold attitude. It's something Molly would say, not me, which is probably why she's surprised. "Hideous? Those were dresses every girl would love to wear on her wedding day."

"That may be true, but they were wrong for me. You've forgotten whose wedding this is. It's mine and Dr—" I stop myself short, every pair of eyes in the room zeroing in on me from the slip of my tongue.

"Wes'," I say through the thick silence. "Mine and Wes'."

"Are you sure about that?"

I swallow hard, pinching my lips together. "Of course I am."

"So sure you almost said you were marrying that hockey friend of yours?"

I meet her eyes through the mirror, the seamstress busying herself by pinning the dress in places. Due to my ample chest, they had to order a dress several sizes larger so it would fit. It's saggy around the waist, but once they take it in, it will fit perfectly. Although it doesn't matter. I won't actually be wearing it to a wedding anytime soon.

"I didn't mean anything by it," I insist, trying to avoid her glare, meeting Judy's eyes, who looks upon me with compassion. "I've said this repeatedly. Drew is a friend. Like a brother, really. I'm marrying Wes."

Mrs. Bradford crosses her arms over her chest, tapping her fingers on her skin. "Mmm-hmm."

A week ago, I would have tried to prove myself worthy of her son's love. I no longer need to do that. It's like a giant weight has been lifted off my shoulders.

Just like Gigi always says, "You'll know you made the right decision when you feel stress leave your body." As I beam at my reflection in the mirror, shrugging off Mrs. Bradford's look of disgust, I know I'm on the right path.

Finally.

CHAPTER FOURTEEN

DREW

THE ATMOSPHERE IN THE house is solemn as everyone arrives for family dinner, a marked contrast to the frivolity that fills this space on a typical Sunday. But this isn't a typical Sunday, not with the news I need to share with Alyssa and Charlotte. There are no smiles and jokes, no tickle monster or games of hide-and-seek. Instead, the mood is somber. Aunt Gigi went so far as to dress in black. Even the girls have picked up on the tense environment. Their normal squeals of joy as they play with whatever new toy their auntie Molly spoiled them with this week seems lackluster, Alyssa's nervous gaze darting to me every few seconds.

I try to pretend everything's normal, that this is just another Sunday dinner, but I can't stop watching my two girls, wondering how they'll cope. Every time I think of it, a lump forms in my throat, the pain bordering on unbearable. Before I became a father, I considered myself to be a selfish individual. But the instant I looked into Alyssa's brown eyes, everything changed. She changed me, made me want to be a better man, a man she'd be proud to call her dad. And I changed again the first time I held Charlotte. The first time her tiny little fist squeezed my finger. The first time she laughed. The first time she called me daddy. I can't stomach the idea of never hearing her call me that again.

"Hey," a compassionate voice murmurs, tearing me out of my thoughts.

I snap my eyes to my left, clearing my throat, trying to regain what little composure I have left. "Hey."

"How ya holding up?" Brooklyn whispers, craning her head to meet my eyes.

I wish I could lie to her, say I'm okay, assure her I'm strong enough to get through this, but Brooklyn knows me better than most people. She's always been able to see past the front I put up and peer into my soul.

"I feel like I'm broken in pieces and the glue that normally holds me together is nowhere to be found."

With more compassion than I deserve, she loops an arm around my waist, resting her head against my chest. I still at the contact. The few times we've been with the rest of my family, we've avoided touching each other, not wanting anyone to read too much into our interactions. But right now, this is what I need. I pull her close, inhaling her comforting lavender scent. It takes all my willpower not to lean down and kiss her.

"It'll be okay," she encourages, running her hands up and down my back, soothing me. "We're all here for you."

"Yes, we are," Molly's voice cuts through.

I expect Brooklyn to jump back, but she doesn't, needing this connection just as much as I do. Molly wraps an arm around me, the three of us standing in a group hug. I close my eyes, a calming sensation enveloping me as I remain enclosed in the love of two of the most important women in my life. I lift my head from Brooklyn, placing a kiss on Molly's temple, grateful for her support.

"We're not going to let this divide us," she struggles to say through her own tears.

"Did someone die?" Alyssa pipes up. We all jump away from each other, staring at the two girls standing in front of us.

"No." Molly wipes at her tears. "No one died."

"Then why are you crying?" Charlotte presses.

"Your auntie Molly just gets a little emotional once in a while. That's what happens when you're pregnant."

"Why are you emotional?" Alyssa asks.

The three of us look between each other, uneasy. I hadn't considered how I would tell them. All I knew was I needed everyone here when they learned the truth. As I peer into their curious eyes that are eager for information, I realize I can't keep this from them any longer.

"Alyssa, Charlotte…" I clear my throat, stepping away

from Molly and Brooklyn. "Can you come sit with me on the couch for a minute?" I hold out my hands, surprised when both girls grab onto one without a single word of protest.

"Are we in trouble?" Charlotte frowns, worrying her lower lip.

"No, sweetie." I sit on the sectional as the girls take their usual place together in the corner. They're both sporting a miniature version of the Bruins jersey I wore during my time with the team. It wasn't even my idea. They insisted, since there's a playoff game tonight. "There's something important I need to tell you. And I wanted the entire family here so you know how much we love you. Both of you." My voice wavers, and Molly chokes out a sob. Noah wraps his arm around her, pulling her into his embrace. It doesn't matter how tough Molly wants everyone to think she is. When it comes to these two girls, she's a softie. We all are. They have every single one of us wrapped around their little fingers. Have since the day they were born.

I glance over my shoulder to see all the important people in my life looking on, long expressions on their faces. Leo hands Gigi his handkerchief, which she brings up to her mouth to hide her quivering chin.

"Can you all join us?"

"Of course, darling," Gigi responds, dabbing at her eyes and sniffling.

Everyone walks toward the living room, the processional reminiscent of a funeral. My eyes meet Brooklyn's as she passes and I reach for her hand. She pauses, narrowing her eyes on me, silently questioning. I wrinkle my brows, begging her to give me this, give me the comfort I need. Nodding, she clutches my hand, sitting on the opposite side of me. I hold her gaze for a moment, drawing strength from the love I see, then release my grip on her, facing my girls. I feel the questions on everyone's faces from witnessing our exchange, but now's not the time. Tonight isn't about Brooklyn and me. It's about these two little girls whose world is about to be tilted on its axis.

"You girls know I love you very much, right?" I say once

everyone's taken their seats on the couch and chairs set throughout the area.

They stare at me with worry, their uncertainty visible in the way their foreheads crease.

"Yes," Alyssa replies in a shaky voice.

"And I would do anything and everything for both of you." I place a hand on each of their tiny legs, marveling at these two little humans, how I raised them and, by some miracle, they survived. How they've become the center of my universe. How not one second of a single day goes by that I don't count myself lucky for being able to be their father. "You girls are my life. You're my reason for breathing." I bite my lip, unable to stop the tears from escaping my eyes.

"Why are you crying, Daddy?" Charlotte looks from me to her sister, searching for some sort of reassurance that everything's okay. I wish I could give her that. Instead, all I can give her is the cruel, unforgiving truth…the truth that's ripping me apart.

A hand squeezes my thigh and I look to Brooklyn. She nods, her compassionate gaze encouraging me to continue. I swipe at my tears, drawing in a deep breath, then turn back to the girls. In retrospect, I wish I had rehearsed what I would say. Every time I stopped to think about it, an excruciating pain settled in my chest. But it's nothing compared to the agony overwhelming me now as I stare into their confused eyes.

"Do you remember asking about Auntie Molly's baby a few months ago? How I explained the baby's in her belly?"

They nod.

"Well, you were both in your mother's belly at one time, too."

Charlotte wrinkles her brow. "Who?"

"Do you remember when we went to the science museum a few weeks ago and you almost bumped into a woman?"

They both nod again.

"Well, the reason I was so upset was because I knew her. Her name is Carla." I pause, drawing in a deep breath. "She's your mother."

Probably not even realizing she's doing it, Alyssa grabs Charlotte's hand in hers, squeezing, offering her the same solace Brooklyn's giving me right now. I can't imagine what they're thinking. My mother left when I was six, but I was old enough to remember her. These girls were so young when Carla abandoned us. Alyssa may have a few weak memories somewhere in her subconscious, but Charlotte has none. For all she knows, she doesn't have a mother. I made it my mission to ensure these girls didn't feel like they needed one. I like to think I succeeded…until now.

"Why isn't she our mother now?" Charlotte asks.

"She still is, sweetie. Your mother and I were married, but we fought a lot. We weren't a good fit, so she left."

"Why? Did she not love us?"

"Oh, Char…" I run my hand down her face. Her skin is so soft, a stark contrast to the roughness in my own hands. "She did, in her own way."

"Why are you telling us about her now?" Alyssa interjects, sensing something is amiss.

I square my shoulders, narrowing my gaze on them. "Because she wants to change the agreement we came to when she left. You see, when parents don't get along anymore, sometimes they get what's called a divorce."

"I understand what a divorce is, Dad," Alyssa bites out, rolling her eyes. I'd normally scold her for her attitude, but it gives me a sense of familiarity I desperately crave right now.

"Of course you do. When we divorced, the court granted me full physical custody of both of you. Now, she's asking to share custody. She wants to be a part of your lives."

The two girls turn to each other, obviously unsure how to react to the prospect of another woman, a complete stranger, taking care of them.

"I may not be able to keep her from you forever, but I'm going to do everything I can to make sure absolutely nothing changes."

"What would change?" Charlotte's lower lip trembles.

I tent my hands in front of me, taking a moment to compose my thoughts, an emptiness forming in the pit of my stomach. Nothing could have prepared me for this, for the pain I'm enduring. It's not just pain at the knowledge that Charlotte isn't my daughter. It's pain for what she's about to go through. What they both are.

"Because, Charlotte, sweetie…" I reach out and grab her hand in mine, rubbing my finger along her knuckles. "Because I just found out I'm not your biological father." I struggle to swallow back my tears as those words ring in the air, the anguish squeezing my heart like a vice.

"What does that mean?" Her wide eyes search mine, then float to the rest of the room, pleading for an explanation. I can see her world falling apart around her and hate that I'm the cause of it.

"You know how Auntie Molly's carrying the baby in her belly until it's big enough?" I wipe at my tears, doing my best to maintain composure so she understands exactly what's going on.

The two girls nod in unison.

"And how your mother carried you in her belly?"

They nod again.

"Well, the mommy gives some DNA, and the daddy gives some, too. At first, the baby is no bigger than a speck of dust. But inside the mommy's belly, the baby gets bigger and bigger. He develops arms, legs, and all the organs he needs to function outside his mommy's belly. I thought I gave your mother the DNA to make both of you, but I didn't."

"So you're not my daddy?"

I bite my lip, struggling to maintain control. A lump in my throat prevents me from uttering a single word. All I can do is shake my head as tears roll down my cheeks. I've always been able to keep my emotions in check, only letting them out in private. But this is too much, more difficult for me to process than when I learned I'd never play hockey again. I thought my life was over back then. I had my two daughters and their love to help me through it. What do I have now?

Charlotte sniffles, her breaths heavy. "Does that mean you don't love me anymore?"

"Oh god, sweetie…" I quickly grab her, pulling her onto

my lap, wishing I could do something so she could physically feel how much I love her. Kissing the top of her head, I rock her gently, just like I did all those nights when she was a baby, when she cried out for the mother who abandoned her. We've come full circle. This time, she's crying because of that mother.

"I love you so much, Charlotte Marie." I pull back, meeting her teary eyes. "Nothing will ever come between that. Nothing." My voice becomes a growl, needing her to hear the meaning behind my words. "Just because you don't have my DNA doesn't mean I love you any less. I will always be your daddy. You will always be part of this family." I wipe at her tears, kissing her nose. "Your mother is trying to change that. She wants you to go live with her all the time, but I will not let that happen."

I shift my eyes to Alyssa, who has tears of her own streaming down her cheeks. I open my arms and she barrels into me, nuzzling against my chest. It's been ages since she's done something like this. She usually thinks she's too mature to need her father. It feels good to be needed again.

"I love you both so much. I promise, no matter what, I will always be your family. Always. But I also need both of you to know the truth, to know who your mother is. As much as I'd like to keep you mine, she is your mother and has certain rights."

"I hate her," Alyssa spits out.

"That's not nice, sweetie. Hate is a very strong word. You don't even know her."

"But she left us! Now she's trying to take us away from you?"

"That won't happen." My voice remains calm as I reassure them this isn't going to change anything. It's all I can do to hope it won't. "Like I said before… You girls are my life." I glance down at Charlotte in my arms. "Both of you are."

She remains still, the entire room silent as every set of eyes is trained on us to see how the girls cope with this news. After a few moments, Charlotte tilts her head, looking up at me, a question on the tip of her tongue. I brace myself, praying I have a good answer for whatever she's about to ask.

"Can we still go to Disney World?" she inquires with all the seriousness she can muster.

In an instant, relieved laughter fills the space, the weight on my shoulders lifting. "You better believe it! Nothing's going to keep us from going on that trip."

She grins, using the sleeve of her jersey to wipe her nose. "Good. Because I really want to go to Disney World."

I lean down and brush my mouth against her temple, hugging my girls tighter, never wanting to let go.

When I first received Carla's motion, I vowed to do everything in my power to fight for my girls. The love I feel from them only strengthens my resolve. These girls are my family. And no one messes with my family.

CHAPTER FIFTEEN

BROOKLYN

"I HEAR YOU HAD your dress fitting," Gigi comments as we all sit around the large rectangular table in Drew's open dining area.

As I expected, the conversation isn't as lively as usual. We all do our best to pretend everything is like it's always been, but the reality of the situation seems to weigh heavily on all of us. The one person who doesn't seem as affected as we thought is little Charlotte. She's spent the entire time informing Drew about yet another boy who likes Alyssa. No matter what, she'll always be the little sister, and my heart warms at the notion.

I look at Gigi, placing my fork on my plate. "Yes. This past Friday." I swallow hard, stealing a glance at Drew, who simply winks.

"That's wonderful, dear," she says, but I can hear her lack of enthusiasm.

Gigi seems to know everything. I wonder if she knows I've been sneaking over here every morning the past ten days to have coffee with Drew. I wonder if she knows that morning coffee has turned into a morning make-out session that's been leaving both of us on edge and desperate for more.

"You must be looking forward to the big day."

I give her a trite smile. "Of course." I try to keep my responses as short and sweet as possible.

She studies me with a furrowed brow, then opens her mouth, about to press further when Drew interrupts.

"Okay, munchkins…"

I blow out a breath, grateful he came to my rescue.

"Time for bed."

The girls groan, just like they do every Sunday. And just like every week, they ask to stay up a little longer with promises to help clean, to which Drew says no. It gives me hope things won't change.

The instant they get up from their chairs, Drew scoops each under an arm, then brings them around the table so we can all say our goodnights. Today, the hugs last a bit longer, the kisses a little more meaningful.

Just as Drew's about to carry the two girls upstairs, he leans down toward me. "Stay," he whispers.

One word, and I'm ravenous with an insatiable hunger. One word, and I'm putty in his hands. One word, and I want to drown in him and never come back up for air.

I subtly nod, struggling to look away as I watch him disappear out of the living area and up the stairs. When I return my gaze to the table, four sets of eyes are on me.

"What?" I push back and busy myself with clearing the plates from the pasta feast we consumed.

"What?" Molly mimics, standing from the table and attempting to help clean, as well, but Noah is up in an instant, ripping the dishes from her. It's sweet to see how much he dotes on her, especially now that she's pregnant. He doesn't like her lifting a finger. I often envied them, wondering if I'd ever have that kind of devotion and affection. Now I do, but I can't tell anyone about it yet, and it's killing me. "If you think we're all oblivious to the sexual tension between you and Drew, think again. You all but have a giant 'fuck me' sign on your forehead whenever he looks at you."

I straighten my spine as I continue cleaning, not wanting to look directly at any of them. "What are you talking about?"

"You and Drew. Three weeks ago, you were running from him." She approaches, lowering her voice to a whisper so only I can hear. "Now it seems you're running toward him, jumping on him, letting him ride you until your legs are sore from being spread that long."

I shake my head, still avoiding her eyes. "That's absurd. I'm engaged to Wes."

"Are you?" She crosses her arms, resting them on her baby bump, which is more like a baby watermelon at this point. "I haven't seen you wearing that gargantuan rock in over a week."

I still, fidgeting with my ring finger. While I don't normally wear jewelry to work, I'm usually diligent about putting my ring back on, at least on nights I know I'll be seeing Wes. Since he left for Dubai, I haven't worn it. At first, I felt naked whenever I took it off. Now, though, it's freeing.

"I must have forgotten to put it back on." A heat washes over me as I rewind to Friday, how I spent the morning with Mrs. Bradford. She never brought up my lack of a ring. Based on what I know, she's probably storing that nugget of information to use against me later. It doesn't matter. She doesn't matter.

"Whatever you say."

"Molly..." I lift my eyes to hers, giving her a look she knows all too well, the one that allows her to read my inner thoughts. When I grin deviously, understanding washes over her.

"Got it." With a wink, she inches toward me, her voice turning into a whisper. "Just tell me one thing and I'll drop it. It's good news, right?"

I hesitate, glancing around the room to make sure no one's listening in. Unfortunately, all eyes are glued to me. I zero in on Aunt Gigi to see so much optimism in her gaze as she awaits my response. As much as I want to avoid answering, I also want to give these people hope after the night they had.

"It's really good news."

Gigi clasps her hands together and stares up at the ceiling. I see her lips moving, as if she's praying. After performing the sign of the cross, she heads toward me, clutching my face in her hands.

"I knew it would all work out, my sweet, sweet girl. God had a plan for you two. I noticed it the second you walked into our house when you were barely five years old."

She brings my head toward her and kisses my forehead, then pulls back, moving her hands to my biceps. The enthusiasm in this woman's face is unmatched by anything I've seen from her in quite a while, probably since Molly announced she was pregnant.

"You've brought absolute joy to my heart, my dear. Bless you."

While I didn't want to say anything until I spoke to Wes, I haven't technically admitted to anything. They could take my response many different ways. I have no control over how it's interpreted...or misinterpreted.

"What's going on?" Drew's booming voice fills the space. I tear my eyes to his, unsure how he'll react to everyone being aware of what's going on between us. When he sees the uncertainty on my face, he shakes his head, laughing. "She figured it out, didn't she?"

I shrug, biting my lower lip. "You know how she can be."

"That I do." He approaches and slings an arm over my shoulders, pulling me against him.

Gigi smiles wide at the sight of us together, clasping her hands over her heart. Then her eyes darken, her mouth forming a tight line. "Don't you dare mess it up this time, Andrew."

"What?" he shoots back, laughing.

"Yeah," I say in agreement, elbowing him in the stomach. "Don't mess it up this time."

He gazes down on me with all the sincerity he possesses. The next words that come out of his mouth make my heart soar higher than it ever has before. "I don't plan to. Everything I do is for you. Always has been. Always will be."

If I didn't have Drew supporting me, I'm pretty sure I'd turn into a puddle on the floor.

"Well, shit," Molly chokes out.

We whip our eyes to hers as she fans herself, trying to fight off her tears. I should have known this might happen. A few days ago, I walked into her house and found her bawling because of an animal cruelty prevention commercial. It took over an hour to finally get her to stop crying.

"That may be the sweetest thing you've ever said to anyone."

Noah shakes his head as he pulls her against him, laughing at his overly emotional fiancée. To anyone else, this entire scenario would seem odd, but we've always been an odd group. It's what makes our bond so strong. We all came from less than optimal beginnings, but we persevered and survived. All our friendships have, too.

I allow the moment to linger for a while before I straighten my expression, becoming serious. "But I don't want one word of this getting out." I smile at Drew, who gives me a reassuring nod, telling me he's in agreement. "Not yet anyway," I add, addressing everyone once more. "Wes is still in Dubai for a few more days. He deserves to learn the truth face to face, not over the phone. So while Drew and I have finally discussed a future between us, we haven't..." I trail off, cringing, unsure how to say this.

"Fucked?" Molly suggests.

Gigi shoots her a pointed glare.

"What? I'm just trying to help her out a little." She returns her eyes to me. "Right? You guys haven't screwed yet?"

I swallow hard, wondering how we went from telling Charlotte the truth about her parentage to discussing my sex life in just a few hours. "That's correct." I lift my eyes back to Drew's momentarily. "We don't want to start this until we both have a clean slate. Until I do..."

"And you will on Friday, correct?" Molly presses.

"That's the plan." I fidget with my hands, nerves settling in my stomach at the prospect of welcoming Wes home, then breaking his heart.

She immediately shifts her attention to Drew. "I'll take the girls Friday night. That way, you two can be as loud as you want. Hell, you can ride him so hard you break the bed frame. Trust me. It's easier than you think."

"Molly..." I lower my head, embarrassed.

"Never a dull moment with you." Noah laughs. At this point, he's probably used to her lack of brain-to-mouth filter.

She tilts back her head, meeting his eyes. "And you love that about me."

"Yes. Yes, I do." He leans down, treating her to a sweet kiss. I sigh, longing for the day when I'll finally be able to do that with Drew for everyone to see.

As if he's thinking the same thing, he pulls me even closer

to him. "Soon," he murmurs, the promise in that one word causing me to sigh again.

"Well, we shouldn't intrude any longer," Gigi says, her voice strong. She heads toward Drew and clasps his face in her hands. "I'm happy for you, my darling boy."

I watch their interaction, my heart full. I adore how close this family is, how close they've always been, even through all their difficulties. I've never gotten that feeling from Wes. The few family dinners I attended when Wes and I visited Atlanta seemed more like a board meeting than a gathering of loved ones. It's not Wes' fault his family is the way they are, but for a girl who grew up with barely any relatives, I've always imagined marrying into a large, rambunctious family. As I beam at Drew, I wonder if I'll finally get my wish.

After we all say our goodbyes and Drew and I are alone, he turns to me. The caring, easy-going man he was moments ago is a distant memory. In its place is another Drew, one who's wanton, lustful…wild. Butterflies dance in my stomach at the heat in his eyes as they rake over every inch of me. I swallow hard, instinct taking over as I step back. But with each retreat, he advances toward me until I hit the wall, unable to escape. I don't want to. I never want to walk away from him. I've made peace with the past hurt he's caused me, the past hurt I've caused him. We're exactly where we're meant to be.

He places his hands on the wall behind me, leaning on them. With each inch he erases between us, my heart rate increases, drumming a thunderous rhythm. There's so much need, so much want, so much passion. I want to pinch myself, this reminiscent of a dream I've had for too long now. It reminds me of the way he looked at me all those years ago at Brody Carmichael's party.

After what seems like a torturously long time, his lips land on mine. I exhale into him, the sensation of his mouth moving with mine the only thing that seems to make sense these days. He pushes his hard body against mine, his hunger for me unmistakable in the way he holds me, cradles me, devours me. I've never felt so coveted, so desired, so craved as I do when I'm with him.

"Stay," he whispers in almost the same tone he used before. This time, it's even more sinful and wicked.

"I'm here."

He pulls back, shaking his head. "No. The night. Don't go."

I swallow hard at the intensity in his gaze. "We agreed we'd wait until—"

He erases my protest with a kiss, then tears away. "No. Not that. I just…" He briefly closes his eyes. I see so much pain and vulnerability, a stark juxtaposition to the hunger he wore mere seconds ago. It's similar to the expression he had the night I found him drunk and brought him into my bedroom. "I need you. I want to fall asleep with you in my arms. That's all. We won't do anything. I respect you too much to put you in any position that will make you uncomfortable."

I search his eyes, opening and closing my mouth. The idea of falling asleep surrounded by Drew's embrace is incredibly inviting. I couldn't deny him that night all those years ago. I can't deny him now, either, even if we are pushing the boundaries too much. After what Drew's been through the past few weeks, especially tonight, he needs to feel loved. He needs to feel my love.

"Okay."

"Okay?" he repeats, surprised.

"Yes." I bring my hand to his face, running my fingers along his stubble. "I'll spend the night with you."

His shoulders visibly relax as he leans his forehead against mine. "Thank you."

Before I utter another word, he grabs my hand, leading me up the stairs and into his bedroom. A bout of nerves rushes over me when I cross the threshold and lay my eyes on his bed, so much promise and fear in that one piece of furniture. My adolescent anxiety comes rushing back, doubt filling me, my body becoming taut.

"Brooklyn?" Drew's voice is sweet as he senses my unease. "What is it?"

Staring at the floor, I ask the same question I did the night

138

we first kissed. "What if I'm not enough for you?"

It's stupid, but after a lifetime of being constantly disappointed, I've learned if something seems too good to be true, it usually is. I've struggled my entire life to live up to everyone's expectations of me. What if I don't measure up to the fantasy in Drew's head?

He grasps my chin, forcing my gaze back to his. "What makes you think you're not?"

I push out a laugh. "I've seen the women you've dated, Drew." I gesture to my body. "I'm not it. I'm, like, a complete one-eighty from your type. I'm not petite, blonde, and shaped like a toothpick. I mean, I'm in good shape, but—"

In an instant, his hand is on my lower back and he tugs me against him. "Did you ever stop to consider there was a reason I dated the women I did?"

Words escape me in response to his powerful tone.

"I thought being with someone who was your polar opposite would help me forget." His voice is soft as he runs the pad of his thumb along my lower lip.

"But you couldn't."

His mouth turns into a small smile. "Never. And for the record…" He brings his lips to my neck, peppering soft kisses along my skin. "You've always been more than enough. All those other women… They've never been able to hold a candle to you, my beautiful Brooklyn Rose. And in just a few more days, you will be mine. Forever."

"I like the sound of forever," I murmur as I lose myself in him once more, a slave to his touch.

"Me, too."

CHAPTER SIXTEEN

DREW

INHALE A DEEP breath as the light of dawn filters into my bedroom, rousing me from the first night of restful sleep I've had in a long time. Everything's right in the world, despite the obstacles facing me with Alyssa and Charlotte. As I nuzzle my face in Brooklyn's tousled hair while she sleeps peacefully in my arms, I'm certain we'll make it through this. How could we not when I have this amazing woman by my side?

"Morning," Brooklyn murmurs.

"Morning," I respond in a raspy voice, pulling her into me, my front to her back. There's no denying how much I want her right now. This waiting is agonizing. How am I going to survive another five days?

"Down boy," she jokes as I rub against her.

Groaning, I push her onto her back, hovering over her. "I can't control myself around you." I bring my lips to hers, kissing her tenderly.

"You won't have to for much longer." She runs her fingers up and down my back, her nails digging into my flesh. Her touch jumpstarts my heart, causing an electric current to flow from my head to my toes, no place on my body unaffected. Our kiss becomes more intense, and she wraps her long legs around me, a rhythmic pulsing, the heat of her more addicting than any drug.

"Just a few more days," I remind myself before pressing my lips back to hers.

"Just a few more days." Her breathy voice is evidence she's struggling with control as much as I am. "And I have a feeling they'll be the longest few days in the history of time."

I pulse against her, burying my head in her neck. "That may be the understatement of the century."

When my teeth scrape against her skin, she moans, needy,

140

wanton, husky. Her fingers dig deeper into my back, increasing my craving to taste, to possess, to consume every part of her.

"Have I told you how much I've fantasized about this?" My voice is low, seductive, tongue trailing along her jawline. My scruffy chin grazes her flesh, her hold on me tightening. I would have thought she'd prefer me without a beard. I've seen the men she's dated, every one of them clean cut, not a single strand of hair out of place. Then again, I dated women who were the polar opposite of Brooklyn. I suppose she did the same.

"Tell me again," she whimpers as my teeth tug on her earlobe.

"I've fantasized about this for years, about making you come harder and faster than you thought possible."

I move to her lips, my mouth poised on hers, about to kiss her in a way that leaves no question as to how deep my need for her runs, when her alarm rips through the space, breaking the moment. She pushes against me, reaching for her phone.

"Don't," I beg.

"I have to. Your girls will be getting up soon. I can't be here when that happens. Not yet." She arches a brow and I sigh, reluctantly rolling off her.

She grabs her cell and silences it, about to stand when I wrap an arm around her waist, forcing her back against me.

"Drew," she scolds, but her tone's playful.

"Five more minutes," I plead, my voice bordering on whining.

"And how will you explain to your young, impressionable daughters why a woman they consider their aunt is sharing a bed with their father?"

I trace a finger down the curvature of her body, my touch sending a shiver through her. Still, she doesn't attempt to shrug me off or get out of bed. "That their auntie Brook cast her spell on me years ago and I'm done fighting it. You devil woman, you." I clamp my teeth on her neck, squeezing her nipple through the oversized t-shirt I gave her to sleep in, which causes her to yelp.

141

"Am I going to have to spend the next five days rejecting your advances?" Her words come out as a needy moan.

My hand disappears under her shirt, roaming her stomach, grazing her chest before landing on her throat. Applying minimal pressure, I force her head against me, a tiny whimper escaping her.

"You're doing a horrible job of that right now."

"I didn't say it would be easy. In fact, I have a feeling it'll be extremely hard." She grinds against me, my grip on her tightening, raw need making me throb. "And with every day, it will most likely get harder…" Reaching behind her, she sensually runs her fingers through my hair. "And harder." Her nails dig into my scalp. The mixture of pleasure and pain blinds me to everything but feeling every inch of her.

Loosening my grip on her neck, my hand journeys down her body, memorizing every curve, every dip, every valley. Savoring the way her hips move and thighs clench. Relishing in everything that is Brooklyn.

With a growl, I roll onto my back, bringing her on top of me, forcing her to straddle me so she can feel how much I need her. What I wouldn't give to rid ourselves of our clothes that are a rather unwelcome barrier.

Moving with the rhythm I set, she parts her lips and closes eyes, her nails burrowing into my chest. "Drew…" The way she utters my name is a mixture of a warning and a moan.

"Tell me you want me."

She takes her lower lip between her teeth, her breathing becoming heavy.

"Brooklyn, look at me."

Her eyes fling open, dark, wanton, hungry.

I dig my hand into her hair, forcing her mouth within a breath of mine. "Tell me you want this, that you want me inside you."

My words make her motions increase, the friction almost impossible to bear.

"I shouldn't," she mewls.

"But you do." It's not a question.

"I do."

142

"Then say it."

"Fuck," she exhales, circling her hips against me with greater urgency. "I want you inside me."

"God, that's hot." I crush her lips to mine, my tongue plunging into her mouth. The way she holds her breath makes it clear she's close to unraveling. I pull her even tighter against me, oblivious to everything else…until I hear the familiar sound of small feet padding down the hallway.

"Shit," I whisper.

Brooklyn inhales sharply, her eyes wide. She looks from me to the door, then quickly shoots off me, scanning the room in a panic. She zeros in on the closet and darts to it.

"You don't have to hide," I insist, running my hand over my face.

"Yes, I do."

"Brooklyn…"

She whirls around. I expect her to agree that she's being overly concerned regarding this. Instead, she rushes over to grab her phone and clothes before darting back into the closet, the door closing just as the one to my bedroom opens.

A deer caught in the headlights, I fling my eyes to the doorway where my two girls stand. I draw in a deep breath, my heart still racing from the rush of Brooklyn on top of me, her perfect body so close to falling over the edge. I wonder if this is the universe's way of making us put on the brakes, of telling us it's too much, too fast.

"Oh man…" Charlotte pouts. "You're awake already."

"Is everything okay?" Alyssa asks, her inquisitive eyes scanning the bedroom, landing on the side of the bed Brooklyn slept on to see the covers rumpled. I usually only sleep on one side of my king-sized bed. When I notice her focus zeroing in on the opposite side, I smooth the comforter.

"I was restless last night and tossed and turned," I say to explain away the disarray of my bed.

Both girls remain frozen in place, analyzing me for what seems like an eternity.

"Okay. Enough standing around." I fling my covers off and rush toward them, swooping them into my arms. Alyssa protests, trying to tell me she's too old for this, but Charlotte squeals with joy, the sound warming my heart, giving me hope the news I shared with her won't affect her like I feared it would. "Time to get ready for school."

I steal a glance at the door to my closet as I walk out and carry them to the opposite side of the house, depositing them in Alyssa's room. When I'm confident she has things under control with getting herself and her little sister ready, I close the door to her room, my steps quick as I make my way back down the long hallway. Safe in my room, I shut the door behind me, blowing out a breath.

"That was close," Brooklyn comments as she hurriedly yanks her jeans up her legs.

"I hate having to sneak around with you." I head toward her and grip her hip, pulling her into my body. She's warm and soft. "Hate having to hide you."

"It's only for a few more days." She meets my eyes as she drapes her arms over my shoulders, bringing her lips to mine. It's a brief kiss, but still deep and fulfilling.

"Come on," I say when she steps away to finish dressing. "I bought you a few minutes to make your escape." Linking my fingers with hers, I pull her from the bedroom, our steps quiet as we pad down the stairs.

Brooklyn opens the front door, hurrying to disappear before the girls come barreling down the stairs, but I pull her against me. Addicted to her lips, my mouth finds hers.

"Last night was the best night I've had in a long time," I whisper. "It was exactly what I needed."

I feel her lips turn up into a grin. "Me, too."

I deepen the kiss, my hand going to her ass and squeezing. "God, I love your ass."

Her smile only grows as she places her hand on my chest, pushing me away. "Don't start something you can't finish."

"Oh, I can finish." I waggle my eyebrows at her.

She shakes her head, laughing as she frees herself from me, heading toward her car.

"Brooklyn," I whisper-shout.

She glances over her shoulder.

"I have a few meetings downtown and the girls have dance tonight. Meet me at the beach at seven?" I arch a brow. "Like old times?"

She bites her lower lip, pure, untainted joy crossing her expression. I can't remember the last time I saw her this happy. "I'd like that."

I beam, unable to hide how absolutely exhilarated I am over the mere idea of spending more time with Brooklyn.

"Goodbye, Drew."

When she's about to duck into her car, I dart toward her. She's taken by complete surprise as I yank her against me one last time, my kiss ravenous and eager.

"I love you." I gradually pull back, leaving a kiss on her nose. "So much."

"I love you, too," she murmurs. "So much."

CHAPTER SEVENTEEN

DREW

"ANDREW," A SOOTHING FEMALE voice says as I enter the cozy office in Boston's Back Bay. "Thank you so much for taking the time to meet with me today." Alice smiles at me warmly.

"No, thank you."

She gestures down the hallway and I walk beside her toward her office. I can't help but smile as I recall how much has changed since the last time I walked this path, Brooklyn at my side. At the time, I was just grateful she didn't kick me out when I barged into her office, begging for help. Never in a million years could I have imagined we'd be where we are, days from finally being together.

Once I enter the office, Alice gestures to a small sitting area, steering me from the formality of the desk where we spoke at our last meeting. I sit down, rubbing the back of my neck, praying she has some good news.

"So, tell me," she says, lowering herself onto the love seat, "How are the girls doing? You mentioned you planned to tell them this past weekend."

"Yes." My legs bounce as I run my hands down my pants. I wish I had asked Brooklyn to be here with me, but she's already stressed about her caseload as it is. I didn't want to add to that any more than I already have. "They took the news alarmingly well. Based on your and Brooklyn's advice, I spoke to the counselor at the girls' school to inform her of the situation."

"Good."

"I expected Charlotte to handle the news badly, but she's bouncing back."

"And Alyssa?" She arches a brow.

I blow out a long breath, tugging on my tie. "It's too early to tell with Alyssa. She says she's okay, but… I don't know. She's not her usual self. I want to say she's just having an off day, but I don't think that's it."

Alice nods, assessing this news. "Alyssa is older. She probably has some memories of her mother. This may bring up some of those memories of being abandoned that have lain dormant since she left."

"Brooklyn mentioned the same thing. She reached out to a child therapist she knows. I have an appointment for both girls to see her this week. We have plans for them to continue seeing her at least once a week to ensure they learn to cope with the changes that are coming. I've cut back my hours at the college. Thankfully, our hockey season is over, so I don't have to worry about all the practices and games. I've also had the assistant coaches take over the scouting trips I had planned. Right now, it's more important that I stick around for my girls."

"Good. That will all work in your favor. We want to demonstrate you're a constant presence in those girls' lives." She smiles, then her expression turns solemn. "Which brings me to the next thing we need to discuss." She opens a file folder sitting on the coffee table and hands me what appears to be a court pleading. "This is our response to the request for custody modification. Now, it's standard procedure to go through mediation first, as you're probably aware from your divorce. In family law cases, you usually only see a judge if the parties can't come to any agreement after multiple mediation sessions. This motion will still be filed and a court date set, which is when we'll meet with the mediator, unless the parties can come to an agreement beforehand." She pauses as her gaze rakes over me, hesitant. "I believe it's in our best interest to offer Carla visitation with both girls."

"What?" I shoot back, eyes wide, muscles tense. "No. Absolutely not. I swore I'd never let her hurt them again."

"I understand your frustration," Alice replies calmly. "But they're her kids, too. The court will only refuse visitation to a biological parent in the instance of abuse or severe neglect."

"I'd say abandoning them for six years would qualify as

severe neglect," I mutter under my breath. I knew this was a likelihood. I even implied as much when I told the girls the truth. But I thought we'd fight harder, not offer them on a silver platter right off the bat. I want to see that Carla truly does want to be a part of their lives, that she'll do whatever it takes to spend time with them. How will I know that's the case if we agree to her demands immediately?

"You may, but the court won't, not when she left them in the care of someone who is exceedingly capable. And you want the court to consider you more than capable of caring for those children, considering that's going to help you maintain at least partial custody of Charlotte. Agreeing to visitation will also help to that end."

I grind my teeth at the idea of sharing these girls with Carla. For the past six years, it's just been us. I can't imagine having to drop them off for weekends with their mother, walking into a lifeless house, waking up to something other than their excited squeals and giggles.

"I'm not suggesting we allow the girls to spend extended periods of time with her. Not right away. They don't know her. To begin with, we'll agree to supervised visitations at pre-arranged times with you present. However, there needs to be a plan in place to slowly allow her unsupervised time with the girls once an assessment has been made and a neutral party at DCF determines she's capable of caring for them."

I bite my lip, my face heating, my muscles constricting. Sensing my frustration, Alice reaches across the coffee table, clutching my hand in hers. I fling my gaze to her.

"I understand you're angry at your ex for abandoning you. And none of this will change your request for non-parental custody of Charlotte. We will still do everything to keep her under your care, even if that custody is split with your ex. But in my experience, putting into motion a plan to grant her time with her own children is the best option to get all parties on the path to healing. Those girls should have the opportunity to get to know their mother, don't you think? Don't you think everyone deserves a second chance?"

I swallow hard at her words. As much as I want to say no,

I can't, not when I've been granted my own second chance, one I've been yearning for. I like to think I've changed since my hockey days. Maybe Carla has, too.

"If you truly think this is the best option, I'll defer to your judgment." My voice is low as I pray this is the right course of action. I know the law's on Carla's side. It doesn't make it any easier, though.

* * *

Having spent more time going over strategy with Alice than I originally planned, I find myself running to my next meeting. I hurry through the lobby of the tall building in the Financial District, rushing into a waiting elevator. As I ride up to the thirtieth floor, I check my watch. Quarter after six. The second the elevator doors open and I step into the posh reception area, the woman sitting behind the extravagant desk greets me with a smile.

"Mr. Brinks, so wonderful to see you again."

I should remember her name, but it's been quite a few years since I've come here. It's been quite a few years since I needed to be here. Usually, the endorsement and commentating gigs haven't been of such a huge magnitude as to require me to sit down with my agent. But the opportunity to be head coach for the Bruins is a different offer, one that could increase my salary to a comfortable seven figures a year.

"You, as well."

"Mr. Acosta is expecting you." She stands, heading around the desk toward me. "I'll show you in."

"Thank you."

She smiles, then turns toward the hallway to her right, walking with purpose. I follow her down the long corridor. Everything is glass and light, modern colors. Framed pictures of the biggest names in sports hang on the walls, a photographic résumé of the stars Daniel Acosta has represented over the years, myself included. It's a name you hear often when you're first climbing the ladder in professional sports. You hope for the day he'll agree to meet with you, let alone cold-call with an offer to represent you, which was what happened with me.

The day after the game that changed my career, turning me from a player who rarely saw any ice time to a household name overnight, I received a phone call from this man. At first, I thought it was just a joke, a friend playing a prank on me. Sure enough, it was Daniel Acosta wanting to represent me, saying if I signed with him, he'd set me up with endorsement deals that could net me another several million a year. Although I had to leave the game six years ago, he's kept those endorsement deals coming in, pocketing himself a nice fifteen percent.

Over the years, he's proven himself to be reliable, trustworthy, and honest, advising me against some offers, regardless that it would earn him some money. He's always looked out for what's best for me, which was why he was the first call I made when the manager of the Bruins reached out a few weeks ago, asking for a meeting to discuss coaching the team. It's not something he's typically involved in, but I trust him to steer me in the right direction, to tell me if I'm making a colossal mistake.

The blonde receptionist knocks on the large wooden door at the end of the hallway before opening it.

"Mr. Acosta, Mr. Brinks has arrived." She steps aside, allowing me to enter the lush office.

It's an enormous space, decorated in understated elegance. A large desk sits in front of an expanse of floor-to-ceiling windows overlooking the city skyline. The rest of the room contains a sitting area with a couch, love seat, and a few chairs, as well as a wet bar. But the most impressive part of this office is the wall that's made up entirely of dozens of TV screens, each one showing a different game, from European soccer, to college softball, to the Celtics game. This isn't even his main office. His offices in New York and Los Angeles are double the size of this one, with an even more impressive video wall.

"Andrew!" Daniel bellows, standing from the couch where he's currently sitting, sipping on an amber liquid. "So good to see you."

"Thanks for meeting with me. I apologize for being late. My last meeting ran longer than I expected. Then traffic getting here was crazy because of the Celtics game tonight." I gesture to one of the large panels displaying tonight's pre-game show.

"No worries. It gave me a chance to look over the contract Pat Winters sent over. Shall we?" Daniel gestures to the chair at the head of the coffee table, the love seat on one side, the couch on the other. "Drink?"

"No. I'm fine." I sit, steeling myself for what I must do. If this meeting had occurred a few weeks ago, the outcome would have been different. But things have changed. It doesn't make it any easier to turn down what amounts to any former hockey player's dream job.

"I understand Parker Hobbs spoke with you about why Winters has been trying to get a meeting with you these past several months."

"He did," I say, rubbing my hands along my pants. "Probably wants to make sure he still has a job after this season."

My response garners a polite laugh from Daniel. I study him, a predator in his natural habitat. Crisp designer suit, a Rolex on his wrist, and shoes made by someone whose name I can't even pronounce. It's all about appearances with him. The more expensive the clothes, the easier it is to get what you want. While I shaved and put on a suit, I still feel underdressed compared to him.

"Well, I've had a chance to look at the offer," Daniel says, reaching for a large stack of papers. "It is quite attractive." He glances at me. "And lucrative. One of the highest coaching offers I've seen."

"No. The highest," I correct.

"Ah. So you've done your homework." His mouth turns into a smirk. "Winters is serious and motivated, as evidenced by the high salary and generous stipend for travel expenses and a car, among other benefits."

"It's everything I've wanted since I was forced into

151

retirement."

A solemn expression crosses his face as he nods. It doesn't matter that it's been six years. It's a game those in hockey circles often speak about, especially those who were there, like Daniel was.

"Then I recommend accepting. There's nothing in this that stands out as being fishy. This is genuine, the offer of a lifetime."

"I know." I pinch my lips together, my head hanging.

"But?" He arches a brow, sensing my hesitation.

"But I'm not sure the timing is right."

"How could it not be? I understand the team's approached you in the past with assistant coaching positions. I can see how those may not be as attractive to you, especially with the lower salary, but this... Head coach? I figured you'd have a boner over the prospect."

"I'll be honest. A year ago...hell, a month ago, I would have jumped at the opportunity, but things are...different now."

"Different? Different how?"

I scrape my hand through my hair, biting the inside of my cheek. "There have been a few recent developments in my personal life that require my full attention." When he wrinkles his brow, I embellish. "It involves my kids."

"Is everything okay?"

I readjust my posture in the chair, straightening my spine. "I haven't told many people, but seeing as you've been so gracious as to take the time and meet with me, you deserve an explanation." I pause, licking my lips. "The truth is, I'm about to be embroiled in what I can only imagine to be an ugly custody battle with Carla."

"I thought she gave you full custody when she left." Rubbing his chin, confusion clouds his expression. Other than my immediate family, he's one of the few people who knows the nitty-gritty details of my divorce.

I nod. "She did. I haven't heard from her in years. But she's back and wants to be part of their lives after not having so much as picked up the phone to call in all this time. That I could deal with, I suppose. She is their mother. Mine ran out on us and never attempted to reconnect. At least Carla's trying."

"But?" Daniel presses.

I rub my temples, sighing. "I just found out Charlotte, the youngest, isn't even mine. So she's asking for shared physical custody of Alyssa and full physical custody of Charlotte. She lied, said she was mine, when this entire time she knew she was—"

"Chase Gardner's," he finishes, putting the pieces together. Although he's my agent, he's always clued in on the players' lives, including mine. Hell, the fact my wife left me for Chase Gardner, the man who took my place on the ice just weeks after I officially announced my retirement, was all over the headlines.

"Exactly. So as much as I'd love to say yes, I don't know if I can. Not right now. I need to put all my effort into making sure those girls stay with me. I'm afraid taking a job that would require extensive traveling may work against me."

Daniel slumps into his chair, absorbing what I've just told him. The mood in the room is more somber than anything. "What can I do to help? Do you need a lawyer?"

"No. One of my good friends works for DCF. She knew who to go see. Granted, she's not a big shot like Carla's lawyer, but I don't care about that. All I care about is having someone represent me who will fight for my rights. So far, she has been."

"Wait a minute." Daniel shakes his head. "Carla has a big shot lawyer?"

"Yeah. It seemed odd to me, too. I haven't kept tabs. Maybe they're doing it pro bono or something. Based on the financials that came with the petition for custody, she's not exactly making a lot of money."

He ponders this for a moment as he pinches his chin between his thumb and forefinger. I can see the wheels spinning in his head, which is never a good thing. "Who's her lawyer?" he asks finally.

"I don't remember off the top of my head." I reach into

my pocket, retrieving my phone. After scrolling through my emails, I find the one with the attached PDF of the petition. Opening the file, I look at the heading. "Hollis and Galloway."

Daniel blinks repeatedly. "Are you sure about that?"

"Of course." I show him the screen. "Says it right there, doesn't it? I may have been knocked on the head a few times, but I can still read," I joke.

"Huh." He stares off into the distance, not laughing. He's usually an easy-going guy, except in negotiations. He likes to be everyone's best friend, as long as you give him what he wants. He's a typical agent, able to smile and schmooze even the most standoffish person. "You'd think there'd be some sort of conflict of interest. There's certainly the appearance of one."

I scrunch my brows. "I'm not sure I follow."

"Graham Hollis," he urges, his tone indicating I should know what he's talking about.

"Sorry." I blink, still just as confused, the name not ringing any bells. "Am I supposed to know who that is, other than someone who's a partner at the firm Carla hired?"

"Yeah, you should. You've been dating Skylar Jensen, correct?"

My curiosity only increases with this line of questioning, a ball of dread forming in the pit of my stomach. "I'm not so sure I'd classify it as dating, but yeah. We were seeing each other off and on over the past several months. I broke things off a few weeks ago."

"Graham Hollis is her step-brother. He's an agent, as well as a sports and entertainment lawyer. In the past few years, he's branched out into a little family law, mainly representing their clients in divorces since these things can be more complicated than a typical divorce."

My jaw grows slack as I process this piece of information, trying to figure out what it means. A sinking feeling settles in my core, heat washing over my face, my mind reeling.

"I'm surprised you didn't know that," he continues when I remain silent. "Hell, that's how she got that gig with the

Celtics. It certainly wasn't because she's a talented dancer. Rumor is there's a little Cruel Intentions vibe going on between the two of them. It's a bit off-putting, but based on what I've observed, Graham will do anything his step-sister asks of him. And I do mean anything."

I rewind to the last time I spoke to Skylar, recalling who showed up at my office just a few minutes after she made her dramatic departure when I told her I wasn't interested in a serious relationship, using my kids as an excuse. My stomach churns, bile rising in my throat, a sour taste in my mouth.

"She... She's behind this."

"Who?"

"Skylar." I swallow hard. "She came to my office, saying she wanted to take our relationship to the next level, one I had absolutely no interest in. Instead of leaving it at that, I said my kids were my priority, that as long as I was still responsible for them I wouldn't date her...or anyone, for that matter."

I bury my head in my hands, wondering how I didn't put two and two together. At first, I thought the universe was merely playing a cruel joke on me. Now I wonder if there's more to it than that. If this is all the result of two scorned women getting their revenge.

Slowly lifting my eyes back to his, I continue. "No more than a couple seconds after Skylar stormed out, Carla stopped by, asking for visitation with the girls. Hell!" I slam my fist on the side table, my temper rising. "They probably passed each other in the damn hallway!"

"So you think...?"

"It makes sense, doesn't it?" I jump to my feet, pacing, tugging on my hair. "Every time Skylar brought up taking things to the next level, I always told her I wasn't interested in a relationship, that I couldn't put my girls through that. What if..." I stop in my tracks, trying to make sense of this in my scrambled mind. "What if the two of them came up with this plan together? Carla gets time with the girls, and somewhere in Skylar's fucked-up mind, she thinks it paves her way to having a relationship with me."

My blood boiling more with every word I speak, I grit my

jaw, pacing once more. It's just a theory, but it couldn't have been simply a coincidence that they both paid me a visit on the same exact day, at almost the same exact time.

In an instant, everything's changed. I'm no longer thinking about anything else. Not of Alice's recommendation to come to an agreement with Carla. Not of the fact that in just a few days, I'll be able to announce to the world that I'm in love with Brooklyn. All of that seems insignificant to getting to the truth, to learning if my gut is right. That I brought this on myself.

"I need to talk to Skylar." I glance at the time, seeing it's a quarter to seven, and curse my luck. "Shit. There's a game tonight." I look at the screen showing the pre-game show, spying one of the tall basketball players whose photo hangs on Daniel's wall of fame. A plan formulating, I whip my eyes toward him, hope building inside me. "Some of your clients play for the Celtics, right?"

"Yes," he replies guardedly, his brow wrinkled in confusion. Then realization crosses his face. He blows out a breath, resigned. "Fine. I'll get you into the game. You'd better not start throwing punches around the dancers, though," he warns. "Some of those girls are my clients, too, and they have modeling contracts that will be canceled in the event of a broken nose."

"I won't. As much as she may deserve it, I'd never hit a woman."

Daniel stands, buttoning his suit jacket. "If Skylar's behind this, she definitely deserves it."

CHAPTER EIGHTEEN

DREW

THERE'S A FRENZIED ATMOSPHERE around the Garden as Daniel's chauffeur pulls in front of it, dropping us off in the VIP area. Sometimes it's good to know people with connections, like Daniel. Name the sport and he can get you amazing seats with just a simple phone call, even moments before the game begins.

"You know this will raise some eyebrows, right?" he says as he ushers me through the roped off area, handing me a lanyard with COURT on the pass. He hangs his around his neck. I do the same.

Since I retired, I've been here dozens of times, but the Garden has a different vibe during basketball games. Yes, there are still thousands of fans wearing jerseys, sloshing beer everywhere as they cheer for their team, sometimes to the point of getting into a physical altercation with a fan who's supporting the opposing team, but it's a different feeling when the arena is covered in polished maple instead of ice. There's no chill in the air, no sound of the blades cutting into ice, no lights flashing as adrenaline rushes through you when they're about to announce your name.

"What do you mean?"

"It's public knowledge Bruins management has been after you to coach for years. When people see you sitting courtside with your agent, they're going to talk. What are you going to tell them?"

"What I always do. That it's none of their damn business," I bark, my tone harsher than I intended. It's taking all my control not to storm into the green room and seek out Skylar right now. If Daniel weren't here with me, I probably would do just that, despite the fact I wouldn't have been able to get in without him. He talked a bit of sense and reason into me during the drive down here, advised me to sit in the stands and smile at Skylar when she looks my way during her routines, let her think I've changed my mind. If she sees the anger inside, her defenses will kick in. This isn't my normal style, but it might work. Daniel's made a career out of always getting exactly what he wants, all because of his ability to read people.

"And this, my friend, is why I take the percentage I do. The damage control I used to have to do for you is the reason I have gray hair." He laughs, gesturing to two seats in the row right behind where the team sits.

"I've been a walk in the park the past several years, yet you're still getting your cut. Let's call it even."

"Deal." He grins, nodding and smiling at a few people sitting around us. Everyone always seems to know Daniel. I've never gone anywhere without at least one person approaching him. When I first became a household name, I loved when people would clamber up to me for an autograph. It quickly got old, especially when I couldn't even have a drink alone to decompress after a rough game. I don't know how Daniel still deals with it. I suppose it's part of the job. Then again, he has the personality to always be the center of attention. I don't.

The instant we take our seats, music blares, the cheers and screams deafening as the dancers run onto the court. I tense when I spot Skylar in the front row of their formation, smiling, pretending she doesn't have a care in the world, acting as if she's not responsible for tearing my family apart. My jaw hardens as I glower at her.

Daniel nudges my side and I whip my head around. When he lifts his brows as a reminder, I relax my posture, plastering a fake smile on my face. At first, I wonder if Skylar will even notice me in the crowd. She has no reason to search for me. I'm quickly proven wrong when her eyes land on mine. She's surprised, perhaps confused. Then she recovers, a seductive smirk building on her plump, red lips, her beckoning gaze remaining locked with mine as she goes through her routine.

During our "relationship", I never watched her perform. I told her repeatedly I had no interest in attending one of her games, considering basketball isn't my sport. But as I watch her, I see what Daniel implied earlier. She's not that great, her lack of talent obvious when I look at the other dancers. I wonder how many people she had to sleep with to get picked for the squad. I wonder how many people her step-brother slept with to get her this job.

Thankfully, the display of gyrating hips and shaking butts soon ends and the announcers go through the process of introducing the players. With each name, the crowd cheers a little louder, a little more enthusiastically. It brings back memories of my time on the ice, the way the rafters shook when my name was announced.

"You miss it, don't you?" Daniel turns to me.

"Miss what?" I glance at him, doing my best to hide the longing on my face. I look at my feet, knowing all too well that just beneath this flooring is the ice I miss so much, the ice I'd give anything to skate on again. But it'll never happen, not unless I want to risk a brain injury I'll never recover from.

"Thousands of strangers cheering for you."

I shrug dismissively, looking back at the court, but not paying attention to what's happening. "It's overrated. People forget about you the instant someone new comes along."

"That's not true. Look around you." He gestures to the crowd sitting close to us. I meet several pairs of curious eyes, people whispering to each other. "These are basketball fans, yet the majority of them know who you are. You think people forgot, but they haven't. Sure, there are some players who are forgotten the instant they disappear from the game, but not you. You're different. You left your mark on that sport. Hell, on this city. You never noticed it, but I did. You should have seen the crowd gathered outside MGH and along the promenade by the Charles when you were injured. They were out there for days, Andrew. Days. I get that having to walk away from the sport hurt you. I've seen it before. But the sport, the league, was everything to you." He lowers his passionate voice, his tone becoming more pleading. He's not just saying this so he'll make a buck. He has nothing to gain if I take this offer. He's saying it because, in his heart, he knows I need this. "It can be that way again."

I open my mouth, about to repeat the same argument I gave him earlier.

He holds up a hand. "I know what you're going to say. You need to put your girls first. Maybe there's a way to balance your family and your career."

"I don't see how, not with what Carla's trying to do. They want an answer before the end of this season so they can announce it."

"Remember what I told you during our first meeting?"

"You said a lot of things during our first meeting. I couldn't get you to shut up," I joke.

"True. No one can." He winks before his expression turns serious once more. "But I told you the same thing I tell all my clients. Everything is negotiable. Management wants you to coach so badly, they're offering you more than any other coach has ever made. In the entire league. I'm pretty sure they'll agree to an extension if you need more time to get your answers."

I shake my head. "I don't know…"

"Remember the rush of skating on that ice and hearing people cheering your name? You can have that again. You can do what you love again. You don't have to waste your talent on coaching college, as admirable as that is. You belong in the big leagues. We all know it. When are you going to realize it?"

I meet Daniel's eyes. "When I know I won't lose my girls. Until then…"

He gestures to where Skylar's standing at the edge of the court, smiling at me. She sticks her chest out a little more, pouting her lips, batting her eyelashes. The only thing it does for me is increase my anger.

"Hopefully, you'll soon have information that will prove Carla's anything but a fit mother, especially if Skylar admits they concocted this scheme together." He leans toward me. "If I were you, I'd set your phone to record the audio when you talk to her."

"Thank you, counselor." I wink.

"That's why you pay me the big bucks. To look out for

your best interests."

* * *

The game seems to drag on as I watch what feels like a ping-pong match. I suppose the same could be said about hockey, but at least we give our fans a little more entertainment value with the occasional fights that break out.

About halfway through the second quarter, Daniel nudges me, nodding toward the dancers. Most of them file off the court, presumably to get ready for their halftime routine. Skylar doesn't follow them. Instead, she heads toward me, smirking.

"Well, if it isn't Andrew Brinks," she coos, placing her hands on her hips. The mere sound of her voice grates on my nerves, but instead of acting like that's the case, I grin, licking my lips. I need to get her alone so we can talk. I can't do it here, not with all these people around.

"Hey, Sky," I reply coolly. "Daniel Acosta, this is Skylar Jennings. Skylar, Daniel Acosta."

Daniel extends his hand toward her, smiling congenially. "Pleasure to meet you." Always the charmer, he brings her hand up to his mouth, kissing it.

"You, too. I've heard great things about you. I guess you could say you and my step-brother are competitors."

"Really?" he responds, pretending he doesn't know anything. "And who's that?"

"Graham Hollis."

"Ah, yes. A very formidable negotiator from what I understand."

"That he is." She holds his gaze for a moment. I can almost sense her undressing Daniel with her eyes. It doesn't matter that he's married with kids. That's never stopped her before.

"Do you have a minute to talk?" I say. She whips her eyes to mine, treating me to the same once-over she gave Daniel.

"You finally came to a game just to talk? You know how the phone works, don't you?"

"Of course. But a few of my circumstances have changed, and I didn't want to wait another second to see you," I lie. Just saying those words cuts me open. But if it's necessary in order to protect my girls, I'll do anything it takes.

"Circumstances have changed?"

I rake my eyes over her, pretending I crave her like I once did. Or at least like my dick once did. "They certainly have. And I believe you may benefit from this."

A sly smile crawling on her lips, she reaches for my hand, pulling me from my chair. "Well then, let's talk."

Leering at her, I give off every indication I want to do something other than talk. I have to hand it to Daniel. He was right. If I had gone off on her the second she approached, she would have denied everything. So far, his method is working like a charm. I hope his next piece of advice does, as well, although the idea of what I'm about to do makes my skin crawl.

She leads me onto the court, skirting the out-of-bounds area, heading toward the corridor leading to the locker rooms. People come and go, but at least there's some semblance of privacy. After turning down another long hallway, she pulls me into one of the catering suites. It's empty, since all the VIPs are courtside.

Once we're alone, she turns to me, everything about her predatory. Remembering Daniel's advice to capture the audio, I pull out my phone. The instant I do, my heart drops to the pit of my stomach, my screen filled with text message and voicemail alerts from Brooklyn. I look at the time. 8:15. I completely forgot I was supposed to meet her over an hour ago. Once I learned Skylar may be involved with what Carla's trying to do, my focus was on one thing and one thing only — vindication.

"What is it?" Skylar coos.

I snap back to the present. As much as I need to call Brooklyn to smooth things over, to explain why I didn't show up at the beach when I asked her to meet me there, I can't, not with Skylar standing less than a foot in front of me, analyzing me. Yes, I could have gone straight to Carla with my theory, but she'd never admit to working with Skylar. But Skylar might…especially if I get her in the right mood. I pray Brooklyn will understand. How could she not? She knows I'll do anything for those girls, including this.

I quickly swipe through my screen, hiding it from Skylar as I start the voice recorder, then shove it back into my pocket.

"Nothing." I curve my lips into a smile, inching toward Skylar, my eyes heated, carnal, riddled with forced desire. "Just a text from Daniel reminding me to use a rubber."

She smirks, her eyes lighting up. "So tell me, Andrew…" She tilts her mouth toward mine.

"Yes?"

"What is this changed circumstance you want to discuss? Last time we saw each other, you made it quite clear you hoped to never see me again. Yet here you are."

"Here I am…"

Licking my lips, I stalk toward her, pressing my body against hers until she's backed against the wall. I swallow down my distaste. This is so wrong, so abhorrent, so vile. I pray it's worth this nauseated feeling coursing through me.

"And why are you here?" Her voice is firm, her mouth formed in a hard line.

"To ask for forgiveness. To admit I was wrong. To admit you were right. You could be good for me."

"And what brought you to that conclusion?" She pouts her lips.

"Like I said, I've had a change in circumstance. My ex…" I pause, summoning the willpower to continue with this act, even though the words feel like knives slashing at my skin, scarring, scabbing, torturing. "She's back in the area and asked for shared custody. Turns out, my youngest isn't even mine."

She tilts her head to the side, her eyebrows raised. "She isn't?" Her tone lacks the surprise it should hold when learning something like that. It's more sanctimonious, more smug.

"I figure why should I have to raise a child who isn't even mine? Her mother can deal with that. She thought her request for custody would hurt me. Well, she was wrong." I feign a relieved smile, my shoulders relaxing. "I can finally have a life again. You have no idea how freeing it is. And I want this new life to start with you." I lean closer, her breath dancing with mine. I have to ward off my gut instinct to grimace at the warmth of her.

"Is that really what you want?"

"Do you think I'd be here if it wasn't?" The corners of my mouth turn up. "You know how much I hate basketball."

"That I do," she murmurs as she grips the back of my head, forcing my lips to hers.

I inhale a sharp breath, instinct kicking in, my body wanting to tear away from her. But there's a reason I'm doing this. This is a sacrifice I need to make to get to the truth, to persuade Skylar to tell me that truth.

Moaning, I fist my hand in her hair, plunging my tongue into her mouth, convincing her I'm into her when I want nothing more than to scald my skin and wash my mouth out with the strongest chemical known to man.

"God, it feels good to be doing this again," I murmur before covering her mouth once more, kissing her with more passion and hunger. She arches into me, rubbing her body against mine. I clutch her hips, lifting her up as I press her against the wall. She wraps her legs around my waist, thrusting against me. "I've never felt so damn free, like the chains that have shackled me to a life I never wanted have been severed."

I nip at her neck, my teeth grazing the skin. She tightens her hold on me, throwing her head back, moaning, circling, driving. I know what she likes, what sets her off, what makes her forget where she is, who she is, the secrets she's hiding. And that sweet spot behind her ear drives her absolutely crazy. With prurient motions, I trail a line along her neck toward her earlobe, taking it between my teeth, tugging.

"Oh, Drew." Her voice is breathy as she claws and scratches at me, desperate for me to pull her skirt down and fuck her right here with no regard as to who could walk in on us. "I knew it would work. I just knew it. No man would want to be stuck raising kids. Once I talked Carla into filing for custody, I knew you'd finally be free and we could be together."

It takes every ounce of restraint I possess not to slam her head into the wall.

"You did this?" I say, my tone more intrigued than accusatory. At least, that's how I hope it comes off as I continue kissing her. She's so lost in her own desire she doesn't even realize my dick's as soft as the Pillsbury Doughboy.

"I didn't think it would work, but figured I'd give it a shot, especially when I overheard your conversation that day at the college. She didn't want to agree, said you were a good father, but she changed her mind. Aren't you glad?" Her nails dig into my back as I clamp my teeth onto her neck. She yelps, her body stiffening. Then she moans, thinking I bit her out of wanton desire, not because I want to hurt her just like her actions have hurt me. "Now we can be together with nothing standing in our way. Nothing will ever be in our way again, Andrew. I'll make sure of that. I'll always make sure of that."

I bury my anger, masking it in lust as I grip her hips tighter, grate my teeth against her skin even harsher, my voice becoming a growl as I allow her to keep thrusting against me.

"So you mean to tell me you did all this for me? Helped my ex file for custody so we could finally be together?"

"I told you I'd do anything for you." Her pants become louder, her skin getting warmer. I know her body well enough to tell she's close to coming undone from the friction alone. "That I'd do whatever it took to have you. Nothing is out of bounds when it comes to you, Andrew. Nothing."

"What you did for me…" I quickly pull back, forcing her legs to loosen their grip around me, my eyes hardening, my lips turning into a sneer. "Thank you, Skylar." I smirk, stepping away, retrieving my cell from my pocket. After ending the recording, I text it to Daniel so there's an extra copy.

"Wha—" She's bewildered, confused, her lips turning into a frown.

I hold up my cell. "You've just given me all the evidence I need to show the judge why my ex shouldn't be allowed to come near my kids." I lean into her, all the animosity and distaste I've been forced to hide the past several minutes set free. "Did you honestly think I'd be grateful for what you did? This is a level of fucked up I didn't think anyone was capable of."

She stares at me for several protracted moments, stunned, before her eyes turn fiery.

"What choice did I have?" she screeches. "Those girls are the reason you refused to get serious with me. I figured this would be a win-win for both of us. She'd get to spend time with those kids…God knows why she'd want that…and I'd get you all to myself."

I shake my head, my throat burning, my skin crawling. Has Skylar always been this crazy? She's young. Maybe I mistook some of her craziness for immaturity. But to be so devious and vindictive as to help my ex get custody on the slight chance I'd want to be with her? I wanted to believe Daniel was just running his mouth when he implied she'd been hooking up with her step-brother. Now I think she's deranged enough to do something like that.

"If you thought the only reason I didn't want to be with you was because of those girls, you're more out of touch with reality than I thought. The reason I didn't want to be with you is because I felt nothing for you. You were just a means to an end. Nothing more. I could never fall for someone who treats people, treats children, like they don't matter." The more I speak, the angrier I become, my shoulders hunched, the vein in my neck throbbing. "So you'd better watch your fucking back. If I ever see you come within a mile of those kids, you'll wish you never thought to try to take the two most important people in my life from me. You may think you're hot shit now, but I will ruin your career. Even a strip club won't touch you with a ten-foot pole."

Fire in my eyes, I spin around, striding down the long corridors and back onto the court. When I emerge, the dance squad is already on the floor doing their halftime routine. I hope Skylar gets fired for missing it.

Daniel meets my gaze and jumps up as I storm along the side of the court toward him.

"Ask Winters for more time before I make my decision. Carla's trying to take my girls from me. I won't let her take my dream job from me, too."

"You got it." He follows as I rush out of the arena, his chauffeur driving up almost the instant we emerge. We both remain silent during the short drive back to his building. Once we arrive, I give him my thanks, then hurry to the parking garage to grab my car.

The entire drive out to Revere Beach, I pray Carla hasn't taken Brooklyn from me, too.

CHAPTER NINETEEN

BROOKLYN

A WIDE GRIN PLASTERED on my face, I push the folders scattered all over my desk into a pile, then shove them into the cabinets, not caring about the lack of organization. Normally, I'd take my time to put each and every file exactly where they're supposed to go, but not tonight, not with the electricity filling me in anticipation of seeing Drew.

Grabbing my bag, I head down the corridor with a spring in my step, about to make my escape when someone calls my name. "Brooklyn! Hold on a second."

I whirl around to see Michelle scurrying after me. "What's going on?" I furrow my brows in concern.

"I won't keep you, since it looks like you're on your way somewhere important." She waggles her eyebrows. "Like a booty call with Wes."

Heat washes over my face as I swallow down my unease at the mention of him. "Is something wrong?"

Her expression falls. "I just got off the phone with the Attorney General's office." She straightens her posture, brushing her dark locks behind her ear, her eyes serious. "Apparently, Zachary Plummer's brother, Marcus, tried to get through security to speak with AAG Stone about the disposition of the TPR from a week ago, wanting to know where Zachary's kids ended up."

"Is she okay?"

"Yes. He wasn't able to get through and walked away when they suggested he speak to Zachary's attorney."

I bite my lower lip, something about this not adding up. "You'd think with the amount of neglect those kids endured, Zachary would have been thrilled when the judge signed the TPR. Not to mention, he's currently serving a twenty-year sentence."

168

"Those brothers only saw dollar signs whenever they looked at those kids. Sick bastards. The DA is still working on building a criminal case against Marcus for trafficking, but Zachary refused to implicate him, so right now, it's only circumstantial. Nothing sufficient for even an arrest warrant."

I nod, my stomach churning at what those kids' lives would be like had DCF not intervened. It doesn't matter how long I've been doing this. Seeing kids abused and neglected never gets any easier.

"Anyway, I guess I just wanted to warn you to keep your eyes peeled. If he's going after Stone, he may try to track you down, too."

"Thanks, Michelle. I'm sure it's nothing to worry about and will all blow over. Like it always does." Any other day, I may have taken her warning a little more seriously, but nothing can dampen my current mood, not when I'm minutes away from seeing Drew in a spot that means so much to both of us.

She pulls her lips together into a tight line. "Probably, but still. Be careful."

"I will." I give her a reassuring smile, then glance at the glass doors leading to the parking lot.

"Well, I won't keep you from your prior engagement any longer." She gives me an exaggerated wink. "And I expect a full report on all the steaminess tomorrow."

I laugh, unable to reel in my smile. "You should know by now, Michelle."

"What's that?"

"I never kiss and tell." Especially considering my date is with a man other than my fiancé.

With a grin, I spin from her, rushing out of the building and through the parking lot, tuning out everything except the exhilaration of being in Drew's arms, knowing I'm mere minutes from experiencing that again.

Once I'm behind the wheel of my car, I crank the engine and head toward Revere Beach. While it's not the best in the state, it's the one closest to where we grew up. It has all the essentials...sand, ocean, a snack bar. Better yet, it's home to thousands of memories of my younger years. Of squealing with joy when I felt that first wave splash over my legs as a child. Of lounging in the sun with my best friend as we talked about everything and nothing at the same time. Of being tossed into the ocean by Drew time and time again. These memories make this place special, and I get the feeling they must hold the same importance for Drew.

I pull into the beach lot, step out of my car, then kick off my heels. It's not dark yet, but the sun no longer illuminates the sky, the faint hint of the half-moon appearing. Now that I'm close to the shore, there's more of a breeze than was noticeable inland. Still, I make no move to secure my hair, allowing it to blow around my face instead.

The sand is warm against my feet as I walk toward what became our spot during our last summer together. With every step, I dig my toes in a little more, something about the feel of the grains against my skin pacifying me.

Approaching the ledge separating the beach from the street, I hoist myself onto it, just as I did so many times during my youth. Just as I did the day before Drew went off to college. I remember sitting with him in this exact spot, neither one of us saying a word. In that moment, I could tell it was as difficult for him to leave me as it was for me to say goodbye to him. In retrospect, maybe it was a blessing in disguise he left without saying goodbye. Maybe he did it because he was struggling with leaving me as much as I was.

As I sit watching planes prepare to land at Logan Airport off in the distance, I'm on edge. My unease only increases with the passing of time. I glance at my watch. 7:15. I tell myself Drew's probably running a little late, that he's stuck in one of his meetings or got caught in game-day traffic trying to get out of the city, which I know from experience can be horrendous.

For the next thirty minutes, I come up with excuse after excuse to explain why he's not here, why he hasn't returned any of my texts or calls. A tiny voice reminds me I did the same thing the morning he left for college, but I silence it. I'm no longer that same girl. And he's not the same guy, either. He wouldn't ask me to meet him here and not show up. Would he?

Withdrawing my phone from my purse, I'm about to call Molly to see if she's heard from him when a chill runs through me. I glance at the parking lot behind me, finding it empty of people, a dozen cars scattered among the numerous spaces. Michelle's warning nags at me. I'm probably just being paranoid. Regardless, it's not the smartest idea to be sitting alone on the beach now that darkness shrouds the shoreline. It's not exactly the safest part of the city.

Jumping off the ledge, I hurry across the sand toward the parking lot, brushing the granules off my feet before sliding my heels back on. A loud cheer startles me and I look toward the noise, spying a sports bar a few blocks away. The place is brightly lit, several people congregated outside, smoking. Thinking it's probably safer to wait in there than in my darkened car in a parking lot, I continue in its direction.

When I step into the crowded bar, I feel out of place. Locals sporting Celtics jerseys fill the room, their eyes glued to one of the many large-screen televisions hanging overhead or mounted to the walls, each one tuned into the basketball game. Scanning the area, I find a vacant stool toward the end of the bar and head toward it.

Once I'm settled, a bartender approaches, placing a cardboard coaster in front of me. "What can I get you?"

"Scotch. Neat."

"You got it."

He turns, grabbing a bottle and pouring the amber liquor into a tumbler. He pushes the glass toward me and smiles. "Cheers."

I place enough cash on the bar to cover the drink and a decent tip, then take a sip, my throat and stomach burning as the alcohol makes its way through me.

"Celtics fan?" a deep voice asks as I place the glass back on the bar.

"No. Just waiting for a friend who's running late," I say, stealing a glance at the man by my side. I hadn't noticed him when I walked in, only caring about finding an empty seat. He looks as out of place as me, his tie loose, copper hair disheveled. He's probably in his early forties, his features distinguished enough to make it appear like he has life experience, but not so withered as to make it seem like he's close to retirement age. "Figured it was safer waiting in here than out on the beach."

My phone buzzes. I quickly retrieve it from my purse, my fingers frantic as I hope for a message from Drew. When it's just a work email coming through, my heart deflates, but I try not to let it show, plastering on a smile.

"How about you? Are you a Celtics fan…?" I lift my brows.

"Tony," he answers, holding out his hand.

I grab it. "Brooklyn."

He nods, then releases his hold on me, returning his attention to the game. "I suppose you could say I'm a fan." He blows out a laugh, his mouth twisting in the corners. "I kind of married into it. My wife's a big fan."

I shift my eyes to the TV screen, feigning interest. I've never followed basketball, considering its season is the same as hockey.

"She just asked for a divorce," he says after a minute.

I shift my gaze back to him. His lips are pinched together, his Adam's apple bobbing up and down in hard swallows.

"I should have known it was coming, but it doesn't make it hurt any less. She's always complained I work too hard."

"What is it you do?"

"I'm a detective with Revere PD," he answers in a thick Boston accent, then brings his bottle up to his mouth. "I've worked hard to give her everything she's ever wanted. But I was too blind to realize all she wanted was me. Now I have to figure out a way to tell my kids why I'm moving out."

"How old are they?" I ask in a small voice.

"Jessica is thirteen. Embry is eight."

I offer him as compassionate a smile as possible, hoping he finds even a small slice of comfort in the gesture. "They'll be okay. Kids are alarmingly resilient." I look forward once more, swirling my glass on the surface of the bar.

As I check the score, I almost do a double take when they

show a wide shot, one of the ridiculously tall basketball players dribbling toward the basket. But that's not what catches my attention. It's who's sitting one row behind the team…Drew and his agent.

I squint, wondering if my eyes are playing tricks on me. Sure enough, the whistle blows and the camera zooms in on Drew, a banner below him on the screen displaying his name, followed by "Former Bruins Center".

"How do you know?" Tony's voice cuts through my stunned silence.

I whip my eyes toward his, my face heating as I try to pretend the idea of Drew standing me up for a basketball game doesn't affect me.

"What?"

"Kids. How do you know they'll be okay?"

I blink repeatedly, my gaze fluctuating between the TV and Tony's, confused, a thousand explanations filling my brain as to why Drew would be at a Celtics game, considering he specifically asked me to meet him tonight. It doesn't make sense. When I look back at the screen, I notice Drew's not paying attention to the game, making me think perhaps his agent dragged him there for some reason. The camera goes to a wide shot again and my heart sinks when I realize what that reason is…

Skylar.

I try to tell myself it's just a coincidence. I want to believe he hasn't been carrying on with her even after all the promises he made these past few days, even after I planned to leave a man who's been nothing but devoted to me to pursue something with Drew. But as I witness Skylar saunter up to him in her ridiculously revealing uniform and pull him toward what I can only assume to be a private location, the way he licks his lips as he visibly undresses her with his eyes, makes me realize I've been so wrong about him.

My grip on the glass tightens, my jaw clenching as I do everything to remain in control. But the more I think about how naïve I've been, the harder it becomes. I wonder what sick game he's playing, what he gets out of toying with people's emotions.

"Brooklyn?" Tony says, noticing my changed demeanor. "Are you okay?"

I look at him once more, my voice caught in my throat. Everything feels foggy, the background noise muffled.

"I…" I shake my head, words refusing to form, my chin quivering.

It shouldn't surprise me. After all, Drew's made a habit out of promising me one thing, then failing to follow through. I wanted to think he was serious about me, wanted to believe he was a different person than the cocky hockey player who was going off to college, or the hotshot celebrity whose face was plastered on billboards, t-shirts, coffee mugs. That's what hurts the most right now. Not that Drew stood me up yet again, but that I was so desperate for him to finally want me that I believed the lies he fed me, even though I should have learned my lesson the last time. And the time before that. And the time before that.

"Brooklyn?" Tony repeats.

"I have to go." A blank expression on my face, I raise myself from my seat and walk through the bar, ignoring Tony's requests asking me if I'm okay. I should be crying at how stupid I've been, but I'm not. I've given Drew too many of my tears. He doesn't deserve them. He never did in the first place.

I've always liked to believe everything happens for a reason. There's a reason Drew never showed up at my house when he promised he would all those years ago. There has to be a reason I decided to step into that bar to wait for him in the hopes he'd show up with a valid explanation as to why he was late. Perhaps this is the universe's way of showing me Drew hasn't changed like I thought he had, like he tried to insist he had.

As I cross the street, I remain alarmingly composed, at least on the outside. On the inside, I've broken down, the walls I'd erected around my heart seventeen years ago returning, this time thicker, stronger, impenetrable. Everything seems subdued and distant as I make my way through the parking lot and approach my car.

When I open the door, an unexpected echo of heavy footsteps against gravel breaks through the fog of my heartbreak, catching my attention. I look around, searching the lot for the source, my heart pounding in my chest, adrenaline filling me.

The last thing I remember is peering into a pair of familiar eyes before two large hands wrap around my throat, my head meeting the car door, rendering me unconscious.

CHAPTER TWENTY

DREW

I TAP ON THE steering wheel, cursing all the stoplights as I make my way toward the beach. I have no idea whether Brooklyn is still there, considering she didn't pick up the myriad of times I tried to call. Didn't respond to any of my texts. Not a single word from her. I pray she'll understand. The instant I put the pieces together and realized Skylar played a part in this, all I saw was red. All my outside responsibilities and commitments took a back seat to uncovering the truth.

As I sit in traffic, I continue trying Brooklyn's cell every few minutes, only for it to go to voicemail. I don't want to read too much into it, but I can't help feeling like something's off. If Brooklyn were just pissed at me, she'd pick up and tell me. But not answering at all? It doesn't sit right.

Finally, I turn my SUV onto the street abutting the shoreline, driving faster than normal. Approaching the parking lot, red and blue lights flash. I slow my speed, counting four police cruisers. Dread fills me, beads of sweat forming on my neck.

I slam on my brakes, leaving my SUV on the side of the road, and dash toward the pandemonium. I pray I'm just overreacting, that it's just my guilt seeping into my subconscious. As I near the flashing lights and see yellow tape roping off Brooklyn's car, my pulse skyrockets. The sound of my heart thrashing in my ears mutes the background noise of crashing waves and passing cars.

On autopilot, I duck under the perimeter, my throat tight, barely able to keep myself upright as I stride toward her car. It doesn't take more than a few seconds for an officer to approach me, putting his hand up, preventing me from taking another step.

176

"Sir, I'm going to need to ask you to leave this area. I can't have anyone contaminating evidence or compromising the integrity of the crime scene."

"Crime scene?" I attempt to look past him at Brooklyn's car, desperate for any indication she's okay. "What happened?" I roar, panicked. "Where is she?"

"She?" He glances behind him. I follow his line of sight just as a crime scene tech shines a flashlight on the door, bringing attention to blood smearing the edge.

"Brooklyn!" I shout, my voice bellowing in the night air. "That's her car!" My eyes bulge and nostrils flare as I tug on my hair.

"Sir, please. If you'll wait behind the tape, I'll send a detective over to talk to you." He grips my elbow, dragging me away, but not before I notice more blood on the pavement. I'm too lightheaded to put up a fight, too weak to shake off his tight hold and rush to the beach to see her sitting in our spot, all of this a misunderstanding.

When we get on the other side of the cordoned off area, other locals and passersby congregating in intrigue, he releases his grip on me. "Wait here, Mr..." He lifts a questioning brow.

"Brinks."

He eyes me with mild recognition before retreating toward a group of men in suits. They talk for a moment, increasing my anxiety level, then one looks at me and heads in my direction. He's tall and lean. The bit of gray dotting his copper hair and lines around his face make him appear to be in his forties.

"Detective Tony Santa Rosa." He holds his hand out toward me, a weariness about him. Unlike the other men, his tie is loosened, his hair disheveled.

"Andrew Brinks," I respond.

"I know." He gestures at Brooklyn's car. "Are you acquainted with the woman who owns that automobile?"

"Her name's Brooklyn. Brooklyn Tanner."

He closes his eyes and inhales a long breath. It doesn't matter this man is a complete stranger. I can tell he's out of sorts.

"What happened?" I ask frantically, desperation taking over. My gaze darts from Brooklyn's car, to the crime scene techs taking photos, to the group of other police officers and detectives. My mouth is dry, my neck stiff, my jaw tight.

"I saw it all myself," he answers, staring off into space. "She came into Jonny's Pub and ordered a scotch. I struck up a conversation with her. She seemed to be in a good mood, then started watching the Celtics game." He gives me a knowing look. "It was around the same time the cameras spied you in the crowd."

I swallow hard, heaviness settling in my stomach.

"She suddenly became distracted, quiet, then left the bar, ignoring my questions asking if she was okay. That's when I noticed this big guy follow her. It could have been nothing, but after fifteen years on the job, I couldn't shake the feeling in my gut that this was not a good person, so I paid my tab and left to make sure she was okay." He runs a hand over his face, pulling his lip between his teeth. "I should have left the bar sooner."

"What happened?" I press through a tightness in my throat, unsure I want to hear his response.

"The man attacked her. Smashed her head into her car door, knocked her out, then dragged her toward his car." He looked behind him, gesturing to a run-down station wagon parked several yards away from Brooklyn's car. "As he was about to throw her into the trunk, I told him to stop, showed him my shield. That's when he drew a gun. I did the same and clipped him in the shoulder."

I swallow hard, absorbing his story as my eyes rake over the scene, a trail of blood from Brooklyn's car to the station wagon making me even more queasy now that I know how it got there. "It's all my fault," I murmur, my stomach hardening.

"Excuse me?" Detective Santa Rosa asks, intrigued.

"I was supposed to meet her here at seven, but something came up."

"The Celtics game?" I hear the disapproval in his voice. I know what he's thinking. That if I hadn't gone to that game, this never would have happened.

I shake my head. "No. Well, yes. But..." I pace, tugging on my hair. I've never felt so much guilt in my life. If I'd just stopped for a moment to think instead of being hell-bent on revenge, I would have remembered the plans I made with Brooklyn. How many more promises will I make to her just for something to prevent me from following through? It already required her to make a giant leap of faith to trust me again. How will she ever trust me after this?

I whip my wild eyes to the detective. "Where is she? Is she okay?"

"I haven't received an updated status yet, but she hadn't regained consciousness by the time the EMTs arrived. They took her to Everett."

Reacting quickly, I turn from him, dashing back to where I left my SUV, speeding away from the beach, mumbling a silent prayer for Brooklyn.

* * *

The automatic doors slide open and I barrel into a packed waiting room, the sound of coughing and wheezing overpowering that of the distorted speakers of a television there to keep people occupied so they don't think about how long they've been waiting.

"Brooklyn Tanner. Where is she?" I bark at the nurse manning the registration desk of the emergency room.

"Are you family?"

"Yes, well...not technically, but we grew up together."

She hands me a clipboard and pen. "Sign in. I'll check to verify whether she's able to consent to see you."

"And if she's not?" I scribble my name down, then push the clipboard toward her.

"You'll have to wait until she is."

I glare, her answer only angering me more. I know it's not her fault. She's just following procedure, but I need to see Brooklyn. Need to make sure she's okay. Need to feel her soft skin on mine. Need to see her chest rise and fall. Need to promise never to let her down again. That's all I care about right now. Nothing else.

"Have a seat."

"How long?" I press.

"Once I check in all these people in need of medical care…" She gestures to the line behind me. "I'll work as fast as I can, but I promise to make you a priority."

I fight the urge to return her sarcasm with a biting comment and spin from her, plopping down into a hard chair with a force that evidences my impatience regarding the situation.

My leg bounces as I chew on my nails. Every few minutes, a nurse opens the security door, calling a name other than mine. I watch as someone with an arm in a sling, or pressing an ice pack to their face, or puking into a pail is escorted into the triage area. I try to peek down the corridor, hoping to catch a glimpse of Brooklyn, but I'm not so lucky.

My hands burrow into my hair, my nostrils flaring. I hate being in this purgatory where I don't know if she's okay. What if she is but requested not to see me? I can't stomach the idea.

When the door opens again, I straighten, the nurse popping out to call yet another name. What I'm about to do is incredibly stupid and may end up with me getting hauled away in handcuffs, but I don't care. Launching to my feet, I dash through the open door, ignoring the shouts as I search for any sign of Brooklyn.

The hallway is littered with people in chairs, some on stretchers as they wait to be seen by a nurse, PA, or doctor. They don't appear to be in that bad of shape, maybe a sprained wrist or a dizzy spell necessitating a visit to the ER since most medical clinics are closed at this hour. Knowing I don't have much longer before security comes after me, I turn down a hallway, peering into every room, none of them containing the woman I'm after.

As I near the end, a familiar moan finds my ears. I've heard that moan before, but when the person was experiencing pleasure. Now the sound is riddled with pain.

Not even thinking twice, I dash inside, closing and locking

the door behind me. The detective told me what happened, but nothing could have prepared me for the sight that greets me. Brooklyn's curled up on her side, blood seeping from a temporary bandage on her head, bruises around her neck, as if someone had tried to strangle her. The detective left that part out.

"Brooklyn," I exhale, rushing to her, desperate to wrap her in my arms and assure her it will all be okay.

The instant I do, she yelps, wincing in agony. I step back, seeing her face scrunched. I survey her, not noticing anything that would cause this reaction. Then I recall the detective's account that she was dragged across the parking lot.

My heart pounding, I slowly shift my gaze to her exposed back, choking out a sob when I see how bruised and bloodied it is, as if whoever attacked her got some twisted pleasure out of harming her like this.

"My god." I shake my head, struggling to keep my tears at bay. "I am so sorry, Brooklyn. I fucked up. Tell me what I can do to make it up to you, and I'll do it." I sit in the chair beside her, brushing her hair out of her face. "Please, just—"

"Don't. Touch. Me." Her voice is scratchy as she glares at me, recoiling from my touch.

I drop my hand, my lips parting. "Brooklyn, I—"

"I saw you." Her tone is alarmingly calm, as if she's speaking to the judge regarding one of her cases, not addressing the man who just broke his promise to her…again.

"It's not—"

"I. Saw. You," she repeats louder. Gradually lifting her head, her wounded gaze locks with mine. I've hurt this woman more times than I care to count, but I've never felt as filled with remorse as I do at this moment.

"Please, Brooklyn," I beg, my voice faltering. "It wasn't what it looked like."

"It doesn't matter." Her words are low, resigned, devoid of all emotion. Everything about her is devoid of emotion. I want her to yell at me, hit me, claw at me, anything to show a sign of life, to show that she's still my Brooklyn. But she doesn't.

"Skylar's the one who encouraged Carla to petition for custody of the girls. When I learned that, I forgot about everything else. All I could think about was getting the truth out of Skylar. You know I'd do anything for my girls. When it comes to them, I become blind to everything else."

"This is just another promise you made that you had no intention of following through with," she murmurs. "I'm used to it at this point. I was weak and fell for your lies. I won't make that mistake again."

"It's not just another promise," I plead, digging my hands into my hair, an ache in my chest, my throat, my heart.

"For years, you tried to protect me from every single guy out there," she continues, her voice still even. I'd give anything to hear even a hint of emotion from her, but I've broken her. "In all reality, the person you should have been protecting me from is you."

Her words hit me harder than any fist to the face or hockey stick to the back I've experienced, knocking the breath from me. I scan her shriveled body as she closes her eyes, sick that I did this to her. Not just the physical wounds she endured tonight, but also the emotional ones she's been carrying for years.

"I love you, Brooklyn." I don't know what else to say at this point. No explanation seems fitting.

"No, you don't. You like the idea of me…until something better comes along. Then I'll be invisible again. Just let me be invisible, Drew."

"I can't do that. I just…" I draw in a deep breath, kneeling in front of her. "I need you to trust me when I say this isn't just another broken promise. There never was a broken promise to begin with. I wanted to be there the day I left for college. So bad. It killed me to leave you, but I didn't have a choice."

She opens her eyes, staring at me with a hint of indecision, something in the pleading tone of my voice cutting through her armor.

"I couldn't sleep the night before, the memory of your kisses better than any dream. I got out of bed early, the minutes seeming to drag as I waited until it was time for me to see you. But as I was packing, your—"

Instantly, the door bursts open, cutting me off. I'm forced to my feet, staring into a familiar pair of eyes.

"Drew," Mr. Tanner says, stoic, severe, unwavering. Two security guards stand behind him. Despite their wide stances, they're not that big. I can easily take both out with no problem, but I doubt that'll win me any points with Brooklyn. "I think it's best if you leave."

I square my shoulders, crossing my arms over my chest, pushing it out to appear more formidable. "I'll go." My eyes find Brooklyn's. "If that's what you want."

He assesses me, mimicking my pose. "Of course it is."

"Not you. Brooklyn."

She perks up, her brows furrowed as she peers at me.

"All you have to do is say the word and I will walk out that door." I point to the open doorway. "And you will never have to see me again. If that's what you want." My Adam's apple bobs up and down, my voice catching as I trail off. "If you truly believe I don't care about you, that I'd intentionally hurt you, that I deliberately broke my promise to you, I'll leave and never look back. If that's what you truly believe."

I hold my breath, waiting for her response, the silence amplified by the monitors measuring her heart and brainwaves.

"Tell me to go, and I'll give you your wish. I'll let you be invisible again."

She parts her lips, her eyes darting between me and her father, but no words come.

"That's enough." Mr. Tanner grasps my shoulder, pushing me toward the doorway. "She needs her rest."

"Fine." I shrug him off, retreating into the hallway, ignoring all the curious eyes from the medical staff congregated around the door. "I'm going." My voice is loud so they all hear. That does nothing to persuade the security personnel, who follow until I'm out of the waiting room area and heading toward the parking lot.

My neck is strained, every muscle in my body tense as I

storm toward my car, wracking my brain for a way I can fix this, a way I can make Brooklyn see I'm not the asshole she considers me to be. Hopefully, she just needs a chance to calm down. Like everything, this will blow over. It has to.

As I'm about to duck into my car and call Gigi to let her know what's happened, someone shouts my name, the voice like nails on a chalkboard. I stop, taking a moment to reel in my rage, then turn around to face Brooklyn's father.

"Drew…," he begins, but I cut him off, not allowing him to say another word.

"Why don't you like me?" My tone is harsh, demanding, evidencing my desperation over the situation. I've done nothing but show this man respect. He's done nothing but try to keep his daughter from me.

He stares at me, considering his response. Then his gaze narrows, his distaste for me clear. "I went through her phone."

"You what?" My eyes bulge out of their sockets. I'm unable to wrap my head around this degree of control over another human, especially an adult.

"I needed to alert Wes to what happened. When I saw all the missed calls from you, it piqued my curiosity, so I went through her texts to see what kind of 'friendship' you two still had," he sneers, using air quotes.

Heat rolls over my face, the ground feeling like it's giving out from beneath me. Over the past week, we've sent dozens of texts to each other, some sweet and sincere, others lust-filled and wanton. He wouldn't have had to go that far back in our texts to find ones neither of us could claim were just harmless and innocent.

"She's engaged," he hisses through a tight jaw, leaning into me.

"She doesn't love him."

"And you think she loves you?"

"I know she does. She told me as much this morning when she kissed me goodbye before leaving my house." My words do nothing except upset him further, but I didn't fight hard enough for Brooklyn all those years ago. She needs to know I'll jump every hurdle facing me this time. Even if that hurdle is her father. "And I love her."

"Love her enough to ditch her for the Celtics game?"

I swallow hard, about to explain myself when he interrupts me.

"I was watching. I saw you sitting courtside. Didn't think anything of it. Then I received a phone call from Revere PD, saying Brooklyn had been rushed to the hospital. When I got here and asked what she was doing at the beach this late at night, she told me she was supposed to meet a friend. From the texts I saw, it appears that friend was you. Isn't that right?"

I nod, the motion subtle.

"Yet, at the same time you were supposed to meet her, you were sitting courtside. If that's love—"

"Something came up. Something important that required my immediate attention."

"Important enough that you couldn't pick up the phone and call Brooklyn to let her know? The first missed call from you didn't appear until after eight! She'd been waiting for you for over an hour! An hour!" He shakes his head, his chin quivering. "She could have died. That bastard was the brother of the father in one of her TPR cases who's serving a twenty-year sentence for trafficking! If Detective Santa Rosa didn't show up when he did, God knows what would have happened to her."

"Don't you think I know that!" I bellow, my voice echoing against the surrounding buildings. "Don't you think I've been thinking the same thing? Because I have! And it makes me sick."

"Stay away from her." His lips curl in the corners as he straightens his posture, returning to the formidable man I've always known him to be. "You've never done anything but hurt her."

"Because of you! You gave me no choice but to hurt her. You can't keep her away from me this time. You can't threaten me with criminal charges anymore. I'm not the scared teenager I once was."

"If you love her like you claim you do, you'll let her move on with her life." He holds my gaze a moment longer, then turns from me, heading back toward the hospital.

"And if you love her, you'll tell her the truth about what happened before I left for college!" I shout.

He comes to an abrupt stop, pausing. On a long exhale, he glances over his shoulder at me. "You know I can't do that."

"I never said a word to her, never told her why I didn't show up when I promised I would. Do you want to know why?"

His hardened expression faltering, he remains silent.

"Because I didn't want her to think any less of you, didn't want her to harbor any animosity toward you. So I've kept it quiet, even though I know the truth would give me the one thing I've always wanted." I struggle to blink back the tears forming in my eyes.

"What's that?" he asks timidly.

"Her. She's all I've ever wanted. Now the woman I've loved my entire life won't believe the truth even if I did tell her. She won't believe me when I tell her I love her, that I want to spend the rest of my life with her, marry her, have a family with her. That I will honor her, provide for her, worship her for the rest of my days. All because I've spent the past seventeen years trying to do the right thing. Now I'm begging you to do the right thing and tell her."

His lips part, turmoil covering the lines of his face.

"If she heard the truth from you, things might be different. Please…" I trail off, my words choked.

He stands there for what feels like an eternity, torn at my request. I'm putting him in a difficult position. But he put me in this same position before I left for college. I've spent the past several decades regretting that I didn't stand up to him, tell him how much I loved his daughter, that I would never do anything to hurt her. He overreacted back then, just like he's overreacting now. He knows it, but is that enough?

"Drew," he says with a long sigh. "You have two daughters of your own now. You may not have experience with these things yet, but you will soon. And you'll want the best for them. Wes comes from a good family. He'll be able to give Brooklyn things I never could have imagined for her. She'll never have to go to sleep worrying about where the money for the next mortgage payment will come from. Whether she'll have enough in her account to put gas in the car to get her to work. Whether she'll have to sleep in a cold house in the dead of winter because she couldn't afford the heating costs."

"She wouldn't have to worry about any of those things with me, either! I've done very well for myself. I've made sacrifices my entire life to be successful. I've just been offered a seven-figure salary to coach for the Bruins."

"She won't have to worry about her spouse being unfaithful."

"I'd never hurt her like that. Never. And at least with me, she'll have love."

"Wes loves her," he responds.

"But she doesn't love him," I say once more. "I know she doesn't." I pause, studying his demeanor, something about the way he's staring at me with apprehension making me think he agrees with my assessment. "And you know she doesn't. Please. You have the power to fix this."

An unspoken apology in his eyes, he turns from me. "But at a price I'm not willing to pay."

CHAPTER TWENTY-ONE

BROOKLYN

I BLINK OPEN MY eyes, staring around the bright room, momentarily disoriented by the strange surroundings until memories of yesterday trickle back... Waking up in Drew's arms. Thinking everything would finally work out between us. Michelle's warning as I left to meet Drew at the beach. Drew never showing up. Seeing him at the Celtics game with Skylar. Hearing a noise and staring into Marcus Plummer's dark eyes before he smashed my head against my car door.

I lift my arm and rub my temple, feeling the bandage, proof that last night did happen, that it wasn't just a nightmare and I'd wake up in Drew's arms. But that's no longer a possibility. I prop myself up, the pain from the bruising and scratches on my back not as overpowering as when I first regained consciousness.

After Drew forced his way into my hospital room, all I wanted to do was go home and pretend the last week never happened, but the doctor wouldn't allow it. Concerned about the severity of the concussion I'd received, he refused to discharge me, keeping me under observation overnight. I've insisted I'm fine, that the dizziness, inability to stand, and bouts of nausea rolling over me are the result of having my trust betrayed yet again. But they won't listen. Maybe it's a blessing in disguise. There's nothing waiting for me at home. Only memories of the one man who's done nothing but hurt me and the one man who will do anything for me...the one I betrayed.

I almost expected Molly to force her way into my hospital room, much like her brother did. But she didn't. The only people who seem concerned about my wellbeing have been my father and his girlfriend, Ana. I'm not sure how to process the fact that my own best friend hasn't come to visit. Then again, it shouldn't surprise me. When I started this thing with Drew, I knew it carried certain risks. Now I'm not only forced to bid farewell to my adolescent dream of marrying my best friend's brother, I've also lost my best friend.

My mouth parched from the dry air in this place, I grab the water on the side table. As I take a sip, my door opens, a familiar, tall figure standing in the doorway, out of breath, eyes wide with worry.

"Oh, Jesus…" Wes rushes toward me, kneeling on the floor next to my bed. He takes my hand in his, peppering kisses along my knuckles. "This is all my fault. I shouldn't have left you."

"Wes," I say through a scratchy throat, trying to get his attention. The sympathy and compassion he has for me is too much. I don't deserve it. Not after how quickly I sought out the arms of another man when the wheels of his plane hadn't yet left the ground.

"I'm going to talk to the prosecutor's office and make sure that bastard gets the maximum sentence. Is what your dad told me true? That the guy's connected to one of the cases where you recommended a termination of parental rights? That he's involved in trafficking women and children?"

I subtly nod.

Wes brings himself to his feet, pacing, running his hands through his hair. He looks weary, exhausted. His jaw is scruffy from not shaving, his clothes disheveled and crumpled. He probably came straight here after landing. He wasn't supposed to leave Dubai for another few days. No man I've ever dated would get on a plane and fly over twelve hours just to see me, make sure I'm okay. It makes my stomach sour even more over what I've done.

Feeling like I'm about to be sick, I reach for the bucket the nurses left by my side for just such an occasion and retch into it. Wes is beside me instantly, rubbing my back. It only makes the pain worse. Noticing my discomfort, he removes his hand as I place the bucket on the floor. Without saying a word, his gaze shifts to my back. I don't stop him when he raises my hospital gown so he can see what caused me so much agony.

When his eyes fall on the bruising and cuts marring my skin, he chokes out a sob.

"You're not going back to work. Not after this."

"Wes…," I say.

"Shh…" He presses a finger against my lips, silencing me. "Let me take care of you."

"Wes," I protest again. "There's something I need to tell you."

He pulls back, peering at me. He shakes his head. "It doesn't matter. All that does is that you're okay." He brings his lips to the bandage covering the stitches on my forehead, kissing me sweetly. "Rest, my sweet, sweet Brooklyn." He brushes my greasy hair behind my ear, the gesture soothing, comforting, relaxing. "We'll talk later. No matter what it is, I love you. No matter what."

Tears spill over my eyelids, his tenderness like a punch in my gut. Mrs. Bradford was right. This man is too good for someone like me.

***

Wes helps me up the front steps of his house, one hand on the small of my back, the other clutching my arm. I don't deserve all the attention he's doting on me. Hell, I barely even remember agreeing to come home with him. He and my father didn't think it wise I return to my house. Somehow, that translated to me staying with Wes. I suppose that's the obvious choice from an outsider's perspective.

There were so many times I opened my mouth, about to tell him everything, but my father constantly stood over his shoulder, eyeing me with suspicion and disapproval, an unspoken warning to stay quiet, making me think he knew about my indiscretions.

If he figured out the truth of what's been going on between Drew and me, I can only imagine what he thinks of me, how disappointed he must be. I've lived my entire life doing everything to meet my father's high expectations. That's why I applied for the doctoral program I'm about to begin. I never wanted to take my education that far. I'm happy just working as a therapist. But I made the mistake of mentioning the next step professionally would be to get my PhD, then MD in Clinical Psychology. The next thing I knew, he started shoving brochures at me for programs in the area.

"Just rest in here," Wes soothes as he leads me into the den, the only room of the house that doesn't feel like it was designed to be featured in an architectural magazine, although it's still a breathtaking space. He helps lower me to the plush leather couch, grabbing a blanket and draping it over my body. "Do you want some tea? Sushi? Anything? You name it and it's yours."

I hate the benevolence he's bestowing upon me. I don't deserve a single breath of it. "Wes, please," I beg.

"I know. You must be exhausted."

"It's not that." My voice lacks the life it once exuded.

I always thought the idea of feeling dead inside was an exaggeration. I was wrong because that's exactly how I feel now. Like my heart no longer beats. Like my lungs no longer breathe. Like my brain no longer fires. I'm lifeless. Heartless. Soulless. Simply going through the motions, doing what I'm told.

"I need to talk to you."

"Just rest," he replies, continuing to fuss with the pillows behind me, ignoring my pleas.

"Wes." I clutch his forearm and he finally looks at me. Something about the way he regards me leads me to believe he knows exactly what I'm about to tell him.

With a defeated sigh, he sits on the bit of free space beside me on the couch, his fingers brushing back a few tendrils of my hair. "What is it?"

I meet his eyes, searching for the right words. I don't know how to put what I need to tell him delicately, how to admit the truth without destroying him.

"Is this about Drew?" he asks when I remain silent.

I blink repeatedly. "You…know?"

He nods, resigned. "I figured it out. I mean, I hoped I was wrong, but after the way we left things before I went to Dubai, then your father telling me you were at Revere Beach when you were attacked… There's only one reason you'd be there. Or, I guess, one person."

I close my eyes, a lone tear trickling down my cheek at how much I hurt Wes, and for what? Because I fell for the lies peddled by a man who's only hurt me? Because I honestly thought he cared? Because I thought he changed? Instead, he was just desperate, scared of losing his daughters. So he latched onto the first compassionate person he crossed paths with — me.

Feeling like more of an intruder in this place than ever, I abruptly stand. I lean my hand on the side table to steady myself, warding off a bout of dizziness that envelopes me. "I'll call my dad to come get me. You've already done more than enough."

Regaining my balance, I head toward the dining area and find my purse, rummaging through it for my phone. Just as I'm about to grab it, I spot the black velvet box containing my engagement ring, in the exact spot it's been since I took off my ring for work over a week ago.

My fingers wrap around it and I remove it from my purse, facing Wes, who stands a few feet away from me. The heartache I've caused him is visible in the way he watches me, his expression pleading with me not to do what I'm about to.

"Here…" I extend my hand.

He keeps his forlorn gaze trained on mine as he slowly reaches for the box, almost reluctant to take it. His posture stooped, he cracks the lid, staring at the ring that once held so much promise.

"I'll just wait outside." My tone is flat. I wish I could cry, wish I could feel something, but I don't. "I'm the last person you want to see right now." I turn from him, reaching for the doorknob, when his voice stops me.

"Did you fuck him?"

I pause for a moment, glancing back. "No." A part of me thinks I should just leave it at that. It doesn't matter now anyway. After everything he's done for me, after everything I've put him through, the least I can do is answer his questions honestly. "We kissed. A lot. The night before the attack, I stayed at his place. But we never slept together." I rub my hands along my arms, warming myself from the sudden chill enveloping me. "I'd hoped he changed, hoped he was a different man than the last time."

"The last time?" Wes steps toward me, concern I don't deserve in his expression.

"This isn't the first time Drew made a promise he had no intention of keeping. It's taken me almost twenty years, but I've finally learned my lesson. I'm just sorry you had to get hurt in the process."

I hold his gaze for another moment, hating myself for doing this to him, for being the reason his shoulders are drooped, his eyes are watering, his chin is trembling. I knew this would happen when he learned the truth, but that didn't stop me, even though it should have. Hell, the fact that I hadn't broken things off should have stopped me.

"I truly am sorry. Goodbye, Wes." I face forward again.

"I'm sorry, too, Brooklyn," he says as I'm about to step through the doorway.

I turn around, furrowing my brow. "You're sorry? What are you sorry for?"

He slowly makes his way toward me, remorse covering his face. "This is all my fault."

"Don't…," I begin, but he holds up his hand, cutting me off.

"The signs were there, but I refused to acknowledge them." His lips pinch together as he shakes his head. "I've been so preoccupied with doing everything in my power to convince my father the company will be in good hands with me, even up here in Boston, I stopped paying attention to you." He closes the distance between us, his voice softening, becoming more serene. Holding my hands in his, he runs his thumb over my knuckles, the gesture soothing, wrapping me in comfort.

"I took you for granted, assumed you'd always be there. I kept promising you things would get better, that once we were past this wedding, I'd be around more. I felt you slipping away, but I still didn't do anything to catch you when you started spiraling downward. I put my career first when all along you've been begging me to put you first. I asked you to be a part of my family, said I'd make you a priority in my life, but I never did."

I pull my hands from his, sick that he's trying to shoulder even an ounce of the blame. "I could have walked away. I knew it was wrong, yet I continued on. I won't let you take responsibility for this."

"Do you regret it?"

I don't even have to stop to contemplate his question, the answer clearer than anything in recent memory. "With every fiber of my being. And I will have to live with this mistake for the rest of my life. You deserve someone who will give you the devotion I wasn't willing to until it was too late. I truly hope you'll find someone like that."

I turn to leave once more, but Wes grabs my arm, preventing me from taking another step. "What if I already have?"

"What do you mean?"

He exhales a breath, clutching both of my biceps. "What if I've already found the person who gives me all the devotion I need, but she's lived her entire life thinking she's not good enough?"

"Wes...," I caution, shaking my head.

"It's true. Over the past several months, you've tried repeatedly to get me to pay attention to you. All the times you called, asking me to meet you for a coffee since you had an appointment in the area. All the times you rearranged your schedule just to make my mother happy with all this wedding planning." He erases the last bit of distance between us, looping an arm around my back and gently pulling me against him. His voice grows softer, more endearing, more compassionate. "All the times you went to bed alone in my house because I was too preoccupied to give you the attention you gave me."

"That's not the same thing." I try to push away, but his hold on me remains firm.

"We both broke our promises to each other."

"You were working. I don't have that excuse. I don't have any excuse. I—"

Before I can say another word, Wes' mouth is on mine. Unsure what to do, I stiffen. I expected Wes would never want to see me again after I told him I'd been fooling around with Drew. I certainly didn't expect him to shoulder the blame of my indiscretions on himself, to be so compassionate…to be kissing me. It's tender, sweet, familiar, like coming home after being gone for months

"I forgive you," he murmurs against my lips. "Now, I'm begging you to forgive me."

I reel back, speechless by this turn of events. "You've done nothing wrong."

"Yes, I have." He grips my cheeks, his voice intense. "Nothing you say will convince me otherwise. I can stand here and pretend to be hurt, and maybe I am a little, but I can't pretend I've been good to you, because I haven't. Maybe this was the wake-up call I needed to see what I would lose if I didn't learn to balance my career with my family. So if you'll still have me…" He releases his hold on me and pulls the ring box out of his pocket, opening it. "I'd like to be your family. And I'd like you to be mine."

I shake my head, having difficulty processing how Wes could be so even-tempered about this situation. "Wes, I—"

"We don't have to get married right away. Like I said before I left, maybe rushing things wasn't the best idea. I was so excited for you be my wife, I wanted it to happen as soon as possible." He pauses, his lips curving into a smile. "And I kind of liked the idea of your doctoral diploma saying Brooklyn Rose Bradford. But if you'd feel more comfortable with a long engagement, I'm happy to give that to you, too. I'll give you anything you need. Just… Let's go back to the start."

Those words knock the air out of me, leaving me stunned, mute, breathless. Just a few words and I'm transported back to my teenage years, to the most popular guy in school begging me to give him a second chance, one I never should have given him. No matter how many times a snake sheds its skin, it will always be a snake.

I remain lost in my past, wishing I'd chosen a different path. Wishing I never got into Drew's car that night he rolled up as I walked home from the movie theater. Wishing I never went to Brody Carmichael's party at the end of that summer. Wishing I never heard the name Andrew Brinks.

The warmth of Wes' lips on mine snaps me out of my memories. I blink, unsure what's happening, why he's sliding the ring back onto my finger. But I'm too broken, too defeated, too tired to question it, to question him.

Love has beaten the fight out of me.

CHAPTER TWENTY-TWO

DREW

TWO WEEKS. TWO LONG, agonizing weeks of pleading, begging, wallowing. The only thing keeping me from having a complete breakdown at the lack of contact from Brooklyn has been my daughters and doing everything to protect them from what Carla and Skylar have done.

In all the drama surrounding Brooklyn's attack, I somehow had the wherewithal to send Alice the voice recording I'd made of Skylar's admission. She reached out to Carla's lawyer to see if he had any knowledge of what Skylar alleged, only to learn he's no longer representing Carla, that she retained new counsel. It feels like for every step forward, we're forced two steps back. This time, I'm not going to agree to anything without a judge telling me I have to. I can feel good about that, at least. That still doesn't help me with Brooklyn.

I've tried to talk to her every day. I've called, texted, and even stopped by her place and Wes', unsure what her status is. She's yet to answer her phone or open the door for me. My luck was no better when I dropped by her office. They informed me she was on a leave of absence until further notice, which I expected.

Molly's tried to find out if she's still with Wes, but Brooklyn hasn't returned any of her phone calls, either. She's shut out all of us, and for what? Because she's worried we might talk some sense into her? That doesn't sound like the Brooklyn I know. I wouldn't be surprised to learn her father's controlling her communication with us, considering he turned away Molly and Gigi when they tried to visit her in the hospital.

Refusing to settle for the silent treatment any longer, I decide to drive to her place in Medford after walking the girls to school on a Tuesday in June. Her street is quiet as I head up the walkway and climb the steps to her small porch, waving at a neighbor I've seen occasionally. I reach into my pocket and retrieve the key, inserting it into the lock. I'd tried to be respectful of her space over the past several weeks, not wanting to barge in on her, but that time has passed. It's time I get answers. Time I hear her tell me she wants nothing to do with me.

When I push the door open, I fully expect to be met with Brooklyn's heated glare as she berates me for letting myself in without knocking. Instead, I'm met with emptiness. No furniture, art, life…anything.

Turning a slow circle, I stare at the empty walls that were once covered with framed prints and photos. The only sign that Brooklyn ever lived here is the dust outline from where the frames once hung. I blink, my heart pounding in my chest at what this could mean. Did she pack her things and leave town? Or did she move out of her house because of a different reason?

I continue into the townhouse that once smelled of lavender and baby powder but now reeks of cleaning supplies and chemicals, searching for any clue. Just like the living room, every room I walk into is empty…except her bedroom.

Boxes are stacked against the far wall, all labeled — donate, destroy, storage…Wes.

Wes.

My heart shatters in my chest, my lungs unable to expand and draw in oxygen. I don't want to believe it, don't want to admit what my eyes are seeing, that this makes it appear as if she's moved in with him.

I walk toward the boxes, a morbid curiosity brewing inside me. A voice in the back of my mind tells me to walk away, but something else pushes me forward, wanting to confirm my suspicions. Any number of these can hold what I'm looking for, but one calls to me more than the others. Grabbing one of the boxes labeled destroy, I bring it to the center of the room and place it on the floor.

I lower myself beside it, the seconds stretching as I lift the lid. When my gaze settles on the contents, I close my eyes, the lump in my throat becoming even more painful. I reach into the box and grab two pieces of a ripped photo, one that Brooklyn once displayed prominently in her home but now discards, along with the rest of this box of memories I hold dear.

I connect the pieces, staring at a faded photo of us from our last summer before I left for college. The first time I saw it, I couldn't hide my surprise, not realizing Molly had taken our photo. From an outsider's perspective, it was just two lifelong friends staring out at the ocean. But it was more than that. My arm is draped along Brooklyn's shoulders, my chin resting on the top of her head, my expression heavy with contemplation. I can almost feel the sun on my skin, the salty sea air blowing around me, the softness of Brooklyn's hair—

"Holy shit!" a voice exclaims, startling me.

I whip my head up, staring at an equally surprised Ana standing in the doorway, her hand over her chest, gray eyes wide. I scramble to my feet, uncertain how to explain my presence in Brooklyn's bedroom to the woman dating her father.

"Ana. I'm sorry. I know this looks bad…"

She blows out a breath, then smiles, walking toward me. "Relax," she assures me, placing a hand on my bicep. "It's okay. I just wasn't expecting to walk in on anyone." She pulls away, analyzing me. "Actually, I was wondering how many more times you were going to stop by here before you just barged in." She smirks, then her light expression falters, her gaze darting to the boxes.

"She's still with him?"

She closes her eyes, pinching her lips together as she nods. In that one gesture I can see she's not happy about it. "She is."

"The wedding?" I ask, unsure I want to hear the response.

"Proceeding as planned."

My shoulders fall as I shake my head, my heart heavy.

"I'll tell you one thing. That girl is stubborn. Gets it from her father."

I roll my eyes, the mere mention of that man making my stomach tense.

"He means well," she says.

I narrow my gaze on her, my brow creasing. Her words are laced with a thousand possible meanings, piquing my curiosity. "What do you—"

"Reece." She pulls her short blonde hair into a small ponytail at the nape of her neck. "He's…protective."

I snort out a laugh. "That's putting it mildly."

"He's a good man, albeit misguided." She meets my eyes, then adds, "Just like Brooklyn."

My pulse quickens, her words giving me the hope I've been searching for since I was escorted out of the hospital by Mr. Tanner. I thought her father was my last chance of clearing up the misunderstanding of our youth. Maybe I was wrong. Gigi always says, "You get to the man through the woman in their lives." Maybe Ana can help me get through to Mr. Tanner.

"You think she's misguided?"

She ponders my question for a moment, her arms crossed over her stomach, then nods. "I think she's confused. I think she's so tired of having her heart broken that she's done fighting. She doesn't smile anymore. There's no life in her eyes, like she's—"

"Dead inside," I finish.

"Exactly."

I pull my lips between my teeth, unsure what to say, unsure what Ana knows about my relationship with Brooklyn, both past and present. I want to shout that I'll mend her heart if she'd just give me the chance. Instead, I remain mute, allowing Ana to continue.

"Little does she realize the person responsible for all that heartache is the man who brought her into this world."

My eyes widen, my breath catching as those words linger in the air between us. They could mean so many different things, but I know that's not the case. Not now. Not here. Not after everything.

"You know?" My chest rises and falls in a quicker pattern,

desperate for confirmation.

She studies me a moment, then nods. "Reece told me the night Brooklyn was attacked. He was torn. Still is. I think a part of him wants to believe Brooklyn will be happy with Wes. That by keeping you from her, it will bury whatever happened in the past."

"And the other part?"

She inhales a deep breath, her brows furrowed in concentration. "I think the other part of him is petrified of losing the last piece of his wife he has left." A small smile forms on her lips. "It's hard to understand if you haven't experienced the loss of a spouse. It changes you, makes you do things you never thought you would. You cling to every last memory you possibly can, often at the detriment of everything else. And you'll do everything to protect that memory. In Reece's eyes, Brooklyn is that last memory. He's spent the past few decades of his life clinging to it, protecting it, refusing to let go."

"So he'd rather watch her marry a man she doesn't love than tell her the truth?"

She ponders my question for a moment. "I think he'll do whatever's necessary to ensure his daughter's happiness."

"Except tell her the truth."

She shrugs. "In his mind, I think he truly believes that Wes does make her happy, that he'll love and cherish her for the rest of his life. You have to admit, your track record doesn't exactly help your case."

"But I told him how much I love her!" I interrupt, throwing up my hands in frustration, tugging on my hair. "When he kicked me out of the hospital room and I begged him to come clean, I—"

"But have you ever shown her?"

I open my mouth, about to protest and argue I have, but not a single instance comes to mind, even though I can list dozens of occurrences that demonstrate how much she loves me. How she didn't even hesitate to help me with the custody request. How she selflessly agreed to be at my side when I shared the news with the girls. How she stayed with me that night because she knew I was hurting and needed comfort. I always thought it was just in Brooklyn's nature to put other people's needs ahead of her own and that's why she always did these things for me. But that's not it at all. Every decision she's made is because she loves me. And how did I return that love? By putting her in harm's way.

"Sometimes it's better to show someone our hearts, our feelings, with actions rather than words," Ana's voice cuts through my thoughts. "If you want to win her heart, you need to put yours out there, too. If you do that, I have a feeling you'll get the girl."

She heads toward the far wall and grabs one of the boxes, then passes me, about to disappear down the hallway.

"How do you know?" I ask, snapping out of my stupor.

The corners of her lips lift slightly, a knowing smirk crossing her mouth. "Want to know what song she's been listening to every time I've stopped by to check on her?"

"What's that?"

Her eyes brighten. "'Crash Into Me'. Something tells me it's not a coincidence, that it has something to do with you. Am I right?" She arches a brow.

I run a finger over my lips, the ghost of her mouth on mine making them tingle. "It was the song playing the first time I kissed her before I left for college."

"There's a part of her that hasn't let go of you yet. You need to do something to bring that part of her back."

She allows her words to sink in, then turns, continuing down the stairs.

I process what she said, my mind racing. A plan forming, I run after her. "Ana!"

She stops, leaning against the doorjamb, about to step onto the porch, a brow cocked.

"Think you can do me a favor?"

A sly grin crosses her mouth. "If it involves snapping that girl out of this funk, I'll do anything."

CHAPTER TWENTY-THREE

BROOKLYN

I STAND ON THE pedestal in the fitting room of the boutique, staring at my reflection as I'm adorned in the wedding dress of my dreams, feeling like I'm watching a movie of someone else's life. That's how everything's been lately. Like I'm simply going through the motions, doing what's expected of me. No protest. No arguments. No life. I'm on an out-of-control freight train, too scared to jump off. Or maybe I just don't care anymore.

Within a few hours of my discharge from the hospital, Wes' mother was at his house, fussing over me, checking my scars and bruises. She tried to appear sympathetic, but I know the reason for her visit was simply to ensure they'd heal in time for the wedding. Wes looked to me, questioning, silently inquiring whether there would still be a wedding. I was too emotionally drained to fight it anymore. I still am, which is probably how I ended up here, three days before my wedding, having my final dress fitting, when just a few weeks ago, I was getting ready to break up with Wes.

I continue to stare at someone who looks alarmingly like me, except her eyes lack any life, her lips refuse to smile. I know what a broken heart feels like now. It's the worst punishment one could be forced to suffer...my penance for how I betrayed Wes. I'm no longer living. I'm just existing, waiting for the time the universe believes I've learned my lesson and I'm allowed to smile, to laugh, to live.

"So you're going through with it then, are you?"

A biting voice cuts through the silence and I snap my head in its direction. I suck in a hard breath when I see Molly standing in the entryway to the fitting room, her arms crossed in front of her stomach.

"How did you know where I was?" I ask in an even voice

once my initial surprise wears off.

"Considering you haven't answered any of my calls and it appears as if you've moved out of your place, I reached out to Ana." She heads toward me, her blue eyes fierce, a stark juxtaposition to the lack of emotion in mine. "She was nice enough to tell me you had your final dress fitting today. As I'm sure you can imagine, my jaw fell to the fucking floor."

Noticing the tension building in the room, the seamstress gets up from where she's checking the small train. "I'll give you two some privacy. The last adjustments are perfect. No need to make any more."

I force a grateful smile. "Thank you."

"Of course." She scurries away.

"It looks good, for what it's worth. But you're walking down the aisle to the wrong person."

I sigh, stepping off the pedestal, bunching the fabric in my hands as I head toward the private dressing area. "No, I'm not. I'm walking toward the person I should have been all along."

"How could you think that? Drew loves you. I've never seen him so depressed, even after Carla left him."

"He has a funny way of showing his love." I start to duck into the dressing area, but Molly jumps in front of me, preventing me from running away from this conversation, one I've been avoiding for weeks.

"You need to pull your head out of your ass, Brooklyn. I love you, but you are so much smarter than this. You know as well as I do there's nothing going on between Drew and Skylar. He found out she put Carla up to filing that petition for custody. He was at that game to get answers, confirmation of his suspicions. This sort of information could help him keep custody. When it comes to those girls, you know damn well Drew has a tendency to be blind to everything else…even prior commitments."

I readjust my posture, waving dismissively. "That doesn't matter. This entire ordeal has helped me realize something I've been in denial about for years."

"Oh really? And what's that?"

"That no matter how hard I try, I'll never be able to trust him."

"And what about Wes?" Her fiery eyes bore into me, her attack relentless, regardless of what I do or say. "Does he still trust you? Or did you not tell him about you and Drew?"

I narrow my gaze on her, my lips forming a tight line. "I told him. I was honest. He found it in his heart to forgive me."

"Huh. Imagine that." A vein in her forehead throbs as she cocks her head to the side.

"What?"

"No." Molly brushes me off. "Must be nice to be with someone who can forgive so easily, not hold a grudge for nearly twenty years because of one misunderstanding."

"What are you talking about?" A chill runs down my spine, my heart beating faster than it has in weeks…making me feel more alive than I have in weeks.

"You know exactly what I'm talking about, Brooklyn." Her voice is a harsh whisper, the seconds seeming to stretch as she closes the distance between us once more. "I know about the night of Brody Carmichael's party."

My eyes widen, my mind racing. "Wha—"

"I know Drew stopped you from taking off your bra in front of a room of horny teenage boys."

"Everyone heard about—"

"I also know he kissed you." She pauses, allowing her words to linger in the air. "And I know you kissed him back. Your first real kiss." A slight smile crosses her face as she grabs my hands in hers, her anger waning. For the first time since the attack, I feel something other than the crushing heartache as the memory of that night returns with such clarity, it could have happened last night, not seventeen years ago. "And I know he made you a promise…to be your first."

My momentary happiness dissipates as I'm reminded of my first heartbreak, one I hope to never relive. I yank my hands from hers. "A promise he broke, the first of many."

Reaffirming my resolve that this is the right decision, I continue back toward the dressing room. Able to feel her eyes on me, I pause, glancing over my shoulder.

"I know it's stupid because it was years ago, but when he broke that promise, he did more than break my heart. He crushed my ability to ever believe a word he said again."

"So you think the answer is marrying someone you don't love?"

"Wes loves me. And I love him. It may not be butterflies and fireworks, but the type of love we share is enough for me." I hold my head high, doing my best to hide any indecision or vulnerability.

"Is this Brooklyn talking, or someone else?" she asks.

"What do you mean?"

"We've been friends for years, Brook. Years. Your father can be a bit overbearing. We all know that. So I want to know if this love you claim for Wes is real, or if someone else is insisting you love him."

I blink repeatedly, my lips parting, on the verge of breaking down and baring my soul to Molly. Tell her I shut down, that I'm confused, that I don't want to be here. But I'm not quite sure where I want to be, either.

"I'm sorry," I say, avoiding her question. "I understand if you no longer want to be at the wedding, since you obviously don't support it. I won't harbor any hard feelings."

"You're ridiculous," she hisses, throwing her arms up in frustration, stomping from me. Just as she's about to turn the corner into the showroom, she stops, meeting my eyes.

"You know, I used to think Drew didn't deserve someone as caring and compassionate as you." Her voice is soft, solemn. Then her eyes harden, her mouth turning into a sneer. "I was wrong. You don't deserve someone as caring and compassionate as Drew." She whirls around, storming away.

"I know I don't," I whisper.

CHAPTER TWENTY-FOUR

BROOKLYN

A CELEBRATORY ATMOSPHERE SURROUNDS me as I stand at Wes' side, scanning the large room in an upscale restaurant on the Waterfront of Boston. Waitstaff in bow ties circle the space, carrying trays of hors d'oeuvres and champagne. This is supposed to be our rehearsal dinner, a small gathering of wedding party members, after going through the ceremony for tomorrow. I should have known Mrs. Bradford would turn it into a huge event. There's over a hundred people in attendance. If this is just the rehearsal dinner, I shudder to consider how long the guest list is for the actual ceremony.

I force a smile as I listen to Wes go on about one of his latest designs. I should be interested in what he does for a living, but it's like he's speaking a foreign language. It's all he's talked about since we arrived here over an hour ago. Now, as I watch him joke and laugh with several of his high-paying clients, the Wes I thought I was marrying nowhere to be found in this complete stranger standing next to me, I've never felt so invisible.

As I shift my gaze around our semi-circle, I observe the women clinging to their husband's arm. They all wear the same expression. Tight lips. Small smile. Vacant eyes. Like they've resigned themselves to a life of only being known as the wife of someone, not as who they are. Do they know who they are? Or have they lost their identity to the man they married? I shiver at the thought of that happening to me. A voice inside tells me perhaps it already has. I've already agreed to give some thought to resigning from my job so I can focus on grad school. How much longer until Wes convinces me to step away from that, as well, so I can accompany him on the multitude of business trips that are scheduled over the next several months?

Removing my hand from Wes' arm, I quietly slip away, not interrupting their conversation. Part of me hopes my departure will force him to stop, maybe ask if I'm okay. But he doesn't. Instead, the circle of men closes, swallowing up where I just stood, as if I'd never been there in the first place.

Needing something stronger than champagne to quiet the doubt filling me, I head to the bar. The instant I approach, a bartender sets a napkin on the counter.

"What can I get you?"

"Three fingers of the best scotch you have. Neat."

He lifts a brow, then turns, reaching for a dark bottle on the top shelf. His height helps him grab it with little effort. When he returns, he places a rocks glass in front of me and pours. "Rough night?" He pushes it toward me.

"Rough couple of decades, I suppose."

"I'll have one of those, too," a familiar voice says as I sip. I peer over my glass, my shoulders relaxing when I see my father's girlfriend standing there.

"Ana…"

I place my drink on the counter, then wrap my arms around her, hugging her tighter than I planned. I have no one else in my life right now, other than Wes and my dad, who Ana's been dating for the past ten years. They met in a grief support group. She'd lost her husband years ago and still has trouble coping with it occasionally. She's been one of the best things to happen to my father. Since they started dating, he's been less focused on me and more focused on living life. I suppose I have her to thank for that.

"Where's Dad?" I pull back, glancing over her shoulder.

"There was a line of cars waiting to valet. He had me come in while he dealt with that."

I laugh sarcastically. "I'm sure he's thrilled about that. He has no patience."

She rolls her eyes, bringing her scotch to her lips. "Ain't that the truth."

Silence settles between us as we stand by the bar and sip on our drinks. The party continues around us, everyone seemingly oblivious to our presence, even though I'm the guest of honor.

"So… Excited about tomorrow?" Ana asks after a while.

I swallow hard, grit out the fake smile I've worn all evening, and give her the same canned response I have memorized at this point. "Absolutely. Wes and I are so excited about starting our lives together."

She studies me for a moment, then shifts her eyes around the room. "I don't see Molly or Gigi." She pauses. I sense what's coming next. "Or Drew."

Bringing my glass back to my mouth, I take a large gulp, grateful for the burn as it travels down my throat and coats my stomach. "I don't expect them to be here."

She scrutinizes me even longer, then gestures out the grand doors leading to the terrace overlooking the water. "Want to go outside? I could use a cigarette."

I smile, grateful for the reprieve from my own party. "Of course."

I know how much my father hates when she smokes. She's tried to quit on more than one occasion, and some days, she can go without craving a single puff. But other days, when the pain of losing her husband is too much, she needs it. I don't blame her. I'm not a smoker, but there have been quite a few times over the past few weeks I've considered taking it up.

Once we're outside, I exhale a breath, basking in the June air. We're not in the heat of the summer yet, so the temperatures are still comfortable, even a little crisp as the sun sets in the west. White party lights hang on strands overhead, making the outdoor patio inviting, but the dark clouds offshore threatening rain keep the party inside.

Ana lights a cigarette and takes a drag. I sip on my drink, looking over the ocean. I feel much less suffocated now that I'm outside, now that I'm with someone who cares about me. I can finally breathe and be me, be the Brooklyn I was before I allowed Drew to break my heart for the last time.

"I ran into Drew earlier this week," Ana says, cutting through the silence.

I whip my eyes toward hers, unable to hide my surprise.

"What?"

"Yup. When I went to get the rest of the boxes from your house, he was there."

I blink, processing this information. "What was he doing there?" My voice is timid, as if I already know the answer.

She takes another drag off her cigarette, exhaling the smoke away from me. "My guess… Hoping to talk to you." Her eyes lock with mine, my stomach feeling sour. The sound of a familiar laugh reaches me and I glance back inside. The expression on Wes' face as he chuckles at something a client must have said is so fake, it makes me question everything I thought I knew about him. I feel like I don't really know him. But do I know Drew? I'm no longer sure of that, either.

"Are you in love with him?" Ana's voice cuts through.

"Drew? Of course not." I lower my eyes, staring at the jewel-studded Jimmy Choo shoes Wes bought me. I'd often longed for the day I'd be able to wear some of the beautiful designer shoes Molly wrote about in her books. I didn't think I'd ever be so lucky.

Ana's hand lands on my forearm and I slowly lift my gaze back to hers. "I'm not talking about Drew. I'm talking about Wes, the man you're less than twenty-four hours away from marrying."

"Of course I do." I swallow hard, my tone anything but convincing.

She nods, the motion almost imperceptible, particularly to anyone who doesn't know Ana well. But I do. She's been a permanent fixture in my life the past decade. Without so much as a word, she can sense my inner turmoil, the turmoil I've spent the past several weeks trying to convince myself didn't exist. No matter how hard I tried, I couldn't erase the pain of Drew's eyes as he pleaded with me to believe him. It was so true, so compelling, so…real. More real than anything else in my life, including the love Wes claims he has for me.

"Did I ever tell you I was engaged to another man before I married Gavin?"

I slowly shake my head. "You've never talked about Gavin much." I take a sip of my scotch. "Or maybe I never asked because I knew how hard it was for my father to talk about my mother."

"That kind of loss never goes away. At first, it's impossible to talk about without your throat feeling like it's closing up, like the pain is drowning you and you'll never breathe again. But, over time, it gets easier. It never disappears. You just hope to find someone to fill that missing part someday."

"Is my father that missing part?" I arch a brow.

She considers my question, then smiles. "He is."

A clap of thunder sounds in the distance, the wind picking up. There's an eerie feeling in the air, a warning to all that a storm is about to descend on us. Regardless, we remain out here, ignoring the celebration raging inside.

"What was his name?" I ask after a while. "The guy you were engaged to before Gavin?"

"Lincoln." Her complexion flushes from the mere mention of his name. "Gosh, I thought I hit the jackpot when he asked me out." She faces me. "Before I went out with him, Gavin and I had dated off and on for years, but life always seemed to get in the way of us being together for longer than a summer fling. College. Work. Moving away. New friends. Not to mention my father didn't exactly approve of him."

That certainly piques my interest. I know all too well how that can be. Wes was the first guy I dated who my father actually approved of. "Why's that?"

"Could have been any number of reasons. I'm the youngest of five children. I have four older brothers."

"And I thought I had it bad with my father being as over-protective as he is."

Ana laughs. "Oh, no. Take that and multiply it by four. No one was good enough for me. Regardless, I never forgot about Gavin. When I heard he'd gotten married, it hurt. Gavin was the first person I slept with. I always had this romantic notion in the back of my mind that we'd end up together. So when I learned about his marriage... I don't know. I guess I thought I needed to settle, that it was time for me to give up on my romantic dreams since it was obvious he didn't feel the same way about me. So I dated, but not one single person held that spark. I figured if I tried a little harder, I'd eventually learn to love them. And Lincoln… He was every girl's dream. Handsome. Intelligent. Hardworking. Professional. Polite. The complete package. He just wasn't my dream."

"What happened?" I ask, my expression almost pleading with her to tell me she learned to love him, despite knowing how the story was destined to end.

"Brooklyn, sweetie…" She reaches toward me, brushing a lock of hair behind my ear. "You can't make yourself love someone. You're a very intelligent young woman with such a good head on your shoulders. I've watched you grow and mature into a young adult, into this caring, compassionate person who I'm truly blessed to have in my life. Love isn't something you can force. Your brain can't make your heart feel something it doesn't. So I need you to be honest with me. No matter what, this will stay between us."

"Okay." My voice trembles with hesitation.

"What does your heart feel right now?"

"That I shouldn't be here," I answer with more honesty than I've spoken with in weeks.

"And your brain?"

"That Wes is a good man, that it's time I forget about my adolescent dreams."

"Why do you think that?"

"Wes is one of the only people in my life who's always been honest with me, who's never hurt me." I struggle to reel in the tears threatening to fall, not wanting to make a scene at my own rehearsal dinner. I should be smiling and laughing as I relish in the love of the man I'm hours away from marrying, not doubt the path I've chosen. Not wonder if I should be on a different path, even though I've been down that path and it brought me nothing but pain. "He won't make me a promise, then break it. He won't promise me everything I've ever wanted, then shatter it. He won't use me. He won't make me feel invisible."

"What if you learned things aren't what they seem? What if you learned there was a very good reason Drew never showed up at your father's house on the morning he was supposed to leave for college?"

I stiffen, inhaling a sharp breath. "How do you know about that?" I didn't even think my father knew about that. How could he? Drew never showed up. I was so embarrassed about falling for his lies that I never told another person about what happened between us. Hell, I hadn't even told Molly. Drew must have done that. "How—"

"Brooklyn?" a deep voice interrupts. I snap my eyes from Ana, staring into deep pools of whiskey, my taut body straightening even more.

In my mind, I like to think I was right about Drew, that he didn't care about me, that when I pushed him away, he continued on like I didn't matter. But as I survey his appearance and take in his disheveled hair, bloodshot eyes, and lackluster expression, I see he's in as much pain as me, maybe more. It doesn't matter that he's recently shaved and put on a dress shirt and a pair of nice pants. He looks as empty as I feel.

"I'll leave you two to talk." Ana squeezes my bicep, giving me a small smile. "Don't settle for less than the love you deserve. Your father won't tell you that, but I will. Life is too short to waste it on any relationship where you don't feel like you're flying. You deserve to fly." She kisses my forehead, then nods at Drew.

"Thanks," he whispers.

"You bet. I'll distract him for a few minutes, but I'm not sure how much time I can give you."

His eyes lock on mine, unwavering and intense, just like everything with him. "That's all I need."

CHAPTER TWENTY-FIVE

DREW

CONFUSED GREEN EYES SEARCH mine, everything still as we stare at each other, probing, analyzing…hoping. It's the first time I've been near Brooklyn since I was graciously kicked out of the hospital, then told by her father to stay away from her. The first time I've delighted in this electricity coursing through me from her proximity. The first time I've inhaled the familiar aroma that's always comforted me, even when I didn't know why.

Laughter and excited conversation filters over the music being piped into speakers on the terrace, the tension between us growing and mounting with every silent heartbeat. I take a cautious step toward her, my movement snapping her out of her trance. She spins around, about to run away, like she always does when she's scared.

"Brooklyn, wait." I grab her arm and she stills, inhaling a sharp breath at the contact. I know she feels it, this reaction her body has whenever I touch her. This sort of attraction doesn't happen all the time. What we have is special, unique. I refuse to give up on this, on us, not after everything it took to finally get here. I don't care if anyone sees us and I'm escorted out of here. At least I'll know I showed her I was willing to fight for her.

She wrenches out of my hold, turning to face me. "I have nothing to say to you." Her voice lacks the determination it needs, like she's saying that because it's what's expected of her.

"You don't have to say anything."

She crosses her arms in front of her chest, making her cleavage even more pronounced. The slinky black dress she wears hugs her curves in just the right places, my eyes heating with hunger the longer I remain in her presence. I can faintly make out the bruising around her neck and scar on her forehead through the layers of makeup. Knowing Mrs. Bradford's reputation as I do, she probably has a professional makeup artist on the payroll all weekend to ensure all evidence of Brooklyn's assault is covered up so it doesn't appear as if anything's wrong.

"Then why did you come here? What do you want?"

My gaze remains locked on hers as I hold out a hand. "Just a dance."

"A...dance?" she clarifies, skeptical, confused.

I nod, leisurely licking my lips. "Just one dance with you, Brooklyn. Then I'll leave."

"You'll...leave?" She can't mask the surprise in her voice.

Perhaps she's hoping I'll put up more of a fight. Most men in my position would probably grovel, desperation taking over. But I know Brooklyn. Begging isn't the way to win her heart. I've already done that. This situation requires something different, something with more finesse, something much more personal. Something that touches her heart and infiltrates her soul. Something that reinvigorates this lifeless person she's turned into these past few weeks. Something that reminds her how deep our connection goes.

"Yes." My tone is even, my hand extended toward her.

"And if I say no?" She tilts her head, placing her hands on her hips.

I consider my response, assessing her. Then I smirk, laughing to myself. I may not know much, but I know Brooklyn. As stubborn as she is, she's even more curious, as evidenced by the furrowed brow and narrowed eyes.

"You won't." As if on cue, the music changes to a slower tune, Roberta Flack's voice singing the opening lines of "The First Time Ever I Saw Your Face" setting the mood.

She closes her eyes, her chest expanding as she inhales a deep breath. "I should walk away right now." I'm not sure if she says that for me or for her. I have a feeling it's the latter.

"You probably should, but we've known each other our entire lives and have never danced together. I say it's time that's rectified."

She releases a long sigh and meets my gaze. After a

protracted moment, she extends her hand, her fingers intertwining with mine. My eyes unwavering, I bring her against me, one hand holding hers, the other placed on the small of her back. If this is the last time I'll be lucky enough to feel her body against mine, I want to remember every little thing — every exhale of her sweet breath against my skin, every beat of her heart with mine, every sway of her hips.

When nearly a minute has passed and I still haven't so much as uttered a single syllable, Brooklyn finally blurts out, "Aren't you going to say something? Beg me to reconsider? Anything?"

My lips lift into a small smile, my demeanor calm despite her obvious agitation. "No. I'm not."

"You're…not?"

"Nope. I've wanted to dance with you for seventeen years, maybe even longer. I'd rather not ruin it."

"So you're not going to apologize?" There's a hint of disappointment in her voice.

"Like I said, no."

Her brows scrunch together, which is the most breathtaking thing I've seen in a long time. It takes all my resolve not to break into a wide grin at how much I adore that look on her. "Why?"

"Because I don't need to."

"You don't think you need to attempt to make amends?"

"This isn't about me trying to make amends. This is about you, Brooklyn. And I know you better than most people, except your father and maybe Molly. But the jury's still out on that. While she's been your best friend since you were playing with Barbie's, I still know you damn well. So I don't need to say anything to you."

"You don't?"

I shake my head, my grip on her tightening. I'd give anything to crush my lips to hers and kiss her the way I doubt Wes ever has. It's what she needs, what she deserves.

"What we have… It's more powerful than words. This isn't about what either one of us did or didn't do. It's bigger than that. I can stand here and waste my breath, but nothing

I say really matters."

"It doesn't?" She swallows hard as I close the distance between our mouths, every inch I erase making her more on edge.

"No. Because in your heart, you feel it, too."

She cranes her head, her lips seeking mine, like they're made for one another. "Feel what?"

"This. I've fought it for so long. We both have. Maybe there's a reason for that. Maybe that's why we've hurt each other, why we keep hurting each other. Then again, maybe that's why we feel the pain when most people wouldn't. Why Carla didn't, why Wes didn't. Because there was never this. I may not have graduated with honors. I may not be the smartest man. But I do know one thing…"

"And what's that?" Her voice is husky as that beautiful blush blooms on her cheeks, prominent against her fair skin. Her chest heaves with her breaths as she subconsciously lifts her chin. Like a dancer who recalls choreography she's done her entire life, she releases her hold on my hand, draping both arms over my shoulders as she arches into me, barely a whisper between us.

"You. I know you, Brooklyn. And that's why all I need is one dance."

"You think one dance will make me change my mind?"

"A wise woman once told me that sometimes it's better to show someone our hearts, our feelings, with actions rather than words."

She pushes out a laugh, the tension breaking. "That sounds like something Aunt Gigi would say."

"Actually, it was Ana."

She blinks, her jaw dropping. "Ana? How—"

"The time for talking is done." My voice is firm, determined. "I've never been good with words anyway. I've always been more a man of action. I'm not going to waste my breath trying to convince you I had my reasons for not showing up all those years ago, just like I had my reasons I was late meeting you at the beach a few weeks ago."

I brush a tendril of hair out of her eyes so she can see me

as clearly as possible. "Despite what your brain is telling you to think, in your heart, you know I've spent the past seventeen years trying to do right by you. And I'll spend the rest of my life doing the same thing." We stop swaying as I move my hands to her face, cupping her cheeks. "I know you love me. And you always will. I know the only reason you're marrying Wes is because I've hurt you more times than any person should have to suffer through in their life. I was your first heartbreak when I should have been your first and only love. The truth is…" I pause, licking my lips, unsure what to say, whether I should finally come clean.

"Yes?" she breathes, craning her head even more, her lips grazing mine.

"The truth is…"

"Yes," she repeats, this time more as an affirmation that this is what she wants.

"The truth is, I—"

A loud throat clearing rips through the space, startling both of us. Brooklyn jumps away, inhaling a sharp breath when she sees her father standing there, his arms crossed in front of his intimidating physique. Ana stands behind him, offering an apologetic smile.

"We were just dancing," Brooklyn explains urgently, her cheeks reddening in shame.

"Wes is looking for you." He narrows his gaze on her, then me. "I suggest finding him before he finds you."

Brooklyn lifts her eyes back to mine, hesitating. I remain silent, keeping my gaze locked on hers, wanting her to see my thoughts and feelings through our connection. It's so deep I believe she can.

"Brooklyn?" Her father's voice cuts through and she whips her gaze back to his. "Go. Now."

Acting like a fifteen-year-old girl instead of the thirty-two-year-old woman she is, she lowers her head, hurrying inside. Ana follows, her gaze shifting between Brooklyn and me until the frivolity of the party swallows them.

The entire situation angers me and I storm after her, no longer caring about the scene I'll make in front of Wes and his guests. A hand wraps around my arm, stopping me.

"Drew."

I shake my head, my jaw clenching. Then I lift my fiery eyes to his, my lips turning into a sneer as I struggle to speak through the frustration building in my throat. "I get that you don't like me. I get that you don't think I'm good enough for your daughter." My irate tone gives him pause, and he releases his hold on me. "I know I'm not. In my opinion, there isn't a single human being walking this planet who is good enough for that woman in there." I lift my arm, pointing in the direction Brooklyn just left. The pain that settled in my chest when I broke into her hospital room mounts, the burn turning to desperation as I plead my case like a man facing execution begging for a last-minute pardon.

"But I'm willing to promise you and her that I will make it my mission in life to try to be that man, to be worthy of even an ounce of her devotion." My chest heaves as everything spills forward, my voice choked with emotion. Tears form in the corners of my eyes, my neck stiff, forearms strained as my hands ball into fists. "Has Wes ever made that promise to you?"

He remains speechless, swallowing hard. His lack of response is all the answer I need. Drawing in a deep breath, I lower my voice, stepping toward him, softening my expression.

"Do you think your wife would have wanted Brooklyn to marry someone who doesn't make her happy just so you could save face?"

His lips part, but still no words come.

"Maybe you should think about that before you walk her down the aisle to a man she doesn't love."

CHAPTER TWENTY-SIX

BROOKLYN

"**B**ROOKLYN, DARLING, I'VE BEEN looking everywhere for you," Wes croons in a lazy voice as I make my way through the crowded room, cheerful people surrounding me. This is supposed to be my party, my time to be happy, to be on top of the world, to relish in the love of this man. Instead, I'm more confused than ever. I thought I had everything figured out, thought I'd made peace with my past and was ready to move on with my future. After seeing Drew, after losing myself in him as we danced together, I feel more alive than I have in weeks, his touch jumpstarting my heart once more.

"I'm not feeling well. I just... I just need a minute." I keep my eyes lowered so he doesn't notice the guilt in my expression.

He grabs my arms, preventing me from taking another step. Tilting my chin, he forces my gaze to his. My heart pounds as he studies me, a hidden accusation in the way he scrutinizes me, like I have a giant scarlet A branded on my chest.

"Are you okay?" He leans closer, his lips brushing with mine. No spark. No electricity. No all-consuming need to deepen the kiss. "Are we okay?"

"Of course." I straighten my spine, blinking. "The doctors warned me against drinking since I'm still dealing with the aftereffects of some of my injuries." I smile, but it's as fake as many of these women's noses. "I just need to splash some water on my face. That's all."

He pinches his lips together, seeming to assess my response. Is this how it will always be between us? Will he always wonder whether I'm telling the truth? I know the answer to that all too well. I've done the same thing with

Drew.

"Okay." He releases his hold on me. "Hurry back. There are a few more people I want to introduce you to."

His words more like a demand than a request, I nod, not giving him another glance as I continue toward the ladies' room. Out of the corner of my eye, I spot Mrs. Bradford's sanctimonious expression trained on me, her lips formed in a permanent scowl of disapproval. For the longest time, I just wanted to be with someone who noticed me, who didn't make me feel invisible. Now I'd give anything to be able to disappear.

Pushing open the door to the ladies' room, I barrel inside the private restroom, letting out a huge breath once I no longer feel the burn of hundreds of eyes analyzing me, looking for a fault. Wes never mentioned my indiscretions to anyone, claimed he didn't want that tiny slip up to define us. But how could it not? How could we both expect to move on and pretend it never happened? As much as I thought I could, thought he could, I realize it's an insurmountable obstacle we'll never overcome.

Dizziness overtaking me, I head to the sink, turning on the faucet. As I splash water on my face, there's a subtle knock. I exhale, about to reiterate to Wes I'm fine when a different voice speaks. This one older, more gruff, one that read me stories and sang me to sleep when I was a little girl.

"Brooklyn, sweetie, are you okay?"

I splash more water on my face, pinching my cheeks so he won't be able to tell I'm on the verge of tears. "Yes. Of course," I say in a shaky voice. "I'll be out in a minute."

There's a door between us, but I can sense his hesitation, his reluctance to believe me. Even a complete stranger can tell I'm anything but okay right now.

"Can you open the door? There's... There's something we need to talk about." Something in his tone gives me pause. Normally, I'd insist I was fine, but nothing about tonight, about this entire ordeal, is normal. Not anymore.

I turn off the faucet, dry my face and hands, then head toward the door, unlocking it. "What is it, Dad?"

He opens his mouth, an unusual reluctance covering his face. This man has always exuded confidence in spades. Not tonight. A sinking feeling forms in the pit of my stomach that whatever he wants to discuss is about to turn my entire world upside down. I don't know if I can handle any more drama tonight. I've hit my lifetime quota of that over the past several weeks.

"Can we go talk somewhere? Maybe back outside?" Hope builds in his expression as he awaits my response. It's strange to have him ask me like this. It's usually more of a demand, especially in my younger years.

Without saying a word, I nod. Instead of heading back toward the party, he leads me down the hallway, opening the door to the terrace. I glance at the spot where, less than five minutes ago, I danced with Drew, still able to feel the ghost of his arms around me, pacifying me…loving me?

Dad goes to the ledge and leans his forearms against it. I do the same, watching the night darken with every passing second. The wind has increased, the approaching storm getting closer. Thunder rumbles in the distance, a few streaks of lightning illuminating the sky miles offshore.

"You know I love you, don't you?" he says after a moment of silent contemplation.

I meet his eyes. "Of course. You're the best father a girl could ask for."

On a long sigh, he straightens his spine and runs his hand over his weary face. "I loved your mother so very much. When I lost her, it felt like I lost a part of myself. I made it my mission to ensure you never felt the hole her absence left. Everything I've done, every decision I've made, has been with that in mind, to protect you."

"I know that." I grab his hands in mine, squeezing. "I may have hated some of your rules at the time, but I understand why you had them."

Our gazes remain locked and I can see the forming of tears in the corners of his eyes, his chin trembling slightly. I swallow hard, a chill trickling down my spine. My father is not an emotional man. I don't think I've seen him cry since the day of my mother's funeral.

"That may be true, but now, my darling Brooklyn, I fear my own heartache may have cost you the one thing your mother always wished for you."

"What's that?" I ask cautiously.

His lips lift in the corners. "Love."

My breathing increases as that word lingers in the air between us. "What do you mean? Wes—"

"Is not the man for you. You don't love him."

"What?" My posture stiffens, my lips parting. The one person who's supported my relationship with Wes has been my father. I need him to support this. "How could you say that? I wouldn't have agreed to marry him if I didn't love him."

My father tilts his head to the side, knowing all too well that my words lack the conviction they should have. "I think we both know that's not true, that perhaps there's a different reason you agreed to marry him. To forget about someone else."

I tear my eyes from his. "There's never been anything between Drew and me," I lie. "Nothing worth remembering anyway." I lift my head, shrugging. "Maybe I thought there was at one point, but I was young and stupid. And Drew turned out to be just like all the boys you warned me about. Only interested in one thing."

Dad closes his eyes, inhaling a deep breath before returning them to me. "Brooklyn, sweetie, he really does love you. I saw that tonight. Hell, I've seen that since you were teenagers. I just… I didn't want to believe it, didn't want to think my little girl was growing up. I thought I was doing the right thing back then. Now I can't help but think I've ruined both of your lives."

I lean back, my sluggish heartbeat echoing in my ears. "What are you talking about, Dad?"

He swallows hard, time seeming to stand still. "I know about your history."

My lips part as I blink, my stomach rolling. That could mean so much. Does he know I've always had feelings for

Drew? Does he know he came to my rescue that night all those years ago when I was about to make a terrible decision? Does he know I invited him into my bedroom, even though he had a wife and child, only to learn he was still the same Drew who broke his promise to me when I was a teenager?

"I've done a lot of things I'm not proud of, but this…" He shakes his head, his remorse-filled gaze locking with mine. "I saw him kiss you."

"When?" My voice is guarded as I try not to give anything away. It could be recent or seventeen years ago.

"The night before he left for college. On the security cameras."

My heart drops, the world seeming to spin around me as another piece of the puzzle snaps into place. I can hear Drew's pleas to believe him when he told me he didn't have a choice, that if he could have been there that morning, he would have.

"What did you do?" I take a step back, every inch of my body trembling.

"When I saw that video of him walking you up the driveway, you in nothing but your underwear with a blanket wrapped around you, I thought—"

"What? That it was because of Drew?"

His expression remains even, apologetic.

"Drew would never hurt me, or any girl."

"I know that now. Back then, all I saw was my sweet, innocent daughter being taken advantage of by someone much older, much more mature, much more experienced. I couldn't stand the idea of him hurting you, so I did what I thought necessary."

"What did you do?" I ask again, my voice strained.

He opens his mouth, blowing out a breath as he rubs his temples. When he returns his gaze to mine, it's filled with regret, shame, heartache. "The following morning, I stopped by his father's house before I headed into work."

"You didn't." I back away, my stomach churning. I know my father well enough that nothing he had to say to Drew or his father that morning could have been good.

"I've spent the past seventeen years wondering if I made

the right decision. I convinced myself I did, that I did what any father of a beautiful young girl would do."

"What did you do?" I ask once more, my voice catching.

"You have to look at things from my perspective," he begs frantically, rushing toward me. He reaches for my hands, but I avoid his touch. "You were so young. I wasn't prepared to deal with all the physical changes you were going through. I thought I did what I had to do to keep you safe."

"What. Did. You. Do?!" I demand a final time, tears streaming down my face.

He swallows hard, his posture slumping. "I told him if he went near you, if he so much as looked at you, I'd turn him in for statutory rape."

His words rip all the oxygen from my body, heat washing over my face. I continue backing away, shaking my head, feeling like the world is closing in on me, despite the fact that we're outside. I try to make sense of what he just confessed, but it doesn't register in my brain. I want to think this is just a dream, that I'll wake up on my wedding day and not be saddled with the truth that I've held a grudge against Drew for seventeen years over something he wasn't responsible for, just like he begged me to believe. That this man who was supposed to love me and support me caused all the tears I've cried. That this man who gave me life is the one responsible for ruining it.

"When I saw that video, I snapped. I didn't know what else to do!"

"You could have asked me about it."

"And what would you have said?"

"I would have told you the truth!" I lean into him, my voice growing louder with each word I speak. "That if he hadn't shown up to that party when he did, something awful could have happened! I probably would have actually been raped! But Drew showed up just when I needed him and hauled me out of there."

I briefly close my eyes, seeing Drew in a different light now that I know the truth. All those times he came home during school breaks and I thought he was ignoring me because he wanted nothing to do with me. All those times he made me feel invisible. All those times I questioned whether that night actually did happen. It's all different now.

I lick my lips, my throat closing up. "You saw how upset I was after he left for college, how much pain I was in when I learned he got married, and you still didn't think you should tell me the truth?!"

"Brooklyn, sweetie…" He reaches for me, but I step back again. I've always been a very reasonable person. It takes a lot to upset me, but this is more than I can handle, especially just hours away from my wedding to another man. "There were so many times I wanted to, but… I don't know. I guess I wanted to believe it didn't matter, that he didn't matter. Now, I know the truth." His eyes lock with mine. "He matters. He always will."

A weight crushing my chest, suffocating me the longer I remain in this man's presence, I push past him, desperate for some sort of clarity, some sort of assurance that this information changes nothing.

"Brooklyn!" he calls out.

I stop, whirling around. "Drew was supposed to be my first." My chin trembles as tears stream down my cheeks, obscuring my vision. "Instead, because you thought you were doing the right thing, do you know who my first was?"

His expression is long as he remains frozen in place, not saying a word.

"His name was Domenic Bianchi. He was a junior when I was a freshman at college." I take slow steps toward him. I swore I'd never talk about this again, but I need him to understand exactly what his over-protectiveness did. "He was the perfect gentleman on the outside. Good family. Charismatic smile. Active in sports. Volunteered at the local soup kitchen. That's actually where we met. We hit it off, and I thought he was my chance at forgetting about Drew, about how he broke my heart. Do you want to know what Domenic did?"

"Did he…?" He trails off, unable to finish his sentence.

"Rape me? No. But what he did hurt just as much. I was

just a square in a game of Bingo the lacrosse team was playing. Once he screwed me, he had no more use for me. So maybe I would have been able to find it in my heart to forgive you for what you did to Drew. But I'll never forgive you for what you did to me. Because of you, because of your selfishness, I'll always have to remember Domenic Bianchi when I would love nothing more than to forget him." I spin back around, opening the door.

"Brooklyn, please. I thought—"

"That's the problem," I interrupt, glancing over my shoulder. "You didn't think. Every action has consequences. This action, this decision, has ruined more lives than you can imagine."

A crack of thunder sounds as the sky opens, rain falling around me. I duck back inside, tears streaming down my cheeks, my heart physically breaking that this man kept this secret from me for so long. I have no idea where I'm going, what I'm supposed to do now that everything I once thought to be true isn't.

The party is in full force as I search the room, people I've never met dancing to an up-tempo song, the background music to my world crashing around me. I turn in circles, looking for guidance, a sign, anything. I catch Ana's eyes as she comforts my father. Does she know? How many people knew? How many people kept it from me because they didn't think I could handle the truth? Maybe they're right. Maybe I can't handle this truth.

I place my hand on a nearby table, ready to collapse from the pressure mounting inside me, when a familiar arm wraps around my waist.

"Brooklyn?" I raise my eyes, meeting Wes' concerned gaze. "Are you okay? You look like you've seen a ghost or something."

I swallow hard, desperate to see something in his expression that tells me how I'm supposed to process this new information, to see a love I've never felt, to see my future. But I don't.

Frantic, I clutch his face in my hands, pressing my lips to

his. These are lips I've kissed so many times, but it feels…wrong. Everything feels wrong.

Cheers and applause echo through the room, all the guests toasting the bride and groom. It makes me kiss him harder, sending up a silent prayer for that bolt of lightning to jumpstart my heart like whenever I kiss Drew, whenever I feel Drew, whenever I think of Drew. But it doesn't. I feel nothing. I've felt nothing since the beginning. I was just too heartbroken to admit it.

My lips lingering on his a moment longer, I close my eyes, a lone tear trickling down my cheek.

"Brook?"

Wes' voice forces my gaze back to his. I can pretend I love him, pretend I'm happy, but my eyes don't lie. I swallow hard, trying to find the words I need. Only three words seem fitting for this situation.

"I'm so sorry."

He studies me for a moment, then his shoulders fall, resignation washing over him. Those words could mean so many things, but Wes is a smart man. He knows why I said them. I bring my hand in front of me, taking my engagement ring between my thumb and forefinger, about to slide it off, when a shrill voice interrupts.

"Sorry?" We both snap our heads to see Wes' mother storming toward us, her eyes fiery, her lips turned into a scowl. "You're sorry? Sorry is not good enough, you little slut. I know all about you and that washed-up hockey player. I know you've been—"

"Mother, please," Wes hisses under his breath. "Not now." With haste, he clutches my hand, dragging me past the crowd of curious onlookers, through the dining area, and into a smaller private function room that's not being used, closing the door behind us.

I remain motionless, studying him as he keeps his back to me, pinching the bridge of his nose, his shoulders slumped.

"It doesn't matter how much you love a person." His voice is quiet and contemplative. Then he turns and lifts his sad eyes to mine. "It won't stop them from loving someone else."

"I tried." I step toward him, urging him to see the truth. "I wanted this to work."

"Me, too, even though I knew it would probably end like this. I guess a part of me hoped I could love you enough for the both of us."

I bring my hand to his face, swiping at the few tears that had escaped. "You know it doesn't work that way." He melts into my touch, savoring it, as if it's the last bit of oxygen he'll ever breathe. "We were always meant to say goodbye." I raise myself onto my toes, placing a soft kiss on his lips.

Cupping my cheeks, he returns my kiss with the same tenderness he's shown me since the day he approached me and struck up a conversation. I like to think there's a purpose for every encounter, every life event, that the people who enter our lives do so for a reason. At first, I thought Wes entered my life to help me bury my past, but I was wrong. He entered my life to make me feel beautiful again. He gave me his love. No limitations. No qualifications. Just pure, untainted love. Better yet, he taught me it was okay to love again, to take a risk on love again. For that, he will always have a special place in my heart.

"I'm glad you figured things out." His voice is filled with masked pain. As much as I wish I could take away his heartache, his anguish, I'm not the one to do that. Not anymore. "He loves you. I noticed it in his eyes the day I first saw you."

I blink back my tears. "I didn't think he did, or maybe I just thought it was too good to be true, that he'd just break yet another promise, but now…" I shake my head.

I've lived the past seventeen years of my life never being able to trust a single word out of Drew's mouth because of that one broken promise. Or what I thought was a broken promise. Everything's different. Everything he's ever done, ever said, has a different meaning.

"Now I know he does. He always has." I draw in a long breath, glancing back at my left hand. I slide the ring off my finger, holding it toward Wes. "I need to go after that. I can't run from it anymore."

He's reluctant as he reaches for it and takes it in his hand. "I can respect that."

I clutch his face, the pads of my thumbs swiping his tears. He brings a hand up to mine, exhaling a long breath before pulling away, forcing me to drop my hold on him.

"So what are you going to do now?" I ask, not wanting to leave until I know he'll be okay.

"You mean after running damage control with my mother?" He chuckles, cutting through the tension.

"Oh god, Wes." I cringe. "I'm so sorry. I'll go back in there, try to explain things—"

"It's okay," he assures me with a forced smile. "This won't be any worse than when my sister eloped a week before her wedding."

"The last thing I wanted was to hurt you, then leave you to clean up the mess."

He shrugs. "It'll give me something to do. Who knows? Maybe this is the universe trying to tell me it's time to head back to Georgia. Run the company from there instead of struggle to do it up here. You were my reason for staying. But now…" He trails off, his words caught in his throat. I try to blink back my own tears, unsuccessfully. Stepping toward me, he brushes his finger against my cheeks, erasing my tears. "Now maybe this is the chance we both need for our new start. My meemaw used to always say, 'Each day is a new chapter that's yet to be written so make the most of it.' No matter how much this hurts, I plan to make the most of this next chapter. I hope you do, too."

Overwhelmed with how understanding and humble this man is, I wrap my arms around his broad shoulders, pressing my lips back to his. "Thank you, Wes."

This time, he doesn't kiss me back. Instead, he leans his forehead on mine, inhaling.

"I did love you," I say, hoping it gives him the small slice of the comfort he needs right now. "I still do."

"Just not like you need to."

I slowly shake my head. "No."

On a shaky inhale, he gradually pulls away. I release my hold on him, my fingers tingling from the lack of warmth. We're all wrong for each other, but that doesn't mean my heart isn't breaking at the thought that this will be the last time I see him, the last time I touch him, the last time I hear his soothing voice.

Wes leans against a long banquet table, running a hand over his face. I take this as my cue to leave and start toward the door.

"I've been scared of losing you since the day you agreed to that first date."

I glance over my shoulder, but remain silent. There's nothing I can say that will dampen the pain. I'll only make it worse.

"But you were never mine to lose in the first place." He pulls his lip between his teeth, the despair covering him almost more than I can bear. Then he meets my eyes. "Live a good life, Brooklyn. And do all the amazing things I know you were put on this earth to do. Just know, no matter what, you will always have a piece of my heart."

His words unleash the waterworks once more. I want to hug him, assure him it'll be okay. Instead, I nod and say the only thing that seems meaningful at this moment. "Thank you."

Without another look back, I walk away from Wes and toward what I hope will be the next chapter in my life.

CHAPTER TWENTY-SEVEN

DREW

DARKNESS SURROUNDS ME AS I sit in my home office, a half-empty glass of scotch in my hand. I glance at the grandfather clock to see it's almost midnight. Tomorrow at this time, Brooklyn will be married and there won't be anything else I can do about it. There's nothing more I can do about it now.

Ever since I got back from crashing her rehearsal dinner, I've sat in this room, nursing this same glass of scotch, replaying the evening in my mind. Was there a better way I could have approached the situation? Should I have blurted out the truth? Would she have believed me? Would it have changed anything? Did I just lose my best friend?

As I stare at the framed photos spanning the years from childhood to adulthood that adorn the walls, a pair of headlights flash into the room. I squint through the rain to see a car pulling up the long drive to my house. I stand, heading to the window. When the car comes to a stop, I notice the Uber sticker on the windshield. The rear passenger door opens and a familiar silhouette steps onto the walkway, stopping and staring at the house. The car waits for a moment, but eventually drives away, leaving my late-night guest in the elements.

I expect her to hurry to the front porch to avoid the rain, but she doesn't, allowing the drops to drench her black dress. Her hair is still haphazardly pinned to her head, as if she's been running and hasn't had a chance to take it out of the style she had it in earlier this evening. The makeup that had been caked on now runs down her face. I'm unsure if it's because of the rain or because she's been crying. By the long expression she wears, I sense it's due to the latter.

Placing my glass on the desk, I walk out of the office and

through the quiet house, anticipation building inside me. When I open the front door, she doesn't immediately look my way, her focus still glued to a window on the second floor...my window.

"Brooklyn?"

The sound of my voice forces her eyes to mine. The way she's looking at me seems different. It's sad, pained, almost mournful. It's like she's able to peer into my soul to see my faults and secrets. Like she's finally seeing me, not the Andrew Brinks she always believed me to be, the one who always let her down, the one who made her feel like she didn't matter, the one who broke his promise to her.

Realization hits me and I haltingly step toward her. "You know."

She nods, wiping away the tears on her face, smudging her makeup even more. "Why didn't you say anything? Why did you let me believe the worst of you?"

I close the distance between us but don't touch her, as much as I want to reach out and pull her into my chest to comfort her. She needs to see the truth in my eyes. "I didn't want to ruin your relationship with your father. I didn't want to hurt you any more than I already had."

"You cared about that so much you were willing to let me marry another man?"

"Your dad was all the family you had left. I couldn't be the reason you hated him."

"You are so stupid, Andrew Brinks. Don't you see?"

I shake my head, confused. "See what?"

"You are my family."

Before I have a chance to utter another word, she grasps my face in her hands, pulling my lips to hers. I still, caught off-guard. Is she here to say goodbye, for one last kiss before she marries Wes?

I reach up and wrap my hands around hers, my breath leaving me when there's no longer a ring on a very important finger like there was just a few hours ago. Groaning, I palm her back, bringing her closer, falling into the kiss, into her, into us.

God, please let there finally be an us.

She digs her hands into my hair, her fingers raking against my scalp, kissing me hard, fast, and desperate. In this moment, I realize I finally have all of Brooklyn. Her past. Her present. Her future. And I want nothing more than to give this woman all those things, too.

Leaving a lingering kiss, I pull back, resting my forehead against hers. "What happened?"

A gentle smile forms on her plump lips. There's a peacefulness about her, one I haven't seen on her since the night she gave me her first kiss. "Dad told me the truth. At first, I didn't think it mattered, that it was years ago. But it does. You've always mattered, Drew. It's time I make up for all the years I was supposed to be kissing you, but couldn't."

All the tension in my body disappears as I hang my head in gratitude, her words like a life vest keeping me afloat. I stare into her blazing eyes, losing myself in her. In the way the rain drips from her hair. The way the porch light shines in her eyes, making them gleam and dance. The way she seems so confident and assured as she gives me her heart. No more secrets. No more lies. No more barriers between us.

"Please, say something," she begs when I remain silent. She lowers her head, stepping back and wrapping her arms around her slender body. "I know I've made a habit of running from you when things got too real, too scary. I thought it was what I had to do to protect myself." A small smile builds on her mouth as she meets my gaze. "But I should have been running toward you. You're the only man who's ever made me feel safe, who's ever made me a priority, who's ever lo—"

I erase the distance and cover her mouth with mine. Our kiss is feverish and heavy as I grip her hips, hoisting her up as if she weighs no more than a feather. Instinct kicks in and her legs circle my waist, like a puzzle piece snapping into place. She tugs on my hair, her soft lips locked on mine, bruising. No matter how deep our kiss, how much passion we put into the exchange, it's still not enough. There's so much I want to do, to say, to feel. I don't know where to begin, my need for her bubbling and overflowing.

My mouth never leaving hers, I carry her up the steps and into my house, our tongues tangling as we greedily take everything the other's willing to give, the buildup to this moment crashing over us. I never want to let her go, never want to stop tasting her lips, never want to stop basking in this love I have for her…and she me.

When we reach the kitchen, I place her on the island, our kiss becoming less frenzied, less hurried, more sensual, more meaningful. She runs her hands through my coarse, wet hair, moaning into my mouth as we take our time to savor and explore each other in a way I thought we never would again.

With a contented sigh, she pulls away, gazing up at me. I still can't believe she's here. Just a few minutes ago, I was drowning my sorrows in a bottle of scotch, resigned to the fact that I'd lost her. That no matter what I did, it would never be enough. That I'd sealed our fate when I got on that plane and left for college, then stayed away. Somehow, the universe thought us worthy of another chance. This time, I'm not messing it up, I'm not letting it go. This is it for me. Brooklyn is it for me.

"You're wet," I say finally.

"So are you."

"But you're beautiful." I run a light finger down the outline of her face, her skin silken compared to the roughness of mine.

"So are you," she murmurs as my thumb traces the line of her bottom lip. She plumps them, her tongue darting out, grazing my skin.

I suck in a breath, my jaw clenching from the contact. A hunger for more fills me and I lean into her, my lips landing on her neck. A chill visibly rolls through her, her legs trembling. I pull back, noticing goosebumps have formed on her skin, her teeth chattering.

"You're shivering." I study her a little closer. Her complexion is pale, her lips a shade too close to purple for my liking. "Let's get you out of this wet dress."

My sense of urgency seems to be lost on her as she smiles

coyly. "Now that, Andrew Brinks…" She trails a finger down my chest, balling my t-shirt in her fist and forcing me close to her, "is one of the best ideas you've had in a long time."

"I'm glad you think so." I waggle my eyebrows. Then, in one quick move, I loop an arm around her back and one under her legs, lifting her off the island and against my chest in a cradle hold.

"Drew," she whisper-shouts, keeping her voice low so she doesn't wake the girls. "What are you doing?" She playfully swats at me as I head up the stairs, but I only tighten my grip.

"I've been imagining this since before I hit puberty and discovered boobs. Then even more when you hit puberty, and I discovered you were a girl with boobs. A girl with fucking incredible boobs, if you don't mind me saying."

"Thanks for your vote of confidence."

I cross the threshold to the master bedroom, heading straight toward the bed. My light expression becoming more serious, I lower her to her feet. She stares at me as I step closer, our chests rising and falling in time with each other.

"I already messed up my first shot with you." I cup her face in my hands. "And probably my second and third."

"And fourth and fifth," she jokes.

"I am not doing that again. I'm doing this right." My voice turns husky and deep as my lips hover close to hers. She seeks them out, but I remain just out of reach. "I'll give you everything you've ever wanted, ever desired, ever craved." I nuzzle into the crook of her neck, inhaling a long breath. "Make you feel things you didn't think possible," I murmur against her, then pull back. "After tonight, you'll never think of another man. Because for years, you've been the only woman I've thought of. For years, I've thought of the promise I made you."

A blush blooms on her cheeks and she turns her head downward.

"Don't." The harshness of my tone forces her eyes back up. With a smile, I lower my voice. "Don't look away. Don't hide from me. Not anymore. Not ever again."

Her lips part as her gaze rakes over my face, as if searching for the truth, whether these are just another bunch of lies she's being fed, more promises I'll never fulfill.

"I promised I'd be your first."

She swallows hard, a lone tear trickling down her cheek, staining her skin. I swipe it away with the pad of my thumb.

"I broke that promise to you. I should have fought harder for you. I have to live with that mistake. But I'll make a new promise, one I will spend the rest of my life fulfilling."

"What's that?"

"To be your last. To do everything in my power to make you forget about every single man who came before me, who didn't treat you with the respect you deserve, who hurt you, who broke your heart...including me." I keep my eyes trained on her, needing this connection. "I will spend the rest of my life earning your love. I'm not sure I deserve it. I'm not sure anyone deserves it, but I will do everything in my power to prove myself worthy, to show you that you've made the right decision in choosing me."

"It wasn't a choice." She drapes her arms over my shoulders, her breath dancing on my skin making me come alive. "It never was. I've loved you since I learned what love was. I've just been fighting it for all these years. No more."

"No more." I run my tongue along her bottom lip, begging for permission to enter. When she opens, I envelope her into my embrace, exploring her mouth as if it's the first time. It doesn't matter how many times I've kissed this woman. Every kiss, every breath, every moan feels new and exhilarating.

Her grip on me tightens as she arches her body into mine, our exchange turning from soft and meaningful to greedy, lustful, desperate. This moment has been a lifetime in the making, one I didn't think I'd experience just a few hours ago. I don't want to rush this, but damn if I'm not anxious for a taste of everything she has to offer.

I tear my lips from hers, staring at her with a sinful gaze as I reach for the bottom of her dress. She nods, not so much as even a hint of hesitation or reluctance in her expression. My eyes remaining glued to hers, I deliberately lift it over her head, then drop it to the floor, the wet material landing with a thud. Her black bra is soaked through, the chill enveloping her even more noticeable from her alert nipples. I run a finger down the line of her face and her teeth chatter.

"We need to warm you up." I step back, ripping my t-shirt over my head. I unbutton my jeans and shove them down my legs before stepping out of them, leaving me standing in just my boxer briefs. Brooklyn's pupils dilate, her cheeks reddening.

With calm steps, I approach her again, barely a breath between us.

"We're really doing this, aren't we?" She lifts her eyes.

Palming her back, I dig my other hand into her hair, my grip tight. I can feel her heart thumping against my chest, fast and firm. "We don't have to. I don't want you to feel pressured. I—"

She cuts me off, covering my mouth with hers. Groaning, I lose myself in her. The feel of her lips on mine, her tongue moving so delicately against mine drives me wild with desperation to have more of her, to taste every inch of her, to know her in a way no man ever will again.

I tug her harder into me, crushing her frame to mine. When she gasps, I quickly loosen my hold. "I'm sorry. Did I hurt you?" I survey her body, looking for signs of distress, unsure if she's still experiencing any pain from her attack.

With a sly grin, she steps back. Coyly biting her bottom lip, she kicks off her heels, then unclasps her bra, her motions slow and deliberate. With every drawn-out movement that reveals more of her skin, all the composure I've struggled to maintain evaporates. I want to make this last, but don't know how much longer I can wait to experience something I've dreamed about for years.

As she drops the material to the floor, standing before me in just her panties, I lose the last bit of control I've clung to. Fast and fevered, I rush to her, devouring her mouth as I push her toward the bed. Once her legs hit the mattress, I lower her onto it, then crawl on top, my lips never leaving hers, my hands never straying from her body.

Her fingers trail down my back, causing a shiver to roll through me. When she digs her nails into my skin, I arch into her. I've been with my fair share of women in my thirty-five years. Before I had kids, I lived by the motto "Work hard and play even harder." And I played very hard. With success came a revolving door of women. I was only too happy to indulge in the fruits of my newfound celebrity status. But no woman ever had the electricity Brooklyn's touch does. I felt it all those years ago. And I feel it again now. I want to kick the younger, more selfish version of myself for being an idiot, for not fighting harder for her, then trying to do everything to forget her.

Then again, maybe everything we went through happened for a reason. Maybe I kept my distance because it wasn't the right time. Maybe I can't remember that one night we shared seven years ago because the universe knew Charlotte needed me. Regardless of the reason, I'm grateful the planets have finally aligned for us.

I stare into her green eyes, overwhelmed. "I love you, Brooklyn."

The most radiant smile I've ever seen crosses her lips. "And I love you."

"I'm so glad you came back," I murmur, sealing our devotion with a kiss.

"I didn't come back."

I cock my head, meeting her eyes.

"I've always been yours, Andrew Brinks," she says as she runs a hand through my hair. "I gave you my heart years ago. You've held onto it since the day you pulled my half-naked body from a game of Strip Uno. Since the day you gave Damian Murphy a broken nose for touching me. Since the day you threatened every boy we went to school with who made comments about my chest." She moves her hands down my face, cupping my cheeks. "Since the first day I went over my best friend's house and met her annoying big brother. I knew you were different. And with each word, each stolen glance, each smile, you captured another piece of my heart. I don't want them back anymore. I'm finally ready, Drew."

239

"Ready?"

She nods. "I'm ready for you to have all of me. My body. My heart. My love."

My chest expanding, I crush my lips to hers, her kiss making me breathless, reckless, thoughtless. "Let me love you, Brooklyn," I plead, breathing into her.

"Yes, Drew." She tilts her head back, her expression heated as my lips travel from hers, tasting her skin. "Yes."

I snake down her frame, nipping at her jawline, her neck, her chest. When my teeth graze her flesh, she moans at the combination of pleasure and pain coursing through her. I fight against the urge to rip off her panties and bury myself inside her, releasing the tension that's been building for years.

My fingers trace her nipple, her skin prickling under my touch. Licking my lips as my eyes lock on hers, I bring my forefinger and thumb up to the alert peak. I squeeze, and she whimpers, closing her eyes, biting her bottom lip. I lower my mouth to her chest, my touch light. Every second that passes, she gets increasingly unhinged, her legs squeezing around me, her muscles clenching, her breathing ragged. When I finally clamp my mouth over her nipple, my teeth tugging slightly, her body stiffens.

"Drew... Please..." She thrusts against me, panting, her nails scratching my scalp.

I pull back, staring down at her. She looks more beautiful than I thought possible, her cheeks flushed, the desire in her eyes for me alone. I love that she's begging for me, that she's desperate to feel me. I'm ready to lose my mind with need for her.

I return my lips to hers, kissing her once more, sweet, compassionate, full of hope. "There's no going back after this. I won't let you."

"I don't want to. I only want to move forward. With you. So please... Let me feel you."

I move from her lips, down her neck, kissing and tasting her delicate skin. She releases a tiny moan, her nails digging even harder into me. With each lick, each taste, each suck, her chest heaves even more. Her grip around me tightens, the warmth emanating from between her legs driving me mad.

My hand roams down her side, briefly settling on her hip before traveling inward. I move my lips from her chest and slide farther south, kissing her stomach, circling her belly button, stopping when I hit the fabric of her panties. I lift my eyes to hers once more.

"I need to taste you." I hook my fingers in the silky material, pausing. She lifts her hips, an unspoken invitation. Once I lower them down her legs, I settle between her thighs, my breath a whisper away. The instant my tongue flicks against her warmth, she whimpers, her body fusing into the mattress.

She reaches down, massaging my scalp as I taste her, savor her, cherish her. "Remember me," she breathes, her pleading voice almost inaudible.

"I'll never forget. Never again," I promise as I slip a finger inside, then another, filling and stretching her. Her moans of appreciation echo in the room. Until this point, we've both tried to be quiet, not wanting to disturb the girls, but I no longer care. I can't hold anything back now, and I don't want her to, either.

I drag my tongue along her pink flesh, pushing her higher and higher. As her breathing increases, her body tenses. She pulses against me, her grip on my hair tightening. "Come on, baby. Let me feel you. Let me see what only I can give you."

My words are all she needs as she shatters around me, screaming my name. It gives me all the satisfaction I need. But I don't stop. I keep tasting and sucking, drawing out her orgasm for as long as I can. When her spasms wane, I meet her eyes, grinning coyly.

"I'll always remember that. Damn, Brooklyn…"

"Get up here." She clutches my cheeks, dragging me up to her, crushing her lips against mine. Her tongue plunges into my mouth with no hesitation, tasting her and me in one impassioned kiss.

Lost in the moment, I'm taken by surprise when she hooks a leg around my waist and flips over, forcing me beneath her. She leans back, unclipping her hair, allowing it to fall past her shoulders. She erases the distance between us, her dark locks shading my face as she grinds against me, hardening my arousal even more.

"Brooklyn...," I groan, closing my eyes. She's so warm. So sweet. So perfect.

"Do you like that?"

"God, yes." I grip her hips, somewhat surprised by her take-charge attitude. Not that I need to be the one in control, but I had her pegged as being more submissive. Just another reminder that the Brooklyn I first kissed all those years ago is no longer a shy little girl, but a woman who knows what she wants. After all these years, she still wants me.

"Drew..." She continues circling against me, leaning even closer. She nips at my lower lip, pulling it. The erotic sensation of her teeth tugging on my skin only makes me burn for her more, a fire in my veins only she can extinguish.

"Yes?"

"We've known each other a long time." She presses a hand against my chest, her eyes fluttering into the back of her head. It reminds me of our last morning together, how she was seconds away from getting off by grinding against me like this...until we were interrupted. Before this moment, it was the most arousing thing I'd ever experienced. I have a feeling that was child's play compared to what I'm about to be treated to.

"Almost our entire lives." My voice is husky, throaty, the combination of Brooklyn on top of me and her taste on my tongue driving me insane with lust.

"I trust you."

I meet her eyes. "And I trust you."

She brings her mouth to mine, the warmth of her lips forcing a shiver to roll down my spine. "I want all of you." She allows those words to linger in the air, then pulls back, giving me a knowing look. "Nothing between us."

Growling, I force my mouth to hers, kissing her. "There will never be anything between us again." I wrap an arm around her waist, using my strength to flip her onto her back once again. The pout on her face is adorable, but I erase it with another kiss. "You can be in control next time."

"A little confident of yourself, aren't you?" She smirks playfully. "What if I'm completely unsatisfied and don't want another time?"

I grab her thigh, squeezing, causing her to yelp.

"You will." I thrust between her legs, teasing her, then bring my mouth back to hers. "After I make love to you, every other guy will be nothing but a distant memory. Because right now, after just a taste of you, every other woman is nothing but a distant memory for me."

Supporting myself on one elbow, I kiss her as I push my briefs down my legs. Once they fall to the floor, I kneel between her thighs, then pause, overwhelmed by the magnitude of this moment. For most people, it would just be sex, but this isn't. This is the moment I can fulfill the promise I made to this woman seventeen years ago.

"Please, Drew," she begs, the flirtatious expression leaving her face, replaced with sincerity as the importance of this washes over her, as well. "Be my last."

"Be my forever," I reply, inching inside her. The instant her warmth envelopes me, all the tension leaves me, leaves her, leaves us as we find our rhythm. Nothing's ever felt so right, so perfect, so amazing. I was meant to be with this woman, and she was meant to be with me. Nothing will ever convince me otherwise.

"Kiss me," she begs.

Without saying a word, I bring my lips to hers as we celebrate in this moment, in making it to this place neither one of us ever thought we'd get to.

"Say you love me."

"I love you, Brooklyn. Always have. Always will."

My words are the only reassurance she needs. She moves against me with greater urgency, the muscles in her body tightening around me. I lean back and move my hand from her hips, along her waist. My thumb finds her center and I gently rub.

"I… I can't," she says through her heavy pants.

"Yes, you can. I feel it." I push into her with more

intensity, driving deeper, fuller. Her muscles grow taut, her eyes closing as she seems to hold her breath.

She moans, matching my rhythm, bringing her hands to her chest.

"Fuck." I want to go slow with her, but I lose all restraint when I see the pleasure covering her face as she plays with her nipples, squeezing and pushing her breasts together. "Don't stop doing that. Don't. Ever. Stop. God." My motions increase to a relentless tempo, sweat beading on my forehead. I'm seconds away from unraveling, but I need to feel her shake around me, need to know I satisfy her more than any other man.

"Drew..." Her breaths come in pants, her hands falling to her sides as she fists the bedsheets. I bring my mouth to her, clamping my teeth around a nipple. The instant I do, she shatters, her cries filling the space. I exhale a breath as I let go, my motions still ferocious, greedy, insatiable, giving her everything I have left.

She runs her fingers through my hair, down my back, pulsing against me, matching my tempo. Tightening her legs around me, she takes control, slowing us down, the moment turning from a frenzied explosion of need to something deeper and more intense. She grabs my face and brings my mouth to hers, kissing me. I've never felt as fulfilled in my life as I do right now.

"Lavender and lilacs," I remark, my chest still heaving, staring down at this incredible woman as we slow to a stop.

She furrows her brow, an adorable look of confusion crossing her face. "What?"

"You smell like lavender and lilacs. It's one of the first things I remember about you. I didn't know what the scent was then, but as I grew older, it became one of my favorite smells. And it's still one of my favorite smells. But..."

"But?"

I smile, lowering my lips to hers. "But I fucking love the smell of your pussy. And don't even get me started on how incredible you taste." Greedy, I kiss her once more, my need for her ravenous.

"Be a good boy and I'll let you have another taste tomorrow." She smirks.

"Tomorrow?" I shoot up. Before she can say anything, I scoop her into my arms and carry her toward the bathroom. "I'm not waiting until tomorrow."

Her carefree laughter surrounds me. "You're an animal. I don't know if I can keep up with you."

"We'll just have to practice. A lot." I wink.

Her lips find the place where my earlobe meets my neck, nipping, making me harden again. "I like the sound of practicing. A lot."

CHAPTER TWENTY-EIGHT

BROOKLYN

SUNLIGHT FIGHTS TO SHINE through the shutters as I lay in Drew's bed, in Drew's arms, snuggling against Drew's body. I want to pinch myself and make sure last night wasn't just a dream. It still doesn't seem like it could be real. Less than twenty-four hours ago, I was engaged to Wes, hours away from walking down the aisle and marrying him.

Now, I no longer wear his ring and am wrapped in the arms of another man...the man I've always loved. I still have to figure out how to deal with what my father did, but I don't want to think about that right now, not when I'm surrounded by the love I've been searching for my entire life.

"What are you thinking about?" Drew's scratchy voice breaks through the quiet solitude.

"How did you know I was awake?"

He brushes my hair in front of my shoulder, exposing my nape. His lips meet my skin, his kiss jumpstarting my libido, a shiver running down my back.

"I know everything about you, Brooklyn."

His hands roam my frame and I close my eyes, his touch making me feel more alive than being with Wes ever did.

"When you're upset."

His mouth lands on that place in the crook of my neck that awakens my body with a yearning I didn't think possible. The tiniest moan leaves my throat as lust, strong and powerful, consumes me. Arching into him, he leans my head against him, his other hand exploring my body. My breath quickens when those talented fingers find my breast, teasing and tugging, making me squirm.

"When you're lying, even to yourself."

A small pain emanates from my neck and I stiffen at the feel of his teeth clamping down on the sensitive flesh. But that

246

momentary discomfort is replaced with immense pleasure, rapture, greed.

"Drew…," I beg, moments away from falling apart, despite the number of orgasms he gave me throughout the night before we succumbed to sleep, too exhausted to continue.

"Yes?"

His lips brush against my shoulder blades, his motions gentle and benevolent once more. I move against him, his erection hardening against my back. I didn't think this kind of reaction were possible, thought this unrelenting craving to be with someone was simply something I read about in Molly's romance novels. But it is real. This spark. This connection. This unyielding hunger. I could start fires with how hot I burn for this man.

"I need you."

"And I need you, Brooklyn." He pushes me onto my back and looms over me, his eyes sincere. "Like a fish needs water. Like a flower needs the rain." He lowers his mouth to mine, his scruffy chin scratching my skin in the most delicious of ways. "Like a bird needs wings to fly. Because when I'm with you, that's how I feel. Like I'm flying. And I never want to stop soaring."

"Oh, Drew…" I grab the back of his neck, forcing his lips to mine. I thought I knew every side of Andrew Brinks. I never expected him to be so suggestive yet sweet in the bedroom.

I breathe into the kiss, into him, into us. It doesn't matter how many times he made love to me over the course of last night and into the early morning hours. My body still yearns for him, to feel his heat, to drown in his love.

Just as I'm about to force him onto his back, the door flings open, startling both of us. I shriek, scrambling to cover myself, Drew shooting up to do the same. Alyssa and Charlotte stop in their tracks, their eyes settling on me.

"Dad?" Alyssa says, her tone cautious. "What's going on?"

I'd like to think she's too young to realize what she walked in on, but she's a smart girl. While she probably doesn't understand the technicalities just yet, she must know something.

"Auntie Brook!" Charlotte says, oblivious to our predicament. "Did you and Daddy have a sleepover?"

I look at Drew, who appears much more calm and collected than I, much to my surprise. I've never felt so exposed, naked in their father's bed, the only thing covering me is his duvet. I'm sure I look a sight, too — hair rumpled, skin flushed, eyes panicked.

"Yes, we did." He catches my gaze, winking.

"Why?" Charlotte presses.

"Yeah. Why?" Alyssa repeats, placing her hands on her hips. "Shouldn't she be getting ready for the wedding? You told us to make sure we got up on time so we could go get our hair done. Aunt Gigi and Auntie Molly are supposed to come pick us up after breakfast."

"Well, you don't have to worry about that anymore." Drew wraps an arm around me, bringing me against him. Confusion clouds the girls' expressions. I can only imagine what they're thinking. "There isn't going to be a wedding today."

"There isn't?"

"No, Alyssa," I say, finally speaking up. "There isn't."

"Why not?" Charlotte interjects.

I lick my lips, unsure how to best handle this line of questioning. One thing I picked up from Drew's parenting style is he always tells them the truth, regardless of how much it hurts them…or him. I suppose that's what I need to do here, too.

"Do you remember when I first told you I was getting married and you asked if I was marrying your daddy?" Drew whips his eyes to mine, surprised. I smile, reassuring him, before looking back at Charlotte. "How I told you I wasn't, and you asked if I loved your daddy?"

She nods. "You said you did, but in a different way."

"And that's true. I do love your daddy differently than the way I love Wes. I admire and respect Wes, and he's treated me very well." I bring my eyes to Drew's, unable to stop from beaming, my heart expanding in my chest at what I see in his gaze. "But I've been in love with your father since I was a teenager. Probably before. I was just too scared to admit it. I'm not anymore."

"Does that mean you're going to marry him and be our new mother?" Alyssa asks.

I shake my head, meeting her confused stare. "No, sweetie. I'll never replace your mother."

"But you are going to get married, right?" Charlotte's brows are furrowed in concern. "I was really looking forward to wearing my pretty dress today," she pouts, crossing her arms over her chest.

Drew bursts out laughing, the deep rumble hitting me in places I didn't even know existed. I shift my eyes to his, the smile on his face evidence of how at peace he is with me in his embrace, despite the awkward situation.

"Tell you what, kiddo. If you help me not mess things up with Brooklyn, I have a feeling you'll be able to wear that dress sometime soon. Can you do that?"

She nods excitedly, a toothy grin crawling across her mouth. "I can do that."

"Good." He shifts his eyes to Alyssa, his expression becoming serious. "Are you okay with this, Lyss?"

She tilts her head, studying us. "Are you happy?" Her question surprises me. I find it rather mature and perceptive for an eight-year-old.

Drew nods. "Happier than I've been in a long time."

"Then I'm happy for you." She holds his gaze for several long moments, then looks at Charlotte. "Come on, Char. It's Saturday. We get TV time in the morning."

"I'll be right down," Drew calls out as they retreat from the bedroom.

Once the door closes behind them, I blow out a long breath, falling back onto the mattress. I throw my arm over my head. "That may be the most embarrassing thing that's ever happened."

When the mattress shifts, I open my eyes to see Drew staring down at me. He rests his weight on an elbow as he smooths my hair behind my ear. "It could have been a lot worse. They could have barged in a few seconds later."

I smirk. "And why would that have been worse?"

His breath warms my lips as he closes the distance between our mouths. "Because I was seconds away from flipping you onto your hands and knees and fucking the memory of every other guy from you."

My body tingles, my libido sparking back to life. "I thought you did that last night." My core clenches as his mouth travels down my neck, his jaw scratching and bruising. A desire to experience that on other parts of my body consumes me.

"Not from behind I didn't. Now…" His breath on my skin lights me on fire as he slithers down my frame. I squirm and writhe in anticipation, but his mouth remains just a breath away, unhinging me even more. I pant, desperate for even the slightest brush of his lips or nip of his teeth. "If you'll be so kind…" When he reaches my waist, he glances up at me. "I'm dying to know what you feel like from behind."

"Jesus Christ," I exhale, propping into a sitting position. "Who knew the boy next door had such a dirty mouth?"

"Only for you." Finally, he crushes that mouth to mine, his tongue plunging into me, then pulls back. "Now, get on your hands and knees. This is going to be quick, but I promise you'll get off."

My heart pounds in my chest, the way those erotic words fall from his mouth causing moisture to pool between my legs. Without saying another word, I do as he asks, shifting onto my hands and knees, resting on my forearms.

"My god," he whispers as he traces a light finger down my back. A shiver follows the line he's drawn, my stomach clenching with anticipation. "You are absolutely stunning." He grows closer to the spot I need to feel him, my eyes fluttering in the back of my head when he touches me, spreading my wetness all around. "And all mine."

I rest my head on the pillow, succumbing to the sensations. "All yours."

"And this…" He inserts a finger, massaging my insides.

"This is all mine."

I moan, moving with the tempo he sets, surrendering to his touch.

"Say it," his voice comes out strained, almost like a growl.

"It's yours. I'm yours." I increase my motions, burning for a release. "My heart. My soul. My body. It's yours. Forever."

"Forever," he repeats as he removes his finger. I pant, about to glance over my shoulder, when he brings his arousal up to me, pushing inside in one quick thrust. We release a simultaneous sigh, evidence our connection runs deeper than just the joining of our two bodies.

When he doesn't move, I look back at him, my fiery gaze locking with his. "Fuck me."

His eyes become heated as he grabs my hair, wrapping it around his fist and forcing my head forward. He moves slowly at first, but within a few seconds, he sets a punishing pace. Last night, every time we made love, it was just that. It was sweet, passionate, all-consuming, but this lust-filled convergence of our bodies is different. I had the tender, endearing side of Andrew Brinks. Right now, I want the greedy, protective man I know him to be.

"I just…" His breathing becomes labored. The harder his breathing, the more forceful his thrusts. I've never felt so fulfilled, so satisfied, so alive. "I can't get enough of you."

Lost in the moment, I shift my weight to one of my forearms, my other hand traveling down my body, finding that sweet spot between my legs.

"Brooklyn," he groans as I toy with myself, the combination of his thickness and my fingers circling me propelling me higher than ever before. "Keep going, baby. God, I love how you feel when you clench around me. Do you like it when I fuck you like this?"

"Harder," I beg, feeling like a different person.

With a growl, his grip on me tightens and he yanks my head back. "Like this?"

"Yes," I exhale, pulling my lip between my teeth to quiet my cries, unsure how much longer I can reel them in. The way Drew moves inside me, the way he makes me feel, erases my ability to control anything.

Instantly, he releases his hold on me, then leans his body over mine, slowing his motions. With each gradual withdrawal, he pushes back into me, deeper, fuller, more intense.

"I love watching you touch yourself. Do you have any idea what a turn-on that is?"

"I have a good idea," I tease flirtatiously.

He brings his teeth to my neck, nibbling. "I'm going to stop moving, but I want you to keep playing with yourself. I want you to make yourself come around my dick while I watch." His motions slow, barely noticeable. But that doesn't stop me from touching myself. I've never done anything remotely this intimate in front of anyone before. But with Drew, it feels right. I can tell he's enjoying it almost as much as I am by the way his grip on my hip tightens, the way his erection gets even thicker inside me. It must be taking every ounce of restraint he possesses not to drive into me. I thought I'd need that, but this, feeling him inside me but not moving, is incredible. It gives me all the control, all the power over my own pleasure.

My eyes roll into the back of my head as the familiar tingling sensation runs through me, the same one I experienced several times in the past few hours. I didn't think I'd be ready again so soon, but Drew seems to have a unique effect on my body. One I can't quite understand.

"That's it." Drew's voice is guttural as he folds his body over mine, clamping his teeth on my neck. "I want your cum soaking my dick."

That's all it takes for me to reach my breaking point, burying my face in the pillow to muffle my cries, my body shivering. Drew doesn't give me a chance to catch my breath as he thrusts into me, his motions determined, his teeth still clamped on my neck. It's painful but so fucking exhilarating. This is what sex is supposed to be like, not something I have to do to stop whomever I'm with from seeing how unhappy I am. This feeling, this sensation, this unparalleled high is what I've been craving for too long. I stopped believing it existed, but it does. It's so real, just like my love for this man moving so passionately and erotically behind me.

"More," I beg, sensing he's close to unraveling. "I need more."

"Goddamn, baby." He pushes into me a few more times before stilling, jerking against me as he finds his own release.

We remain motionless, the only sound that of our heavy breaths echoing in the space. Finally, when I don't think my legs can take the pressure much longer, he withdraws, placing his hand on my stomach to support me as I lower my body onto the mattress.

"That was incredible," he manages to say.

I wipe at the beads of sweat forming on my forehead. "I think I can cancel my gym membership. Especially if you keep fucking me like that."

His laughter fills the room. "That can be arranged." He leaves me with a soft kiss, then gets up, heading toward the dresser.

I roll onto my side, propping my head in my hand as I admire his physique. He's always been in incredible shape. Broad shoulders. Firm chest. Sculpted abs. All tapering into that chiseled V that causes most women to forget their first name. He grabs a pair of shorts and slides them on before yanking a t-shirt over his head. After rummaging through his drawers for a few more seconds, he pulls out another t-shirt and a pair of shorts. He turns around and approaches me, tossing the clothes onto the bed.

"They'll be enormous on you, but it's better than putting your wet dress back on. Do you need me to go grab some things for you somewhere?"

"Most of my stuff is at Wes', although I did leave an overnight bag at my dad's yesterday. I was supposed to stay there last night. You know. The old tradition that the bride and groom not spend the night before their wedding together. But I kind of ran out on the rehearsal dinner after he told me what he did."

Concern crosses his expression and he sits on the corner of the bed, brushing my hair away from my eyes. I marvel at how he can be a passionate lover with an erotic tongue one minute, then turn into this empathetic, devoted man the next.

"So you left things unresolved?"

I nod. "I didn't know what else to do. I couldn't be around him, knowing he kept that from me for so long, knowing he watched me suffer, watched me cry myself to sleep for weeks, months, and he was the reason for it."

"And that's why he didn't want you to know," he says, offering my father more sympathy than he deserves, especially after what he put him through. "Why I didn't want to tell you."

"He always told me to trust him, said he knew what was best for me. And I did that blindly for years when I should have questioned him all along."

He brings his mouth toward the top of my head, inhaling, then leaves a kiss on my temple. "We'll work it all out. I'll be by your side through all of it. Promise."

I smile, linking my fingers with his. Before, I had trouble believing any promise he made me. Now I can. If Drew says he'll be by my side, I'm confident he'll be there. "Thank you."

"Anything for you." He stands, heading toward the door. Just as he's about to disappear down the hallway, he looks back at me. "And for the record, if I were in your father's shoes and it was one of my daughters…" He shakes his head, taking a moment to consider his words. "I don't know. At first, I was convinced I'd never do something like that, especially to someone my kids knew for as long as we've known each other. But we both know I wasn't a good guy in high school. I dated a lot of girls. And I slept with a lot of them, too. Your father knew that. If my girls ever brought home someone like me, I'd think the same thing your father did. That they're only after one thing. So, as much as you want to hate him, I understand why he did it."

The corners of his lips turn into a smile as he meets my eyes. Then he closes the door.

CHAPTER TWENTY-NINE

BROOKLYN

LAUGHTER MAKES ITS WAY to my ears as I head down the steps, the aroma of bacon and maple syrup assaulting me the instant I emerge onto the first floor. I take a minute, adjusting my damp hair into a messy bun on the top of my head and rolling the waist of Drew's shorts so they're not so enormous on me.

"Auntie Brook!" Charlotte's voice calls out. I swing my eyes to see her looking at me from her position on one of the stools in front of Drew's massive eat-in island. "Do you want waffles, too?"

With a smile, I square my shoulders and walk toward them, acting as if their father hadn't just fucked me like he did.

"Wait," she blurts out, turning her furrowed brow to Drew. "Am I still supposed to call her Auntie Brook if she's your girlfriend?"

I cock my head at Drew, placing my hands on my hips. "I'm your girlfriend?"

He turns off the gas on the stove, moving the pan of bacon to the counter and placing it on a trivet. "Well, girlfriend doesn't seem right for what you are to me, but I suppose it's the best title...for now." Winking, he grabs a set of tongs and serves the girls a few pieces of bacon.

"For now?" I approach, still uneasy about how to act around him while in the presence of his kids. This is new territory for me. I've never dated or slept with anyone who had kids. I awkwardly attempt to keep my distance, wishing I had something other than his clothes to wear, but Drew wraps an arm around me, dragging me against him.

"I like to consider it a temporary title." He gradually lowers his mouth toward mine, treating me to yet another one of his kisses. I doubt I'll ever get my fill.

I remember my younger days, how desperate I was to experience my first kiss, how I didn't think I'd ever hit the number of kisses most people experienced in their lifetime. Now I know I will. In fact, I have a feeling I'll far exceed the two weeks most people spend kissing. I could kiss Andrew Brinks for two weeks straight and still hunger for more.

Momentarily forgetting where I am, I melt into him, allowing him to deepen the kiss. Then the sound of giggling cuts through and I pull back, although Drew tries to prevent me, despite our audience.

"Oooh! You guys are kissing!" Alyssa teases. It brings a smile to my face. I was most worried about her being okay with this. She's older and much more reluctant to trust people. I don't fault her. I was the same way. To hear her joke makes me think it's all going to be okay. That we're all going to be okay.

Drew returns his attention to the waffle maker and opens it, scooping the waffle onto a plate, adding it to the pile he'd already made.

"Hey, Dad?" Alyssa's tone turns serious.

He shifts his gaze to hers. "What is it, sweetie?"

"Since there's no wedding, I was wondering…" She trails off as she brings her fork to her waffle, hesitating.

"What is it?" he presses once more.

"Well…" She pulls her bottom lip between her teeth. "It's just…" She inhales a deep breath, returning her eyes to Drew's. "Tonight's game seven of the Stanley Cup and it's here. I'd hoped…"

We laugh at the seriousness on her face. "That we could go?" he finishes.

She nods.

"Do you think we'd miss it? No way!"

Both girls squeal in excitement, dancing in their stools.

"They truly are your daughters," I comment in mock irritation.

"Every girl needs a little hockey in her life." He winks as he heads toward the counter, grabbing the freshly pressed pot of coffee and pouring some into a mug. After preparing it the way I prefer, he hands it to me, leaning toward my ear, his voice a whisper. "And every woman needs a hockey player in their bed."

"Is that right?" I smirk, pulling back. "So this is community service for you?"

He shakes his head with a lascivious grin. "No. It's more like Brooklyn service. All Brooklyn. All the time."

I bite my lower lip. "I like the sound of Brooklyn service."

He brushes his mouth against mine, making my flesh tingle. "So do I."

Girlish snickers sound from the island. "You guys are kissing again," Charlotte comments.

"Get used to it," Drew shoots back, then presses his firm lips against mine. I can't help but sigh, loving how he makes no move to hide his affection for me, even in front of his kids.

His hand finds my ass and he gives it a squeeze.

"Shut the front door!" a familiar voice exclaims, breaking the moment.

Drew and I whirl around, staring at a very bewildered Molly and an extremely satisfied Gigi standing just off the entryway. Molly's eyes are wide, her mouth even wider as she gapes at us. Gigi crosses her arms, smirking, as if she predicted this would happen.

"Hi, Auntie Molly!" Charlotte says, barely looking up from her waffles. "Auntie Brooklyn isn't going to marry Wes anymore. Instead, she's Daddy's girlfriend. They had a sleepover last night."

Molly shifts her stunned expression back to me, her surprise waning as she waggles her brows. "You did, did you?" She takes a few steps toward us. "Did you have a pillow fight, too?" She leans closer. "Did Drew win?"

"It looked like he was winning," Charlotte answers around a mouthful of waffle.

Her comment catching me off-guard, I choke on my coffee, shifting my gaze to Drew, his face an adorable shade of red.

"He wasn't winning," Alyssa claims. "They were doing it."

"It?" Charlotte inquires.

I eye Drew, praying he'll put an end to this.

"Yeah. It."

"What do you mean?"

"Okay, you two," Drew interrupts. Finally. "Finish up, or no hockey game tonight." That's all they need to hear. All conversation ceases as they focus on their breakfast. "I'm investing in some better locks," he murmurs, his mouth brushing against my temple.

"Good." I tilt my eyes toward his, chewing on my bottom lip.

"Tell me…" Molly's voice cuts through our moment and we both look at her. "How did you go from marrying Wes to having a 'sleepover' with Drew?"

"He asked me to dance," I respond with a shrug. It sounds silly and insignificant, but it's the truth. Drew was right. No words could have told me what his heart did. "The instant I was in his arms again, I knew it was where I was meant to be." I take a small sip of my coffee, lowering my eyes. "Of course, as we all know, I can be stubborn, so I still tried to fight it. It wasn't until my father…" I trail off, the happiness of being with Drew dampened by the truth of what my father did.

Drew drapes an arm around my shoulders and squeezes, reassuring me it'll all work out. Molly steals a glance at him, questioning. He nods, their interaction leading me to believe Drew told Molly what my father did. I shouldn't be surprised. They have an oddly close relationship. They tell each other everything.

"I'm really sorry, Molly," I say, unsure my words are adequate to relay how awful I feel for the way I've treated her.

"Don't be." She shrugs it off. "I knew you'd come to your senses eventually." She steps toward me, lowering her voice. "How's Wes?"

"He knew it was coming." A lump forms in my throat as I recall his sad eyes when I kissed him goodbye. The way he handled last night with such grace and admiration surprised me. It probably shouldn't have, considering that's how he handled himself throughout our entire relationship. "He was sweet about it, said he tried to love me enough for the both of us, but knew it wasn't enough."

"So he's okay?"

I consider her question for a moment. "Yeah. He is."

"What about mom-zilla?"

"Oh, I expect her to come banging on the door at any minute so she can save face in front of all her friends. Just like she tried to do last night at the rehearsal dinner when I went to give Wes the ring back."

Molly's eyes practically bulge out of their sockets. "You broke up with him at the rehearsal dinner?"

I pinch my lips together. "I was tired of living a lie."

She considers my response, then narrows her eyes, her gaze filled with concern. "And your dad?"

I exhale a long breath, my throat tightening. "I need some time."

"Forgiveness is a difficult thing." Gigi walks toward me, taking my hand in hers. "But so is living with regret."

I swallow hard, nodding.

"I am so happy you finally found your way back to each other." She clutches my cheeks, forcing my eyes to hers. "That's the important thing. Not anything that may have happened in the past. If one thing were different, you may not be here today." She loosens her hold on me, glancing across the island at Alyssa and Charlotte. "They may not be here today. Could you imagine your life without them?"

I shake my head.

"Just remember that."

CHAPTER THIRTY

DREW

I LOOK AROUND MY living room later that morning, heat radiating in my chest, a permanent smile plastered on my face. Alyssa and Charlotte build something with their Legos as a movie of their choosing plays on TV. Molly called Noah and told him there had been a change of plans. Now, instead of getting ready for Brooklyn's wedding, we're all at my house, Uncle Leo included, celebrating something else…our family.

As the girls put their finishing touches on the lopsided tower they've constructed, the doorbell rings. Brooklyn shoots her wide eyes to mine, concern filling them. She's been edgy all morning, worried the doorbell would ring and either Mrs. Bradford or her father would be here to talk to her. While I support her desire to never see Wes' mom again, especially after she shared with me the choice words she had for her last night, I hate being the reason she's avoiding her father. All I can do is make sure she eventually clears the air between them.

I lean toward her, kissing her cheek. "I'll go take care of it." I squeeze her leg when she offers me a relieved smile.

"Thank you."

I hold her gaze for a moment longer, then get up, heading toward the entryway. I open the door, preparing myself to deal with an irate Mrs. Bradford or an apologetic Mr. Tanner, taken by surprise when someone else stands on my porch.

"Carla," I hiss, stepping outside, closing the door behind me to keep that barrier between her and my girls, especially now that I know Skylar encouraged her to try to take them from me. "What the hell are you doing here?" I should have known something like this would happen. It's the story of my life. Just when everything's going great, something happens to bring me down from my high.

"I'm sorry for barging in on you like this. I just… I need to talk to you."

I cross my arms. "Don't you have a lawyer for that?"

She pulls her lip between her teeth, nodding in what seems to be resignation. "I deserve that." There's a slight quiver in her chin as she wipes beneath one of her eyes. Then her voice turns urgent, pleading. "You have to understand where I'm coming from here, Andrew—"

"Oh, I understand. I understand you're trying to take my kids from me when I've done nothing but raise them, care for them, love them…" My voice trails off. I take a moment to collect myself, my despair turning to rage. "You've done nothing but turn my entire world upside down." My lip curling, I lean into her. "You had the audacity to beg me to come back to you when you were pregnant. I thought I was doing the right thing by keeping our family together. Little did I know, you were just tricking me into raising someone else's child!"

"And you should hate me for that," she chokes out, tears falling down her cheeks. In all our years together, I don't think I saw her cry once. "I hate myself for that. I can't take back what I did to you all those years ago." She pauses, inhaling a long breath. "But I can make it right going forward."

"Make it right? You think asking for custody modification is making it right?" I whisper-shout, doing my best to keep my voice down so my girls don't overhear and come running to see who I'm talking to. "You think trying to take Charlotte from me altogether is making it right?"

"No," she shoots back, her eyes widening. "I'm here to make amends for that, too. To fix my momentary lapse of judgment."

"Did you know who Skylar was?" I demand, the vein in my neck twitching. "Is that why you accepted her help? Figured the two of you could join forces?"

"Andrew, please." She clasps her hands together, imploring me to listen. "When she approached me, I had no idea who she was. I was on my lunch break the day after I went to see you. I was looking up family law attorneys on my laptop to see what I could do to have a little time with them when a woman walked up and claimed her step-brother was one of the best family law attorneys in the state. She was so kind and compassionate, I soon found myself sharing the whole story with her, even the part about Charlotte not being yours. When I finished, she hugged me, reassuring me that everything would be okay, that she'd help me get visitation with them. She even agreed to pay all my legal fees."

"And you didn't think that was a giant red flag?"

Her lips part as her dark eyes search mine. I'm on the brink of laying into her even more, stopping when I see something I never thought I would. Regret. Remorse. Sorrow.

"Of course I did," she exclaims, her hands balling into fists. "But I was hurting after you refused to even consider my proposition, refused to allow me anywhere near those girls. I am not the same woman I was when we knew each other, but you were too stubborn to acknowledge that people change." She pinches the bridge of her nose, shaking her head, her shoulders slumping. "It's no excuse. In retrospect I wish I'd taken a step back to analyze the situation before jumping into petitioning for custody, knowing full well what it would to do you. I just wanted to spend time with those girls. That's all. I had no idea my lawyer would bring up what I told him about Chase and Charlotte, that he would make it appear like I wanted to take her from you. After I learned that, I demanded he retract the motion, but he claimed it was too late. It was at this point I told my husband everything."

"He didn't know?" I furrow my brow, blinking. How could she be married to someone and keep something as big as this from him?

"He was aware of you and the girls. I just hadn't told him I filed for custody."

"What prompted the change of heart?"

"I saw the Celtics game a few weeks ago, the one you attended." I swallow hard at the mention of the game that almost cost me everything. "People still know you, especially considering your name's been in the news recently regarding the possibility of coaching for the Bruins. Then I saw Skylar.

I didn't know who she was, other than being the woman who offered to help me. When I saw her approach you, I'd never felt so sick in my entire life." She covers her heart with her hand, her complexion paling, her voice cracking.

"That's when I realized it was too good to be true. I came clean to my husband, and the following day, he helped me hire a new lawyer."

"So you can continue seeking custody?" I bark out.

She vehemently shakes her head. "No. I hired someone new to help make it all right. Not just what I've put you through this past month, but the past seven years." She reaches into her oversized purse and hands me a large envelope.

"What is this?" I glare, my lip turning up in a sneer. "The last time someone showed up at my door and handed me an envelope—"

"Please, Andrew. Just open it. Of course, someone will show up at your door Monday morning to deliver the official copy. I just…" She pauses, tilting her head to the sky. A breeze picks up, her dark hair blowing in her face, a peacefulness about her. When she returns her eyes to mine, she swallows hard. "As difficult as it was for me to come here, I didn't want you to go another second worrying about what the future holds for you and your girls." She sniffles, using her arm to wipe her tears that are now falling relentlessly. Apart from the deep, dark eyes, this woman bears absolutely no resemblance to the woman I married, in temperament or appearance.

Studying her with guarded skepticism, I shift my gaze downward, withdrawing a set of papers from the envelope. This scenario is too reminiscent of that day back in May when I was served with her request for custody modification. This time, the stack of papers stapled together is much thinner, containing only two pieces. At the top is the caption "Withdrawal of Custody Modification Petition Without Prejudice".

I snap my head up, inhaling sharply, my heart thumping in my chest. "Does this mean what I think it does?"

"I'm not going to fight you for them. I hope you'll

eventually find it in your heart to forgive me for putting you through this and will let me be a part of their lives. I understand if you can't do that right now, but I hope you will someday."

I shake my head, continuing to read the words on the page, a huge weight lifted off me. But there's still the problem of Charlotte.

"What about—"

Sensing my next question, she interrupts. "My lawyer seems to think this will be sufficient." She hands me a second envelope.

With shaky hands, I unclasp it, pulling out several more sheets of paper. My eyes gloss over the words. This time, I'm even more confused as I read a statement by Chase Gardner relinquishing his parental rights. Then I sift through the rest of the papers. One caption reads "Affidavit in Support of Consent to Adopt".

"My lawyer's dealt with adoption cases before," Carla explains, noticing my furrowed brow. "Most of them aren't as complicated as this one, but in order for you to adopt Charlotte, all this state requires is for her biological father to relinquish his parental rights and for the biological mother to consent to the adoption. Normally, it occurs in the case of a step-parent adoption, but there's no reason for Charlotte not to be yours officially. You just have to file the petition."

I return my eyes to hers, my words caught in my throat. Despite everything she put me through, this gift is more than I ever thought her capable of. It demonstrates she's not the same woman I married, the same woman who ran out on my girls and me, the same woman who had no regard for us.

Overwhelmed with gratitude, I wrap my arms around her, hugging her tightly, all the tension leaving my body. "Thank you," I barely manage to say. "Thank you so much, Carla." I keep her enclosed in my embrace, my heart full for the first time since I received her original request for custody. I don't know if I'll ever be able to explain exactly how much her doing all of this to make amends means to me. She could have stopped at retracting her petition for custody. But this, giving me everything I need to make Charlotte mine makes me view Carla in a completely different light.

"I'm so sorry for what I did," she laments into my chest. "I've been so selfish. I don't deserve your compassion or forgiveness. I just hope I can make it up to you."

I pull away, smiling as I wave the envelopes in my hand. "This is a pretty good start." I push out a laugh, cutting through the thick tension.

"I hope so." She steps back, swiping at her tears. "I'll let you get back to your day. I just wanted to give these to you." She holds my gaze for another moment, then turns toward her car, her posture slumped. "Just keep me posted on how they're doing, if you can." She gives me a tight smile as she opens the door.

"Carla, wait!"

She meets my eyes, her brow lifted. "Yes?"

I hesitate, chewing on my bottom lip. I never thought I'd be able to stand being in this woman's presence without growing wild with rage at how much she hurt me and those little girls. I never thought I'd ever be able to forgive her. Just like I want Brooklyn to forgive her father for what he did, I need to do the same here.

"Do you want to come in? Spend a little time with them?"

She chokes out a sob, her hand going to her mouth to cover her quivering chin. "Are you sure?" She can't hide her disbelief at this turn of events. I almost can't, either.

I nod, smiling warmly. "A wise woman once told me that forgiveness is a difficult thing, but so is living with regret."

She laughs as she dabs at her tears. "That sounds like something Gigi would say."

"I don't want to live with any more regret." My tone becomes serious. "Just give me a minute to talk to them first. Okay?"

"Of course," she answers quickly. "I'll wait out here. If it's too much, too soon, I understand. I'm just thankful you're willing to do this. You have no idea what it means."

I nod, retreating up the front porch, pausing as I'm about to open the door. "Actually, I do."

CHAPTER THIRTY-ONE

DREW

"WHAT IS SHE DOING here?" Molly barks out the instant I walk into the kitchen.

I come to a dead stop, bewildered. Brooklyn stands with Molly and Gigi by the island, each one wearing a different expression. As expected, Molly is pissed, Gigi is concerned, but Brooklyn appears more empathetic.

"Shh." I place a finger over my mouth, glancing into the living room where Noah and Uncle Leo seem to have the girls occupied.

"Seriously. What makes her think she can just—"

"She came to drop off these." I toss the documents onto the countertop. Three sets of eyes zero in on them. Molly and Gigi furrow their brow, but it only takes Brooklyn a few seconds to read the captions on each of them to realize what it means, the importance of these papers.

"Oh, Drew," she exhales, wrapping her arms around me. I place a hand on her back, relishing in the warmth of her body against mine. Nothing's ever felt so right. And it feels even better now that I no longer have to worry about my girls, either. For months, I've been dreading June ninth, worried I'd forever remember it as the day I lost everything. Instead, it's the day I've gained everything.

"I don't get it," Molly says. "There's a reason I never wanted to be a lawyer."

"Carla's withdrawing her request for custody modification," Brooklyn explains, facing her. I keep my arm around her waist. "She's also given Drew her consent to adopt Charlotte and even went so far as to obtain Chase's relinquishment of parental rights."

"English, please."

"It means Drew can adopt Charlotte. Officially. And

Carla and Chase won't stand in the way."

"Daddy?" a small voice says. We all turn to see Charlotte standing off to the side, Alyssa beside her. "What's going on?"

I open my mouth, unsure how to explain all this so they'll understand and not hate their biological mother. They've always been compassionate and understanding, thanks to all the positive influences in their lives. I pray they'll be compassionate and understanding of this situation now, too.

"Come here, girls." I squat to their level, gesturing for them to come closer.

With long expressions, they head toward me, their steps sluggish and uncertain. I grab each of their hands in mine, smiling at them. "You know how I told you about your real mother a few weeks ago? How she was asking the judge to allow her to spend time with you?"

"Yeah," Alyssa replies, her tone filled with hostility, her distaste for the situation mirroring Molly's. There's no doubt where she got her attitude.

"Well, she came over to tell me she wasn't going to do that anymore, that she hopes we can work this out between ourselves instead. After she saw you girls at the museum a few months ago, she asked if I'd let her spend time with you. I was so hurt by what she did to me and you, how she left all of us, that I didn't consider her needs. I didn't believe her when she insisted she changed, refused to acknowledge how much she did change. I was selfish and told her no. I hurt her, just like she hurt me, hurt us."

"Good," Alyssa sneers.

"Lyss." I narrow my gaze on her. "I want you to listen to what I have to say, because whether you like it or not, this woman gave birth to you, and she will always be a part of you."

"But she's trying to take us away from you. And she lied to you about Charlotte."

I run my thumb over their knuckles, looking between the two of them. "That may be true, but she also did something to make up for that, something she didn't have to do. She's given me her consent to adopt Charlotte as my own."

"Adopt?" Charlotte asks, her brow furrowed.

"Yes, sweetie. There are still a few steps we'll need to go through, but I plan to call my lawyer first thing on Monday to get the wheels in motion to make you mine officially, something that wouldn't have been possible without your mother's consent."

"So I'm not going to have to go live with someone else?"

With a smile, I shake my head. "No, sweetie. This is your home. And it always will be. I understand how confusing this must be for you." I shift my gaze to Alyssa. "For both of you. I know you're angry about what she did, and you have every right to be…" I trail off, struggling at how best to encourage them to look past Carla's mistakes. Brooklyn squeezes my shoulder. I tilt my head, briefly meeting her supportive smile before I return my eyes to the girls. "You remember how I told you I've loved your auntie Brooklyn a very long time?"

They both nod.

"Well, you see, I hurt her…bad. So bad, in fact, that she had every right to never want to talk to me again. I made her a promise that I'd always be there for her, but I broke that promise." I squeeze their hands tighter. "But she found it in her heart to forgive me, to give me a second chance. That's part of life, girls. Everyone makes mistakes. No one's perfect. I don't want you going through life hating your mother because of this. She loves you both so much. Enough to sacrifice her own happiness for yours. As much as she wants to get to know you, she's withdrawn her request for custody so you can stay here. Take it from me. That gesture is so selfless, especially considering she has the right to be a part of your lives.

"You are smart, caring, empathetic girls. I have no idea what I did to raise such amazing people. What I'm about to ask of you may be difficult, but I beg you to reach deep down and find the compassion I know you both possess. I want you to meet her. I want her to get to know how incredible you two are. And I want you to get to know your little brother."

They shoot their wide eyes to each other, inhaling a breath at the same time. Then Alyssa slowly looks back at me.

"We have a little brother?"

I nod. "I'm sure she'll tell you all about him, if you give her this chance. So, can you do this for me? Can you keep your hearts open?"

Charlotte gazes at Alyssa, looking to her for guidance.

"Okay," Alyssa says, nodding. "We'll meet her."

I smile and pull them into my arms, squeezing them. "Thank you." I kiss the top of their heads. "I love you both so much. And your mother does, too. Just give her a chance."

"Okay," they respond again. I keep them in my embrace for several more moments. This will be an adjustment for everybody. There will most likely be some slips and falls along the way, but I know we'll all be better in the end.

Gradually releasing my hold on them, I stand. Brooklyn kisses my cheek, encouraging me, and I turn toward the front door, a nervous flutter in my stomach at how this will all play out. All I can do is support my girls through this big change.

The instant I open the door, Carla whips her head toward me, the trail worn into the sandy path evidence of her pacing. She looks at me with a questioning expression.

"Come on in."

All it takes is three words and the tension she's carried since we first ran into each other all those months ago melts off her. She takes a deep breath, then starts toward me, her eyes darting around.

I grab her hand in mine, the feel of her fingers intertwining with mine odd. There's no spark, no fireworks, no electricity. But there never was with us.

"It'll be okay."

She pushes out an anxiety-ridden laugh as I lead her through the entryway. "I don't think I've ever been this nervous." She lowers her voice, leaning into me. "I didn't expect to see them today. I would have brought them a gift or something."

"Trust me." My light tone cuts through the strain. "They have more than enough toys."

"I don't doubt that for a minute. You spoiled me when we were together. I can only imagine how you dote on those little girls."

We turn the corner into the kitchen, our conversation ceasing as we come face to face with Alyssa and Charlotte, who wear the same curious expression. You could hear a pin drop as we all remain still. The girls survey Carla, seeming to analyze everything about her. Carla trembles beside me, swiping away her tears with her free hand.

"Why are you sad?" Charlotte asks quietly.

"Oh, baby. I'm not sad," she responds, as if it were just yesterday when she sang "Rock-A-Bye Baby" to her, making up new lyrics for every verse. She releases her hold on me, stepping toward them. "Quite the opposite. I'm so happy to be here, to see you and Alyssa." She looks at Alyssa. "I am so sorry for what I did, for leaving you. It was the biggest mistake of my life. I just… I hope you'll let me get to know you. I'll take whatever you can give me. No pressure. Okay?"

"We have a brother?" Alyssa presses.

"Yes." Carla smiles, her eyes lighting up. "You two are going to be such amazing big sisters."

"What's his name?"

"Thomas." There's a glow about her as she answers, the way she says his name proof of how much she adores her son.

"How old is he?" Charlotte inquires.

"Two-and-a-half."

She ponders that response for a moment. Then, seemingly satisfied, approaches Carla, holding her hand toward her. "Do want to see my American Girl doll Daddy just got me?"

Carla hesitates, looking back at me, as if for permission. I nod, never feeling as proud of my daughter as I do right now.

Thank you, she mouths as she allows Charlotte to pull her toward the living area, Alyssa close on their heels. I can't help but smile as I watch them take turns showing her their favorite toys. It only takes a matter of minutes before they're laughing and joking, the past six years evaporating.

"You're a good man, Andrew Brinks," Brooklyn says, looping an arm around my waist.

"No, I'm not," I respond as I observe the changed family dynamic. Even Molly seems to be giving Carla the benefit of the doubt. "I'm just trying to make up for a lifetime of regrets. Everyone deserves a second chance." I kiss the top of her head, inhaling a soothing breath. "You taught me that lesson. And I'll forever be grateful you found it in your heart to give me that second chance."

"Or third or fourth," she jokes, as she always does when we talk about this.

"Nuance, my dear Brooklyn. Simply a nuance." Our eyes lock and I bring my mouth to hers, our kiss delicate and unhurried.

"For the record, I'd give you a tenth chance if need be."

"Good to know, but let's hope it never gets to that."

"Why not?" She pulls back, biting on her lower lip, a flirtatious air about her. "I hear makeup sex is really hot." She waggles her brows.

My eyes grow heated as I lower my voice. "Well then, let's pick something to disagree about and find out how hot it can be, although I'm not sure anything can top this morning."

"You're probably right, but we can spend the rest of our lives trying."

I pull her against me. "I like the sound of that."

CHAPTER THIRTY-TWO

BROOKLYN

"**Y**OU'RE A NATURAL AT that." Drew leans over my shoulder as I bounce the small blue bundle in my arms.

I bring the three-day-old baby up to my nose, nuzzling him, inhaling that powder fresh scent that's like an aphrodisiac. "It's been an eternity since I've held a baby this small." I kiss his wrinkled forehead, my lips lingering. "The last time was probably when Charlotte was born."

"I know how you can fix that," Molly jokes.

"Absolutely not, Molly," I respond quickly, shooting my eyes to where she relaxes on the love seat opposite me, all of us congregated in the living room of her house. She gave birth to Vincent Andrew McAllister earlier this week. We all respected her wishes for privacy while she was at the hospital, but now that she's home, I can't get enough of my little nephew. She doesn't mind the extra half-dozen hands, either, especially when Gigi stops by with food, most notably those famous chocolate chip muffins.

"Why? What's stopping you? You don't have school to worry about anymore."

I shrug, trying not to feel guilty about pulling out of my PhD program. For the longest time, I convinced myself it was something I wanted to do, but it was never my passion. It was something my father wanted. Maybe at some point down the road, I'll consider it again, but I'm happy where I am, both in my personal and professional life. I don't need a fancy office where I help patients with their ongoing problems. I'm content with a closet of an office and having to rush from foster home to foster home to check in on some of the most vulnerable kids there are, even if it might put me at risk, too.

My father has no idea I made this decision, although he

probably figured I would. It's early August, and I still haven't spoken to him since learning what he did to Drew. I keep telling myself I will. I just don't know what to say.

"Drew already has his hands full. No need to turn us into the Brady Bunch."

"He has plenty of help." She gestures out the French doors to the back yard where Alyssa and Charlotte blow bubbles with Carla and her son, Thomas. Over the summer, they've really gotten close to their mother, which worked to Drew's advantage, allowing him to accept the coaching position with the Bruins. Now, it's hard to remember what life was like before Carla. Then again, the woman we've all gotten to know isn't the Carla she was all those years ago. She's kind, loving, warm, and the love she has for those two girls is unparalleled...except by Drew.

"We're not married."

"That didn't stop Noah and me," she reminds me playfully.

"We've only been together a few months. It's far too early to discuss the subject."

"That's not entirely true," Drew flirts, winking. He leans into me, his voice a low growl. "I'm pretty sure when you moaned my name last night you said you were never going to leave me."

I roll my eyes, pushing him away. "That's not the same thing."

"True, but think about all the fun we could have trying to make one of these." He reaches for little Enzo, the nickname Gigi bestowed on him in remembrance of Molly and Drew's father. He brings him up to his face, snuggling the little bundle. As I watch him, I'm pretty sure my ovaries explode at how loving he is.

Every woman dreams of finding a man they hope will be a wonderful father to their children. I know I've found one. He's been nothing short of a doting father to Alyssa and Charlotte, an amazing brother to Molly, and an incredible friend to me. I don't know what the future holds for us, but if children are involved, I know he'll be just as devoted to them as he has been to all of us.

"And pregnancy sex?" Molly interjects, overhearing the conversation I thought we kept private. "I think Noah's relieved the doctor told me no funny business for six weeks."

"Jesus, Molly," Drew exclaims, just like he always does when she talks about things no brother wants to hear his sister discuss. "Enough."

"Enough with you taking the Lord's name in vain in front of my little bambino." She points a finger at him, feigning annoyance.

He rolls his eyes. "If you ever stepped foot in a church, it would probably erupt in flames."

"What can I say? I learned from the best. There are only two reasons to go to church."

Drew and Molly share a smile. "Funerals and weddings," they say simultaneously, then erupt in laughter. It doesn't disturb little Enzo, who still slumbers in Drew's arms.

"Hello?" a familiar voice rips through the jovial atmosphere.

I stiffen, shooting my wide eyes to the kitchen to see my father walking in, carrying a powder blue gift bag, along with a stuffed bunny. I jump to my feet, my breath catching, my heart racing, looking for an escape from this conversation.

"Relax, Brooklyn," Molly says, getting up from her position, wincing from the movement. She heads toward me, running her hands down my arms. "I invited him."

"What? Why—"

"I love you, even though you're stubborn sometimes."

I glance over her shoulder to where my father's standing off to the side, uncertain. He appears tired, worn out, weary, like he hasn't slept in months. I know it's because of me, because I've refused to talk to him, see him, acknowledge him.

"I would have given anything to have a few more minutes with my father."

"We both would."

I shift my gaze to Drew, my brows furrowed, a heaviness in my stomach.

"Yours is still here. Don't squander that opportunity,"

Molly continues.

I have no problem telling the kids in my care to confront their problems, their demons, their monsters. When it comes to my life, I have trouble listening to my own advice.

"Remember what you said? Everyone deserves a second chance."

I knew this day would eventually come. Drew found it in his heart to come to terms with what Carla did. If he can find the strength to forgive her, I need to find it in my heart to start the conversation with my father.

Drawing a deep breath, I step away from Molly. "Hey, Dad."

He smiles, as if the sound of my voice quiets the turmoil. "Hey, Brooklyn," he barely manages to choke out. He swallows hard, then composes himself before looking at Molly, holding out the bag and bunny. "Congratulations." He gestures toward the baby in Drew's arms. "He's beautiful."

"Would you like to hold him?" Drew asks.

Dad looks from Drew to Molly, silently asking permission.

She nods enthusiastically. "Of course you can hold him. He needs to get used to you, since the way these two are headed…" She gestures between Drew and me, "you'll officially be part of our family soon."

Drew hands little Enzo to my father, who brings him close, inhaling. "There's nothing like that new baby smell."

I can't help but laugh, considering I thought the same thing. "I know, right?"

He meets my gaze, moisture pooling in the corners of his eyes. "I'm so sorry, Brook. Truly. When I told you the truth, I tried to excuse away my behavior. No more. I have no excuse, only sincere remorse. I hope you can somehow find it in your heart to forgive me."

"Everything can always be lost," I murmur, recalling words Aunt Gigi has said repeatedly whenever I'd argue with Drew or Molly as kids. Something she continues to remind Alyssa and Charlotte of when they fight.

I could hold this against my father for the rest of his life, but where would that get me? What would I gain? Absolutely nothing. If my father didn't do what he did, there's no telling where I would be now, who would be here now.

I steal a glance outside at Alyssa and Charlotte, the likelihood they wouldn't be here strong. Or maybe Drew and I would have gone our separate ways and never found our way back to each other. I couldn't imagine my life any other way. As much as I didn't want to admit it, my father's actions have had a direct impact on the happiness I'm blessed with.

"I'm sorry, too, Dad."

"Are we…" He takes a breath, his Adam's apple bobbing up and down. "Are we okay?" There's a tremble in his voice, this man in front of me a stark contrast to the man I always thought him to be. I haven't seen him this broken and upset since my mother died. It's refreshing to know he's human, too. That he makes mistakes. That he's not perfect. It takes the pressure off me.

"We're okay."

Drew drapes an arm around my shoulders, kissing my temple. I raise my eyes to his.

"If you hadn't done what you did, we may not be here right now."

"And you're happy?" Dad presses.

"Happier than I've ever been."

He smiles a genuine smile. "That's all I care about."

"I should get home. Ana will be getting out of work soon," Dad says later after Gigi has stuffed our bellies with more food than necessary. "Can you walk out with me? There's something I want to talk to you about."

His tone gives me pause, but I agree. "Of course." I lean toward Drew, grazing his lips with mine. "I'll be right back."

"Ooooh…," Charlotte teases, as she's been prone to do every time we kiss in front of her.

"If you keep doing that, your face will get stuck that way," Carla admonishes.

I glance across the table at her. To have her here when

just months ago, we thought she was trying to tear our family apart reminds me I did the right thing with my dad. Drew gave Carla a second chance, even after what she tried to do. My dad did what he did out of love, misguided as it may have been. I can't fault him for that.

"There's nothing wrong with kissing, Charlotte. It's what people do when they're in love."

"I thought that's why they sleep together naked."

The entire room goes silent for a moment, every pair of adult eyes wide. I have no idea how to react or respond, feeling more awkward than normal, considering my father's here. Then he bursts into a hearty laugh, everyone else following suit.

"See what you've missed out on?" Drew says to Carla, throwing his napkin on his plate. "Be glad you weren't present when they asked if Molly ate her baby and that's why her belly was getting bigger."

"What did you say to that?" she asks in hushed tones.

"I let them believe it. I'm not going into detail about how all that works. That's your job now."

"Great." She reaches for her iced tea, rolling her eyes, but I can tell she's thrilled to take on that role.

"Shall we?" Dad's voice forces my attention back to him.

"Of course." I stand, watching as he says his goodbyes, then follow him through the house and out the front door. We walk in silence, simply enjoying each other's presence after too long apart. As we approach his truck, I notice his nerves increase. "What is it, Dad?"

We stop walking and he faces me, grabbing my hand in his, running his fingers along my knuckles. "I've had a lot of time to think these past few months." He pauses, laughing slightly. "You certainly gave me a lot to think about." His light expression turns serious. "I loved your mother very, very much."

"I know that, Dad."

"I made a lot of mistakes because I was trying to make up for the mother's love you were missing out on. I suppose it was my way of holding onto her. In the grief counseling meetings

I attend, they discuss the importance of moving on, of living your life. For the longest time, I didn't want to move on, thought it meant disrespecting the memory of your mother."

"That's not true."

"I understand that now. But it took quite a while for me to do so."

"Well, you've always been stubborn," I joke lovingly. "It's where I get it from."

"Your mother was much more stubborn than me. I can almost imagine her yelling at Saint Peter when she got up to Heaven, arguing it wasn't her time yet." A twinkle in his eye, his lips pinch together in a nostalgic smile before he continues. "But now, it's time for me to move on. To cherish your mother's memory the way she'd want me to."

"What do you mean?" My voice is guarded as my stomach knots with nerves, worried I'm not going to like what he needs to tell me.

"Ana and I are moving in together, and she's agreed to marry me."

My jaw drops as I process this dramatic change in events, rendered speechless. It's unexpected but amazing at the same time.

"I just… I want your blessing first."

I fling my arms around his neck, hugging him. "You don't need my blessing! This is great news! It's what Mom would've wanted."

"I know," he says, placing his hand on my lower back and bringing me closer to him, our hug lasting longer than usual. "I see that now."

"I'm so happy for you." I pull back, squeezing his biceps. "Honestly."

He pauses, his eyes locked on mine. "There's one more thing."

"What?"

He draws in a deep breath, assessing me. "Since Ana and I both lost someone, we decided our best chance was a fresh start, a clean slate, one where we're not surrounded by the memories."

My pulse picks up as I prepare myself for the words I know are about to come.

"We've bought a new place together. I'm putting the house up for sale."

"Oh."

I release my hold on him, swallowing hard. This news hits me differently than him marrying Ana, like he just told me a loved one had died. I suppose having to say goodbye to your childhood home is similar to losing a lifelong friend, one who stood by you through all the ups and downs of your early years, was witness to triumphs and defeats, moments of happiness and sadness.

"I know it's not the news you want to hear." He pulls me into a hug once more, kissing my temple. "But you have a new life now, too. If I've learned anything over the past almost thirty years, it's better to look forward than be stuck in the past." He points toward the front door of Molly's house, his voice strong and powerful. "Your future is sitting in there with more love for you than I could have ever dreamed. No matter what, you'll still have all those great memories we made in that house. Now it's time to make new ones. For all of us. It's what we all deserve."

I nod against his chest, relishing in the sound of his beating heart. "Yes, it is."

CHAPTER THIRTY-THREE

BROOKLYN

MY HEART HEAVY, I make my way from my car and up the steep hill to my father's house the last Sunday in August. It's only 6:30 in the morning, but the moving truck is already backed up in the driveway, boxes piled in the open garage. Last night was restless for me with what today would bring, the idea of saying goodbye to my childhood home causing me to toss and turn.

As the sun rose, I got up to go for a drive before coming over here. Feeling nostalgic, I took a detour by Wes' house in Cambridge, slowing when I saw moving trucks parked in his driveway, too. I hadn't spoken to him since I called off our wedding, but as I was about to drive past, his eyes found mine. He smiled, a simple gesture, but in that one motion, I knew he'd be okay, that he'd find someone who would love him the way he deserves to be loved.

Morning dew covers the grass as I head toward the front door, bringing my key up to the lock. It's a little bittersweet, knowing this is the last time I'll be able to use this key to let myself in. The last time I'll enter the house and breathe in the aroma that is uniquely home. The last time I'll bask in the security these four walls have always provided me.

Blinking back my tears, I insert my key, turning the knob, letting myself into the small house I grew up in. Now, the place is barely recognizable. Much of the furniture has been sold and no longer clutters the tiny living space. Boxes are stacked almost to the ceiling, all labeled with the room they belong in. The walls are barren, devoid of the multitude of family photos my father displayed with pride.

I shift my eyes out the front window, a lump building in my throat when I see the swing blowing slightly. That swing brings back so many memories, ones I wish I could keep with me forever. It feels like it was just yesterday when Drew pushed me on that very swing, then was inches away from kissing me. I can almost see the ghosts of our past out there, laughing nervously as we realized we weren't just the friends we thought we were.

"Morning, Brooklyn," Dad says in a chipper voice. Wiping my cheeks, I whirl around, forcing a smile.

"Hey, Dad." I walk into the small kitchen as he pours two cups of coffee. "How ya doing?"

He places the pot back on the burner, contemplating my question for a moment. "Surprisingly okay. It may be a different story once this stuff is out of the house and all I see are the walls full of memories, but this is the right thing. Ana's already said goodbye to her house and her memories. It's time I do the same."

He pours some milk into my mug, then adds a packet of sweetener before handing me my coffee, bringing his to his mouth. He takes his black. I wonder if it's a firefighter thing. Every single one of the guys at the station seems to take it that way.

"Well, what can I do to help?" I ask after we've both had a few sips, the silence thick.

"My bedroom's still a disaster. Let's start there."

"Sounds like a plan." He heads down the corridor and I follow, stealing a glance at my old bedroom that's now completely empty. I slow my steps, staring at the barren walls. This space is full of so many memories, some bad, most good. The more I think about it, even the memories I considered bad aren't, now that I've found my happiness, now that Drew and I found our way back to each other.

"Brook?" Dad's voice catches my attention.

"Sorry. Coming."

I continue into the master bedroom, where my dad puts me to work boxing up his bookshelves while he works in the bathroom.

As I'm wrapping up a few of the awards my father's received during his career, the doorbell rings.

"Brooklyn, sweetie," he calls out. "Do you mind getting

that? I'm in the middle of something."

"Sure thing," I answer, raising myself to my feet and padding down the hallway.

Without looking through the peephole, I open the door, then inhale a sharp breath when I see Drew standing on the front stoop. But that's not what takes me by surprise. It's the fact that he's clean-shaven, dressed in a suit, his hair groomed. His girls stand on either side of him, smiling a toothy grin, wearing identical sundresses.

"Drew?" I narrow my eyes at him. "What's going on?"

"Remember how I promised months ago that I'd do everything to make you think I'm deserving of your love?"

"Yes...," I answer in a drawn-out voice, my gaze nervously darting around.

"Well, that's what this is. I'm here to fulfill the first promise I made to you." He brings his wrist up, studying his watch. "Although I'm seventeen years late."

I shoot my eyes to my own watch. 7:01 a.m. I spy the date, August 26th. My hand flies to my mouth, my breath catching. When he drops to one knee, I lose the little composure I have left, tears spilling over.

"My beautiful Brooklyn Rose, I've made a lot of mistakes in my lifetime. And I'd like to say I regret them. I suppose I do to some extent, but every single horrible choice I made led me here, to this moment...to you." His eyes remain locked on mine. It's the only thing keeping me upright, my knees weak, my heart hammering in my chest. "Truthfully, I never thought this moment would come, that I'd ever have this chance. I've imagined this more times than I care to admit, but now that I'm here, now that we're here, I'm afraid what I planned to say is woefully inadequate."

It doesn't matter it's just after seven in the morning. The neighborhood is full of activity, and many of the neighbors have stopped their morning routine, congregating at the foot of the hill to watch this moment. A moment that's been seventeen years in the making. Regardless, I don't care that they're witnessing this. I want them here, want to give people hope that they can find the happiness they're looking for, just like we did.

"When I kissed you all those years ago, I was convinced you were my once in a lifetime. Now, as I kneel before you, I am absolutely certain I was right. I don't want to go another minute of my life without you being mine in every sense of the word. I don't want to fall asleep another night without you in my arms. And I don't want to wake up another day without feeling your love radiating for me and me alone."

He reaches into his pocket and brings out a velvet box, flipping it open to reveal a stunning round cut solitaire. The sun hits it, making it reflect in my eyes. He looks to his girls, nodding at them. They also open a velvet box each, a pair of tanzanite earrings from Alyssa, amethyst from Charlotte. The girls' birthstones.

"Brooklyn Rose Tanner, will you marry us? Be part of our family? Build a new life with us? Complete us?"

Tears obscure my vision as I look from Drew to his girls. Charlotte and Alyssa grin wide, their eyes filled with excitement as they bounce on their feet. In the past half-year, I've now been proposed to three times. But this one is filled with so much more meaning, so much more emotion, so much more heart. I sense a presence approach and glance behind me to see my father standing there, smiling in approval.

"Say yes," Charlotte whispers. "Daddy says we can go to Disney World again if we get you to say yes."

I can't help but laugh at that. My eyes returning to Drew's, which are warm with affection, I nod enthusiastically. "Yes, Drew. And Alyssa and Charlotte. I'll marry you. All of you."

Drew blows out a relieved breath as the girls squeal. In an instant, he's on his feet, pulling me into his arms as he slides the ring onto my finger. Unlike when Wes did the same thing, this no longer feels like a chain shackling me to a life I'm unsure I want. When Drew's ring locks into place, it's like the piece I've been searching for all my life has been found.

He brings his lips toward mine, kissing me sweetly, reverently, thoughtfully. It's fitting he proposed on the date and time he broke the promise that seemed to impact our relationship for years. Drew was my first love, my first kiss. And he'll be my last.

"Now do you believe me?" he murmurs against my mouth.

"What's that?"

"You were never just my sister's best friend."

I run my hands through his hair, arching into him. "I do now."

Thank you so much for reading REDEMPTION! I hope you've enjoyed Brooklyn and Drew's story!

Want to know if Wes finds his happily ever after? His story is next.

We come from two different worlds.
But the instant our paths crossed, our hearts beat as one, our connection undeniable.
Is that connection strong enough to weather the storm trying to upend our relationship? Or will people only see the color of my skin?

Reserve your copy today!
www.tkleighauthor.com/possession

I appreciate your help in spreading the word about my books. Please leave a review on your favorite book site.

PLAYLIST

Little Do You Know - Alex & Sierra
Naked - James Arthur
Dancing on my Own - Callum Scott
Jealous - Labrinth
The Hollow in Retrospect - Corey Kilgannon
A Little Fire - Parker Millsap
Can't You See - Matthew and the Atlas
In Love Again - Colbie Caillat
Waves and the Both of Us - Charlotte Sometimes
Hole in my Heart - Gavin James
Can I Stay - Ray LaMontagne
Mess I Made - Parachute
Sorry - Aquilo
Broken - Lifehouse
The First Time Ever I Saw Your Face - Roberta Flack
Say Something - A Great Big World
Bring on the Rain - Keri Noble
Breathe Again - Sara Bareilles
Colour Me In - Damien Rice
Move Together - James Bay
The Shape of Us - Ian Britt
Perfect Duet - Ed Sheeran & Beyonce

ACKNOWLEDGMENTS

I published my very first book in August of 2013, the book that people still know me best for... A Beautiful Mess. Back then, I thought that story would be the only one I'd ever write. I didn't think I'd have another story in me. Hell, crafting a book is hard work. I thought I'd be a "one and done" kind of author.

Apparently not.

I just celebrated my five year "publiversary" and can't believe the people I've given life to. You often hear authors discuss our "book babies", and there's certainly some underlying truth to those words. We spend months nurturing these stories and characters, then set them free, hoping people love them as much as we do. It's hard work, and often stressful at times, but it's honestly the best job I've ever had. I still can't believe I'm lucky enough to be doing this, even five years later.

Of course, I have my husband to thank for that. Since he learned I'd written a book, he's done nothing but offer me all of his support. I hear stories about how some authors' spouses look at writing as a hobby. He knows this is a career for me, and I couldn't be more grateful for him.

On that same note, thanks to my fantastic nannies who treat Miss Harper Leigh with all the love she deserves so I can work on my books. Sharon and Brooke, I wouldn't be able to do this without you!

There's only one woman I ever trust with my manuscripts — Kim Young. Thanks for an amazing five years. Here's to five more!

Thanks to my wonderful admin team who help me manage my social media presence — Melissa, Joelle, Vicky, Lea. And to my fabulous beta readers - Stacy, Lin, Melissa, Joelle, Vicky, Sylvia.

Thanks to Emily from Social Butterfly PR for dealing with the insanity that is my brain. When I told her what was a stand-alone had turned into a duet, then said I was writing a prequel novella, she went with the flow, nothing fazing her at all! You make my job so much easier.

A special shout out to my street team. Thanks so much for taking time out of your busy schedules to help promote me! And to my lovely reader group! Thanks for giving me a place to be myself, horrible jokes and tasteless memes and all!

Last but not least, thanks to YOU! Without readers, I'd have no one to write for, so thanks for taking a chance on my books! Whether you've just found me or have been with me since the beginning, I'm forever grateful!

Peace & Love,

~ T.K.

ABOUT THE AUTHOR

T.K. Leigh, otherwise known as Tracy Leigh Kellam, is the USA Today Bestselling author of the Beautiful Mess series, in addition to several other works ranging from fun and flirty to sexy and sinful. Originally from New England, she now resides in sunny Southern California with her husband, beautiful daughter, and three cats. When she's not planted in front of her computer, writing away, she can be found training for her next marathon (of which she has run over twenty fulls and far too many halfs to recall) or chasing her daughter around the house.

T.K. Leigh is represented by Jane Dystel of Dystel, Goderich & Bourret Literary Management. All publishing inquiries, including audio, foreign, and film rights, should be directed to her.

www.ingramcontent.com/pod-product-compliance
Lightning Source LLC
Chambersburg PA
CBHW020947120726
47905CB00008B/2721